OUTLAW SCHOOL

Other Books by
Rebecca Ore

GAIA'S TOYS
SLOW FUNERAL
THE ILLEGAL REBIRTH OF BILLY THE KID
BECOMING ALIEN
BEING ALIEN
HUMAN TO HUMAN

OUTLAW SCHOOL

REBECCA ORE

An Imprint of HarperCollinsPublishers

This is a work of fiction. Names, characters, places, and incidents are the products of the author's imagination or are used fictitiously and are not to be construed as real. Any resemblance to actual events, locales, organizations, or persons, living or dead, is entirely coincidental.

EOS
An Imprint of HarperCollins*Publishers*
10 East 53rd Street
New York, New York 10022-5299

Copyright © 2000 by Rebecca Ore
Cover art by Tom Canty
ISBN: 0-380-79250-8
www.eosbooks.com

Library of Congress Cataloging-in-Publication Data
Ore, Rebecca.
  Outlaw school / Rebecca Ore.
    p. cm.
  ISBN 0-380-79250-8 (trade pbk.)
  I. Title.

PS3565.R385 O8 2000
813'.54—dc21   00-034839

First Eos trade paperback printing: November 2000

Eos Trademark Reg. U.S. Pat. Off. and in Other Countries, Marca Registrada, Hecho en U.S.A.
HarperCollins® is a trademark of HarperCollins Publishers Inc.

Printed in the U. S. A.

RRD 10 9 8 7 6 5 4 3 2

Acknowledgments

Thanks to Fluffy, Jeremy Nixon, Sean Eric Fagan, Steve Baur, Hubert Bartels, Dominick DiBernardi, and especially to Michael Swanwick, for ideas and criticism. And for aiding and abetting through various difficulties, much gratitude to my father, John R. Brown.

And to everyone who was patient, again, thanks.

Rebecca Ore
Philadelphia, PA
October 14, 1998–March 10, 1999

1
Babyhood

Jayne's first memory was of terror. Cuffed by doubled bracelets from one of the mother's jewel boxes, Jayne as a three-year-old child screamed from the post where she'd been manacled. Two five-year-old children, one girl, one boy, danced around her laughing, their bare feet green around the tocs from crushed grass, their hands full of weapons Jayne thought were real.

The two mothers, lying with beers on plastic lawn chaises, smiled at the child play. It took Jayne years to connect the two mothers and their nonchalance with the scene where she was screaming in her manacles.

"Don't the children play together well?" the other mother, whose children were in charge, said. Jayne's mother nodded, rubbing a beer can against her bare sweaty leg.

The boy aimed at Jayne's head with a rubber-tipped arrow and fired. She tried to dodge it, but it bruised her. As Jayne screamed louder, the older girl darted forward and sucked on Jayne's arm until blood pooled under the skin. Two bruises. The blood could burst out from her skin.

Jayne finally caught her mother's eyes, but Mom looked away. "Don't be such a crybaby," her mother said.

"Ah, Jayne's just laughing," the other mother said.

The torture would go on, Jayne thought, forever.

"You were a cranky baby," Jayne's mother told her at five as she brushed Jayne's hair after she cut it. "Psychologists tell us a healthy baby helps its mother if the mom's unhappy. Not you. You'd just scream harder when I was nervous. But you'll have a mother when you're eight. Not me. I was an orphan." Jayne's mother was dressing her to go see a friend of Jayne's who'd fractured her skull. *The universe is like this,* Jayne decided. *You find friends who don't torture you, and they fracture their skulls and disappear.* "Just think how lucky you are to have such nice hair when Susan is lying there all shaved down from surgery."

Jayne's mother always cut Jayne's hair short. Jayne wondered if this would make brain surgery easier if she herself needed it. Jayne put on her patent-leather shoes last and looked back at her mother. Perhaps her mother wanted to make sure she knew the universe could break little girls' skulls if they didn't stay on the sidewalks.

Years later, Jayne's memory could always play a still image of a little girl lying in a baby cot, a tube in her arm. Susan's family tended her at home. When Jayne was older, she suspected they'd done that to keep insurance premiums under control. In memory, her mother said, "It's for the best," while Jayne looked at her friend who didn't move, not an eyelid, not a muscle around the mouth. She always remembered this as though she was seeing it all over again, not as though she was watching herself from a slight distance the way she remembered being cuffed to a tree with bracelets and tortured. Death locked this memory straight behind the eyes inside a body that would die. Jayne wondered if her mother had said that about Susan's injury being for the best before she died, when they were visiting the dying girl, or whether her mother had said this later, or had not said it at all in regard to Susan.

Even if her mother had not said "it's for the best" at the

bedside or after the death, Jayne knew that was what her mother always said she believed. Becoming an orphan put her mother in boarding school. A dead friend at age five meant Jayne learned the universe was unreliable. While she was still young, she wondered if it were out to get her, but learned by fifth grade to hide that fear as it made other people nervous. They must have thought, Jayne suspected, that the universe was concentrating on them.

The other option is that the universe was no more concerned about her individuality than she was of the ants whose nests she destroyed with magnifying glasses. Jayne began to suspect that was the correct option, as it reduced her and all her childhood friends and enemies to trivial insects.

Jayne's memory revealed no trace of a funeral for her friend, just her mother's announcement that the girl must have had some organic defect and the fall down the hole only triggered it since accidents like that generally weren't lethal. So it had happened for the best.

After that, Jayne didn't remember much until she learned to read and the older kids stopped her by the creek at the short-cut from school to quiz her about the Compton's Encyclopedia she found on the home computer. When she answered the questions correctly, they, being professors' children, threw rocks at her for being too smart for a middle manager's child.

Her mother, who was having an affair with one of the professors at that time, told Jayne, "They throw rocks at you because they like you."

Jayne's father approved of a family woman being punished, as he couldn't beat up his wife. Her mother always intimidated her father even though neither of them said anything about it. Besides, the affair taught her mother how to become a better lover.

Years later, before she began teaching illegally, Jayne decided the children threw rocks at her because their parents wanted to throw more lethal rocks at her mother. Stoning adulteresses was what the Bible prescribed, but the townspeople preferred to leave such passions to their children. While the Bible said to kill both the man and the woman in cases like this, the professor was socially valuable.

Separated from these memories, although the adult Jayne knew the real time line was intertwined, Jayne at five reinvented the loom, hammering nails into a two-by-four frame, stringing up sewing thread, and darning together a tiny square that looked like real cloth. This was as scary, in a more exciting way, as the memories of being chained to a tree and being bruised by an arrow and a mouth. Nothing is permanent. What was threads had become cloth, would become rags, would tatter away into dust. Things, then, were a trick. The components of being were temporary.

Like all children, Jayne recapitulated the species' technological evolution, making bows and arrows, hurling slings, huts, small hand-sewn items of cloth and leather, bits of knitting done on pencils, frying insects with a magnifying glass. One day, Jayne focused the sun on her hand until the skin smoked. The pain made her drop the glass. How far was the sun if something as hot as the encyclopedia said it was couldn't instantly incinerate her hand when focused by a lens? She found a printed figure for the distance before she found the formula for calculating the loss of energy through distance.

The encyclopedia's figures stripped her of importance and turned her into a biological nanomachine crawling at the bottom of a thin skin of air.

Jayne could never figure out what age she was when she realized this. These memories floated off with connections only to science she learned later.

One alien memory intruded. "You're a tomboy, ain't ya?" A young millworker whose parents still lived in the neighborhood because they'd inherited their house.

Later, memories almost fused into a constant sense of self. At seven, Jayne looked down at her body in the tub and found adulthood a difficult thing to imagine. How could this body lose its baby belly and grow tits and coarse private hair and still be her body?

Then, after she stopped frying ants and her own skin with the focused sun, she accidentally killed a cat. How oddly the fur shrugged off the hot road tar she held on a stick, bending, not sticking. But after brushing a little too hard, the tar stuck to the cat. The cat died because Jayne had been curious.

Jayne realized she was part of the uncaring universe. But she did care. She felt guilty for years. She was obligated to her guilt.

As a child, Jayne knew she'd become famous, like a professor her father seemed to hate when the scientist won the Nobel prize. Her mother had worked for the man when both parents lived in Boston. To please her mother, Jayne would have to become famous. To please her father, she couldn't.

Jayne's father had no idea a girl-child could imagine becoming famous. Women failed to be faithful. Men failed to become famous.

The best way to please both parents would be to teach a male how to become famous. Somehow, Jayne thought, she wanted more. A teacher said Jayne should become a scientist, but Jayne found that figures transposed themselves when she wasn't very careful. Since her encyclopedia told her that women didn't get dyslexia, she had a stupidity for math. She was sorry, because she really did like science. Her school barred calculators in math classes, saying all middle-class children should be capable doing math mentally. Girls could use pencils.

Her home computer found some obscure references to equal numbers of male and female dyslexics, but insisted that the condition affected spelling and reading only.

*   *   *

Geometry didn't hurt as much as quadratic equations. Lines, points, and triangles held their numerical descriptions to logic. Jayne could see when she was wrong and work through the square of the hypotenuse and the squares of the other two sides again.

In the third grade, a teacher accused her of plagiarism when she reinvented the spun-off plasma theory of planetary evolution. She hated the teacher for not believing a girl could think of that on her own, especially since the computer's astronomy text said the theory was wrong.

At this time, she read faster than any professor's child, scored higher on the aptitude and the achievement tests, and was held up to ridicule by a teacher who claimed that Jayne could never know what to do with her brains because her daddy was middle management and lacked culture. When she went to the special books kept for the second brightest student in the class—a child whose parents would move to New York City next year because Jayne's superiority over their daughter embarrassed them—the teacher said, "Those books are not for you."

In fourth grade, Jayne realized that most people like her parents taught their children to defer to the higher-class children, whose genes were supposed to be better. The millworkers' children deferred to Jayne or ignored her, but she thought this was only natural.

The teacher said, "It isn't right to harass those less gifted than you by demanding that they learn like professors' children."

But I've given them my stupidity in math, Jayne thought. *They can't have my curiosity, too.*

When the second smartest girl in the school left for New York, Jayne went home after class every day and cried. Her mother refused to admit the other children didn't like Jayne.

After all, they threw rocks at her. People only teased people they liked.

Telescope, microscope, and marsh. Jayne's best friends moved in from the outside, generally ROTC trainers' children who couldn't care less about fitting in since their daddies would be rotated out in two years anyway. Whether they shared her obsessions or wanted a friend badly enough to fake it, Jayne clung to them until they moved.

The telescope was a private obsession. Her parents bought her a cheap reflector for children with a mirror that went out of alignment, then blackened. Jayne memorized enough about the constellations to earn her Girl Scout Star Badge, but didn't remember how she got from astronomy to Girl Scouts except that her mother, determined to make Jayne fit in after telling Jayne that being liked meant people would hurt her, forced her to go. Jayne suspected that the only thing that kept her from being completely asocial was that she only connected being hurt with being liked by groups. Best friends sneaked in there before the local gang of professors' children started liking her with rocks. Best friends disappeared, killed by collapsing sidewalks, taken to New York by parents who couldn't believe a local manager's child honestly scored higher than their daughter, transferred away.

This all prepared Jayne for the loves of outlaw educators.

The microscope was a link with older people, mainly an eccentric biology professor who must have had a bit of the outlaw teacher in him, too. He gave her reagents and biostains, let her sit in on a session with a scanning electron microscope, and showed her the lab's DNA sequencer.

"My parameciums lysed when I tried using isopropyl alcohol," Jayne told him. She remembered the cell membranes breaking and spewing organelle and protoplasm under the slide. "I want to try osmotic acid as a fixative."

The biology instructor said, "Osmotic acid is not a good

fixative for a young girl to use, but I have something that
would work."

The fixative killed and pickled Jayne's microorganisms
quite well. She stained them blue and ordered her own copy
of the biological supply house catalog.

The marsh was on a different memory track. That friendship got twisted by what Jayne only found out later was typ-
ical pubescent sex play. The two girls tried to see if they
looked normal before turning to the main objects of desire.
Jayne had, however, been stripped and felt up two years before puberty to punish her for her interest in computers and
radios. The community could tolerate an interest in biology,
especially ecology and the mere observing of protozoa, in a
girl. But radios were too close to physics and computers, so
a boy was deputized to prove that her only real interest was
in the boy holding her panties, not the radios she claimed she
wanted to learn. It was an initiation, he told her, but the electronics club disappeared after she complied.

Besides, she couldn't master the math. So, Jayne retreated
back to the biology labs and to the marsh with Christine, her
second friend from the ranks of officers' daughters.

The marsh. Jayne had followed the creek behind suburbia
for miles earlier, but only where the other children played.
Then with Christine, she went farther, to an old road falling
apart, to an abandoned spring flowing from an arched brick
opening into a pool with muskrats swimming in it. All this
was just behind houses draining sewage into the creek a couple yards farther on. Tubifex worms wiggled like red plush in
the water just beyond the sewage drain. All the live-food text
in aquarium books turned real, tubifex in sewage water.
Jayne and Chris went no farther that day, but came back and
went beyond the sewage outlet a few days later. The stench
faded as the creek used tubifex, bacteria, algae, and diatoms
to neutralize the fecal matter.

So the two girls found the marsh, a place outside the usual
child hideouts. The creek widened into braided channels,

with cattails, skin-lacerating sedges, and bullfrog tadpoles that swam across barely wet sand between pools seemingly too tiny for their nine-inch lengths.

A rabbit with smaller than usual ears jumped through water and land both. *Marsh cottontail,* Jayne thought.

Children had legends about the houses across the highway, where the black boys fought the white boys with BB guns, and nobody told the parents or the NAACP, of abandoned sawdust piles riddled with caves children smoked in, of the dams with real ceramic drains that the boy who molested girls built.

But no child ever talked about the marsh. Jayne understood the people with cattails at the back of their lots knew about the marsh, but they never went in. She could imagine that nobody since the Cherokee were driven from this place walked in the marsh until she and Chris followed the creek into it.

The marsh was their escape zone. They got wet, put leaves under their shirts to conceal their nipples, and went though the sedges as carefully as they could, but still got razored. Most children wouldn't bleed to go into a marsh, but Jayne loved the life of it, its difference from both the high Piedmont around them and the suburban yards with their fake Pleistocene veldts proving the evolutionist right. But the marsh filled its own place in the human visual cortex, pumped Jayne's with dreams of cattail stews, fiber nets, arrowhead tubers dug. The marsh, like the African plains suburban lawns imitated, was an old human place.

Even as Jayne discovered this place, she knew the marsh was doomed. The Corps of Engineers scheduled a lake to drown the marsh. Given that, she wanted to commit it to memory before it died, walking it with leaves over her nipples, with Chris, down to where the marsh became a creek again, to a rock in the creek with a shed snakeskin on it. Some miles farther beyond where the two girls went the creek merged with the river. The river continued down to join the Savannah, then the dam closed around the Savannah.

The Corps of Engineers couldn't just let the marsh drown peacefully. Yellow bulldozers scraped it with steel blades, like knives scraping corn for the milk. Jayne came in to find the marsh flattened, the cattails wrecked. In tread marks, she found a cut-apart bumblebee and a leopard frog trying to limp on two shattered legs.

Jayne cried over the dying frog, then stepped down firmly on its head to put it out of its misery. She walked through the ruined marsh, cursing the yellow machines and the men who sent them.

Jayne walked down to the biology building and climbed stairs to the floor where her friend had his office. She asked him to give her the address of the biological supply house. When the catalog came, she plotted all the equipment she'd need for her own private lab: microtome, centrifuge, binocular Zeiss microscope with a mechanical stage and oil-immersion lens, incubator, culture medium and petri dishes, plankton nets, and small building to house it all in.

Without any guidance from teachers, she put together an exhibit for the eighth-grade science fair of her paramecia and her notebook full of drawings of rotifers and hydras from a spring that fed a branch of the creek that became the marsh before the bulldozers scraped that away, and all the chemicals she used to kill, fix, and stain things. A teacher loaned her a projecting microscope to throw a circle filled with dead blue paramecia on the wall. Jayne was pleased that the flagella were visible.

Three professors' daughters made a model of a cell in plastic clay, copied from a textbook, and stuck each organelle with its name written on a wooden stick. They won the first prize for the science fair.

That night, Jayne and Christine practiced working in a brothel. Jayne never saw what she and her friend, and other girls, did before they began to date boys—an intense undress rehearsal only mentioned by a few French women novelists, but not an initiation into gay sex, but fierce play with sexual concepts that could singe them in an instant if they played these games out with their real targets. *Are we okay? Do we look like other women? Do we have breasts large enough, too large? What is that fringe of flesh sticking out from the vulva?*

And if they love you, they'll hurt you. Love them, hurt them first, was the big temptation.

Odd. The French writers never mentioned the anxiety.

Chris lolled over a *Playboy*. "Ice makes the nipples stand up like that," she said.

"Or she's really aroused," Jayne said.

"Nah, she's looking at a photographer, and he's got assistants around," Chris said. "Mom said it's got to be ice."

Jayne's mother told her around that time, but before Jayne's first period, that sometimes women commit adultery and regret it. Jayne understood instantly that her mother was talking about herself, but didn't realize further that her mother knew the children stoned Jayne because the parents were too sophisticated to stone her mother. So, all that time, Jayne's mother was being punished for adultery, being reminded of it even though she'd quit. Of course, she was forced to pretend nothing was really happening to Jayne.

So Jayne learned early that in order to have regular meals, children are forced to defend their parents' delusions and protect them from real life.

"Your father has a wonderful sense of humor," her mother said sometime around the adultery revelation.

Jayne knew already her dad's jokes came from *Reader's Digest*. But then, how could she complain? When the harassment stopped for summer vacation, the ghost stories she used to terrify the other children in the summer came from old issues of *Life* magazine.

During the summer, she wasn't a pariah. Other children played in her yard, listened to her ghost stories, acted in her plays, helped her run her horror shows in the dank room with the dirt floor under her porch. Then school time came, and the children realized again they were supposed to be the leaders, not Jayne, and also the smart ones, not a girl with a middle-manager father who came from the country.

Jayne could put the memories together by dint of logic and applied calendars, but mostly she organized her memories in stories with similar themes.

One snow time, the theme was running behind the buildings in town. Boys were chasing Jayne and Chris through the snow, though that might have been a false memory. Chris darted between two buildings. Jayne followed into an urban equivalent of the marsh, a space behind the storefronts that she'd never thought about before, alleys and courtyards and narrow passages like DeChirico paintings, threatening and strangely beautiful.

As a child, Jayne saw visions of New York that she knew weren't real, a vivid imagination throwing pattern into the car lights rotating through her bedroom window. This tiny scrap of city, three blocks to a side, made Jayne crave New York even though she'd never been there. These urban rear facades gave her hope that she could run all the way to New York and become anonymous and famous all at the same time, could go to see in real oil and canvas all the famous paintings she'd seen only in books. The mean town was a limited thing. New York would be better.

"Why didn't they follow us back here?" Jayne asked Chris.

"Homeless people pick the garbage," Chris said. She leaned against a wall and pulled out a pack of cigarettes, lit one, and handed another to Jayne.

Jayne smoked, coughed, and felt nauseous. "Anyone sell us some marijuana?" she asked.

"No. The dealers think you're weird and talk too much."

Two inhuman loves, then, the marsh, which was dead, and the city, which, though built by humans, would outlive whatever they did, this side of nuclear war. Even then, Manhattan could regrow another city. Jayne imagined Manhattan to be heaven, dangerous to well-dressed people and filled with art museums.

Chris moved away, as usual, but not before the two mothers quarreled and broke up their friendship. So for months, Jayne saw Chris and couldn't talk to her, even though the marsh regrew before the lake water finally drowned all but the cattails. Those worked inland on their rhizomes into what had been associate professors' lawns.

Jayne had a sister, but she had nothing to do with her life at this age. She had been an only child for the first two years of her life and didn't remember her sister as anything other than a doll her parents preferred to her until she was in high school.

Her mother trained Carolyn, the baby, to be a Judas Girl. Jayne found out later that Carolyn got her first club pin at age eight for signing a pledge to report all girls with unseemly interests to school counseling.

Jayne wondered if Carolyn lost her club pin when someone else other than her sister reported her to the school therapist.

"Normal people want to conform," the counselor said. "You're always off on a tangent. Perhaps it's time for aversive therapy."

Jayne remembered photos in *Life* magazine of autistic children being shocked screaming by a psychologist who put them barefoot on a metal grill. Head-banging, screaming earned them shocks.

Years later, an autistic boy swung in a swing over a Broadway performance of Letter to Queen Victoria, performing rituals with clocks.

In the late twentieth century, before the Suicide Laws, autistics started to explain themselves. Jayne wondered if any of the shocked children contributed to the Autistic Liberation movement at the beginning of the century.

"Aversive therapy," the counselor said to Jayne again in her sophomore year of high school. "Or chemotherapy."

"My mother beats my head against the wall when she doesn't like what I do," Jayne said.

"We're talking about you, not about your mother," the therapist said. "If you were a more charming child, she wouldn't beat you."

"Did my sister turn me in?" Jayne asked, having learned by high school that her sister was in the Girls.

The therapist said, "You're oblivious as to how obvious you are." She marked down a higher dose on Jayne's prescription pad. "You'll need to get this okayed by your primary-care physician." School therapists couldn't legally prescribe drugs, but HMO doctors always countersigned the prescriptions—arguing with them took time and money.

Carolyn hated what being Jayne's sister did to her standing with the Girls.

In the backyard, Jayne's father and mother were playing golf chicken, chipping balls at each other and hazing each other for flinching.

"I've been given a prescription for school," Jayne told them.

Her parents looked up as though they'd been expecting to hear this. Her father said, "I hope it will make you happier."

Jayne said, "I'd be happier if I'd been born in the 1950s just before feminism."

Her father said, "It led to crack cocaine and a 30 percent illegitimacy rate among white teenagers."

Jayne wondered if her father knew that the Civil War led to heroin addiction. Even as she realized she should have known better, she realized she knew her father would support the school authorities. A woman was being punished, again. Perhaps not the right one, but then women were all the same. Jayne said, "At least Carolyn didn't turn me in."

Her mother said, "You make life very hard for the rest of us, being different."

Her father said, lining up another golf ball, "Jayne, we

want the best for you." He hit his wife in the sternum with it, but Jayne's mother didn't flinch. "I'll see if this can't wait until next year."

Jayne felt absurdly grateful to him.

Elsewhere, Jayne's world developed: Skill Doctors, privatized schools run by area employers, alternative service for juvenile defendants, citizenship for virtual personalities, physician-assisted suicide houses for the life-quality deficient, psychosurgery with real-time monitored drug dosage, womb monitors, prenatal genetic testing for homosexuality, abortion decriminalized for certain preexisting conditions, tax breaks for home health care by family members, mandatory testing (including drug and sexual secretions testing), selling credit-card debt on credit to homeowners only, and licensing of all educators.

Homosexuals could not only marry; they were required to be married and monogamous if they worked in jobs that put them in contact with the public.

Life was better. Life was worse. The senator who sponsored the alternative-service bill would be murdered when he refused to give a pension to his houseboy who'd been sentenced to his service forty years earlier. Only a few historians remembered the Spanish Nobel laureate who'd invented the lobotomy. A lobotomized mental patient had killed him.

Jayne's school counselor told her, "Our crazies volunteer to be put to sleep. And the Dutch started it by euthanizing AIDS patients and hopelessly anorexic girls, but only at their request. I'm sure that all the gay babies saved by abortion from homophobic homes would thank us."

Jayne couldn't be forced into a lobotomy, but if she wanted to finish college-prep high school, she had to take the proper medication.

"However, if you want a lobotomy and your parents are opposed, your rights to one are protected. We can arrange a guardian."

"I hate being drugged," Jayne said. "I certainly don't want a lobotomy."

"You can't continue at this school unless you agree to take appropriate medication."

Jayne found that the other students on educational drugs had bet themselves as to when she'd be joining them. Drugs didn't give her any friends among the Girls or the guys already scheduled for corporate-sponsored scholarships, but the educational-drug kids expected her to eat with them now. They had a cafeteria table by the door, under fluorescent lamps that seemed to be giving off a slightly bluer spectrum than the rest of the lights.

Jayne wished she didn't feel like just giving up and sitting with them, but the drugs were talking. "Hi," one guy with minor scarification over his eyebrows said.

"Hi."

"When do you get your drug holidays?" a girl with scalloped nostrils said.

Jayne hadn't known she had a right to drug holidays, so talking to these people wasn't a waste. Fuck-ups together, but the drugs kept that from mattering. After about the first month of adjusting to the haze, hating feeling dulled, Jayne realized that she wasn't worried about her future anymore. Her body seemed to grip her, every muscle warmly log-like.

During the drug holidays, she sat in a chair in her bedroom and wondered if she had any future at all. Mick, the boy with the scarifications, who been the first to greet her at the drug table, came over her second drug holiday. Jayne stared at him, wondering how she'd come to see him as a friend. *I'm not like them,* she thought. *Not really.*

Mick said, "Drug holidays are a bitch, aren't they? All your friends look so weird. Come with me, and I'll show you where everybody gets together."

"I don't look weird."

"You look like you wanna be a Judas Girl. Come on out. Don't waste yourself."

Jayne said, "I don't want to fit in anywhere."

"You think I like the scars all the time. My parents won't pay for the surgery unless I get through school."

His name was Mick, and he took Jayne to a four-car garage out in the country where both the rich and smart kids and the poor and dumb or drugged kids, all interested in drugs and music, went and talked stiffly and loudly with each other about drugs and sometimes less stiffly, between sets played by local bands, about music. Jayne didn't quite want to do any kind of drug on her school drug holidays, so she backed herself against a wall to watch and listen.

Not everybody, she thought. *The school-council types and the Judas Girls are missing.* Then she saw one of the Girls walk in alone—Sidna Blair, in Judicious Girl clothes with sensible shoes, circle pin, bluest skirt and whitest blouse, surgically perfect eyes four thousand light-years off observing the natives. Jayne saw Sidna as enemy and envy object. Sidna, like her sister, would never be drugged, would never be told she couldn't be bright because her family was middle management. Sidna could come to a garage band rock and no one would mistake her for one of the gullible girls who sucked down drugs and semen. Sidna was bonded in future pledge to a Yale freshman, now Judicious Girl in curiosity heat, protected by the random chance that all she saw was going out digital narrowband. Not all Judas Girls were tapped all the time. Jayne's sister told her once that it was, after all, for the whole community's protection.

Mick came up to Jayne, and said, "Some of us are going to be screwed tomorrow. You wanna leave?"

"I haven't done anything a Judas Girl would disapprove of."

Mick leaned against the wall beside Jayne, rocked back on his heels, and pointed his booted toes to the ceiling. He leaned on his hands, and said, "And the bitch is so pretty it hurts."

Jayne said, "Sometimes, I wonder why I didn't join the Girls. My mother did everything she could to get me in." People respected Judicious Girls.

Mick seemed alarmed. "You didn't stay in long enough to get protective-wired, did you?"

"Just memory, not silicon, behind my eyeballs," Jayne said. "Mick, when do you want to leave?"

"Must be nasty to have a little snitch in the house," Mick said. "We could have privacy at my house."

Sidna moved through the crowd as though queen. Nobody could be quite sure she wasn't transmitting to the cops. Jayne said to Mick, "Let's go then, but let me go out to your car first."

Shivering by the car, Jayne wondered if Mick would remember that she wanted to leave. The moon looked sickly, lopsided in the fog a few nights after a full moon Jayne hadn't even noticed through her drug haze. Just as she was beginning to cry, Mick came out.

"What's wrong?" he said.

"How do we back out of who we are and become who they want?"

Mick said, "They don't want us to change. That's why we're drugged."

"I hate being drugged."

"Come on, get in the car, and we'll talk at my house," Mick said. He unlocked and opened Jayne's passenger-side door.

His house was in a poorer neighborhood than Jayne's, under power lines. If Jayne had been a Judicious Girl, she would have noticed where Mick lived from his car license number. Even if she'd just been apprehensive, she'd have noticed that.

"Can your parents afford to have your scars removed?" Jayne said when she saw that the door opened straight into a living room/kitchen combination. "Do you have your own room?"

Mick said, "I share with my brothers, but they work late."

Jayne remembered that one way out of being school-drugged was to get pregnant. The drugging had to stop since the fetus had no choice in the matter. She looked closely at Mick, trying to see through the scarifications. "Why did they put you on drugs?"

"School drugs keep me from being so bored I'd cut classes and hitch halfway to New Mexico before I got caught. Three times. My parents kept telling me to finish school, do well, not end up in debt forever to the Skill Doctors like them."

Jayne realized Mick's parents couldn't keep their promise to him. He had his scars forever. "Oh. Can I touch them? Are they sensitive or dull? I mean numb."

Wordlessly, he took her hand and placed her fingers on the scars. The scars bounced under her fingertips like trapunto work, fibrous raised flesh.

Jayne had heard that when the eggs were ready, even fairly modest girls could turn sexual aggressor. She felt that must be the case with her and her ovaries now. She said, "I want off the school meds. Can you help me?"

Her face swam in his eyes. "I don't want a mark. My brother Joe has two marks. Another one, they cut his balls."

"No, he'd just be sterilized."

"Bitches didn't even have his kids," Mick said.

Jayne said, "I'm a virgin. Virgins don't get pregnant the first time." Judicious Girls knew that was a lie. Virgins overcome by lust were in the power of the species. The eggs were ready.

"Do you really want me? Or am I just a way to get pregnant and off the meds?"

"Touch my lips. With your finger."

Both of them could feel Jayne's lips swell under his finger. "The human body is amazing," Mick said. "Promise me, if you can, you'll get someone to take my scars off. If you ever can?"

"I promise," Jayne said.

Thanks to various earlier applied hairbrushes, Jayne's hymen didn't exist.

As she rocked Mick's body in her hips, Jayne felt very maternal. Her own spasm rather scared her, but then wasn't the womb supposed to suck up the sperm for her egg?

After, Jayne felt trapped and panicky. Mick drove her home, but nobody was waiting up. As she unlocked the door, she turned to wave at Mick, but he'd driven off. She took off her shoes and stepped quietly so as to not disturb anyone. She could smell Mick's sweat on her as though it had soaked into her pores. Nobody had ever told her what a sweaty business sex was. Semen oozed into her panties. She went down to the basement and used the maid's shower. Her family hadn't had a live-in for years, but her mother told Jayne the shower was permanently nasty from the decade of maids who'd used the shower before her family bought the house.

In the morning, Jayne came down to breakfast later than usual for Sunday morning. Her father had gone out to buy the Sunday paper, and her mother and Carolyn were cutting and squeezing oranges. Carolyn said, "Sidna said you went to a garage rock with that scarred creep from your adjustment circle."

"Yes, I saw Sidna." Jayne pushed a slice of bread into the toaster, and the gesture screamed to her of blatant symbolism. The toaster sucked the bread in and pushed it out nine seconds later all browned.

"Just because you're taking medications, Jayne, doesn't mean you are like the poor people's kids on meds," her mother said.

"No. They seem to take it a lot less hard."

"If you're willing to go to summer adjustment camp this summer, the school counselor says she might consider taking you off drugs."

"Maybe I'm lobotomized enough," Jayne said. She began to feel defiant, but knew she was trapped in her body with a fetus, trapped in her identity. The drugs gave her counselor the idea she'd done something helpful for Jayne, made her numb to the teasing, gave her a strange connection to the poor kids she'd never seen as human before. Jayne realized she still had trouble seeing them as fully human. The drugs didn't make her that liberal.

Carolyn said, "His brother's sired two babies."

Jayne replied, "They weren't born, Mick said." She wished her mother and sister would support her against the school, against the world. Now she was going to humiliate them, herself. For a panicky moment, she wanted to confess. Then she wondered if her mother would care about any aspect of fucking Mick other than the risk of disease and pregnancy.

Carolyn said, "Probably the sperm was defective. It's a blessing to abort children who'd have opted for suicide had they been able to make the decision."

Her mother said, "We'd really like to see you off medications. You were such a happy child."

Jayne said, "I don't remember being a happy child."

Carolyn said, "You used to be even more embarrassing than you are now, but my group leader said we should be kind to you since you've probably got a chemically imbalanced brain."

"On school meds, I sure do," Jayne said. Her brain now felt momentarily clear and bitter, then another wave of panic hit. But her mother seemed oblivious, and her sister only cared about her own standing in the Girls.

"I've been sorry for things I've done, but I haven't really been sorry I had you," her mother said, handing Jayne a glass of juice. "Fix your own eggs."

I have, Jayne almost wanted to say, but she took down the frying pan, and asked, "Carolyn, can I scramble enough for both of us?" Even that sounded double-edged.

"Thank you. First time I remember you offering."

"I've just done it for you before," Jayne said. She thought Carolyn might have guessed more about the past night than her mother. The smell seemed so obvious. Jayne wondered if she had gotten pregnant or if she'd confused blood for semen. A hymen wasn't likely, though; she'd masturbated before the school meds killed most of her interest in sex.

Three eggs in a bowl, a bit of water, no salt, stirred with a fork, dumped into a coated frying pan and stirred with an olive-wood spatula. The prewarmed pan sizzled as the eggs hit it, bubbled around the edges until Jayne began scrambling. She realized she hadn't thought about being pregnant for a few seconds. Maybe she just had pregnancy paranoia?

Getting pregnant to quit meds had been a dumb idea. She could have gotten off meds by living through this year and going to modification camp. The scrambling took her attention again. Sex with Mick felt more maternal than erotic—a child rooting in her belly.

How was she going to live through this if she was truly pregnant? Jayne turned out portions on plates for her sister and herself, then wondered how her family would react. Perhaps she should run away to some unwed mothers' home, tell people there her parents wanted to take her to Europe for an abortion.

If her parents would cooperate about her passport and the airfare, she could go to Europe for an abortion.

How soon could pregnancy tests tell a zygote was in the womb? By now, if Jayne were pregnant, the cells were dividing as cilia moved the egg down the fallopian tubes. Jayne wanted to check her anatomy and physiology texts to see precisely where she could be in the process. If she did get pregnant.

Virgins could get pregnant. Often.

Her father came in then, cheery with the Sunday paper and a blast of chilly air from outside. Jayne's family bought a print paper on Sunday and spread it around the family in sections. Her mother handed her the magazine section and Carolyn the fashion supplement.

Jayne saw that the magazine's lead article was about

schools that helped marginal children become achievers. Reading in this, she saw that the school required completion of a summer rehab program. She wondered how much the school paid to place the article, then turned to a different article exposing con artists who posed as teachers.

Unlicensed teachers. Jayne wished she could just jump the curriculum and wallow in knowledge and strange facts. She said, "Why do teachers have to be licensed?"

"Because people need structured education. And would you go to an unlicensed doctor?"

Jayne wondered if this was a good analogy. Or even worth considering since her HMO doctor seemed to just prescribe what school counselors with only four years of college suggested. She suspected that the counselors prescribed what the teachers suggested. And that was influenced by parents and Judicious Girls. "How often does anyone see a real MD anyhow?"

"Real MDs supervise the nurse practitioners and surgical technicians," her father said.

Jayne wondered why she didn't feel more like suicide. All life had to offer was school drugs or a shameful pregnancy. "I'd like to learn just for the fun of it. Not worry about why."

"You can always use the net, dear," her mother said. "We've got some illogic locks against magical philosophy, but . . ."

Her father was shaking his head. *No, we're not going to take off the illogic locks just yet.*

Jayne wanted very badly to tell her father that she wasn't a virgin anymore, but couldn't quite do this in front of her sister. She'd tell her mother. Maybe her mother, being a former adulteress, would be more understanding.

"I think I'm sick, so I can't go to school tomorrow," Jayne said.

"You'll probably feel better by tomorrow," her mother said. "Maybe you should keep taking your school meds during the weekends?"

"I need to talk to you, Mom. Can we go somewhere?"

"I was planning to play golf with your father this afternoon," her mom said.

Jayne's dad said, "Go ahead with Jayne."

"She can't play golf or tennis," Jayne's mother said.

Carolyn said, "She needs to talk to you, Mom."

For an instant, Jayne wondered if Carolyn knew, then she realized *she* didn't even know for sure. She should keep her mouth shut and buy a pregnancy test kit. So, the kit would inform on her if she didn't enter a marriage-license number. If she weren't really pregnant, she'd just get lectured for nothing.

"It's too cold to play golf, Mom," Jayne finally said, realizing as she spoke that her mother had lied to her.

Carolyn said, "I want to talk to you."

Her parents were suddenly busy with the paper. Her sister who agreed with the world stared at Jayne. Not for the first time, Jayne wondered if her parents had stolen her from a much more subversive family than this one. Jayne said, "I want to talk to Mom. Alone."

Her mother said, "After Carolyn talks to you."

Jayne got up unsteadily and walked up the stair to her room. She lay down on her bed and stared out at the backyard with the dead tomato plants and lost golf balls and the five different styles of identical houses behind the privacy fence. Maybe the egg wasn't ready?

And how soon could a pregnancy test diagnose a pregnancy? Pregnant or not, the kit would inform on Jayne. Maybe, if she wasn't pregnant, she could persuade her family that she only bought it to get attention.

Tomboys and dildo masturbators don't have hymens. Mick'd never believe she was a virgin the way she'd kneaded his buttocks. Jayne's father came up the stairs, sounding resigned to some foolish woman thing. He knocked on her door. "Can you talk to your daddy?"

Daddy? "I don't think so, but if you could be my father, maybe." Jayne realized too late how cruel that sounded.

"Jayne, we only want what's best for you."

"Can you imagine being drugged all the time is best for me?"

"I'm not going to continue talking to you through the door."

"Okay, Dad, come in." If he said the wrong thing, Jayne felt she'd burst into tears. Of frustration.

Her father opened the door and came in. He stood awkwardly, rather outscale for the armchair. Jayne realized it was a little too small even for her.

"We want you to get off the drugs, but the school insists that the only way is to attend that summer camp."

Jayne wondered then if her father ever wanted this to be happening. He'd been one of the last generations to hitch an IQ test ride out of the working class. One of his cousins was a servant. She said, "Okay, Dad, I'll agree to go to Conditioning Camp."

Her dad said, "When you get my age, you'll realize you can live through anything."

Jayne realized her dad knew about his wife's affair, that he didn't approve of Carolyn's virginity fetish if it stole her sense of humor and compassion, that he wished Jayne could rebel without getting caught, that he feared he'd brain his wife one day at golf chicken. Still, she said, "I dunno. I think my life is over." Well, those sounds made another case of the ear being sharper than the nerves that fired the tongue off.

"Jayne, you'll learn," her dad said, facing time alone with his wife and her older female moods. He said, softer, "You've got your whole life in front of you."

"Not if I die," Jayne said, tired of her tone, too, but still unable to find a more sensible approach to life that didn't involve selling out to the Judas Girls.

"Your mother said she worries about you doing something stupid like that. Because you're on school drugs already, you're not high priority for an intervention."

Jayne wondered if her family wanted her to commit suicide. No unwed mother in their family, not their dead daughter. "Why does she think something like that?"

"You know your mother. She worries. You wanted to talk to her earlier. Alone."

"Oh, shit," Jayne said. "I think it can wait. What about Carolyn?"

"I think you'll want to hear what she has to say." Her father left the room then. Jayne waited on her bed. She heard her parents close and lock the door, then the sound of their car driving off. Golf? Just away to leave her to her sister.

For a while, nobody moved. Jayne suspected Carolyn had been listening for her. Carolyn turned on the sink, putting water in pans so they wouldn't crust up, then clicked across the floor. Jayne wondered if her sister could turn off her Judicious Girl monitoring equipment. Radio-controlled virgins, some people called them.

Her sister came up the stairs. Jayne sat up on her bed as she reached the hall. She pushed her back against the headboard.

"Jayne, can I come in?"

"Sure," Jayne said, hearing her voice as though far off. Carolyn was the perfect child who didn't argue with her place. Not as bright as she, Jayne thought, so she could stand it.

Carolyn came in and sat in Jayne's little chair. She fit right in it. She said, "You could get off school drugs if you joined the Girls. I'd feel like less of a freak."

"I didn't hear that at school."

"I've talked to people. For your own sake, Jayne. You're embarrassing me."

Jayne said, "How soon off drugs?"

Carolyn said, "Come with me tonight to the meeting. We'll all vouch for you."

Jayne wondered if a pregnant sister would get Carolyn in trouble with the Girls. "But I wouldn't be wired."

"You could get off drugs as soon as you pledge."

"What if . . ."

"If you're not a virgin, that can be corrected," Carolyn said. "Surgically."

"So, if I pledge tonight, the Judicious Girls will intervene with the school counselor."

"It would show a real change of heart."

And might be a wonderful way to get her prissy younger sister in trouble. "I'll do it," Jayne said. Carolyn's head hit the back of the chair as though this had proven to be altogether too easy. Jayne knew she'd have to change to a skirt and blouse or dress for the meeting. She asked, "Tell me what would look best to wear."

Carolyn said, "You have to be sincere."

Sine hymen, but not without wax. "I'll do anything to get off school drugs," Jayne said. She wondered if the indoctrination included a pregnancy test. "I don't think I've ever had a natural hymen," she said, "so maybe the Girls will just leave me alone there."

"Judicious Girls all have hymens even if we have to make them," Carolyn said. "So you'll pledge. Really."

"So I can get off drugs," Jayne said. *So my baby, if there is one, isn't damaged from zygote exposure to teratogenic substances.* Bad enough children are turned into monsters. Jayne felt a bit guilty about what her pregnancy might mean to Carolyn, but just slightly, just as she was only slightly older and much less mature as everyone kept pointing out to her. Jayne said, "I realize I'll have to wear a dress."

Carolyn nodded, very dubiously.

2
"But . . ."

The local chapter of the Judicious Girls met at an Episcopal church. Carolyn put Jayne in one of her own dresses for the meeting, but Jayne had to drive since Carolyn wasn't old enough yet for a driver's license. As Jayne parked, she saw Judas Girl after Judas Girl opening car door after car door, escorted, driven by parents, driving in female pairs—the whole flock of them in beige calf-length coats and hats.

Their left eyeballs were Janusian—electronically looking back to a past of women protected because they were both fragile and good. Jayne doubted this past really existed. The artificial eyes also looked for a future where technology forever guarded women, enforcers of delicacy and modest, who'd sacrificed an eye to protect themselves forever.

(Some boys thought that the Judas Girls also had wired cunts—demolition jobs that would kill both the seducer and seduced.)

The Judas Girls, milling around on the church steps, seemed to be waiting for someone. Jayne realized they were waiting for her. She saw Sidna, and wondered how many of them were transmitting. Jayne climbed out of the car, watched Carolyn shrug into her own beige coat. No matter how much thermoelectric circuitry, the exterior looked like camel hair.

I haven't got the right coat. Jayne half laughed at her body's stomach thud, but she felt marked in her foil-and-pile thermoelectric coat.

Up close, the camel coats weren't all real wool and camel hair. Some were synthetics. But they all fit. Judas Girls altered their clothes.

"We'd like to invite you to join us," Sidna said. She looked at Carolyn. Jayne felt Carolyn's hand bump her elbow.

"I appreciate the opportunity," Jayne said.

Sidna twisted her Yalie's ring as she said, "We don't expect everyone to maintain our standards. The average girls, 75 percent of the population, can be sluts if they want. But if you join us, you'll find it very painful to lapse into promiscuity or drug use again. Actually, that won't be painful, but what happens next will be."

Maybe these girls really are radio-controlled? "Is the punishment through the electronic gear?" Jayne asked.

"No. It's done by the guys who've pledged to Judicious Girls," Sidna said. Jayne imagined Sidna would have made a mean whorehouse madam.

Carolyn said, "If you've done these things in the past, you can stop doing them now."

"Before she comes in," Sidna said.

One of the girls in the circle around Jayne said, "We really want you to join us." The invitation turned into a choral murmur.

"What if I'm pregnant?" Jayne asked.

Carolyn said, "Our parents will die, Jayne. They'll positively die."

Sidna asked, "Did you fuck other drug creeps?"

Jayne said, "Just the one last night. The one you saw me with, Mick. I really was a virgin until then." She wanted to say *and he isn't a creep,* but right then she saw all this the way

Sidna must see it: Some whore sister of a baby Girl desperately wants to join to avoid social demotion.

Sidna put a finger against one of her ears. She appeared to be listening to a microphone. "It's impossible to tell this soon whether you're pregnant or not."

"Don't ask her to wait until the test can be done," Carolyn begged. "She wants to be good. Really."

Sidna said, "We don't condone abortion. You could stay at a preadoptive mother house if you paid a sufficient initiation fee." The other Girls seemed to be completely without opinions on the matter. Only one, on the edge of the group half-circling Jayne, frowned slightly. Sidna waited for advice from her prompter, who watched from Sidna's missing eye. Jayne knew she'd lose binocular vision if she joined the Girls. She remembered when her sister first began carrying her head differently, the eye that fed biosignals more central than the spy eye.

Maybe only a few have working spy eyes, Jayne thought. *Maybe most of them sacrificed an eye without knowing if they're being monitored by gangs of future husbands or not.*

Sidna said, "Carolyn, you might want to go sit in your car."

Jayne looked at Carolyn. Her sister turned on the balls of her high-heeled feet and went back without comment to the car. When she got there, she realized Jayne had the keys, but seemed too nervous to come back for them.

Sidna said, "If you got yourself pregnant, you did a terrible thing to your sister."

"I didn't know I had any other options for getting off school drugs," Jayne said.

"Perhaps the baby will prove at first amniocentesis to be defective," Sidna said. "Then your initiation will be only $10,000 instead of the $25,000 plus surgical costs for tightening you up and inserting a hymen."

Jayne said, "I don't have that kind of money."

Sidna said, "We don't care. You're not really one of us."

"I don't want to lose an eye."

"My parents didn't force me to trade an eye for this sister-hood. I traded an eye for a better vision of who I could be."

Just as Jayne understood why women joined the Judicious Girls, she realized she couldn't. *Acceptance, friends bound to you for life by dead eyes—wave it away, Jayne, they'll destroy what's unique about you.*

Then Jayne wondered if she exaggerated what was unique about herself. Eyes could be lost to less significant causes than the Judicious Girls.

"You can sign an agreement that we take it out of your marriage portion," Sidna said.

"What if I don't get married?" Jayne said.

"If you don't join, everyone in school knows tomorrow morning precisely why you didn't join. Not willing to give up sleeping around. Every male asshole will hit on you."

Damn Carolyn. But these people were Carolyn's faux sisters, not Jayne's.

"You'll be so alone," Sidna said.

"If I sign?"

"We send you to a home tonight. We take your eye and install monitoring equipment tomorrow."

"Maybe there are other homes," Jayne said.

"Not for people who've been on school drugs," Sidna said. "And none cheap."

"Right. Last century, people would pay me good money for this baby."

"Oh, not that good. It could, after all, be drug-damaged."

Jayne was afraid she'd either cave in or hit Sidna if she talked more, so she turned away from the flesh magnet that was the semicircle of girls. Sidna called her name, but the sound seemed to be coming from miles away. Jayne walked back to her sister in the car, and said, "If you're going to make your meeting, you need to go now. Call me when you need a ride home."

"Why won't you listen? We offered you respectability, stability."

"And maiming," Jayne said.

"A Judicious Eye is better than a biological eye," Carolyn said. "Jayne, please join us."

"Nope. Want to stay for the meeting or not? I'll come back for you at ten."

Carolyn got out of the car and ran to the other Girls. Jayne started the car and drove away, not intending to go straight home.

What next? Where to next? Jayne considered running away. She decided to drive until her family worried about her, or didn't, which would make what came next in her life clearer, though perhaps, if they weren't worried about her, clearer than she'd like. She drove from the town where she lived onto the interstate headed for Charlotte.

The night beyond the city would be dark and starred. Jayne drove, the city wheeling by, fast food, fast drinks, fast dry cleaning, digital pickup, cellular faxes, and net connections advertised on liquid-crystal billboards. Jayne wondered if the liquid crystal would leak if someone fired a gun into one. She visualized multicolored lights dripping down from the sign, running down the pylon legs that held the billboards high enough to reach miles of eyeballs, large enough to read at interstate speeds.

She wanted to see this whole world melt like Dali's *Persistence of Memory,* liquid-crystal billboards flowing down, melting in waves of blended colors.

Probably if she shot one of the damn things, the bullet would bounce off. The billboards grew fewer as Jayne drove farther into the dark starred night.

She saw the exit to Crowders Mountain Park, the remnants of a range that existed before the Blue Ridge, she'd heard, but then news was entertainment, not bound to absolute facts.

Some of Jayne's teachers didn't believe absolute facts existed anywhere in this continuum. The spirit of Plato wrote out absolute facts on ideal paper while sitting at pure concepts of table and chair. Everything here was contingent.

We don't ask everyone to be as moral as we are, Sidna said from memory. Jayne parked the car at an overlook and stared back at the spiral whorl of lights that was the city. It broke half the darkness under the stars, extended to glow beyond the land curving down the globe. The planet Jayne rode curved away under the city, its suburbs, its locked developments and industrial parks where machines took phone orders for a hundred catalog companies and people like Mick checked merchandise and loaded trucks because they were cheaper than machines for that. Behind the Earth's curve, her safe small town waited to attack her.

A car pulled up. Jayne looked over nervously, but the couple in the car seem oblivious to anything beyond their fumbling lips and fingers. *I don't have either the advantage of a steady lover or the protection of virginity,* Jayne thought as she watched the couple slide down below the windows. She felt maternal toward the couple making it in the car, negotiating space between the world's machines and demands and their bodies. After fifteen minutes, the couple slowly came up from supine and prone. They must be sweating despite the cold. Jayne felt chilly and turned up the car heater. The catalysis wouldn't exhaust for another hour.

Good luck, Jayne wished the couple in the car. They seemed to be drinking now and smoking. It was 10 o'clock, time to go home if that was what she was going to do, time to move on regardless. Childhood was over.

The world beyond Jayne's focus group and guarded town had strange fringes and margins, people who didn't agree with the system and helped each other evade the laws. Jayne wished she knew how to find them, the real ones, not the decoys the police set up to lure in people who needed behavior-mod summer camp and school drugs.

Even the idea of getting pregnant to get off school drugs

seemed stupid. *My life is functionally over.* If she didn't start for home soon, Jayne realized, each hour would make turning back more difficult. But here she was, driving farther, going fast enough to reach the Mississippi by dawn.

They'll think I'm really crazy if I did that. Jayne turned the car around and started back toward her family. Otherwise, St. Louis, then a design decision: New Orleans or Colorado? She imagined a self in another continuum, one closer to the Platonic Plato in his Real Chair, driving on, then splitting between the self who went to New Orleans and became a madam and the self who went to Boulder to become a Tibetan Buddhist nun.

Going back to the world of contingent definitions and real missing eyeballs.

And real missing periods. Jayne would know soon enough. She saw the city spread out before her, and realized she'd never known it. What she looked for might be there below her, strange people leading tiny lives in the corners beyond where Judas Girls walked with their half-blind faces. But, she was a female, vulnerable, not trained in self-defense. The Judas eyes did that for women, kept their protectors aware of what happened to women. Jayne had heard that some Judas Girls, not really judicious enough, went to dangerous neighborhoods where untrained servants came from. Those Girls were ambushed in silence, from the rear. Their attackers left them alive, with empty sockets where the electronic goods had been.

Jayne wondered how much of that was true. She should go straight home, but she decided to drive in through the Charlotte neighborhoods she'd been warned about.

And nothing happened. The people in that neighborhood were leading lives of their own, men and women hanging around steps and porches, talking to each other. Stores sold various grades of newspapers and snack foods. Jayne wondered if she could stop going home forever and join them, but the car might be reported stolen.

A kid noticed her, but he just spat against the curb. Jayne hoped they could tell she wasn't a Judicious Girl, then hoped they had that fear of her direct gaze.

Women don't go out alone at night, her mother's voice said from memory.

It was way too late to go back to the church and pick up Carolyn, but surely someone had gotten her back to the house.

Dad's going to be mad. Everyone in her family and all the Judas Girls in her subdivision knew by now. Jayne realized by their terms, the Judas Girls had offered her absolution. She'd refused. They'd be pissed.

The city disappeared in the suburban details, then Jayne was in the country, approaching her town. At the municipal gate, she wondered for a moment if she'd be barred, but the guards on duty simply waved her on in. To them, guarding was just a job that expected them to risk death for richer people's things.

"I'm home," Jayne told the front door speaker as she unlocked the dead bolt. Her dad came heavily to the door. He looked disappointed, old. Jayne was sorry she couldn't reassure him.

"They're in the kitchen," her father said. "No matter what, remember we really love you. Your mother, too. She really is upset for you."

In their way, Jayne realized, or at least her dad did. "I didn't join the Girls," Jayne said.

"I know," her dad said. "That would have protected you, I think, but I didn't believe you'd accept the cost."

Jayne went in the kitchen. The others, including the school counselor, had been waiting for some time. As soon as the school counselor saw Jayne, she picked the phone, speed-dialed a number, and said, "She looks calm enough."

"I am calm enough," Jayne said.

"Any suicidal thoughts?" the counselor asked, still on the phone with what Jayne presumed was a psych ambulance crew.

"No."

"Why were you gone so long?" her mother asked. Her sister had been crying. Jayne was sorry she'd worried them, but then, if she were pregnant, it would only get worse.

"I had to think," Jayne said.

"About what?" the guidance counselor said.

"One last chance to change your mind," her mother said. "Your sister's done so much to try to help you."

Jayne took off her coat. Her father got up and took it away to the hall closet, as though happy he had an excuse to leave the room.

The school counselor asked, "Have you been promiscuous?"

"They're lying," Jayne said.

"Who?" the counselor said.

Jayne realized the implications of that and wondered if her sister was going to cover for Sidna. "Sidna, the Judicious Girl group leader, said they'd slander me if I didn't join."

Carolyn nodded, then said, "They were only teasing."

"But they did say it," Jayne said. "I've only been with one guy. Not that he'd believed I was a virgin. I didn't bleed."

"You've been autoerotically acting out since you were fourteen," the school counselor said.

Her dad came back and wouldn't look at her. Jayne wanted to make some smart remark, but thought saying, "So if I joined the Judas Girls, people would watch all the time."

"You don't have to masturbate," the school counselor said.

"Look, I only slept with one guy once."

"You know even real virgins who bleed can get pregnant the first time."

"Yesterday, the first time," Jayne said. "I didn't know the Judicious Girls could get me off school meds, so I figured I either had to get pregnant or go to behavior-mod camp."

"You practically raped him. Are you trying to get this baby aborted by claiming a lower genetic quality father?"

"Mick talked to you?"

"We sent Judicious proctors to talk to him. He said you used him." The counselor was relentless. "If you were properly contrite, you'd be rushing to join the Judicious Girls right now."

"I refuse to trade being half-drugged out of my mind for being half-blind."

Her mother said, "They're working on a way to share the signals with your brain and transmit them, too. Tapping the optic nerve."

Even that wouldn't tempt her to join the Judas Girls. Carolyn looked queasy, born too young and too eager to be one of the Girls to have both a functional eye and a spy port.

Jayne said, "Can you force me to join the Judas Girls?"

"It's a privilege, Jayne, not a sentence," the counselor said. Jayne wondered if she was annoyed that Carolyn backed Jayne's story about the Girls' threats.

"Will they tell everyone I'm a slut?"

"When I was a Girl," the counselor said, with the capital G between her teeth, "we didn't have these technological advances that make life safer for women."

Jayne said. "Except those times people attack Judas Girls in the dark from the rear."

"Working on that, too," the counselor said.

"Why don't we have honest news? Why don't we give people an education without forcing them to steal a library card?"

"There's no guaranteed reality outside what we make it this side of the Platonic realm," the counselor said.

"Why is that an excuse for turning people's heads to mush and news into entertainment?"

"News was always entertainment. Haven't you read Thoreau on that hacked library card? News to a real American genius was just a distraction?"

"Fuck," Jayne said.

"No, you're fucked. We'll let you off the school drugs until you test pregnant or not. If you prove to be pregnant, you can either join the Judicious Girls or go to a state unwed mothers' home."

Carolyn said, "Did you ever think of how embarrassing this would be to me? Didn't you have any self-respect?"

Jayne said, "I should have just palmed the pills and bought urine for the test."

"If you'd been utterly confident that you didn't really belong on meds, you would have done that," the school counselor said.

"You didn't try suicide," her mother said suddenly. "Didn't even think about it?"

"No." Jayne hated suicide even though she was sure the life she'd wanted was functionally over. "I have no desire to be that weak."

"Your mother tried pills once," her father said.

"You can't be angry with me because I didn't do something." Jayne caught herself about to say "something that stupid."

"You'll marry him and go down in class," her mother said.

"I'm not going to marry him," Jayne said. "I just wanted . . ."

"Didn't know what you wanted, did you?" the counselor said. "Attention deficit disorder. Not capable of making coherent plans."

For a moment, Jayne felt the counselor was right. She deserved to spend her life limited by the brain drugs, married to a guy who was too weird to get a normal woman and too poor to get a Judas Girl. Or, now with the baby, she could become a house servant. Then she decided to refuse to let her counselor be right. "I was stupid Saturday night, okay. But you people have been stupid about me for years."

"The world knows better than any ADD child what's best for it," the school counselor said.

"If I'd been really an ADD child, I wouldn't have come home tonight."

"If you were really crazy, you'd have kept driving. ADD is

a life sentence, but it's correctable with drugs. Real insanity, well, it's a mercy that the insane can elect to die."

Death was a bit closer than Jayne liked. "Can I get home tutoring until the test shows what my condition is?"

"No, you should go to school and face reality."

Her dad said, "I'll pay for tutoring for a week or two."

"People must gossip," the counselor said. "Social pressure keeps society together."

"Not all society," Jayne said. "We've still got subcultures."

"Awful for women. Dirty and dangerous," the social worker said.

"I drove through one on the way back," Jayne said.

"Give a slum a week, and you'll know. If you're still alive."

Jayne looked at her father. Maybe the right thing to do then was go to school, wait. "Would the Judicious Girls let me wait until the pregnancy test?"

"We'd have to make other arrangements. You could stay with some of my other people."

"Jayne, we don't have that kind of money," her father said.

"She could be pledged," Carolyn said.

"Lose an eye and get a husband who isn't able to pledge a real virgin," Jayne said.

"So what were you planning to do with a ADD high-school diploma?" the counselor asked.

"Women still have jobs," Jayne's mother said. Jayne hadn't expected support. Seconds ago, her mother wanted her to marry someone, anyone.

Jayne said, "If I'm pregnant, I get to put it up for adoption, right?"

Everyone nodded. Jayne wondered if any of Mick's people might want the child. If there was a child coming.

"We can know in a week. If you're not pregnant, we'll put you on an injection schedule for school drugs," the counselor said. She looked for her purse, then looked at Jayne's father for her coat. He went to fetch it as if he'd been trained by glances. As Jayne was neither suicidal nor psychotic, the counselor would finish her business with Jayne at school. "If you need a tutor, call me in the morning." She directed that at Jayne's parents.

"Jayne said she'd go to school," her mother said.

Jayne didn't know what would be best. But if she stayed home, she'd be in the house all day with her mother. "I can take a sick day and think about it, can't I?"

The school counselor paused at the door. "Well, but if you do that, going back will be harder. Why don't you decide by morning, one or the other?"

Jayne, feeling perverse, said, "I'll go in Monday, then take a sick day to think about it." The counselor didn't answer her, just looked back at her. Jayne's mother poured a shot of single-malt Scotch. Jayne wondered if it would hurt the baby if she got drunk, too.

Her father said, "Jayne, I'm sorry."

"Dad, I will die if I stay on school drugs."

"Jayne, one-time mistake," her dad said. "We should have reassured you more. Told you what a neat kid you were."

"S'okay, Dad. Good night."

He looked embarrassed, as though he shouldn't have said anything more, or should have said worlds more. Jayne wondered why he was her father, not her mother. She'd have liked having a mother like him. He put a hand out toward her, dropped it, and went upstairs.

Carolyn looked as though someone had just told her she'd gone zombie and got knocked up herself. She, too, went upstairs.

Jayne realized her mother was just winding up and wondered if speaking was a good idea, but said anyway, "I'll go to school. If I don't, they'll lay into Carolyn."

"Too late to think about Carolyn," her mother said. Jayne sat down, realizing as soon as her thighs were horizontal that she'd been standing since she'd gotten home. "We'd been seeing various suitors on-screen. Wonderful men who'd really liked her prospectus."

"Mom, you can at least remember a time when people weren't so stuffy. Or you heard about it. You . . ."

"Why should I have any sympathy for you?"

"Because you're my mother. Because . . ." Jayne couldn't say *because you've cheated on Dad. Because you grew up at a looser time than I grew up in.*

"You're a bitch," Jayne's mother said in rough, low voice. Jayne's mother had an anger gesture. She tucked the tip of her tongue behind her lower incisors and pressed her tongue against bared teeth. She turned from her whiskey to show Jayne that face full of teeth and pressed tongue.

Jayne remembered she'd been beaten by her mother before. Most of her life, she didn't remember this.

"You didn't even think of the family, did you?" her mother said. "A remorseful woman would have at least attempted suicide."

Her mother's threats made Jayne angry. She hated the younger self who always cowered before this woman. "I don't play at suicide, Mother."

"You think I played at suicide?" Her mother's face went white. Jayne knew her mother wanted Jayne dead. She wished her daugher had been murdered in the slums, had been raped and strangled by a lower-class thug, had committed suicide rather than to have thrown this back at her— *I'm like you, Mom.*

Mother and daughter, alone. Tired of the emotional bullying, tired of her mother's hysteria, Jayne thought she'd just look away and not answer. It seemed grown-up to ignore her mother. But the white face and clawing hands lurched forward.

Jayne felt her mother's nails punching through her skin. *She's attacking me.* Jayne remembered the other attacks, the ones that made the nightmare alligators her almost friends.

Her mother slammed Jayne against a wall, banging her head against pictures, shattering glass. Jayne almost raised her own hands, but couldn't attack her mother. *Can't. Why can't?*

The attack was over as soon as it began. Jayne realized her mother was more upset about breaking the glass over her pictures than she was about beating her daughter. Glass crunched underfoot as Jayne's mother let her go and backed off.

"Jayne, you broke my pictures," her mother said.

"You beat me." Jayne realized her mother didn't beat her often, but when she did, she bounced Jayne's head off walls.

"I was trying to knock some sense into you."

"You beat my head against glass. If that had been a window . . ."

"I'd never beat your head against glass. You moved so I . . ."

Jayne's father came down then, and said, "Linda, come to bed."

"Dad, she's been beating me for years."

"Linda, Jayne. I'm sorry." Her dad came down and put his hands on his wife's shoulders. He turned her toward his chest and wrapped his arms around her, holding her in more than an embrace.

"I thought she'd be more understanding, considering what she's done," Jayne said.

Her father said, "Don't be hurtful."

Jayne looked down at the glass under her feet, and said, "I'll clean up. I'll go to school in the morning."

Her mother mumbled against her father's pajamas, "A halfway-decent woman would have shown so much more remorse."

"Hysterics don't do me any good," her father said to both of them, Jayne realized, and led her mother away. She heard from the hall, "I shouldn't have left you with her. I thought. Oh, well."

Jayne wondered if her mother would beat her until the baby burst out. She turned off the living-room lights and sat in the dark thinking about how little she knew about the world. Maybe giving an eye for protection was a deal. But Sidna— Jayne didn't want to give in to the Sidnas of her world.

Still dressed in her sister's dress, Jayne fell asleep downstairs on the sofa. Her father woke her, gently shaking her. "Jayne, you don't have to go to school today," he said.

"If I don't, they'll take it out on Carolyn."

"Carolyn can take care of herself."

"I feel like I should."

"If it's too terrible, call me at the office," her father said. He looked like someone who didn't know what he'd done wrong. Jayne wanted to tell him it wasn't his fault just to get that expression off his face. Women did that for their men, she realized.

"Dad, if I didn't die over the humiliation of being drugged my junior year, then I think I can live through this."

"I don't think you're really going to be pregnant," her father said as though his belief would hold sperm away from the egg.

"We won't know for a while," Jayne said.

"Wouldn't you want to marry the boy?"

"No. I'm sorry I told Carolyn. I'm sorry there had to be a scene. I thought Mom would be more understanding. I didn't think you'd be at all understanding. I'm sorry."

"Do you have any feelings for the boy?"

"Yeah. I feel sorry for him, too."

Jayne felt as though all this was happening to a body two feet below her. As her dad went back upstairs, she heard her mother come down. As her mother fixed breakfast, Jayne went back upstairs and changed into one of her own tunics and pants. She checked to see what homework she hadn't gotten done. Getting chewed out for not doing homework seemed so nugatory now. If she hadn't gotten lured into trying out the Judas Girls, she could have done it Sunday night. Or if she hadn't gone to the party, her life would have been completely different.

How fast could the Girls spread gossip?

Carolyn came down and refused to look at Jayne. Jayne's mother put a plate in front of her father's place, and said to Jayne, "Your father spoiled you."

Carolyn said, "Mom, once she was on drugs, all she could do was hang out with the drug kids."

"We should have disciplined her when she read ahead in the readers," her mother said.

So, if Jayne had been exempted out of her class, this might make the mother look more adulterous. Genes told.

"Mom, you could have applied for an exemption, gotten me in a higher class." Jayne wondered if her mother thought Jayne might have a different father. She'd always thought her mother's adultery was a one-time thing, but perhaps it wasn't.

"You ask a lot of this family," her mother said. "I want to make sure you never do anything like this again, but I am happy that you weren't with a girl."

Carolyn looked as though both Jayne and her mother embarrassed her. Jayne wondered if Carolyn knew about the adultery. They'd never discussed it.

"So off to school with you two. Happy time," their mother finally said. Her voice seemed to be that of a demented actress, strange mix of fake and delusional suspension of belief. "Don't exaggerate. With that good thought, make sure you don't forget your homework."

Jayne wondered if her mother knew she hadn't done hers. The teacher's scolding would be just a pimple on the social abscess she'd already gotten. As she and her sister walked to the bus, Jayne said, "If you get on first, I'll be the first off at school."

Carolyn nodded. The others waiting for the bus stopped talking when the two walked up. Jayne looked around the circle of them. Some of the guys licked their lips. Jayne couldn't tell if they were lascivious or nervous tongue moves. Only a few of the girls avoided Jayne's eyes.

Nobody spoke until the bus came. Then one of the younger girls said, almost interrogatively, "The school counselor was over at your house last night."

Jayne said, "Yes," and let her sister get on the bus first. When she got on, the bus driver said, "Sit up front near me."

Jayne nodded and sat down. She felt like everyone behind her was whispering about her, but then since the neighbors noticed the school counselor's visit, thinking that wasn't paranoid. The kids would talk.

Mick? Why had Mick made her sound so sluttish? Or had he simply been afraid of the Judicious proctors? Maybe one of them knew his boss or even *was* his boss. Jayne couldn't decide whether she wanted to talk to Mick or not.

He was waiting for her at the bus entrance. And Sidna was watching from just a little farther on. Jayne got off the bus, ignoring all the other staring eyes, only aware of Mick and Sidna. When Mick realized Jayne was looking at someone else more than she looked at him, he looked back at Sidna and turned pale under his scars. Jayne noticed then that a JG proctor draped in a black chesterfield coat stood by Sidna. His receiving glasses opaqued his eyes. Jayne wondered what he saw on his own or if both lenses played Sidna's point of view.

The little bitches have power, Jayne thought. She nodded at Mick, not trusting what she might say, nodded at Sidna's proctor (I won't pretend you're invisible), and walked on. Nobody spoke to her. Then she heard Mick say, "Wait," and the sound of his footsteps.

Sidna is afraid. That's why she had a proctor with her today. Jayne wondered if she seemed that bad a bitch to the Judicious Girls or if Mick had a reputation beyond his school drugs and brothers with illicit children.

"Jayne, can we talk?"

"Mick, I'm sorry." Jayne wondered if he'd propose marriage next, felt that was possible. She didn't think she'd want to hear that, but even worse would be listening to him justify why he squealed to the proctors.

"Jayne, don't leave us."

Jayne realized she was the star among the school-drug kids, the middle-class exceptional child. "Oh, Mick."

"Those people can cost me so much."

The Judicious proctor came up, and said, "Is this person bothering you, miss?" Sidna smiled. *We can protect you.*

Mick looked crushed, sure that Jayne would let the proctor sweep him back against the wall, into the metaphorical gutter, enlarge the ADD/LD loser label, rip away what was left of Mick's self-respect. The proctor's eyeglasses cleared so he could see his target.

"I'm his lover," Jayne said.

"Oh, Jayne, you shouldn't have said that," Mick said.

The proctor smiled, and his eyeglasses went opaque again.

Sidna said, "You had your chance, Jayne."

The proctor said, "Sidna, other people have a say in this."

Mick said, "Jayne, don't pick fights with these people and think you're doing me any favors."

Jayne said, "I've got to go to class," and stepped away from them all. She felt a million years beyond mere adulthood and simultaneously foolish.

Nobody did anything lewd. Nobody said anything to her. At lunch, she sat down with computer nerds who drew back, aghast at having her plunk her devirginated body down among their fantasies. She looked across the lunchroom to where the drug kids sat. Mick looked miserable. One of the other school-drug girls patted him on the leg and gave him a hug.

He had a world. I don't. Jayne ate fiercely, almost biting her own fingers by mistake.

The computer boys, normally a noisy lot, said nothing until lunch was almost over. Then a reasonably nice-looking one, who could have broken Jayne's heart under better circumstances, said, "Jayne, what about next Saturday night?"

Jayne said, "I don't know that I'll still be here next Saturday night."

"Alive?" the boy asked.

"In this stupid town," Jayne said. "I think I might move away."

Another computer guy, a large guy who specialized in hardware, said, "Yeah." The computer guys all started laughing as though they knew what was funny. Jayne took her garbage to the can and recycling bins. Her weird move to sit with the computer guys seemed to have broken everyone's inhibitions about hazing her. As she walked through the cafeteria, hands reached out and rubbed against her. The Girls scanned her with their half-electronic vision. The drug kids looked at her as though she'd faked being one of them only to get close enough to betray them all.

A foot tripped her. She sprawled to her knees, her trash flying out in front of her. The chatter stopped. A voice, male or female—Jayne couldn't tell for shock—rang out, "On her knees or on her back, Mick?"

One of the teachers scurried over, picked Jayne up as though she'd instigated her own harassment, and said, "Don't pick up. Just get out."

"I was going to the library," Jayne said.

"Go," the teacher said. She beckoned for a cafeteria staff woman in a stolen-food-thickened body. The staffers even resented Jayne.

Middle-class kids only go physical when truly provoked, everyone seemed to agree.

Jayne left in a bubble of toxic space. If the librarian wasn't compassionate today, Jayne wasn't quite sure she shouldn't make a despairing gesture with a razor or pills.

"You can sit in back," the librarian said, voice almost forced-neutral. Jayne loved that neutrality. Compassion would have driven her to tears. She didn't trust herself to speak, nodded, and went into the back room where all the restricted-access materials were.

If I were just another school-drug girl, getting pregnant would be what was expected of me. But I don't want to become just an-

other school-drug girl. Jayne realized she'd rather have gotten knocked up by the cutest of the computer guys than by Mick and felt guilty for being such a snob.

The librarian came in, and asked, "You're not hurt, are you?"

"No, it's not that bad." *Don't pity me. I'm a snob.*

"If you keep your head up, everyone will decide by graduation that whatever you did was just a rumor."

"I hate being forced to be dumb."

"I imagine your parents moved here to keep their children safe," the librarian said. "Where I came from . . ." The woman sighed as though she'd descended from heaven to this partitioned hell. "What your parents did wasn't so important as who your people were. Even if they were poor now, if they'd come from the right people."

"Where's that?"

"New Orleans."

"I heard it was dangerous," Jayne said.

"That's the arrangement the city made with the Feds and the State. Pressure valves."

"Can I go there?"

"Jayne, you need to do the best you can until you finish here."

"I don't want a drug diploma."

"Is a pregnancy diploma any better?"

Jayne got out, "I feel so trapped," before she began crying. Maybe, except for losing a eye and joining the Girls, nothing she did would drag her life from the moment she was trapped in.

The librarian handed Jayne a tissue and went to the front desk. Jayne hoped she could spend the rest of the day in the back room with the restricted materials, but she was too proud to ask the librarian to arrange it.

The librarian came back, and said, "If you want to stay in here for the rest of the day, it'll be okay."

"I should go to class." Jayne felt her body quiver.

"I heard you forgot your homework in earlier classes." The librarian added, "I'll pay for a taxi if you don't want to ride the bus home."

Jayne wanted to stay in the library's back room forever and ever.

"Can I do independent study for the rest of the term? In here?"

"Jayne," the librarian said in that adult tone that means a person has asked for too many indulgences. "I wish you'd used your nerve and grit in a better cause than doing something silly to get off school drugs."

"The options were reconditioning camp, the Judas Girls, or being expelled from school."

"Jayne, you . . ." Jayne knew the librarian was about to say, you could have cooperated more. The librarian's face softened. She smiled at Jayne very slightly, and said, "You need to disguise yourself, protect yourself. You can be different inside and fool people who don't need to know the real Jayne. Even the Judas Girls don't have electronics monitoring their fantasies. Not all the Judas Girls are real Judas Girls. I know. I've talked to them."

"Why couldn't you be the school counselor?" Jayne asked.

"Not licensed," the librarian said.

"I drove my classmates to physical violence," Jayne said, imagining how the school counselor would react.

The librarian said, "Guy who tripped you didn't do it to you personally. He tripped his idea of a bad girl that he'd like to have slept with."

"I didn't even have that much fun. I felt maternal," Jayne said. Masturbation was more exciting, but she was suddenly too shy to say that to the librarian. "Can I look at anything I want?"

"Let me log on for you," the librarian said. She bent over one of the terminals and entered code too fast for Jayne to memorize it. "Check out alt.ed.criminal.courtrecords."

Jayne called up alt.psych.criminal.courtrecords first,

and looked for her librarian's name. She didn't find it, but that didn't prove anything. A few of the records caught her attention, and she called up the whole post, reading quickly to boil the salient facts from the mass of yes/no answers.

Do courts expect the truth or will entertainment do?

Jayne read enough of the accounts to realize society wanted to control belief systems. The defendant in one case was an herbalist who believed in passes of hands around a crazy person's head. He had one belief system. The school counselor who put Jayne on school drugs had another. If an Asian went to the herbalist, the belief system was okay, but the herbalist, being Scottish, wasn't authorized to believe in or profit from that system. Despite the yes/no answers, the court got eloquent about this as a problem.

You only can believe what your information license says you can believe. No, that's not it. You can only act on beliefs that you're licensed to believe in openly and profit from.

Lower-class girls of all races can get pregnant. Upper-class girls with one natural eye who get pregnant are tortured. Middle-class girls . . .

Hysteria over space aliens was for deracinated losers. They were encouraged to believe in space aliens since the last century. It kept them busy, happy, and disassociated.

Educational systems. Jayne switched to alt.ed.criminal. courtrecords. A judge in Manhattan sentenced his illegal teachers to community service in licensed schools; a judge in Houston sentenced his to penal servitude. Jayne saw this as regional entertainment for courtroom buffs, but it was . . . she quickly cut into Louisiana records.

Life probation at legal schools. What better place for the legal educational system to keep its dissidents?

Jail for second offenders. Maybe working in the library was less tempting than standing in front of a classroom? Jayne ached to know if her librarian had been an illegal teacher, but she couldn't find the woman's married name in the criminal registers. Perhaps under a different name. Jayne knew she couldn't ask the librarian anything about unlicensed teaching, but she could imagine a kindred rebel behind the gray gentry suits and the English dress shoes.

If I could find an illegal teacher who could teach me science, philosophy, 1950s Beat literature, all that real stuff. Jayne wondered if she'd get the librarian in trouble if she called up file on the nineties—nihilistic end of the century that it was, sludged out with extremist Republicans and Anarchists, the very time to have been young.

The librarian had been young, Jayne realized, when stores sold condoms and pregnancy test kits without controls, when common carriers didn't have to be licensed and available only to the proper subscribers.

The official explanation was that people lived better in coherent belief systems that were entertaining and satisfying at whatever level each belief group could manage. Coherence was esthetically pleasing. Esthetic pleasure was part of entertainment.

Aleatory politics appealed only to people who'd convinced themselves they liked hearing Slinky toys and random noise being played as music. Chance politics and anarchy appealed to the most mandarin who'd never experienced chance or anarchy.

Jayne decided she needed to become a mandarin. She read on in criminal records.

The school counselor called Jayne in the next morning. She said, "We're not going to test you this week. We can't do a cell sample until the fetus, if there is a fetus, is further along."

"So how long do I stay in limbo?" Jayne realized that in hating the uncertainty, she proved the political theorists right. If she were truer to her wish to desystematize, she'd revel in the uncertainty.

"Actually, we've arranged for you to come to school and do independent study in the library. The librarian agreed."

So Jayne went to school with her sister Carolyn. As she got off the bus, she was ritually hazed. But since she'd been ritually hazed all through grade school, she was used to it. She went to homeroom, then to the library.

But should she spend all that time researching out weird topics? Jayne knew the school counselor knew she was using the librarian's pass code. The school wasn't so large that it had more than a couple of female rebels, and at this moment in time, Jayne suspected she was the most serious one.

Jayne spent her second day in the library studying human reproductive biology through the medical nets. Some things weren't matters of opinion. DNA was the genetic code; fertilization occurred in the fallopian tube; the fertilized egg adhered to the womb lining and retained an attachment through the umbilical cord. If Jayne proved to be pregnant, the cell was down in the womb attaching already.

Was this just a belief system? Jayne wondered if the Chinese, who believed in chi and acupuncture, knew some other way to get pregnant. But then they sexed out their unborn with amniocentesis. Jayne's dad said that amniocentesis saved the world from being overrun by starving Asians and that Jayne should be grateful she was born in a country that respected the rights of unborn girls.

After five days of obsessive biology, the school counselor called Jayne into her office. "You don't miss interacting with the other children?"

Since the last interaction that morning had been the usual morning hassles, Jayne thought she'd be crazy to want further interactions with the other children. She did wish she had some friends. She remembered her friend from grade school, who'd played naked games with her, but didn't think she ought to tell the school counselor about that. "I wish I lived somewhere with people like me. Be an alternative like in the nineties. Paris in the twenties."

"Those people were downwardly mobile upper-class," the school counselor said. "You're middle-class."

Except for possibly George Orwell, Jayne's culture heroes sneered at the middle classes. "We can't afford servants."

"Servants are a more valuable commodity than the downwardly mobile upper-class alternatives," the counselor said. "We've tested Mick. He could sire a reasonably happy child. Your genetic possibilities are decent, too. So, if you do turn out to be pregnant, I suspect you can forget about abortion."

"Unless the amniocentesis itself damages the baby," Jayne said, full of her researches of the morning.

"You're obsessing about pregnancy. I even wonder if you are pregnant or just wish you could humiliate yourself this way."

"My mother thought I ought to have cut my wrists carefully to show contrition," Jayne said.

"You're walling me out. You won't give me a chance to help you."

"Can I go back to the library now?" Jayne asked.

"I've blocked the librarian's code. You'll have to stay in appropriate material."

Jayne decided she'd read the appropriate material subversively, ask what self-deceptions, necessary and otherwise, did this appropriate material require or reinforce. "Okay."

"You have schoolwork to do. If you finish school. Dropping out is an option."

Jayne realized that pregnancy wouldn't doom her as much as dropping out. "Since I'm not likely to marry, I need to think about a career," Jayne said. "Even if that seems pessimistic." The counselor looked at Jayne as though she thought Jayne was taunting her as a woman who sacrificed an eye to purity and then still didn't get married.

"Some Judicious Girls choose careers."

Jayne almost said, I'm sure they do, but realized just in time how wise-ass that would sound. "Maybe I'm tired of my posturing and all."

The counselor looked at Jayne with both eyes—data streaming out of her electric eye to some database analyzing the likelihood that Jayne was serious. Jayne expected momentarily to be strapped into a lie detector, but the counselor simply said, "It would be nice if you were serious," and marked on a pad with a stylus. "We'll send you a lesson plan to your terminal in the library back room. You can go back there now. By the way, what do you plan to do for lunch?"

"I'm bringing it," Jayne said.

"You like being alone too much," the counselor said. The door opened, and Jayne walked back to the library.

The librarian Jayne liked wasn't sitting at the desk; nor was she around for the rest of the day. Jayne feared she'd gotten the woman in trouble, but didn't want to ask about her in case that would get the librarian in more trouble.

Lesson I: How sexual excesses lead to poor economic performance. A social history comparing sixteenth-century Japan with twentieth-century Japan, nineteenth-century and early-twentieth-century America with end-of-the-century America, especially St. Louis, Missouri.

Jayne decided to go to the drugstore and buy a pregnancy test kit. Since her parents wouldn't let her drive now (if driving led to teenage pregnancy, this was too late), Jayne walked to the drugstore across the street from the school and bought a pregnancy test kit from someone who seemed utterly unfazed by her purchase. Not everyone was an informant for the Judas Girls. Jayne wondered if the man also sold condoms and, if so, was the quality control any good.

"Think about who you want to be when you sign the register," the man said.

Since everyone knew already, Jayne signed as herself, then wondered if it would have been better to have signed as her mother or even as Sidna.

"You want a scrape?" Jayne asked.

"Machine's broke," the man said. "You insist on giving a DNA sample?"

"I signed in under my own name."

The man shrugged, and said, "It's be $12.96 plus excess tax."

Jayne paid the $18 for the kit and followed a bus onto school grounds. The ID machine either didn't quite keep as accurate records as Jayne thought or it, too, was broken. Jayne was so busy wondering if she was going to get caught for sneaking off the grounds for a pregnancy test kit, she didn't realize that the other students weren't hassling her as much as they had. She went into homeroom, where the teacher had one eye, at least, that wasn't subject to mechanical failure.

"Little late, Jayne?"

"I don't know," Jayne said. She noticed that the other students were looking to see if she was going to pull something really weird. But they weren't hassling her. Jayne finally recalled that the students in the bus yard and in the hall hadn't hassled her, either. Maybe she looked dangerous?

That night, she urinated on the dipstick, and the results were inconclusive. When she looked at the box carefully, she noticed it was out-of-date. Jayne wondered if this meant she was pregnant. She wanted to get the waiting over with. The next day at school, she asked to see the school counselor or the nurse. The counselor sent for her. "Jayne, what do you want to tell me?"

"I want to know whether I'm pregnant or not. I bought a test kit, but it was out-of-date and the results were inconclusive."

"You can't trust illicit sources," the counselor said.

"But you could have me tested. It would do so much for my peace of mind." Jayne realized she shouldn't have said this.

"We won't give you drugs until we know whether you're carrying a healthy child who wouldn't come under the physician-assisted-suicide guidelines."

"You're telling me to be patient, then," Jayne said.

"Are you going to try for an abortion?" Jayne wished she had someone to talk to. Her mother was impossible, the librarian somewhat skittish, perhaps for her own protection. Jayne refused to make the school counselor her confidante. This was the person who poisoned the first half of her junior year.

"Jayne, I am suggesting to your HMO doctor that a consultation with a psychiatrist is in order," the school counselor said. "You refused to trust Judicious Girls. Perhaps you need a strong father surrogate?"

Talking to her own father about this would be too icky. "I guess. Or a woman who wasn't in the Girls." Jayne wondered if this was a trap.

"The state doesn't license counselors who weren't Judicious Girls," the counselor said.

"So are all the guy counselors and therapists ex-proctors?" Jayne asked.

The counselor said, "Males aren't expected to be completely Judicious."

Jayne paced while the psychiatrist talked. "The issue is whether you're a danger to self or others," the psychiatrist, a middle-aged man, said. She hated the idea of being in either of his patients' chairs, the couch or armless chair.

Jayne nodded at him and continued walking. His office was HMO standard, with a big leather chair for him. On his desk was the computer wired to the practice policies. Neatly stacked in piles on the desk were dusty CD jewel boxes. Jayne picked one up and saw it was a real antique in a late-twentieth-century format, full of hypertexts he'd bought but probably hadn't ever accessed. He had a personal imago on his screen who typed with fingers only two pixels wide as the machine itself transcribed what Dr. Meeks had just said to Jayne. The little secretary figure continued typing in the silence. Jayne got up and walked to see the screen better. It read PATIENT HAS BEEN GIVEN INFORMATION ON INVOLUNTARY COMMITMENTS. HER HMO PLAN ALLOWS ONLY 45 CONSECUTIVE DAYS OF IN-HOSPITAL TREATMENT FOR SCHIZOPHRENIA, MANIC-DEPRESSIVE DISORDER, ACUTE PANIC ATTACKS. (COPAYMENTS HIGHER FOR AT-TEMPTED SUICIDE.)

"Imago, find Jayne's school file and keep it closed for now," Dr. Meeks said. Jayne was disappointed that he didn't have a more imaginative name for his personal assistant. He continued speaking to Jayne even though the screen began showing what he said while the imago popped out. The imago hung Jayne's file above her keyboard and continued typing. "Do you feel compelled to see information not intended for you?" Dr. Meeks said.

"I don't like having things done behind my back." Jayne wondered if the computer would only respond to Dr. Meeks's voice, but the imago typed what she'd just said. "Access Jayne's file."

The imago voice came from the speakers. "Wrong voice for commands."

Jayne said, "I thought we'd interact in a virtual reality or something."

Dr. Meeks asked, "Do you often invent private realities yourself?"

Jayne said, "What I want is a pregnancy test. You can do that for my peace of mind."

"Would you want an abortion for your sanity's sake?"

"Is a girl's sanity a valid reason for an abortion anymore?" Jayne said. "I admit this was a dumb way to get off school drugs."

"We want to observe you without the drugs, see if there are other processes going on with you, Jayne."

Jayne said, "Why do you let me walk around your office instead of asking me to take a seat?"

Dr. Meeks paused. The PA imago looked up, then a small bookcase materialized. The tiny book she opened caused twelve-point text to display SOME PATIENTS NEED TO TEST LIMITS. OTHERS ARE IN PARANOID MIND STATES. SOME PATIENTS ARE ANTIAUTHORITARIAN.

They know a lot about me from school. Jayne said, "I'm either pregnant or not. If I'm pregnant, I know I can't raise the child."

The library and text dematerialized on the screen. The imago typed on. Dr. Meeks asked, "Why don't you think you can raise the child?"

"I'll be an unwed mother."

"Why do you want to be pregnant and give a child up for adoption?"

"Maybe I'm not pregnant."

"How would that make you feel?"

"Neither being pregnant nor being on school drugs seems like a worthwhile life outcome to me right now."

"Any suicidal tendencies? Reincarnation fantasies, heh? You've read in Buddhist texts even though your household is prescribed Christianity."

"No," Jayne said.

"What are your earliest memories of childhood?"

Jayne didn't say anything as her first memory was of her handcuffed screaming baby self as her mother watched on. The psychiatrist watched her. She said, "Riding in a stroller."

The imago said, "Lie, 92 percent."

Jayne said, "Oh, shit."

"I think you're jammed in a false memory. We'll look at it as adults and see how illogical it is."

As she spoke, she knew he'd be sure she'd made it up. "I was chained to a tree with jewelry while other children tormented me." False memory jam.

"Why jewelry? Do you think you're a captured princess?"

Jayne sighed. The computer voice said, "Stress and other emotions."

3
"Falling by Body"

Maybe I haven't paid enough attention to the social world about to gobble me, Jayne thought as she went back to the psychiatrist for the second time.

Observe these aliens. She decided to ask the psychiatrist about himself rather than simply sitting there letting him truss her up with questions while his computer PA typed her answers and coded them for truthfulness.

Maybe the control mechanisms are perfect. But then how does my social order explain me?

Jayne suspected that the answer was that her rebellion didn't matter. She was a girl.

As soon as Jayne sat down in the patient's chair, Dr. Meeks asked, "How would you feel about having your class designation changed?"

Jayne doubted he meant to a higher status grade. "I'd like to be able to go to a better college."

"What about being able to drop out of high school now? A mere high-school diploma's been meaningless since the 1980s. You could then keep the baby. If you really are pregnant. I understand that Mick isn't sure now that he really had an ejaculation."

Jayne wondered where that came from. "I'm smart. I

tested higher than I was supposed to on the third-grade IQ test."

Before the imago could report on how strongly Jayne believed this, Dr. Meeks said, "Voice-stress analysis off speakers."

Jayne said, "You don't want anyone to agree with me, not even a computer imago."

"Jayne, the third-grade test could be a fluke. Whatever, you were offered a rare opportunity to a girl in your condition, and you turned it down."

"You mean with the Judas Girls." Suddenly, Jayne wondered if she wasn't making too big a fuss over an eye. And then she wondered what the imago was telling Dr. Meeks about her voice-stress patterns.

"Judicious Girls."

They stared at each other a moment. Jayne found herself almost wanting to say anything to fill this silence. She guessed that not speaking would also count against her. "One of them, Sidna, said that she'd gossip about me all over school."

"Why did you tell your sister about your sexual escapade? Have you adopted an ethic about sex that makes losing virginity a value?"

"No. I felt guilty, actually."

"But not guilty enough to want to join the Judicious Girls and get taught self-control."

Jayne wanted to get up and see what the imago did during moments of silence, but somehow she doesn't feel free to walk around Dr. Meeks's office this time. *He'll interpret it.* "So society is right, and I'm wrong?" Jayne means this to be a question. It comes out a confession, but she doesn't really believe it. The whole human race can't be divided between slut-servants and Judicious Girls.

"This false memory of an infant princess chained by jewelry, have you thought about that anymore?"

Jayne said, "It happened. I doubt they were expensive bracelets."

Dr. Meeks said, "And this was your first memory? What was the emotional overlay?"

"Terror. And people have been picking on me ever since."

"All the time? Was Mick picking on you?"

"No. The drug kids didn't pick on me."

"Perhaps because you fit in with them?"

"They pick on me now."

"You betrayed an intimacy."

"Look, insight is very well and good, but I have a mother who beat me because I didn't make a suicide gesture the way she did when Dad caught her at adultery. A mother who took me at age three or four to see a friend that was dying."

"We're here to talk about you, not your mother."

Jayne felt as though the man had slapped her. Maybe all mothers took their children to see friends die and beat their children's heads against the wall for refusing to make suicide gestures? "Are children supposed to raise themselves, then? Without mothers?"

"Healthy children shape an unhealthy mother's behavior."

"What do you want to do to me?"

"We'd like to hospitalize you for observation. Obviously you want to be punished for your sexual acting out."

"Maybe if I'd been a better girl, little g, not capital, I would have known better how to be in this world. But I was interested in things that weren't supposed to be for girls. I'm really interested in them."

Jayne noticed that the imago didn't accuse her of lying. She also couldn't remember when she last looked at an amoeba. The school drugs destroyed her enthusiasms.

"Share with me?" Dr. Meeks asked.

"I don't trust you," Jayne said.

"You have a limited capacity for reality testing," Dr. Meeks said. "We need to know if it's innate or learned."

"Next week, then."

The imago piped up, "Probablity of lie 67 percent."

"Jayne, we may have to hold you as a danger to your fetus."

"Now you're reinforcing my pregnancy delusion," Jayne said. To her horror, the machine didn't call her on a lie. Dr. Meeks looked at the machine, then back at Jayne, and smiled.

"I'm not sure whether I'm pregnant or not, but I should be," Jayne said. The machine let that one pass, too.

"We now have the whip of shame to keep young girls in line, at least young girls with something to lose if they can't marry well."

Jayne said, "Mick's sisters had lovers."

"That's why I offered to demote you to servant or working class," Dr. Meeks said. "Their community is more tolerant."

"I want to go up, not down. I wanted to be a scientist."

"Past tense," Dr. Meeks said.

Jayne realized she'd thought she was taking charge of her own life when she seduced Mick, but that hadn't worked out. But she didn't know if she trusted anyone more than she trusted herself. The whole world from the inside of her head out was suspect now. She needed to have the pregnancy resolved: yes, no. Why was everyone waiting? Jayne called Mick. "Hi, Mick, I'm sorry if this has been too much fuss for you."

"What do you want, Jayne?" Mick sounded more tired than hostile.

"Can you drive me to Charlotte after school tomorrow?"

"Gotta work," Mick said.

"You're home now. What about now?"

"Can you pay for my gas and dinner?" Mick said.

Jayne hated the whine overtones to his question, but said, "Yes." Her mother came in just then. Jayne said, "I'll meet you at the gate in half an hour."

Her mother asked, "Who was that? And where do you think you're going?"

"I'm going to do what needs to be done, Mother, with Mick."

"Getting married? Dr. Meeks told us you might function better if fewer social demands were placed on you. A simpler class might be less demanding. You told Dr. Meeks I neglected you as a child, let other kids beat you. Well, I told you that was just their way of showing affection."

Jayne thought this said something terrible about affection and her mother. "He told me I suffered from false memories. We've got to talk, Mick and me. See what might work for us both."

Jayne's mother said, "I could raise it. Pretend it was mine." Her mother seemed deadly sincere.

This women-collaborating-against-the-world tone made Jayne extraordinarily nervous. She said, "Mother, I don't want a fake younger sibling. All I wanted was to get off school drugs."

Jayne's mother said, "I can't defend you."

"We've always understood that you cheated on Dad." Jayne expected to be hit, but her mother simply leaned against the kitchen counter. Jayne felt cheap and cruel for saying that.

"It was punishment enough that your dad forgave me," her mother said. "I'll walk you out to see Mick. And here." Jayne's mother pulled out a credit card, signed a temporary permit on it. "The bill comes to me. Your dad won't see it. Have as good a time as you can, but do come home before curfew. Please marry someone before the baby comes."

Jayne didn't want her mother to see Mick, but there it was. Each helped the other on with her coat, then, without saying much more, they walked out, Jayne turning back to lock and alarm the house. She hoped her mother remembered the code in the state that she was in.

The guard offered them hot coffee, but neither of them was interested. When Mick pulled up, his scars seemed exaggerated in the sodium lights around the guard kiosk.

Jayne's mother whispered to her, "He looks like a child stuck behind a mask."

Sometimes my mother can be insightful. Mick's eyes looked detached from the scarred face. Even when she had sex with him, Jayne hadn't realized how long and delicate his eyelashes were. She remembered with a visual flash a picture of a woman with tentacle lashes—on the Net? On video. Jayne couldn't remember. But these were real lashes on two functional eyes.

"I'm Jayne's mother," her mother said.

"I'm a friend of Jayne's."

"Be good to her."

"Mother, please."

"I didn't mean for all this gossip to happen," Mick said.

"Jayne's careless about whom she confides in," Jayne's mother said. "I learned it's best never to confide in anyone."

Mick was white under the even paler scars. The guard looked at him as though he was a bad younger brother. Not entirely impossible that they could have been brothers.

Jayne's mother said, "Do you like your scars, Mick?"

Mick said, "If I pass school, my parents said they'd pay to have them removed."

Jayne's mother nodded. Jayne wasn't sure her mother realized as she had that Mick's parents couldn't afford to have the scars removed.

As they drove off, Mick said, "So who did you tell?"

"My little Judas of a younger sister," Jayne said. "She wanted me to join, but it was too late."

"None of my sisters ever got asked," Mick said. "Did you have any feeling for me or what?"

"I feel so awkward. You were kind to me after they put me on school drugs."

"My parents told me they were thinking of bonding me out for training as a butler. Great opportunity, my dad said. Butlers get kickbacks from food and beverage contractors."

"Society puts you in a position where the only way to do well is to be dishonest."

"Honesty is for people who already have the money," Mick said. "I hate this fucking country. I wish I was enough nigger so they'd have sent me back to Africa or to a ghetto city."

"What are they doing there?"

"Can't afford to see for myself, and everyone knows the whole story is a lie. Maybe they didn't even send them back, you know. Maybe they're all dead."

"Black children are still being born to people who tested out white," Jayne said.

"Ever seen one? Bet they abort them since they'd be victims of racism. You gonna have it aborted?"

Jayne said, "The school counselor said your sperm seems okay enough."

"I fucking never took their nasty drugs. Not all the time."

Jayne felt like she'd been a double fool. "You didn't? What about the blood tests?"

"Well, like you get someone in cleaning to find out when the medicos are coming to test. So, yeah, I took the drugs for those days. Like how often were you tested?"

"My dad's HMO tested my school-drug blood level, not the school." Jayne realized she wasn't privileged but privilege's captive. "Once a week."

"Shit. Oh, shit," Mick said.

"I wouldn't have known anyone on the cleaning staff, anyway," Jayne said.

"You won't inform on me about this, will you?"

"No. I am so sorry. The HMO now has a psychiatrist wanting to demote me." Jayne realized she wanted desperately to cling to the middle-class privileges even if they hurt her.

"We could get married," Mick said. "Jayne?"

"I want to find out about unlicensed education."

"Just more mind-warp for money," Mick said. "Can I at

least be with you when you find out whether you're pregnant or not? If I am the father?"

"You're the father. If I am pregnant."

"You didn't bleed. The school counselor thinks you're protecting someone nice."

Jayne said, "I had reasons not to have a hymen, but you were the first flesh in. Is there a neighborhood in Charlotte where people like me go when we're adults?"

"What are you?"

"Weird and nonconforming."

"Took your pills every day, so nonconforming?"

"I want to be weird and nonconforming."

"Can we take a razor to your face and rub in scar factor?"

Jayne hoped not answering either way would push that subject aside.

"Did you do me despite the scars?"

"You want the scars off?"

"Yeah. If I indenture for servant, the family can have them removed if they want."

"Do families generally clean up their servants' faces?"

"Sometimes. Mostly, they think scars keep their virgins safer. Didn't stop you, did it?"

"We don't have a servant."

"Could, couldn't you? Bet your dad's got the license."

"Mom won't have help unless she can afford live-in."

"Harder to steal if you have to take the loot to a room the boss can inspect," Mick said. "So, you want to find a drugstore first or eat dinner?"

Jayne wanted to get all this over with, but she did feel something—pity, sympathy, sexual bonding, whatever—for Mick. "Let's eat first. Mom gave me her private card. She said to have as good a time as we want but to be home before curfew."

"Your mom seems okay," Mick said. "Pretty decent."

"Pretty, but not always decent."

"Don't talk trash about your own mom."

"Sorry. What do you want to try eating that you haven't been able . . . had before." Not so diplomatic to say haven't been able to afford.

Mick said, "What I'd really like to do is eat raw fish. My dad said he ate raw fish when he was in the army. The army sent him to Hawaii."

"Sushi," Jayne said. And it didn't take long to prepare. "When you get gas, I'll find out where the nearest sushi place is."

"Bad sushi's dangerous," Mick said. "I dunno. Dad said you want to see them cut it in front of you. See the fish eyes, make sure they're clear and the gills are nice and red."

"I'm sure they have chemicals that take care of the bacteria these days," Jayne said. She'd had sushi once, when her parents took her to Washington, DC. Perhaps Mick's scars would be more the problem in getting service.

They pulled into a fuel store with gasoline pumps. While Mick filled the tank, Jayne looked up Japanese restaurants on a public display. She had the terminal print a map, then paid for the gas and the map. Mick took a look at the map, and said, "Well, reading is good for finding places, isn't it?"

"You can entertain yourself with reading," Jayne said.

"This country's been half-about entertained to death," Mick said. "Let's go eat some industrial development nation food."

The Japanese restaurant looked like a general steak house from the outside. Inside a man playing an antique pinball machine with real metal balls and incandescent lights stopped and took them inside. He didn't seem to notice Mick's scars at all. "Sushi," Jayne said, as they were about to pass the sushi bar. The Japanese man grunted and nodded to the cook, who was yelling at a waitress.

Mick said, "It looks like plastic food."

"It is. They make your real food up from what you point to."

Mick looked at the food and interrupted the cook at his haranguing of the waitress. "What's the best?"

"Sushi love boat."

Jayne looked at the price on the model love boat, then saw the sashimi platter beside it, and said, "We could split the sashimi platter."

Mick saw the price on the love boat and nodded. "I don't want to do your mom's credit. We could even just get a couple pieces and fill up on rice or something."

"Thanks, but half a platter would be okay."

The waitress took the opportunity to pick up her order and take it to her table.

"Are you really Japanese?" Mick asked the cook.

"Are you really white?" the cook asked back as he cut up fish. He flipped everything onto rice spread on a straw mat, rolled, sliced, ladled out wasabi and grated radish. Mick didn't answer. Jayne wondered if perhaps everyone was lying about their ancestors. The man in front of them could be a Korean. Her parents could have African or Creek ancestors; Mick could be a Bulgarian refugee's great-grandson. Everyone could be pretending.

She could go to the Girls and get her virginity back.

Tuna with a pickle wedge, flying fish egg, California roll, Philadelphia roll with imitation low-fat cream cheese, and barbecue-pork sushi rolls—what was authentic? Maybe the octopus?

Mick said, "I thought it would taste rawer."

Jayne said, "The octopus wasn't raw at all."

"It's hard to feel like you're eating something raw when it's all wrapped up in rice and cut so formal," Mick said.

"Try this," the cook said, extending a hunk of raw tuna on a bamboo skewer.

Jayne signed the card and passed it to the man playing pinball on the way out. Now she almost wished she could postpone buying the pregnancy test kit. "Where are we going to do the pregnancy test?" she asked.

"My sister'll let us use her room," Mick said.

After all that, he wants to go to bed with me again, Jayne thought, hoping her instincts were wrong. It was going to be so awkward. "I have to be back by curfew."

"We'll do it," Mick said. "It's only seven-thirty now." They got back in the car and drove to a drugstore. Mick bought the pregnancy test kit under his own name and even paid for it. Jayne wondered if she was his best chance of a child that would have better options in this world than he or his siblings had. Maybe his best chance of a child who wouldn't get aborted.

As they walked back to the car, Mick said, "My sister'd be willing to raise it."

"My mom said the same thing."

By 8:27, Mick pulled into an apartment complex on Central Boulevard. Men stood around miniature pickup trucks, beer in coolers at their feet. A man appeared to be selling drugs under a streetlight at the corner. Mick looked at Jayne, then back at what must have been a familiar scene to him. He looked as though he just recognized it through Jayne's eyes.

"Your sister lives here?" Jayne asked, though it was obvious she did. "Isn't that guy selling drugs?"

"Yeah. Yeah. Point man for getting a federal score-card. Have to prove you're an addict before you can get on the king's dope."

Jayne wondered if Mick's sister used heavy drugs, if that was why she lived here. "You don't use, do you?"

"My genes ain't broke yet," Mick said.

"It affects you genetically?"

"King's dope does, so I hear. Then they don't have to have addicted babies to deal with. Embryo's too broke to make baby."

Jayne remembered that his brothers couldn't sire viable children. "Oh."

Mick didn't answer. He pulled up into a parking space across from the apartments. They walked across the parking lot together, Mick slightly in front, holding the bag with the pregnancy test kit.

Jayne said, "How does it know who to inform on?"

"The test can't inform on you." He had a key to his sister's apartment. Jayne wondered about that. "You middle-class girls sure do believe a lot of shit."

The main room of the apartment was about nine feet on a side. On one wall was a galley-sized kitchen with one burner, a frying pan and a little sink and microwave. The table hinged down from the wall. Under the picture window with the steel grate was a futon bed. Jayne hoped the woman had a separate bedroom at least. Mick's sister wasn't there, but she'd left a bong and a bonded marijuana package on the table in a neat and deliberate way, semiotics for have fun. A note said, MICK, BE SURE TO LOCK BACK UP.

Jayne said, "Let me go on to the bathroom."

Mick looked away from Jayne then. "Will you really let me know?"

"Yes."

Jayne went into the tiny bathroom and peed over the test stick. She wondered if she'd done it right.

A cross materialized on the stick. Pregnant. She went out and saw Mick still staring at the same point in random space. "Yes," Jayne said.

He looked at her, looked away, then came over and squeezed her hand. He said, "Don't kill it, please."

Jayne said, "I don't know how even to begin." She'd been right when she felt maternal after fucking Mick.

He reached up for her shoulders. "And don't cry."

"Have you gotten other girls pregnant?" Jayne asked.

"No." His hands began circling on her back.

Jayne sensed he needed comfort. She wasn't sure she wanted to sleep with him again. But she was pregnant, so it probably didn't matter unless he'd been unclean since. AIDS? He put his hand, the back of his knuckles against her cheek and rubbed. They were almost the same height, eye to eye, bodies almost together. She sensed that she was more likely to survive pregnancy okay than he would survive his life.

There was a tiny bedroom, filled with mattress and rods overhead for clothes. She licked his scars rather than kissing him. He jiggled her left breast, and said, "Human bodies are so wonderful."

Afterward, Jayne felt terribly bored. She said, "Now, can you take me home?"

"Curfew?"

"Yeah, curfew."

"You could live as a working-class woman."

"Mick, what everyone wants for me makes me nervous."

"So you want to go home forever?"

"I'll probaby have to go to a Federal Unwed Mother Home or to the Judicious Girls."

"They sell the babies," Mick said.

"You know that for a fact?"

"Everyone knows. Maybe what everyone knows doesn't rate as a fact." He pulled on his pants.

"My dad would have to pay them so much money."

"If I wasn't the father, if you'd gotten knocked by some college professor's son, the kid would be more valuable."

"I can't believe they sell the babies."

"Ask an adoption broker where the babies come from."

"Judas Girls sell their bastards?"

"Can't hardly get middle-class white babies any other way."

If Mick was telling the truth and not lying to keep her out of the Judas Girls, Jayne shouldn't turn herself over to them. Any placement money should go to the mother, maybe the dad, but not to the Judas Girls if they were collecting $60,000 up front to rebuild her hymen.

Then it hit Jayne. She was pregnant. Her honest life was over. She'd be forced to use deception and guile forever to keep her status. Seeing Mick's sister's place made degradation a horror.

Halfway across the parking lot, she burst into tears for the honest straightforward person she could never be again. Mick stood by the car until she collected herself enough to finish walking across it. He opened the car door for her, and said, "Feeling sorry for yourself's no good, you know."

Even with his semen oozing out, she felt remote from him. She even wondered if he'd picked up a disease since she first slept with him and had gotten her back to infect. No, she'd called him.

On the left, they passed one of Charlotte's ghettos. From the highway, the houses looked like ordinary houses, more mixed. "Is it that bad there?" she asked Mick.

"Where?"

"In that ghetto we've almost passed."

"Ghettos are real various. I had a pass once to hear a couple bands. Some of the people even look white enough."

"Some working-class whites look mulatto. Even some of us, the middle-class whites."

"Bad manners, don't you know, to mention that," Mick said.

"I've led a sheltered life."

"I'm sorry."

Jayne wasn't sure whether he was sorry she'd lost her sheltered life or that she'd missed so much. "I've always resented what was offered me, but I sure didn't want less than manager class."

"Did you think to play the games better. They think if you don't, you aren't capable."

"That's not true."

"Yeah? Sure you and I don't have a developmental defect that wrecks our concentration without school drugs? Hell, I'm not sure I don't believe it and I cheek the drugs. You have the ability, you rise. You don't, you sink."

"It's not true. The Aztecs were more of a meritocratic society than this one."

"So you know this little history factoid. But how does this apply to being alive now?"

"If you refused to play by their rules, the whole system could be shattered."

"Yeah, breaking the rules got worked into the very rules themselves. Like you can be a race traitor and go live in the ghetto. And the owners come visit on the weekends. Ghetto's the human zoo."

Mick'd handed Jayne a conceptual knot to pick. "What do you mean, breaking the rules is part of the rules?"

"Well, like you. Break the rules and prove that the Judicious Girls are tolerant and forgiving even to women who kill an eye too late. Break the rules and—so what are you going to do?"

"Figure out something they don't expect me to do," Jayne said. "Keep moving."

"Our owners have seen it all, babe," Mick said. "Like Lennon said before they shot him, 'a working-class hero's nothing to be. They hate you if you're clever and they despise a fool.' Game's been rigged since before my great-granddaddy was born."

"I'm not a working-class hero," Jayne said.

"No? The women I grew up around would yank your nipples out for a dumb cunt."

They made it back to the guardhouse well before curfew, but the guard wouldn't let Mick in. As Mick turned around, the guard called Jayne's mother to come and pick her up. While Jayne waited, the guard said, "I wouldn't have let my daughter go out with a guy like that."

Jayne thought the guard was pretentious. Then she felt guilty for the whole night. Until the psychiatrist wanted to put her down a class, Jayne had thought she was class-crashing, daring. Faced with a life in a trailer or in Mick's sister's apartment, Jayne wanted all of her privileges.

"You didn't quarrel with him," Jayne's mother said when Jayne got in the family car.

"Mother, I'm not going to marry him. And I am pregnant."

"It wouldn't be that bad. Losing status isn't important when you have a good man."

"I'm not going to marry him."

"Oh, Jayne. Judas Girl homes aren't covered by HMOs. You just want to bleed your poor father's retirement. I could find a naturopath down in South Carolina to abort you. You might die, though. And it is illegal."

Jayne had an ugly vision of dying from an illegal abortion, holding her mother's hand. "Don't want that either. Maybe the genome will justify an abortion."

"The psychiatrist said you were too fragile for an abortion. The guilt would make you crazy. He'll sign to have you bear a slightly defective fetus. But we could spare you the federal home. Dr. Meeks said that the HMO will pay for nonconsecutive forty-five-day stays in a hospital. You'll have to work for your board for the fourteen days between stays."

"In a hospital? What kind of a hospital?"

"A rehabilitation hospital for people like you who abused drugs, sex, alcohol. He thinks you used your counselor to abuse drugs. I never thought you were really brain-damaged. You were such a happy child."

"The psychiatrist who kept telling me I fantasized about being pregnant now tells you I'm too fragile for an abortion? He told you this?"

"Jayne, rehabilitation will be good for you. You'll be working off some of the cost for the off-HMO days by helping around the facility."

"Am I being committed?"

"Yes. For the sake of the baby," her mother said.

"This is nuts," Jayne said.

"I think you're pretending to be crazy. But that's good. If you stop pretending to be crazy, you have to marry Mick or take yourself to a federal home," her mother said. "We're sacrificing some of our nursing-home time for you, so be glad we found some way to deal with you that's less scary than a federal home."

"What will you do if I move away?"

"If you cooperate with us, you'll be able to put this behind you. The hospital has a licensed tutor. We'll find, somehow, a college that will take you."

Jayne wondered if moving was a word her mother simply couldn't hear. *Move, as in leaving the social universe I know and hate.* Just in case, she asked again, "What would you do if I moved out?"

Her mother said, "If you tried to run away, you'd look even more dangerous to self and fetus."

"What if I got away? And stayed away?"

"If you ran away and died of it, we'd forget you. We're healthy people. Healthy people don't dwell on misery. Life expectancy on the street for sexual deliquents is two years. For crazies, up to ten years, tops. Those statistics include hardened street children from criminal families, children who learned from their parents how to survive by their wits. Two years, max, and you'd be dead."

The social utility of these statistics was too obvious, but perhaps some statistics were true enough. "I'm tired. I need to go to bed." Jayne had seen real poor people's housing with her own eyes. Sinking even below that would be too costly a defiance. Jayne didn't want her defiant gestures to kill her in two years. She began climbing the stairs to her bedroom.

Jayne's mother said, "I love you. Everything works out for the best."

Jayne said, over her shoulder and down the stairs, "Mother, everything works out. That's all."

"By the time you're fifty, science may have conquered death and old age."

Jayne kept going up the stairs. Unlimited life was quite the bribe, right up there with unlimited potential. She realized as she stripped for her shower that she smelled like Mick. Her mother must have known she'd slept with him again.

Perhaps overattachment to life wasn't called for now. But Mick's sister's apartment had appalled her.

Jayne dressed herself in a long cotton nightgown and imagined herself dead in it and visibly pregnant. Then she saw herself dead in it, aborted, the cotton soaking up the blood as only a natural fiber could.

She put her hands on her stomach. Still flat. But her breasts seemed heavier. If thoughts really were reality, babies could be spontaneously reabsorbed. Jayne tried to press around the outline of her womb with her fingers. Invisible complexities that didn't respond to media lived in her belly.

The next morning, Jayne woke up sick and threw up sushi fragments into the toilet. She shouldn't have last night's sushi still in her stomach. Her whole body seemed to have slowed down above the fetus and womb.

Her mother brought her crackers, and said, "The hormones and the baby take over your body now." Jayne saw the fetus as a tiny thing with teeth eating at her. Her mother said again, as though trying to hypnotize her, "Hormones will take over now. You'll lose energy."

Sitting sick on the floor, listening to her mother, Jayne wanted a legal abortion. But even an abortion couldn't undo what she was now. Birthing a baby or not, she'd broken the social code for her class. Lust follows class.

What world would she find if she ran away? If she couldn't beat the statistic for runaways, she was the fuck-down the Judas Girls and the rest of the world thought she was.

Jayne ate the crackers her mother brought her. They came up on the water she'd used to wash them down. She thought, *Reality check. It's hard to be a runaway when you have morning sickness.*

Over the next month, hormones put the baby hooks to Jayne, altering Jayne's neurologics, setting up the enhanced circulation responsible for pregnancy glow.

Despite her mother's objections about the cost, her father

assured her that going to the Judicious Girls was still an option. He loved her dearly and wanted her to be a virgin again.

Revirgination was possible. Her sister invited her to come
to a Girls' ritual for a secondary virgin. Jayne, who didn't
want to totally alienate the Girls, went.

The sisters went to the same church as before. The Girls
ignored Jayne as they welcomed in the woman, presealed by
a hospital-built hymen, who was taking secondary-virgin
vows. Puffy bruises surrounded her left eye socket. Her nose
looked like the surgeon had used it for leverage when he
pried bone away from the orbit. The good eye shivered, probably frightened by its fellow eye's replacement. The eyebrows
and head hair hadn't been shaved. Having expected to see a
totally bald woman, Jayne thought this an odd touch. A
shaved head for a revirgin somehow seemed more appropriate.

Her sister said, "In the old days, the Judicious Girls sometimes performed a ritual 'Pulling the Steel.' Women who had
active sex lives pierced their body parts. You had to pull the
steel to prove you were going to be chaste in the flesh."

"That's easy," Jayne said. "You could just unfasten the
navel ring or whatever." She realized then that some women
pieced their labia. "And slide it out."

"No, the woman had to pull it out in front of witnesses,"
her sister said, sounding grimmer than Jayne had ever heard.
"You could use a yanking machine, but you had to set the
machine up yourself."

Jayne thought the present ritual was obscene enough.
Sidna and another woman took the revirgin into another
room. Jayne assumed they put her up in stirrups and checked
the surgeon's work. When they came out, Sidna said, "A virgin again, by act of God through man."

The Girls circled the revirgin, each kissing her on the
cheeks and passing her by the shoulders to the next girl.
Judas kisses, Jayne thought. The ritual had sinister charm.
Jayne could imagine how cool the Girls thought they were.

Even though it wasn't morning, she felt vomit rise. On her way to the toilet, the Girls parted around her as though she were toxic.

Sidna, though, followed her into the toilets. Jayne wondered if she'd be allowed to throw up in private, but Sidna waited beyond the stall door. Jayne wiped the drool off her chin and came out.

"Sidna, you want to talk to me."

"We can find a good home for the baby."

"Even with a low-IQ daddy?"

Sidna's mouth twitched.

"I have other options beside the government home or the Judicious Girl one."

"Your sister told us. Rehab will do you more damage than we will—sensory deprivation, shock treatments, drugs. We could even let you return to society as you are now, without making you one of us. For the baby's sake, consider it. Rehab works major structural changes in personality. They'll bring you to hate what you were before Rehab."

"If they only could really make me like the world I'm forced to live in." Jayne didn't trust Sidna's sudden concern for her welfare, but she shocked herself by admitting she wished she could have her personality changed.

But what was rehab really like? Maybe it left a person mentally whipped without changing the underlying angers and hostilities.

Sidna said, "You might as well learn to accept us. Eventually, you'll come to love us. I know you don't have enough guts to strike out on your own."

Jayne decided to see if she could run away in a self-preserving fashion.

This world that Jayne hadn't paid much attention to had her slotted and ready to be locked up.

Jayne found out that running away without money was a logistical nightmare. Her parents had saved under her name, but that was for college. *If I don't go to school, the money should be mine anyway,* Jayne thought. But what if the running away didn't work. She'd still be pregnant, would have blown the money her parents put aside for college, and would have disappointed them more thoroughly than ever.

If she didn't touch the money her parents set aside for her education, or not all of it, she'd have to buy a fake work card. *Ah, but Dr. Meeks offered me a real demotion in class.* Jayne realized she'd be a fool to fake a work/tech ID when she could get one just for asking.

While Jayne sat in the library, thinking furiously in circles, her librarian friend came in, and said, "Rehab hospital wouldn't be so bad. Psychiatrists are, on the average, smarter than school counselors. You'd have a chance to persuade them you were smarter than your family."

"I feel stupider than anyone ever could be. I got myself pregnant."

"Don't jump over walls you can look over first. Check things out before you commit to doing them."

Jayne realized she could take a bus to Charlotte and see what jobs were available. If she got a job, she'd move out. If not, then she'd stall on further decisions as long as possible. By September, she'd be showing; but everyone knew what had happened to her anyway. "I wish my parents would move away from here."

"Your dad can't just get another job like that," the librarian said. "Let me know where you end up. I'll write."

Jayne wondered if the librarian would loan her money for the bus trips she'd need to take. "I need to find after school work. How would I go about looking?"

"It's a pity all children don't have part-time jobs more often. You learn that school's not everything and that there's more to life than whatever official news web you follow. Unfortunately, you'll have to talk to the counselor about getting a permit since you're not a working-class child."

Jayne wished she could ask the librarian about her own life in New Orleans. "I wish I had unusual skills."

"Not everyone out there even has basic computer skills."

Jayne decided she'd look for a job, then apply for the permit. She could tell, she thought, if people were interested in hiring her. For a second, she wondered if she just wanted people to tell her what to do, then she decided she was taking a sensible course—neither running away nor refusing, yet, the options others offered.

Look over the walls before jumping. That was a great concept.

On the morning bus to Charlotte, the bus driver didn't ask Jayne why she was cutting school. At the professors' compound, a little boy child about ten got on. The bus driver didn't even card him.

Jayne felt her social realities shift. The bus driver knew he drove hooky players to the city. Not all of the world was dedicated to making her behave. The ten-year-old boy stared back at Jayne as though daring her to say anything. Perhaps he feared she was a Judas Girl. Then he stuck out his tongue at her and blatted a wrong-ended fart at her.

At the highway, the bus locked on to the traffic grid, and the driver leaned back in his seat. He had a small microwave under his seat and used it to make popcorn.

"Want some?" he asked the boy-child.

The boy-child came up and began eating popcorn out of the popping bag. The driver popped another bag and looked at Jayne, lifting it in the air and tilting it toward her.

Jayne felt vaguely threatened. But the man wasn't flirting. But if he were, she was already pregnant. The strange chink in society's rules seemed like a media event, something she watched from far away. A professor's son, or a servant's?

If the boy was a servant's child, this scene made more sense, but Jayne wished the boy was a professor's son and the bus driver was luring him out of his class prejudices, perhaps even trying to lure him out of his class. Jayne asked, "How is it being a bus driver?"

"Not so shabby," the bus driver said.

"And do you want to be a bus driver when you grow up?" Jayne asked the boy.

A woman said, "He's on independent study."

"Funny, so am I," Jayne said.

The boy said, "I'm going to be president when I grow up."

As though sharing a secret, the bus driver smiled at Jayne. She wasn't sure what the secret was. Perhaps the boy was mad. Perhaps the boy was scheduled to become president when he reached the age of thirty-five. Where's Reality Central?

From the back of the bus, a woman's voice said, "We don't have real presidents anymore, sonny. They're all expert systems."

Jayne thought the bus driver would touch his head in the she-must-be-crazy gesture, but he said, "Heidi, you must tell babies there ain't no Santa Claus."

"Santa Claus started it," Heidi said.

Jayne knew at one level that television was entertainment, not reality, but she suspected that social animals had to share consensus realities or lose neurons from lack of stimulation. Whether that consensus reflected pixelated entities by digital masters or pure Platonic ideals beyond the byte-thrown shadows didn't matter to the human animal.

All human neurons required was a belief system flexible enough to keep its holders fed and sheltered. Zeus, Coyote, Yahweh—real? Unreal? Did the belief system allow its believers to eat, find shelter, and breed? Memes were necessary, not true.

And how real is that?

Jayne watched the city thicken around the highway, sprouting streetlights bending over the roads like minimalist steel mothers. Finally, the bus pulled into the terminal near the Square. Charlotte's Square was a misrepresentation, just the two roads crossing. On each corner were sculptures: bankers, gold panners, railroad and textile workers, heroic mothers.

The sculptures struck Jayne as silly and sinister, the white dream of a city wired on hype and Christian cargo cults. Under them, the homeless slept on massive concrete street benches.

Jayne went off the homeless ground-level streets up into the skywalks between office buildings. She found a phone and began calling temporary placement agencies.

"You'll have three forms of ID, two with current address and photo, third small-form birth certificate."

"I'm in school, so I thought I'd see if I could get a job before applying for an afterwork permit," Jayne said. "I have my school swipe pass and my driver's license. Can't I at least see how I'd do on the computer tests?"

"We don't have time for this," the woman said.

On the advice of the third woman Jayne called, she finally found someone who'd consider her proposition. The agency, not a national franchise, did have a listed phone number. Jayne got the address and was quite relieved to find that she could walk there without going back to ground level again.

Jayne took a slidewalk across a street and into an office building. There she changed to an elevator for the seventeenth-floor office of the temporary employment agency.

The elevator had been tagged by mural hit people. The interior walls glowed with a fluorescent frog contemplating a woman with three stacked vaginas: one that replaced her navel, one that might have been a hysterectomy scar, then the vaginal vagina. The woman was wild-eyed. The hit artist or artists weren't without talent.

The paint looked very fresh. Jayne touched it. It seemed mildly tacky, but that might have been her sweating finger. No color stuck.

The elevator's front wall was painted over. Earlier hits bled faintly through white primer. Jayne knew this particular building was on the slum fringe of the walkway complex. *Nobody knows where I am.* Jayne made sure she had her two forms of ID with her.

The agency was at the end of a hall filled with astrologers, Christian socialists, Theosophists, small record companies, and short-term desk and computer rentals. Jayne followed the numbers until she reached it. The door was blank, only the number.

Go home. Go home.

Jayne opened the door and said to the woman on the desk, "You have an interesting elevator."

"No, it's gross," the woman said. "You have an appointment? You hiring out or hiring?"

"Hiring out. I called maybe twenty minutes ago. Someone said to come over."

"Take this into the john and pee in it," the woman said, handing Jayne a clear plastic container with a liquid-crystal thermometer strip against the side and a pill and plastic strip inside. "Don't try to lose the pill or the strip. The pill shows color whatever results."

Jayne took the plastic urinal into the bathroom the woman unlocked for her. While Jayne urinated in the plastic container, the woman waited by the sinks.

Jayne handed the plastic container filled with now green liquid to the woman. The woman said, "You're pregnant."

"I know. That's why I'm looking for a job."

"Yeah," the woman said as though she'd expected Jayne had a problem and was hung between being disappointed and mildly relieved that it wasn't drugs. Green was obviously the go-ahead color for that half of the test. "Yeah, you looking for long-term temporary or just until the baby's born or what. We got some clients might help for consideration."

"I've got good keyboard skills and can talk through interactive programs," Jayne said.

"College prep before this? Not an LD kid or dyslexic?"

"Yeah." Jayne remembered this as the first day she managed a lie without suspecting the other person disbelieved her.

"Going back after?"

"Oh, yeah. I'm not going to let this ruin my life."

The woman said, "Fill out the forms. Only thing is I have to verify you're an American citizen, so on this form, use your real name whatever you put down on the other forms."

Jayne realized her age and class wouldn't be a problem here.

"You like shooting pictures? We're always looking for commission photogs who have cars and can travel. Baby pictures, totally legal. In department stores."

Jayne wondered if her parents would buy her a car so she could work taking baby pictures in department stores until her own baby was born. "Let me think about it."

"Alway openings. Commission work, but they reimburse you for mileage." The woman looked up at Jayne, and said, "Really."

"I was thinking of something in an office," Jayne said. Being exposed as pregnant for months on end didn't seem really desirable. "Not on a front desk, in a back office."

"Where you can hide out for almost seven months?"

"Yeah."

The woman looked at her computer and touched the screen for different entries. She tapped one, sighed, tapped another. Jayne wanted to see what she was calling up, but the desk bulk prevented that.

"Slow," the woman said. "One here you might try, but the photog job would pay you more if you could sell. Being pregnant might soften women's sales resistance, but you'd have to wear a ring. Fake being married, say to someone in the service."

"I don't have a car."

"See if you can get one," the woman said. She tapped the screen again, and said, "This one's willing to work with all sort of handicapped and minimally dysfunctionals."

Jayne said, trying to sound brazen, "See if pregnancy is considered a handicap."

"Can you work nights? You'd be making follow-up calls to leads developed by direct e-mailing machines."

Just then, Jayne realized how impossible all this was. She didn't have a car, nor an apartment, nor, if she used a fake identity, an HMO. "I need to find a place to stay first, then get a car."

"This address no good or fake?" the woman asked.

"It's my parents'."

"Oh. I know some rooming houses you might get a bed in quite cheap. Got a camera or disk system, or your computer if you don't mind being off-line, you sell it and you'd have a bed and box." The woman scribbled down an address. "A bus runs by every half hour. I'll call her for you, tell her to give you a special rate."

The bus was full of poor people who smelled of sweat, liquor, and mildew. It ran automatically, a well-bred voice coming from the computer to announce each stop.

Jayne got off on Queens Road at a block of large old houses turned into bed rentals. She'd heard about bed rentals—how the poor had no choice in roommates, how what little they had got stolen. Terrified of finding herself an old woman dying in a rented bed surrounded by strangers, Jayne rang the bell.

A woman said, "Jillian sent you, right?"

"At the temporary agency," Jayne said.

"Yes," the woman said. She did't look that much poorer than Jayne's own mother and about the same age. "You're looking for a job and a place to stay. Your folks kick you out?"

Jayne realized Jillian at the temp agency also told this woman she was pregnant. She couldn't stand the pity in the woman's voice. "No, but I thought I ought to leave before I had to choose between the Feds or a rehabilitation hospital or the Judas Girls."

"You could join the Judas Girls? Shit, don't waste a

chance. They'll fix you up with a new hymen, arrange a marriage. You'd throw away that for an eye. Hell, you can always lose an eye on the street for nothing."

"But they'd charge my father so much to take the baby and rebuild my hymen that it isn't worth it."

"Well," the woman said, turning to show Jayne the rooms. "Oh, well."

Jayne felt compelled to explain herself. "After being a disappointment to my parents, I didn't want to be an extra burden." Looking for a job, walking behind this woman to see beds for rent seemed brave and stupid.

"You'd share a room with only two other girls, and you'd have your own bed, so it's not so bad. Bed and board would be $75 a week, cheaper than the Y. A rack space out by the airport is about the same, but this is so much more homey. We've got a kitchen and sitting room."

Jayne remembered that minimum wage was now $2.40 an hour. The door opened on three beds in a room with a dormer window—flowered bedspreads, large boxes at the foot of each bed, a closet the size of Jayne's at home. Shabby and cheerful. Jayne expected she'd get as much at the rehabilitation hospital.

"I could let the bed under the window go for $250 a month, but you'd need first and last months' rent and a month's security."

Five hundred dollars, she didn't think even her stereo and camera together would sell for that much.

"Talk to your parents. They might be more supportive than you think. We have a couple of girls like you come through every year. If you want, I can help arrange an adoption. I could waive the rent in advance and the security if we found the right parents for your child."

In other words, there still was a market for a white girl's baby. "Oh." Jayne didn't want this life. She wanted to go to college and study Greek and Latin, anthropology, art, psychology, music, science. She felt disgraced.

"Well, do you want to take it?"

"I want to look around a bit more."

"Do you want my advice?"

Jayne nodded. She felt that if she spoke right then, she'd burst into unstoppable tears.

The woman said, "Join the Judicious Girls."

Suddenly, Jayne felt remote from crying. "I want a life, not a husband."

"Life is easy. Living well ain't," the woman said, looking at the beds as though fully aware of how shabby their cheerful covers really were.

Jayne wished she'd only fantasized about running away and getting a job. Then, whatever happened, she'd have had a warm imagination for her alternative self to run wild in. She was glad she hadn't pawned her stereo and camera and gone out wild. She might get home without her mother even noticing that she'd gone missing.

As they walked back to the door, the woman said, "Did you hear about the president? He's been meeting secretly with aliens."

If the president had been meeting secretly with aliens, this woman would never know about it.

The bus was forever in coming. Jayne hoped she wouldn't be attacked while she waited. Several cars slowed down to inspect her, but she didn't answer the "oh, baby, baby"-ing men.

But the men in cars seemed to expect women to be more responsive than Jayne was. As the bus pulled up, Jayne thought, *It was bed rentals, not a brothel, wasn't it?* She decided she was being paranoid. Brothels had to be licensed.

Not that everyone pays taxes and license fees. In the bus terminal, two persistent guys forced Jayne to wait in the women's rest room until the three-thirty buses began going back to the enclaves.

An ambulance was waiting by the guardhouse. Jayne didn't realize it was for her until two strong young women in tan uniforms that looked almost like khakis put their hands on her arms. Her parents clung to each other. Her mother said, "Dr. Meeks signed the advisory papers at noon when you didn't show up at school. You're not legally committed, but we've signed you in voluntarily as a minor."

Jayne, too stunned to pull against the two attendants, said, "I'm not running away. I'm coming home."

Perhaps her parents would abandon her now, let these people drive off with her.

Her mother climbed into the ambulance with her. Perhaps her mother had been declared crazy, too.

4
Bridge Among the Mad

The ambulance took Jayne to Dr. Meeks's office, and the attendants walked her in. As though exorcising a demon, Dr. Meeks stood up at his desk and pronounced, "You are a danger to yourself and others. So, you must be sent to a rehab center for the child's protection."

Jayne thought she'd been reasonable. After looking for work and a place to live, she'd come home. "I was exploring my options."

The computer voice said, "She really believes it."

For an instant, Jayne felt grateful that a computer PA understood her. Then she wondered how she'd gotten sucked into reifying a computer program. It didn't side with her; it didn't even have a self.

"Can't I wait at home until I begin to show?" Jayne said. She wondered if she'd be given shock or locked-in VR treatment.

"Putting you in a controlled environment is best for you." The psychiatrist hit some keys, then said, "I've forwarded your records. You'll be at the rehab hospital in two hours."

It was like being declared a leper. *Unclean, unclean, you are now dead to society but alive to God.*

At the ambulance, her mother hugged her, and said, "We'll follow in your father's car. We still love you."

The aides' bodies swayed together as the ambulance maneuvered onto the traffic grid and headed west. Jayne finally said, "What's the place like?"

"It's pretty," one of the aides said. "Old resort hotel."

"Thanks," Jayne said.

"Most of the people are regulars," the other aide said.

Jayne didn't know quite how to answer this friendliness. They were only a little older than she was. "I'm sorry I was so startled when I first heard."

"Never been binned before?" the first aide asked.

"No."

"Well, this place has everything necessary for the business. Maybe not the latest equipment, but functional."

The other aide said, "Except they don't do cutlis there. We have orders to take you in the front. That's good."

"Be glad you're not living in Virginia in the 1950s. They used to sterilize girls like you and send them out as sex slaves."

Jayne realized they'd been being familiar with her, not friendly. She wasn't a complete social unit; she was a crazy whose problems provided them with work. She said, "Where is this place again?"

"In Crystal Springs," the first aide said. "Near Asheville."

Whatever Crystal Springs had been, it was now home to a large chemical plant and waste-reclamation center. Jayne hoped that the locals found better jobs in those plants, because Crystal Springs was built in the Appalachians where the local mountains weren't so massive. The factories repelled the tourists and forced the town to find other uses for the old hotels. Rehabilitation North Carolina, Inc., bought one of the largest, set now on top of a hill. Jayne saw the hospital looming above the trees and semisuburban houses like a fantastic château, visible intermittently when lawns lined up to give a vista. *Who gets the turret rooms?*

When Jayne arrived, her parents weren't there yet. The ambulance had priority on the road grid, she realized, even though they hadn't rushed her here to save her life, just to save an hour of the aides' and driver's time.

A uniformed secretary took Jayne into a small room with leather-upholstered chairs, bookcases, and a dark wood desk topped with a brass lamp. In the room's corner was a paper-covered examining table and a blood pressure machine. The woman said, "Your doctor will be responsible for all medical needs, physical and psychiatric. He's coming in to evaluate you."

Jayne said, "You've got my records."

"Yes, but we make up our own minds here."

This was the first promising sound Jayne had heard in years. Jayne thought the woman was talking to her as though she was normal. "Should I change to an examining gown?"

"Let Dr. Ames's nurse tell you. I just need your HMO card, please."

"My parents have it," Jayne said.

"Oh."

The door clicked shut and locked. While waiting, Jayne looked around the little room. The books and disks looked promising: *Metamorphoses* by Kafka, *Steppenwolf* by Hermann Hesse, *Dr. Faustus and Other Plays* by Christopher Marlowe, *The Conformist* directed by Bertolucci, and other old serious works, salted with the sorts of books and tapes that indicated a reader neither subscribed to official taste nor bought the books by the yard. Jayne wondered if this was her doctor's office. She wanted to grow up to an office like this. She pulled out a hardcover edition, *Genome and Blot: Further Explorations of the Cerebrosphere,* unsure as to whether the book was a medical text or fiction. But then, did that matter?

Genome and Blot looked interesting, but the main characters were concepts, so Jayne put it back on the shelf and pulled out *Steppenwolf.* Just then, she realized the mirror over the desk could be one-way. Or perhaps the bookends had wide-angle lenses in them. She doubted that the hospital would have left her alone and unwatched in this room that long.

Or was that paranoid? She put *Steppenwolf* back, then realized she was getting bored.

So she was being watched. So what. All they'd learn is that she sanely picked up a book to read rather than sit wondering about the mirror. All she'd known about the book before was that Hesse was an old 1960s writer. Looked like from the copyright that he had to have been writing really late in life to have written in the 1960s. She took the book back off the shelf. *So, I'm fidgeting. It's normal under these circumstances, waiting to be admitted to a rehab house.*

Just as Jayne was getting into the book, Dr. Ames came in. He wore a sweater over corduroy pants, but Jayne knew he was the doctor because he was too old and self-assured to be an aide and too male to be a nurse. He was in his forties, with half gray hair and bald spot. He said, "Hi. How are you feeling?"

"Dubious," Jayne said. That sounded insane. She closed the book and said, "I'm here to be rehabbed because I got pregnant to get off school drugs."

"Why do you think you're crazy?"

Jayne put the book back on the shelf to give herself a bit of time. She blew out a breath, took in another one, and said, "I don't think I'm crazy, but I obviously don't negotiate the world altogether that well."

"What eighteen-year-old does?"

"I'm not quite eighteen," Jayne said. "Judas Girls negotiate the world better than I do."

"You'll be eighteen soon enough," the doctor said. "Perhaps you just need a refuge from criticism until you deliver your baby."

"You're going to lock me up and not give me therapy?"

"We'll be observing you for the next few weeks. I'm going

to insist that you spend time talking to other patients. Isolation can be a habit as well as a symptom."

Jayne didn't answer. The whole deal seemed screwy. "I'm sure I need something. Reality checks at bedtime."

"We don't let you use insanity as an attention-getting device, here," Dr. Ames said. "Most of our clients here are older. You might find the ones who aren't psychotic to be very interesting. And they miss their own children. I'm assigning you a room on the front hall, open door. You can sign out to go on the grounds."

"What about therapy sessions?"

"Our occupational therapist will let you know what your schedule is going to be. Now, I'm going to do a physical."

It was just a physical for lungs and head. Dr. Ames didn't even feel Jayne's belly.

"Can I borrow this book?" she asked him, as he wrote notes on an electric pad.

"Sure," he said. "Your tutor is a patient here. She's great. You'll want to finish high school." From Dr. Ames, that wasn't a question. "While you're getting settled in, I'm going to talk to your parents." He tapped the electric pad. "Ocean, your new student is here."

A woman in a tweed suit with a black-velveteen collar came in. Jayne couldn't figure out whether she was a hard-used woman in her late thirties or a well-preserved woman in her fifties. She smiled at Jayne. Jayne couldn't figure out whether the smile was forced or not. It seemed basically sad.

Dr. Ames said, "Jayne, this is Ocean Tatum. Ocean, Jayne. Your pupil. She's going to be in room 211."

"Ms. Tatum."

"Call me Ocean." The woman said to Dr. Ames, "Next to Alice? Is that the best of ideas? I know the first day is rough, so let's get it over with. Jayne? Right, I'll show you to your room."

The room in the madhouse was more spacious than the

bed-rent in Charlotte. "You'll share a bathroom," Ocean said.

Even if the mountains had been more scenic, these shared bathrooms condemned the hotel to use as a rehab center/madhouse. She asked Ocean, "Where are my clothes?"

"You can't have your clothes in your room yet. The aides will bring you fresh clothes each day."

"Okay."

"The men are upstairs. The back hall is for people who are really crazy. Junior staffers board on the third floor."

"Okay." Jayne wondered what she was supposed to do next. "Who gets the turret rooms?"

"Senior staff if they want. I'll tell Alice you're here. She's been waiting for someone her age to show up. We're more pleasant than most HMO detox centers. Don't let Alice bully you, though."

"Will I be helping people during detox?" Jayne asked. She remembered an unpleasant text about drug people quitting drugs—constipation, enemas, diarrhea.

"I don't have anything to do with that," Ocean said. Jayne wondered if she tutored to pay for her own stay here. "I'll go get Alice."

Jayne sat down on the bed and decided she was socially dead. Then she went to see what the bathroom looked like. The taps dated back to the last century or before, with separate faucets for hot and cold water. The door to the other room was locked now. The dresser in Jane's room was empty. The closet also had nothing in it. Just as Jayne was thinking that Alice wasn't going to show up, she heard a knock on her door. "Come in."

Alice wore black. Her hair was the unrelieved blackness of dyed hair, curling all over her head. One eye was covered with a black patch that blended with her hair. On her visible eyelid, she'd drawn black lines over the lashes. She'd painted her right big toenail black or had bruised it. Her visible eye was dark. Her skin was translucent. "I'm Alice. You're Jayne. Ocean wanted me to show you around."

"Hi, who else is our ages here?"

"Just us on the front hall. I'll need to get my shoes on," Alice said. She limped slightly on the right foot, Jayne noticed, so the nail was bruised, not painted. "Why are you here?" Alice asked.

"I'm pregnant, and since a girl has to be crazy to get pregnant out of wedlock these days, well, here I am," Jayne said, faking more bravado than she felt. But after all, everyone here would see her belly swell if they stayed long enough or came back that often.

"Oh, really," Alice said. "Everyone else has had an abortion. But we're genetically difficult material."

They walked down to Alice's room, where she pulled on a pair of sandals that left her toe free to drain, then Alice began popping her head in various rooms, introducing Jayne to the middle-aged and older women who were still in their rooms. Some looked drugged.

Jayne said, "I won't remember all their names."

Alice said, "I would have," and continued on down the wide stairs that led to the ground floor. "If you tell me something, I remember it. And I hate hearing repetitions. So don't tell me things twice."

"Okay," Jayne said.

Her parents were waiting in the lobby. Jayne's mother said, "We were told someone would bring you from your room. So you've found a friend."

Alice said, "She's found a local informant," and left Jayne with her parents. Jayne wondered if they'd say good-bye in front of all the old patients who'd paused in their bridge playing at the card table in the corner. Ocean was now sitting among them, looking more like fifty than she'd looked earlier. She looked at Jayne's mother as though not quite approving.

Jayne's father said, "Your doctor seems nice. He said they

wouldn't have to give you shock treatment and you seem under control, so virtual isn't an option."

Her mother said, "Shock treatment wouldn't have hurt the baby. It's one of the few things they could have done for you."

Jayne felt cold to think that shock treatment might have been an option. "I wish I could have an abortion," she said. "The other girls here have had them."

Jayne's mother asked, "Has she gone gray prematurely that she dyes her hair?"

"Mother, I didn't ask."

"Well, I'll be up to see you often," Jayne's mother said. Her father didn't say anything. After a furtive glance toward her belly, he didn't look at her again. Jayne suspected seeing his daughter pregnant in a madhouse was so heartbreaking he wouldn't repeat the experience. She got up dutifully to hug them good-bye. As they walked out, her mother look over her shoulder and gave Jayne a thumbs-up. What was that, the hurrah-for-breeders sign? The women-sneaking-around-respectability sign?

Ocean was sitting by a little middle-aged man who looked like a rich hillbilly. She nodded at him, and he stood up from the bridge table, and asked, "How good are you at bridge?"

"I don't know it at all," Jayne said. She wondered where Alice had gone.

"Come, then, and talk to the dummy."

God, they're so blunt. Jayne found out quickly that the dummy was the bridge player who didn't do anything with the cards after the bidding. After Jayne began to feel less nervous, Alice came in and sat on the sofa near them. She curled her legs under her and didn't speak.

"When will I get my clothes?" Jayne asked.

"When the aides have stolen what they want," Alice said.

Ocean looked up from her cards, and said, "For all the clothes they steal, at least they can find it in their hearts to sell you a drink or two when you need one."

"Being an aide is a shit job," Henry, the man who'd asked
Jayne to join the bridge group, said. "No future in it at all."

"Do you remember everyone's names?" Alice asked Jayne.

Jayne said, "Ocean, Henry. The others, I'm sorry."

Alice said, "This is Jayne. She's pregnant. Jayne, Henry
manages to get back here for a rest every three months or so.
Ocean has cut a deal with the Feds. She'll stay here for a
while if they'll ignore what she'd been doing. She's rather
mysterious about what that was. Her parents were trust
fundies who left her with drugs and the old wild computer
systems. The woman on her right with the cards spread out
in front of her is Mrs. Grace Adams, who had the most elegant tattoos and piercings in her youth, including a pierced
tongue. The other woman is Miss Margaret Turner, never
married, never suicidal, never pierced by anything except
perhaps tongues."

Miss Turner, a tall woman in her late fifties, said, "Alice,
quit trying to upset her."

Alice sat up on the couch, and asked, "Tell me, Jayne, who
are these people?"

"Henry, Ocean, Grace Adams, and Miss Turner."

Ocean said, "Alice, if you're going to blab about us, tell her
your sad story, why don't you?" The bridge group seemed
annoyed much less with Alice than Jayne was. She seemed to
be their snappish terrier, even more amusing for her at-
tempts at biting.

Alice said, "My mother has kept me locked up since junior high. I ran away from home, but you've heard all this before, so I'll tell it to Jayne in private."

Maggie Turner said, "Alice's mother is the very eyeball of
Judas women."

Jayne said, "My sister's a Judicious Girl."

Ocean said, "Alice's mother founded the organization."

Alice said, "My mother believes half the bastard babies
are okay. The others are like me. If she could have figured
out from in the womb which fetuses were like me and not

my glorious brother, she'd have killed me before I was born."

"Aren't you being melodramatic?" Jayne said.

Alice curled into an almost fetal ball. She said, "That's what I'm in for. Melodrama." The patch was buried in the sofa cushion, the good eye looked up.

Henry looked as if he wanted to cuddle Alice. To Jayne, Alice seemed like a dangerous cuddler. Ocean looked at Jayne. The older woman's mouth twitched, a corner deliberately pulled back toward her right ear. She looked at Alice, then back at Jayne. Silence hit for a few moments, then Ocean said, "We are playing bridge, aren't we?" Attention returned to the cards.

Alice said, "Poker nights are more interesting. Come on, Jayne, I've got more things to show you." She uncurled and walked out without saying more. Jayne, somewhat nonplussed that she was taking orders from this strange girl, nodded good-bye to the bridge group. Ocean smiled as she reshuffled the deck, but she seemed slightly disappointed in Jayne. As Henry cut the cards, Jayne walked fast toward the front door and Alice's disappearing back.

Jayne said, "I need to sign out." She couldn't figure out where she'd do that. Perhaps she needed to go back upstairs to the nurses' station.

"I'm with you," Alice said. "I'm just going to show you the grounds. I'm glad you came. They've been considering putting me on the back hall."

Jayne didn't want to ask why but suspected the bruised toe. This other woman was, after all, a mental patient, and she wasn't pregnant out of wedlock or anything else Jayne could see was an excuse for hiding out in a rehab hospital. "Are they all crazy?"

"Most of the ones in the front hall aren't. Old drunks and dopers, with a few psychotics who've learned how to behave themselves. Back hall has some people ransomed from state institutions that are really wacko."

"Ransomed from state institutions?" Jayne asked, meaning intonation to mark the question.

"You didn't hear?"

"Yes, I heard. Don't you get intonation? What does that mean?"

"Don't get snappish with me. Someone died and the family got money. Or someone got retroactive health insurance that covered a relative's preexisting condition. Lithium's probably what you need. Getting pregnant and then committed sounds like a manic-depressive event."

Could be, Jayne thought.

They had rounded the building and were at the tennis and volleyball courts in the rear of the building. A car parked behind the chain-link fence blew its horn at them.

"Townies," Alice said. She picked at one of her cuticles. "So what do you think of the place?"

"What are the therapy sessions like?"

"This is a nice enough warehouse. The docs are selling it to a virtual reprogramming corporation. Things will change."

Jayne asked, "What about virtual reprogramming?"

Alice said, "Doesn't really work as well as they'd like. When I was at the other place, I always knew I was in an illusion because the scene streaked when I turned my head fast. Not quite at reality's eighty million polygons per second, but closing, so they tell me. But if they rig you for medium-term cyberia and forget to program, well, if you weren't nuts before, getting sensory dep in a cyberia will strip you of delusions of sanity. But as long as the program's good, you can stay under forever. But it's useless for rehab, really, another thing like lobotomy that doctors hoped would work. Cheap warehouses use it all the time. Saves on basket-weaving material."

"How long were you locked in a cyberia?"

The car blew its horn again, flicked its headlights on bright. Alice smiled back at the headlights. The smile looked like the tongue behind it was counting teeth. Then Alice ran toward the fence, thrashing her arms about on the chain links. Before she could start climbing over, the car backed up suddenly and pulled away. Alice leaned her head against the fence, fingers curled through the chain links. She looked at Jayne with her unpatched eye, the patch against the fence. She said, calmly though slightly out of breath, "Couple of weeks in the first hospital. A day or three when I was in jail. I hate townie kids like that. Don't they realize true crazies are quite sensitive?" She uncurled her fingers from the chain link and laughed.

Almost ready to say, *you were in jail,* Jayne felt nervous using intonation as interrogative. "If you don't mind my asking, why were you in jail?"

"I shot a guy who beat me. Until he killed my dog, I thought I'd done something to deserve it. But my dog didn't deserve it."

Jayne wondered why Alice wasn't either in jail or totally free. "Did you kill him?"

"No. Don't ever shoot anyone and leave him screaming. My friends bailed me out," Alice said. "But I ran out of options in a few months and called home. Mom thought I'd liked my other hospital too much."

"Have they ever offered you . . ." The euthanasia question was too nasty to finish.

"Mommy has suggested euthanasia since she was convinced by the time I was fifteen that I was a permanent case. But after I shot a man, thus showing some promise, Mommy put me on the wait list for a progressive rehab hospital. She said the hospital I'd been in earlier didn't supervise me well enough, so she put me in here until I get in the good place. I'm still waiting to be transferred. Should happen in another three months."

"But I was told this was a rehab hospital." Jayne expected to get her mind shattered and rebuilt into a different person who'd fit in. The prospect both terrified and tempted her. Her duel with the world would be over. The old Jayne would die; the new Jayne would join the Judas Girls. The curiosity that drove her to be independent as a child had already died, so what was the point?

When they'd walked back toward the front, Jayne noticed that the chain-link fence stopped before it showed in the front. Toward the side were trees and apartments and stores without a barrier between them.

"We should go down there and get some wine to celebrate your arrival here," Alice said.

"I can't drink because of the baby," Jayne said. "I've been on school drugs already."

"What interesting person hasn't?" Alice said. "But they had absolutely no impact on me whatsoever."

"Did you actually take them?" Jayne asked.

"By the handful," Alice said.

As they came in, a woman wearing street clothes and a white cap came up to Jayne. "Jayne, I'm sorry if we didn't explain ground privileges to you well enough. Until you get unlimited privileges, you must sign out at the nurses' station. Alice, don't pull tricks on our new patients. But show Jayne to supper and then to the media room?"

Jayne was feeling overwhelmed by all the people she'd been meeting. She couldn't quite sort them all out. "Ocean is the daughter of trust fundies?"

Alice said, "The kind of trust fundies with drugs, tattoos, and genital steel. They had Ocean pierced when she was eleven. Tattoos were out of fashion by then."

Jayne remembered what she'd been told about Judas Girls pulling piercing steel when a woman converted. "Do people tell you these things?" Ripped through the flesh.

Alice said, "All we crazies do is talk."

So to supper. The food was served cafeteria style, but was a cut above what was served at school. Alice steered them to Ocean and Henry. Jayne realized Alice hadn't said much about Henry.

"Now, see them," Alice said, raising her fork from mashed potatoes to point at a line of people coming in.

Aides herded in the patients. The truly mad moved in jerks like their joints were crusty. Even their eyes were stiff. "The cooperative backward ones get to eat with the rest of us."

In the same dining room, but not at the same tables. Even here, us and them.

A soft-looking guy with slightly bulging eyes waved at them. He looked at the aides as if he wanted to come and sit with them, but knew he wasn't allowed.

"That's Lou," Alice said. "He's slightly retarded. I've played pool with him. Maybe we should call him over." The expression on her face reminded Jayne of her face in the townie's car headlights just before she charged the fence, a bright pointed smile.

Ocean said, "Don't try to get people in trouble, Alice."

"I don't try to get people in trouble," Alice said. "We just have fun and get caught, is all."

Again, Ocean twitched back a corner of her mouth and looked at Jayne. Jayne already knew that Alice could lead her into trouble.

But whatever trouble Jayne got into, she could blame it on Alice. The thought was like a drug going off in her head. She was a poor pregnant crazy fool that nobody was going to take seriously. Use that image as a mask for the real Jayne, she decided, the trickster. Ah . . .

Maybe. Reality had teeth and drugs and binding tools.

Ocean said, "You do try to get people in trouble."

Alice said, "Ocean, repetition just makes me think other people are too dumb to remember what they've said."

Jayne wondered if Alice really remembered or had a delusion of memory. But she'd learned enough already not to challenge what Alice said.

Ocean said, "So, Jayne, how does all this strike you?"

Not realizing until she spoke what she felt, Jayne said, "I feel like my old life is dead and that I'm in a new one."

Nobody spoke for a few moments, then Ocean said, "I

learned lives are never over until you're dead. Beyond that, we don't know."

Alice said, "Those are platitudes."

"All I think I meant was that I couldn't go back to being who I was before I got pregnant," Jayne said. "My life won't be the same after this."

Ocean said, "Couldn't a change be for the better?"

"Another fucking platitude," Alice said. "All I see is hospitals on top of hospitals, hospitals all the way down. Like the idea that the world is on the back of a turtle and it's turtles all the way down. Only it's hospitals."

Ocean leaned away from the table. "Alice, choosing the wrong lover isn't new in the world, nor is shooting him." She turned to Jayne, and said, "Jayne, this is a hard place to be an apprentice adult. But, perhaps not an impossible place. Nor the worst place."

Suddenly Alice was crying. Jayne wanted to ask why the crying, but Ocean warned her with a tiny head shake not to comment.

Hospitals all the way down. Jayne visualized that, the whole world as a hospital on top of other dimensions of hospitals. All life was the insanity of molecules, delusions matter had. Um, better not say that out loud. She wondered if Alice had quite as sophisticated a view of her image.

Alice said, "After supper, we need to take a walk."

Ocean said, "But there's a movie."

Jayne said, "I think I'd better see the movie, Alice. I'm still new here."

Henry reached over and squeezed Alice's shoulder. She put her hand on his hand, holding it on her shoulder. Henry didn't seem to have meant the gesture erotically. Henry removed his hand, and said, "I'm just who I am."

Alice's unpatched eye darkened.

We're in limbo. In Jayne's new universe, once-elegant hotels faded into mental hospitals, mental hospitals all the way down.

*   *   *

Lou managed to be moved to the men's front hall, which meant he could come into the parlor and go out on the porch. Alice seemed to regard him as a combination pet and pest. He made Jayne nervous. Even though she suspected he had ground privileges, he seemed terrified to go off the front porch, as though the world beyond threatened him.

"I'm moderately retarded," he told her one day as he sat rocking on the porch. His rocking was mechanical and fast.

"Oh," Jayne said.

"People can be mean, can't they?"

"Yes."

"Do you like the squirrel?"

Jayne thought this was quite a brain jump, then she saw a black squirrel running across the front lawn. "It's a black squirrel."

"Yes," Lou said. "It was born that way, you know." He smiled and continued to watch the squirrel until it disappeared. Jayne felt very mean.

Ocean came out and sat for a while with them, all of them rocking, then said, "Jayne, time for your lesson."

Lou's face turned toward Jayne. He looked like he wished he could have lessons, too. Then he looked away and rocked harder.

Jayne got up and followed Ocean into the library, where an old computer stood with the screen on. A window showed File, Edit, Apps, Options, Buffers, Tools with pictures below and smaller letters.

"XEmacs," Ocean said. "It's an old program, free software when I was young before the hardware companies got the rules changed. It helps you learn. I want you to start breaking out of the patterns you've trapped yourself in."

"I'm not good at stuff like this."

"That trap," Ocean said. "There's code from the last century embedded in the present-day programs, whole operating systems commented out and forgotten. We will start with this, in C."

```
#include <stdio.h> void main ( ) {      printf ("Hello,
world!\n"); }
```

Jayne had trouble at first keeping the curly braces separated from the parentheses, but the old machine and program Ocean had found finally worked her through it.

"So where from here?"

"Much more," Ocean said.

"It's neat," Jayne said, "but I'm not supposed to be in track for programming." She felt foolish saying that. She wasn't supposed to have a child out of wedlock either.

"It's just a way to describe categories and hierarchies," Ocean said. "Everyone should learn as much programming as possible. Then you can find holes in the system and un-comment out space for change."

Hello, world!

As the sale of the hospital progressed, Jayne saw various people come in and look the patients over as though calculating what they'd bring on the meat market if cannibalism was legal. They didn't speak to any of the patients, but looked through all the back-ward charts, according to the more talkative of the nursing students.

Ocean seemed dismayed when she saw them and seemed to avoid them. Jayne thought she overhead Ocean bribing one of the nurses to lose various charts, but didn't get close enough to catch the names, but Jayne's own name wasn't one of them.

The sale went through and men brought in hand trucks full of boxes from electronics firms Jayne had never heard of. Alice looked at them, and said, "Cyberia rigs. They make patient management so much easier. We need to go out and celebrate while we still have time. I'm going down the hill. I wonder what Lou would be like drunk."

It was an appalling idea. Jayne said, "I'm not going with you."

"I'll take Lou."

"He doesn't even leave the front porch."

Alice tried to talk Lou into going out on the lawn the next day as Dr. Ames bid farewell to the patients. The new doctor didn't seem to be talking to any of the patients.

Jayne didn't know if she should go with Alice down the hill to protect her from her delight in getting caught, or if she should stay with Lou, to talk him out of doing what Alice wanted.

Alice went on down the hill and was gone for an hour. Jayne wondered what precisely she was doing.

Lou sat with some of the men, all rocking in rockers when Alice came in from the side of the porch. "We've got treats," she said as she walked by them, her jacket folded over her arm even though the weather was crisp. Jayne got up and walked in with Alice, amazed that Alice had broken the rules so blatantly. Alice was shivering, but she kept going up the stairs to the women's floor. Jayne didn't know if she should go up, too, or not.

Ocean called up from the bridge table, "Don't let her ride you."

"I don't have any other people my age here to be with," Jayne said.

"We were all young once," Ocean said. "And some of us are still sixteen years old inside."

"She's . . ."

"Yes, I know, compelling," Ocean said. "And she likes to be caught and humiliated. Do you?"

Jayne didn't know how to answer. Ocean went back to her bridge game. Jayne waited; Alice finally came down.

"We'll have to be in bed soon, so we'll have to postpone the celebration," Alice said, thrusting a purse at Jayne. She whispered, "Hide this."

Maybe I am paranoid. Jayne opened the purse and saw a

vodka bottle and a packet of powder in the purse Alice gave her. *But why did she give this to me?*

Alice was talking to the women around the bridge table when Jayne decided to take the purse upstairs and put it in Alice's room. She didn't want to hold these things.

Jayne went into Alice's room and felt strange, as though she was burglarizing it, only she was putting something in it, not taking things out.

Alice came as Jayne was turning to leave. "Why did you put it in my room?"

"They still search my room," Jayne said. "I can't hide things there."

"You're so stupid. You could have hidden it in so many other places. Don't come in again without telling me," Alice said.

Jayne realized she didn't have to take Alice's temper seriously. "Okay."

"I'm going to make Lou a happy man," Alice said. "Really. But now that you've drawn attention to my little expedition, we'll have to wait. You could have hidden it outside. Unless you know a way to smuggle us to his room or him to ours, we're going to have to drink it with him outside."

"What's the powder?"

"A drug. You don't need to know."

"Are you going to try to drug him, too?"

"Oh, no."

"Well, how are we going to manage this?"

Alice said, "We pour it into cups and drink it with orange juice. It's all so simple."

"Right in front of everyone?"

Alice shrugged. "What will they do if they catch us? Breaking the rules because you're crazy is one of the liberating things about being crazy. The new management expects to be tested. I've known people who just moved out of reality forever to places like this."

Jayne was uneasy. She had asked the morning nurse to

schedule an appointment with the new doctor to discuss therapy. The morning nurse noted it down and smiled, then said, "We think you're ready to have your clothes," but nobody had told her what her chores would be in the mandated periods between hospitalizations. Now Alice was both scaring her and enticing her into some outlaw postures Jayne wasn't sure she wanted to live up to.

"If there is a real reality out there. Plato says no," Jayne said. "One's belief in what's real is conditional on class and intelligence." She would have rather talked for hours about media shaping society and the impossibility of proving that class was genetic than to begin to deal with the vodka and drugs hidden in among Alice's bras and panties.

"Tomorrow, party," Alice said. "Real enough for me."

As Alice, the only one with money, punched the orange juice containers out of the machine in the basement recreation room, someone put Bach's *Goldberg Variations* on the multimedia deck. The back-ward patients sitting in the chairs seemed just as stiff as they seemed earlier when fierce dance music played.

"Who likes Bach?" Jayne asked as she took her and Lou's juices from Alice.

"Ocean," Alice said. "Bring the bottle out here. We'll go to the back." Where the townies parked and blew their horns at the crazies, Jayne realized.

The Bach haunted Jayne all the way upstairs where the vodka waited. Theme and variation forever. *Hospitals all the way down.*

Jayne said, "I don't know if we should be doing this."

"We shouldn't," Alice said. "That's what makes it amusing."

"But to Lou?"

"He's never been drunk. The world owes him the experience."

"He's never been laid, either, I bet."

"That's not as amusing," Alice said. "Unless you want to do that for him. Hell, you're already pregnant and he's been hospitalized since he was a kid, so you're not going to catch anything."

Lou wouldn't come with them out in front of the porch, but he had been to the back grounds, so that seemed okay and familiar to him. They walked behind the volleyball courts to the ruins of a clay tennis court. Ants had built mounds in it; moles and grass loosened its edges. The net poles leaned over. Behind the tennis court was the chain link and a thin woods. Beyond that, the road where townies parked and watched for crazies.

Not tonight, please.

Alice unscrewed the vodka cap and held the bottle up high. She poured orange juice into a paper cup, then added an equal portion of vodka and handed it to Jayne, then poured a second cup for Lou.

Then Alice made her own drink with noticeably less vodka than was in the other two cups. *Be careful.*

Lou winced at the taste and tried to hand the cup back to Alice, but she said, "You'll like it after you drink it down. Drink."

Lou looked as though he was ordered to drink and drained the glass. Alice poured pure vodka into his cup. "So, we're all damned here. You know, Lou, I've always wanted to ask. What did they do to you on the back ward when you were bad?"

Jayne wanted to say, stop mind-fucking him. She said, "Alice, this is supposed to be a party."

"Why should this question be cruel? I spent time in restraints and cyberia. You'll spend time in restraints and cyberia eventually. They don't know how to fix us. After a hundred years of National Mental Health programs, they still can't fix us. We're broken."

Lou said, with considerable dignity, "I'm not broken. I'm just occasionally a little crazy and moderately retarded."

Jayne said, "I want to be rehabilitated."

Alice said, "I'm going to the best place in the country for that. If they can't do it, I'm fucked forever. Are you drunk yet?"

A car drove slowly down the road behind the hospital. Jayne hoped it wouldn't stop. The horn blared. Alice turned to watch, then said, "All they can see is our silhouettes."

The horn blew again. Lou turned and ran. Jayne almost ran after him, but Alice caught her by the arm. "Don't. They won't hurt him."

"He'll tell them we got him drunk."

"We did, didn't we?" Alice smiled. She poured herself another drink, then offered one to Jayne, who shook her head.

"I'm completely sober now."

The car pulled back and drove away, headlight beams broken through the thin woods between the car and the fence.

Alice said, "I wish I was drunker."

When they walked in, they heard that Lou was again on the back ward. Alice said, "He's so weird, I don't think anyone even suspected he could have been drinking." She sounded disappointed.

The new doctor, Dr. McGuire, met with Jayne briefly at the nurses' station. "Why do you think you need to be rehabilitated? I don't think you're likely to go off a second time and get pregnant. Do you? We'll need you to help us to pay off the times when your HMO suspends you."

"I want to completely and unconsciously fit in," Jayne said.

"Well, your earlier doctors disagreed about the severity of your problem. I think you could start helping with patients now. We'll give you a day's credit anytime you help us with an unruly patient."

Jayne wondered if the other patients would consider her a stool pigeon. "What if I refused?"

"We might consider that the first doctor knew you better

than the second doctor." Dr. McGuire smiled. Jayne wondered if he knew how threatening he was being. No, he could have been more threatening. He could have threatened to put her in cyberia restraints if she didn't cooperate. And Jayne was tired of feeling guilty about not stopping Alice.

The next night, one of the aides woke Jayne up to have her start helping them. They were putting Lou in cyberia restraints.

"Jayne, I'm just slightly retarded," he said. "I don't want the world to disappear."

"He's been hitting people," the aide who'd gotten Jayne out of bed said.

"I just want to go home," Lou said. "I don't want to be here. I'd be okay if I could just get back home."

He reached for Jayne, and she held his hands, wishing he could be okay and miles away from there. *Alice, you are evil.*

The other aides slipped the hood over him, and sedated him. "He'll be entertained," the nurse who sold Ocean liquor from time to time said.

I can't undo what I let happen to him. Jayne was shaking. The aide noticed and walked her back to her room as though she was again a patient.

"I want to be okay. I want the bad things about me fixed," Jayne said.

"Even the Judicious Girls aren't always judicious," Ocean said. "If they were perfect virgins, they wouldn't need watchers and enforcers."

"But they weren't sent here," Jayne said. "I was sent here. Getting sent here has to mean something."

"Don't bother the doctors. Let's go on down to the library."

The library was full of books and woodwork. It had a real ladder and rail to allow a reader to get books from the tallest shelves. In one corner were a couple of computer terminals set up on oak desks.

"We've got net access and CDs and a large server in there, but it's all bonded and ID-user'ed," Ocean said, pointing out double wooden doors. "The Ames family has been collecting systems for over fifty years, but the oldest ones are in the attic. The new management doesn't know anything about them. Doesn't care, really, which is a relief. Now these aren't that old, but they're not networked and user-ID'ed."

"What happened to Alice's eye?"

"She said she took it out. Judas eye. Don't understand why they don't put in a false eye, but she might not ever believe they put in something that didn't narc on her."

"Lou got drunk before his last setback."

"Oh. Did you hear about it or were you an eyewitness?"

"Alice got the liquor. I didn't tell anyone."

Ocean turned on two of the computers. "Except me. What am I, the keeper of your conscience?" She sounded somewhat bitterly amused. "You helped put him in cyberia restraints."

"He's out now."

"Heavily sedated. What will you do when they bring me in drunk and rowdy?" Ocean smiled slightly.

"I don't want to be in that position."

"I have seen the enemy and she is me, perhaps?"

"Yes."

Ocean sighed. "One function of mental hospitals is to break people of having social weight. Humans tend to be so competitive with each other. A stay in a mental hospital— you're not competition anymore, you're a crazy." The older woman found a disk and loaded it into one of the CD drives. She wrote on the smartpad as she continued talking. "Some people here aren't crazy at all. I don't think you are. But did you like putting Lou in restraints?"

Jayne was horrified. "No. But there has to be something wrong with me. I have so many problems."

Ocean said, "Let's see how you do at algebra."

"It keeps me from being a scientist," Jayne said.

"Maybe you just need to learn it in a different way. Several different ways."

Jayne said, "I didn't realize computers could be fun, though."

"Computers are morally indifferent. Computers also make Judas Girls possible. Programmatic scanning, algorithms for events."

An eyeball sacrificed to connect to a program that forced women to be pure. Jayne said, "I thought they had live scanners."

Ocean said, "Just of the hits."

Jayne understood that the Judicious Institution couldn't save women under assault, just avenge the damage. "What do they do to the women who get carried away or try to sneak around the scanning algorithms?"

"Sometimes the sponsors arrange a gang rape," Ocean said. "Alice was more fortunate. They just threw her away."

So Jayne found her life split in two—one memory track of sitting down with Ocean, learning, partially from self-guided computer programs and from Ocean's more particular explanations.

Her belly swelled and when the baby turned it was like being fucked from the inside. Jayne's dreams shivered her body.

In the other memory track, Jayne gave up and went down the hill with Alice out of sheer loneliness and guilt, again and again, prowling. Henry went home, but returned to Crystal Springs to meet Alice secretly in motels where the two girls smoked marijuana and Henry injected himself with a drug he wouldn't name. He seemed happy with it.

"If you don't do too much at once, there's no danger to it," he said, looking up from the needle. His hands shook. "I do all my office work okay."

Alice seemed enchanted, but Henry didn't want her to try his drug. Jayne couldn't believe he could work and do drugs that injected.

They were sitting in a motel room by the paper factory, the pot making the fumes even more repulsive. Henry said, "They wanted to put me on methadone, but I refused the king's dope. People in Mexico grow this for me. I can feel the resin on the poppy . . ."

Heroin, Jayne realized, knowing she'd known all along. But Henry wasn't a fiend.

". . . and a warm brown hand pulls a knife across the seed pod, skims the resin. The mountainside is beautiful, warm, poppies and irrigation ditches under snow-tipped volcanoes. The women gathering the resin seem dazed. Maybe heat. Maybe they absorb the resin through their skin."

Alice said, "I don't know if I want to try it or not."

Henry said, "Alice, I want to kick for you next time I'm here. You don't have to join me."

Jayne asked, "Have you really seen the Mexican poppy fields?"

"I know my drug all the way to the plant," Henry said.

Alice said, "Just weeks ago Jayne wouldn't go down to the store a half mile from the hospital. Now, look at her."

Jayne swayed her tunnel vision around the motel room. The paper fumes seemed to slow down everything. "We shouldn't be doing this."

But Jayne began to understand why she did this. The hospital decided she was a shy girl who'd been taken advantage of by some lout. Being bad defied that simpering loser definition. For Alice, being bad kept her from being just another crazy. Henry?

Jayne imagined he injected his drug in the bathrooms of country clubs that used his great-granddaddy as a greens-keeper.

"I'm always careful," Henry said. "I never nod."

What was the point of a major narcotic if you don't nod?

And Henry drank, too, contrary to the myth about junkies. Alice brought huge bottles of Chianti and caught a taxi to his motel. Jayne felt she had to go with Alice, as chaperone, as witness, because nothing was quite so strange as Alice's courtship of Henry.

Since Alice slept in a huddle under all her covers, Jayne could fix the bed so Alice appeared to be sleeping. She slept in late mornings anyway.

"So, do it for me," Alice said, the Chianti in her arms as she got out of the taxi.

Without promising anything, Jayne followed Alice into Henry's room. They all drank, Henry sipping the wine, Alice hardly touching it at all. Jayne drank, threw up, and wiped the drool from her chin as she listened to Alice murmuring at Henry.

If she were a guy, she'd be dangerous.

A motel person, a big guy with the Irish slant eyes, came to the door and asked them to leave.

By midafternoon, they'd put Henry in another motel, and went back to the hospital for dinner and bed checks.

Jayne went to Alice's room and found she'd gone out. So she faked the bed up.

A lump under covers, the world's oldest trick, and then Jayne went down the hill and caught a cab to the next motel. A man in a suit with waxed mustaches was talking to Henry as Alice sulked against a headboard.

At the third motel, Henry cooked his heroin in a neat outfit heated by a butane lighter. He pulled out an old metal-and-glass syringe, a true classic.

"Needles are hard to get," he said. "But it's so elegant." A tiny bead of liquid trembled at the slant end of the needle.

Alice said, "I want to do it for you, Henry."

Henry looked at her, his face slack, his eyes empty of catch lights, dusty jelly hanging in two pits. "You can tie me off. I always put in my own needles. If I OD, then I did it."

"Don't you trust me?"

"That wasn't my usual supplier," Henry said. Alice moved

up with the tourniquet. Henry watched the veins, then sank the tip of the needle into his left elbow. "Loosen it."

Alice did. Henry lay back, his head between Alice's legs. "Wonder if they've got a greenhouse somewhere." He stared off into space.

"Henry," Alice said.

"Um," he said. "I . . . like . . . old-fashioned . . . drugs."

"I thought you didn't nod." Alice sounded as though she was on the edge of hysteria.

"S'okay," Henry said. "Decadent."

Jayne wondered if what she'd heard about reviving an OD case was factual enough to really save someone. Henry's eyes blinked for several hours.

"I've got to get back to the hospital," Jayne said.

"Bye," Henry said.

"You've got to get back, too, Alice. I bet they found the lump in the bed wasn't you by now."

"Taxi money in m'wallet," Henry said.

"Don't give him more," Jayne said to Alice. Alice found Henry's wallet and gave Jayne taxi money plus enough to come back again the next day.

"We probably won't be here tomorrow," Alice said. "I'll call you."

Jayne almost said, Come back with me, but Henry obviously needed to be watched. He seemed incapable of doing anything. He opened his eyes as she stood there. The pupils were expanded slightly. "Okay. What shall I tell them?"

"They won't have called anyone yet. People have died on the mental hospital's grounds and not been reported missing until the skeletons showed up during major landscaping."

Henry spoke without changing his expression. "Police would have been here. Check motels first. Too obvious."

Jayne was horrified, but she called a cab and went back to the hospital.

Ocean pounced on her as soon as she came in. "Is Alice alive?"

"Yes."

Ocean took Jayne's chin in her hand, and said, "Where? I know they're not fucking because Henry's much too scag-balled for that."

"How do you know she's with Henry?"

"Seemed obvious. He wasn't here, and he's due back soon. The last couple days, she flinched every time someone mentioned him."

"Are you going to tell Dr. McGuire?"

"Neither you nor Alice is legally committed. If you really wanted to walk out, you could."

"Shit." Jayne felt like she'd been duped again.

"But in your case, I think this is a better deal than what might happen to you as an unwed pregnant woman on the outside."

"I thought I was legally committed," Jayne said.

"Nope. If you didn't go before a judge with a court-appointed lawyer, nothing but good manners keeps you here."

"So they haven't called. . . ."

"What if they call the police? Alice and Henry get busted with drugs. Henry is a frequent patient here. So the hospital gets the reputation for attracting junkies who don't quietly check in but who get rowdy with teenage madwomen."

"So, did they call her mother?"

"Her mother's paying cash. Many of us are. When we need recuperation, refuge, we get it. And even though the help steals, it's courteous. A real advantage to be able to pay cash."

"But everyone comes back. Nobody seems to get cured."

"We get to leave. If we really want to turn into reformed drunks, the option is open."

"I think we're going to have to bring Henry in before he ODs. We can't take care of him."

"That's what the hospital does. They've got drinks and injections to ease a person from the chemicals. Ah, yes, the chemicals."

"He drinks, too. I didn't know junkies could do that."

Ocean laughed. "Pity it's her mother with the money, not her. She's out of resources and friends. Bring her back before they do panic and put her on the back ward in restraints. I'll do what I can to protect you from the new management."

5
"Attention Spans and Frames"

all a cab, sign out for a little shopping trip in town although everyone knows you're bringing back Henry and Alice, and go.

Jayne was learning that she could survive much more than she'd ever expected. When she got put on school drugs, she thought her life was over. But now, even getting pregnant didn't shift her into a zone where she was constantly aware of her belly and failures. She remembered her belly only with a jolt from the cab, and realized she'd forgotten for hours that she was pregnant out of wedlock.

Alice and Henry were at a motel under the stench of a paper mill. It had all the features of a bad motel—a pond for suicides, a woods for private drug abuse, and a wood fence hiding the parking lot from the highway.

The taxi took off as soon as Jayne paid the fare. She walked down to Room 33, not quite sure what she'd find.

As soon as Jayne knocked, Alice came to the door. "Hi. Where were you?"

"We've got to get back to the hospital." Henry was staring at the ceiling and breathing erratically. Yes, they really needed to get back fast.

Alice said, "He started that this morning."

"Let's call another cab."

"Did you tell them where I was?"

"I told Ocean. The hospital didn't call the police or your mother because they don't want to be embarrassed."

"I'm going to be transferred to the other hospital in two weeks. I called Henry. That's why he's here. That hospital keeps people for years. Nobody gets off grounds in less than six months unless they want to be kicked out. I'd lose everything I stand to inherit if I just ran. Plus I couldn't cope before. Oh, Jayne."

Not feeling terrific about any of this, Jayne said, "Well, you'll be together in the hospital for the last two weeks."

Alice sat down by Henry and took his hand. "And he just lies here. I wanted to see him, but I didn't want to see him like this."

"We've got to get him dressed."

"He just doesn't stop doing drugs and drinking."

Jayne began by sweeping Henry's covers off. He wasn't naked, though she didn't ask how long he'd been wearing the same briefs. "Where are his pants?"

"I'll call the taxi. It will be here by the time you've finished dressing him."

"Help me. He's like a lump of suet."

Alice called the cab first, then helped Jayne pull Henry through his pant legs. The shirt was comparatively easy. He sank back down on the bed with his legs dangling, which made getting his shoes on easy.

The cab honked.

Alice asked, "Should we call the hospital to tell them we're coming in?"

Jayne said, "Meter's running. Let's just do it. They'll know soon enough." The two women pulled Henry up between them and sat him in the backseat. When Alice gave the hospital address, the driver looked in the rearview mirror back at Henry, then radioed in his location and the hospital address.

Alice had Henry's wallet. She showed Jayne that he had a couple hundred with him. "I'd better take it or the aides will steal it."

The driver said, "Shouldn't he be going by ambulance?"

Alice said, "He's been semicomatose for a couple of hours, but hasn't gotten worse." Nobody spoke more until the cab pulled up at the hospital.

As the cab stopped, two aides with a wheelchair came through the front doors. They lugged Henry into it, then wheeled him up the ramp. Alice paid for the cab and put Henry's wallet in her purse.

In the hospital lobby they fell down into chairs laughing. The aides wheeled Henry by them. Drooling, he dangled in the chair. They laughed even harder. Except for Ocean, the bridge players were dismayed.

"God, he is a junkie," Alice said. "He really is."

Ocean came over and put her hand on Jayne's elbow. "You need to go upstairs. To your room. Get out of sight."

Three female aides and a male aide came in for Alice. She stood up, still laughing, and walked into Dr. McGuire's office with them.

Ocean said, "Can you go to your room without help?"

Jayne's laughter dropped away instantly. Real threat was in that voice. "Yes." She turned and went toward her room.

When Jayne passed the nursing station, one aide smiled at her. Jayne didn't feel like smiling back, but she did so to be polite to someone who minutes later might be tying her into restraints. She went into her room but left her door open so she could hear gossip.

Pregnant out to where?

Dr. McGuire came to her room and leaned against the door frame. He said, "You'll help us put her in cyberia or we'll put you in, too."

Jayne said, "Alice told me she's being transferred in two weeks."

"She may spend all of it in cyberia. She's a terrible influence on all the patients here."

Jayne said, "I'm not going to help you put cyberia restraints on her." She felt that Alice deserved them, almost, certainly more than Lou, but she was afraid of Alice. *More afraid of Alice than of cyberia restraints? Yes.*

And then she felt guilty because she'd helped them put Lou in cyberia.

"So, you get them, too. I don't think you'll fight us, though. You're too intelligent for that."

Jayne waited. The aide who'd woken her to help them with Lou and two other aides, one a guy, walked into her room with a full cyberia rig, complete with catheters.

"Two days," the aide said.

Jayne stood up and closed her eyes as the hood went down to her neck.

They injected her with something, then she felt numb and the world disappeared into a strange cartoon moving in streaks forever.

Sometime later, she found herself walking to the bathroom, feeling sore. The aides were packing up the cyberia rig. "Where's Alice?" Jayne asked.

"In the back now for two days. Will you fuck up again?"

Jayne shook her head, but she resented all the show of force, the days lost to the stupid cartoon show that faded like a dream now that she wasn't in the virtual rig.

But it hadn't been that hideous. Nothing could be that hideous anymore.

Jayne's mother showed up for a visit the next day. For some reason that Jayne felt she almost understood, Linda came in looking breezy, cheerful, and about thirty-two. Ocean's old eyes took in Jayne's mother, then looked at Jayne. Her mouth corner twitched slightly again. Jayne knew Ocean was disappointed in her since the Henry business, but didn't quite understand why. Now Ocean didn't approve of her mother. Okay, Jayne wasn't quite sure she approved of her mother either, all bright and vivacious during her daughter's illicit pregnancy.

Then Dr. McGuire came out, smiling, and led Jayne's mother to his office. Jayne felt angry. Her mother, who wasn't the patient, got to see Dr. McGuire in his office. She only saw Dr. McGuire at the nurses' station, surrounded by dilapidated patients who craved audiences with the doctors whisking by, going on to the important things in a psychiatrist's life, like making sure the family or insurance company would pay and prescribing drugs to outpatients. Or what?

Ocean said, "Your mother?"

Jayne nodded.

Ocean said, "I don't think I like her. But I do understand why you and Alice collapsed into laughter when you brought Henry back in."

Jayne realized some of the patients might have had a problem with that. "I was relieved it was all over."

Ocean said, "And you like getting caught."

Jayne said, "No, but I knew I could blame it on Alice. She was the one who got caught. I was just chaperoning them."

Ocean said, "A man with that much drugs and liquor in him is no sexual threat."

"The cyberia wasn't that bad," Jayne said.

"Alice is still in it," Ocean said.

Linda came out of the doctor's office smiling and checked Jayne out of the hospital for a day.

"You're not wearing the gold band we got you," her mother said.

"I didn't get it back when I got my clothes back. I had to surrender any jewelry, remember."

"We'll have to stop at a jewelry store or Woolworth's and get you a band," Linda said.

"I don't think I'll ever be back here," Jayne said.

"You're making me a grandmother before I was ready," Linda said. "Wear a goddamn band just for today." Her mother was pressing her tongue against her bared teeth, a bad sign.

"Okay, okay," Jayne said.

The band they found at a local estate-jewelry store looked weird, gold with black-enameled bands top and bottom. Jayne thought it would be appropriate for a wedding between a bisexual woman and bisexual man to regularize the children born to the woman and her female lover. But it was a gold wedding band and cheap enough for her mother to settle there and not keep looking for a Woolworth's.

For lunch, they drove up the Blue Ridge Parkway to a restaurant near Craggy Gardens. Jayne just looked while her mother told her all about how the rest of the family was doing.

"Sidna asked about you," Linda said.

"Oh."

"Carolyn said Sidna has asked about you several times."

"I don't like Sidna," Jayne said.

"She told Carolyn you'd be much happier if you only cooperated with the Girls. Your father would pay for the surgery to make you a virgin again. It would cost less than the time at a Judicious Girls' unwed mothers' home. We could afford it."

"Mother, you're . . ." Jayne didn't want to finish *you're one to talk*. "I don't want Sidna's attention."

"You know, Dr. McGuire told me about what you and Alice did. He was concerned. I told him that after all, Alice was the only person here your age who wasn't really crazy."

"She's sort of crazy, only it isn't something biochemical. It's existential."

"So, I told him that if you had better companions, you'd be more like them. You're really a sweet girl, and you had a happy childhood. Dr. McGuire wants you to help them with the unruly patients to pay the times when the HMO isn't covering you. You must cooperate with the doctors and nurses."

Okay, Mom. They didn't talk about madness during lunch. Jayne heard more about Carolyn, about Sidna's broken engagement (still, however, a virgin with her investments and very eligible).

On the drive back, Jayne told her mother about hiding Henry in a series of motels until he became too stoned to lug around easily. When she told it, the story sounded funny, and her mother laughed.

It was funny. It wasn't funny. Three lost lives tangled in cheap motels and mental hospitals.

Ocean checked herself out just before Alice came out of a week in cyberia restraints. Alice and Henry had a week together in the hospital before Alice went on to the next hospital.

About four days after Alice left, Jayne heard Ocean was back, drying out from a drunk, in one of the front rooms. Only patients who had money and were trusted got to dry out on the front hall.

The aide who'd told Jayne about this said, "She'd like to see you. Go," the aide said. "She needs someone to drop by while she's down like she is."

Ocean sober was so strong the other patients didn't want to see her helplessly drunk, Jayne realized. But then, she didn't want to see Ocean like that either.

However, Jayne went.

Jayne went to see Ocean in her dark room, where the aides brought her drinks every two hours, each one weaker and weaker.

"They make nice drinks here," Ocean said. She looked bruised around the eyes. Jayne wondered if someone had beaten her. "Don't wince, Jayne. I know I look hideous." Ocean sounded as though she'd been punched in the vocal cords, too.

What happened, Jayne wanted to ask. But she didn't know if Ocean herself knew. Could anyone in the hospital say precisely when they started heading for the hospital?

"Why did you come back here?"

Ocean pushed her head back into the pillows propping her

up. "Nasty question. I got too drunk again. Happens. Can't win sometimes for trying."

"Why do you drink?"

"Matches me with the times. Depressing. My parents. . . . Terrible thing to be the child of old hippies. At fifteen or so, you find out the universe of discourse they live in is so terribly tiny."

"But everything is so much more complex than anyone's parents tell them," Jayne said. *You're my self-selected grown-up parent surrogate, why are you having these problems?*

"Ah, yes, why should anyone's parents want them to challenge the system? As Kafka said, 'In your quarrel with the world, bet on the world.' "

"Maybe it doesn't have to be that way," Jayne said. She remembered that Mick said the system even made a place for rebellion these days.

"I'm afraid in the most perfect of systems, I'd still be a drunk. It's my nature. Drink brings out this sly wild person I don't acknowledge when I'm sober."

Jayne said, "You just sound depressed to me."

"You see, now I'm too drunk. I have to get sober to get drunk again and find that self."

Jayne thought that most people drunk were just themselves, only sloppy. While she couldn't see the wild sly person Ocean claimed to be as a drunk, Jayne didn't think Ocean was quite herself. "You're more ironic when you're sober."

Ocean said, "You can't know an alcoholic unless you know both the drunk and the parson sides of the personality."

Jayne said, "Why don't they encourage girls to study computers these days?"

Ocean said, "Awful lot of nasty code between us and any use we might have for computers, don't you think? Damned world, finds so many excuses to cheat people."

"Could you teach me more programming and math? You are my licensed tutor for home studies."

"I'm too drunk right now," Ocean said. "Man, I miss being young. Twenty years of being young and I just wasted it."

"Drink?" the aide coming in the door said.

Ocean said, "This one's not the equal of the one I had two hours ago, and the next one will be like the ice melted in it for days." She winked at Jayne. "I should complain to the management."

The aide said, "If you didn't want to sober up, you could have kept drinking at home."

"Spoilsport," Ocean said. She sipped at her drink, eyes half-crossed as she stared at it. Jayne slipped out the door and didn't see Ocean again until she was sober.

Meanwhile, Jayne dreamed with the baby in her belly, a growing entity that possessed her in her sleep, leading to the most erotic dreams she'd ever had. Babies rotten with eroticism make their mothers have them.

No one ever told Jayne about this part of pregnancy. Even though she was still sick in the mornings if the aide forgot the little pill that kept breakfast in her stomach, the baby rolling in her belly felt not quite pleasantly erotic. Nature's way, perhaps, of securing a bond between mother and child. The dreams left Jayne feeling both pleasured and slightly violated by a biological imperative.

Her ovaries didn't care if she was married or not. The egg had been ready, sucking semen and Jayne into its plan.

One night before she went to bed, Jayne stopped by Ocean's room. "How important is it to not want to get caught?" Jayne asked.

"Depends on how many other people you drag down with you," Ocean said.

"I don't like getting caught, but I feel fairly defiant," Jayne said. "This isn't a fair world." She wasn't quite sure whether the world was unfair because it didn't finally rehab her or because it made her an outcast in the first place.

"It's certainly not a fair world. Lou from men's back is going to the state hospital tomorrow."

"Why?" Jayne asked. Then she realized—euthanasia.

"The world talked him into it. He's moderately retarded, moderately psychotic, and just intact and intelligent enough to know that at best he'll live the rest of his life in a backward room somewhere. I don't know if his family is utterly wrong."

Jayne remembered Lou, drinking so trustingly from Alice's cup. The world disappearing when she put the hood on him, locking him into a cartoon world he couldn't understand was an illusion. *I've done someone infinite damage.*

"Yet, was everything tried?" Ocean said. "In Germany in the last century, citizens protested the killing of crazy veterans. Let the Jews die, but not Crazy Otto. Now, it's the other way around. Hospitals are for people who can be treated. I guess you could say IAE treats the condition?"

"IAE?"

"Involuntary Active Euthanasia."

"But didn't Lou consent?"

"Oh, how can Lou know what he's consenting to? He probably thinks he's going to be reborn with full brainpower and a nice different body or is going to live with the angels."

"What does Dr. McGuire think about this?" Jayne asked.

"He doesn't," Ocean said. "He keeps them as long as possible, but he isn't running a free shelter."

Jayne said, "I feel threatened by just having been here."

Ocean said, "Yes, being mad's the desecration of all your prior ideals. They were, after all, what a madwoman believed."

"Oh."

"After a while, voluntary active euthanasia doesn't seem that much different than voluntary poverty," Ocean said. "We'll all watch Lou go. At least all of us on the front. The back halls get locked down on days when someone transfers to the state hospitals."

"What do you do when you're on the outside?" Jayne asked.

"Pretend none of this ever happened," Ocean said.

"How? It's been the most intense time in my life."

"Yes. Your apprentice adulthood. And nobody will understand, not even people who share your politics, your dreams."

"But you're just a drunk, not a crazy. You weren't on school drugs, were you?"

Ocean didn't answer that, just said, "Be on the porch tomorrow at 10 A.M."

The ambulance that pulled into the hospital passed by the porch and went around to the rear. The people on the front porch, aides and patients both, followed it. The men in the ambulance looked nervous, but the aides said, "It's okay."

"Let him walk out," Henry said. The other patients began whispering it, then speaking up.

One of the aides went inside. The ambulance drivers stayed where they were. Let him walk out. Don't bundle him out in a straitjacket on a stretcher.

The Big Dangle, Henry called society's offer of a kind death. Perhaps more than half of the people waiting for Lou had been tempted by it. In health, Jayne had been told that euthanasia only happens in the most extreme circumstances. She saw the old video of the Dutch anorexic begging for death.

Four aides brought Lou out in restraints that bound his arms to his sides, but he was walking. Sweaty hair fell into his eyes.

"Can he say good-bye to people?" Henry asked.

The aides nodded. Henry went up and put his head against Lou's head, his hand to the back of Lou's head. Jayne sensed it was a ritual they'd done before.

The aides helped Lou into the ambulance. The crowd let it drive away in absolute silence.

Jayne wondered if Lou would be dead within minutes of arriving at the state hospital or if they'd do a further evaluation. She hoped they'd have an ombudsman, because the poor fool who walked to the ambulance looked calm enough.

Ocean said, "A mercy killing. Shit." Her vocal cords could have been smashed with broken bottles. She said, "Sometimes you have to live for other people."

And sometimes die for them, Jayne thought with a chill. No, the papers were signed and sealed. No need to waste more food on a dead crazy. Would Lou even make the hospital alive? The ambulance crew could be equipped for the job, do it before Lou, if he even had expectations, expected it.

The next day, Ocean said to Jayne, "Come, let's bug Dr. McGuire." They went out in the hall waiting for him to pass them in rounds, acting like the neurotic patients who always wanted him to talk to them. Dr. McGuire saw them in the hall. His eyes jerked at them; he looked alarmed.

"Notice, he keeps on going," Ocean said.

What Jayne noticed was the usual neurotics weren't in the hall, just them.

They went back to Ocean's room. In twenty minutes, Dr. McGuire popped his head in the door. "What do you want?" He seemed uneasy to see Jayne in the same room.

Ocean said, "Just wanted to bug you."

Dr. McGuire said, "Well, that's nothing," and left.

Ocean said, "Well, he thinks his ass is clean." Jayne wondered if Ocean had found some liquor. Considering, getting drunk wasn't a bad idea except that alcohol was a depressant.

"Henry told me that Lou thought dying was like on TV, that he'd be in another show somewhere else."

Ocean said, "Don't dwell on that. Please, don't dwell on that. So many things to fix."

"I want to prove them wrong about me, about Lou, about people like Mick." Mick had been kind to her. She had fucked him.

Ocean said, "And you want to prove a whole society wrong, make it realize what it thought were acts of kindness were cruelties equal to those of the twentieth century. What do you win if you do this?"

Jayne said, "My own peace of mind."

"Do you want to die for a cause?"

Jayne suspected dying for a cause involved getting caught. Ocean didn't approve of getting caught. "No." She could visualize herself walking to a firing squad, though, if it came to that.

Ocean said, "If only there was absolute right and wrong."

Jayne said, "What I saw was wrong. What I did to Lou was wrong. I'd have felt better about doing it to Alice."

"Are you so terribly sure?"

Jayne said, "Yes. And you shouldn't drink when you're facing depressing things."

"Ah, Jayne, more observant than I realized."

"You're never coarse when you're sober."

"Well, it was awful about Lou."

"Do you think they let him meet with his folks before they killed him? How do . . ."

"I don't want to dwell on this. Jayne, his parents didn't want to see him suffer, so they were highly unlikely to see him at the state hospital. Has your father been to see you here?"

"No. But he writes. He loves me."

"He loves his idea of you, his idea of himself as the good father who could have saved you if only. Lou, well, sometimes, someone at the state hospital intervenes. And sometimes, they just want to get it over and forget about what they did. We had an executioner here once."

"Did he . . ."

"He said he'd never do it again. He signed out of the white race and went to New Mexico to join the Flagellentes. He died on the cross. Now, was that a suicide or what?"

Jayne was sorry she'd pried. "I'm sorry."

"Oh, but you're not drunk. Get drunk with me, Jayne." Ocean pulled a black flask from under her pillow.

"No," Jayne said. "I'm not into flagellation and self-pity myself. I want to prove society wrong about girls like me, guys like Lou, guys like Mick."

"Mick?"

Jayne touched her belly.

Ocean took a drink from her bottle, and said, "My, such passion. You'll get over it."

"We saw a murder yesterday," Jayne said.

"That's precisely why I'm drinking. I couldn't do a damn thing to stop it. Could you?"

6
Nonhistory and Time, Memory and Violence

When Jayne went into labor, the hospital where Dr. McGuire sent her put her in cyberia for the duration.

The next day, she had no memories of having given birth but a dim sense of living through a nightmare under the cute cartoons of talking dragons and boys sailing the ocean.

She left the hospital knowing something about computers and systems for managing them, and a sense that she'd been robbed.

Ocean told Jayne she'd had a boy. Everyone thought it was good that she didn't have to remember labor and that she didn't see the baby.

Back home, Jayne did her uterus-reduction exercises faithfully. The doctor who said he'd delivered the baby told her never to tell her husband what had happened when she married.

That was manifestly impossible. The baby had scarred her belly with stretch marks.

The social universe Jayne knew expected her to hide her experiences and go on to get married. That was, if she was to redeem herself as a good girl. Jayne decided she could never be their idea of a good girl. She'd had apprentice adult conversations with people who remembered the nineties, who had parents who remembered the sixties and fifties. Maybe Kafka was right and she should bet on the world in her quarrel with it. But what the world offered her was boring.

But to her parents' community, Jayne was a pitiful person. And the horror was they thought she had to be pitiful because they wanted to approve of her for her sibling's and parents' sake.

After Jayne spent several hours telling her father about the hospital, he said, "I guess confessing to me helps you, but don't tell anyone else about that. That woman Ocean got in touch with us, offered to help with a scholarship to college if you'd agree to go to one she knew about, but I told her we could manage ourselves."

"Ocean got in touch with you?"

"Yes. If you pass your GED, we can look into community college. You'd have to do it in-state, but if your grades were high enough, you could apply to a four-year school. The other option is a technical program, learn a career. We'd be happy to pay your way and help with a cheap apartment. You can work part-time."

Arrgh. Jayne had a number for Ocean, but hadn't called until now, when she sneaked out.

"How are you?" Ocean said when Jayne identified herself.

"My father turned down a scholarship? You didn't get in touch with me directly."

"Jayne, you must be bored."

"It's like sensory deprivation. Shit, I want back in the madhouse."

"Ah, yes, the vividness. But if you run off, your parents will file a missing persons report and you could get anyone who shelters you in trouble."

"I embarrass my family. They wouldn't give a rat's ass."

"You're wrong there, Jayne. They might not know how to care in a way you like, but they do care."

"But they turned down a scholarship for me."

"I can only manage to get them in certain schools. You'd have had to have gone to school in California or the Midwest."

"I'd love to."

"But your parents want to see you more often. They want to make sure you're going to survive on your own. Do the time there, then I'll get you transferred. I'm concerned about you, Jayne. Don't create excitements you can't manage right now. Green Pines Community College is not bad. I'll come see you."

California. Somewhere in a city. Gone for two years. Jayne had waited four months in a madhouse to give birth to a baby, but two years lasted half of high school.

"Do you like dogs or horses?" Ocean asked. "I know people who could use help with either."

So Jayne spent the next tenth of her life in the comic opera of a community college full of Judas Girls with bad grades who'd failed to get their pledges to marry them, rehabilitated drug kids who were learning horse keeping and landscape gardening, nonrehabilitated drug people who were taking freshman English for the third time, ex-convicts who wanted to transfer to Carolina, and various people for whom a two-year program was the last chance they'd ever have to change their lives, and rich kids who wanted to play before transferring to the rest of their lives.

For the first time in her life, Jayne fit right in with people who weren't institutionalized. She lived with five other people in a loft over a clothing store. They rode bicycles out the to community college. Three of the guys drove pedicabs around Pinehurst during the rich season. One of the other women also worked the golfers, whoring part-time. The third woman was thirty-two years old, with the broken hands of a scullery maid and a keen interest in pretending to be other people when online. Somehow, she'd gotten the money together to try this.

The house collected computers abandoned by richer students and occasionally made forays up to Chapel Hill for the last year's models that Carolina students left on the curb.

Everyone in the house hacked around in turn-of-the-century programs that hadn't been built by machines. Jayne began pulling pieces of the old programs out of the commented-out chunks of what had been abandoned or hidden when ideas became copyrighted and the Free Software Foundation lost their lawsuit against the backbone providers and chip makers.

Chunks of history floated through the data mist. Jayne came across the comment: ;;Open Source Rules. The code below was an encryption program with unix manual pages that Jayne carried for years on various media.

It had all been so rapidly moving then, ideas, social changes, that the whole technological expansion turned on itself like a Klein bottle, technology driving the forces of its own containment, surface to interior to surface, automatically interpenetrating, never collapsing, but the expansions only feeding the containment.

Another commented out section from 2009: ;;We are the singularity we're escaping.

One of the guys brought in lock cracks to open restricted news programs. Unrestricted news played all day long in randomly shifting patterns on the five monitors in the main living space. Jayne began to pick up information on what the past might have been.

One excuse for the present was that it stopped information overload. Slowing ideas stabilized the economy. People settled for more reasonable dreams, and institutions had futures they could imagine.

Jayne wondered how much happened from not being willing to admit mistakes, of building from one fuck-up to another. So the world she lived in was the fossilized version of the millennium. *We had dreams; they had investments in structure—they won.*

And someone left the message "Open Source Rules" buried with an encryption program in a copy of an overly complex net browser.

Jayne found no comments about Open Source after 2014.

Guys proposed instant love to her avatars in the chat spaces and followed her home by voice. After a very short trial, Jayne quit electron play spaces. She wondered why the other rommates spent so much time there.

So this was a reversal of high school. Dumb Judas Girls sulked through their classes, teased by the majority, and went back to stay with the people their parents had arranged to board them, waiting for the options on their virginities to get picked up while Jayne hung out with people as interesting as the people she'd met in the hospital.

But her ex–scullery maid housemate said, "In the end, the Judas Girls win. I'd sell my eye to have people like me in my kitchen. But hell, I ain't gonna fit in as a good bride to any-one rich. I'm going to be alone, supporting myself."

The five monitors played programs telling about the literal veracity of the Bible to the medical show demonstrating active-ethuanasia practices least likely to scare patients into changing their minds at the last moment.

One monitor displayed what was advertised as a live per-manent feed from Congress. Jayne noticed that the con-gressmen's heads streaked when they moved quickly. Perhaps community college was a holo rig. Perhaps the con-gressmen themselves weren't quite operating at eighty mil-lion polygons per second.

Cyberias made her shudder. ₆

Jayne thought, *Could be a holo rig. It's a little too wonderful.* Junior college all over the world was the last break from real life, people going down, people going up, many at least mi-noring in horizontal biology. At Green Pines, the teachers were either bored rich wives who didn't want to go that far from home or graduate students from Duke who didn't get

Duke classes to teach in their fourth years of grad school and had to drive ninety miles to find work. Last chance for them, too, Jayne realized.

Since Jayne was smart, the ambitious grad-student teachers liked her. On their résumés, they counted their students who transferred into four-year schools. The Dukelings needed Jayne to win worse than the predictors of her high-school life needed her to fail.

Pedicabs and computers and midnight painting and jam sessions and haunting shops full of excessively expensive beautiful things —Jayne got a break from the nightmare, but she expected that the world as it was would reclaim her.

Her mother and sister tricked her into coming home for Sidna's wedding. Jayne felt she'd be too disrespectful if she didn't go, so she got in the car with the rest of the family and saw Sidna get married. The groom looked like a decadent country squire who'd escaped from the eighteenth century without his peruke.

During spring exams, Ocean came to visit, sitting on a street-picked chair, looking at the walls Jayne's housemates had painted in the night-long painting sessions, all whirling enthusiasm and genitalia. "If you want," Ocean said to Jayne, "I can get you your scholarship when you finish here."

Jayne asked, "Is college like junior college?"

Ocean said, "No."

The four-year school didn't give Jayne two years of credit for her community college work. The first year was like high school without the torture. Jayne explored the flat Midwestern town enough to know she didn't want to stay there when she finished. Unlike in community college, everyone studied hard. The first year ended with good enough grades and a summer internship in Charleston, South Carolina, arranged by Ocean's people.

The instant Jayne got out of the bus, she smelled some-

thing weird—maybe three hundred years of chamber pots
and later cheap plumbing. Composted human garbage.
Charleston looked quake-shocked and vaguely third-world.
Ocean had told her that she'd arranged a pedicab to get out
to where she'd be doing her internship. Pedicabs weren't a
flourish there—they were genuine transportation. Jayne finally found the one with the double yellow-and-black rib-
bons twisted around the handlebars, and said, "Can you get
me across the bridge before dark?"

"Jayne, right?"

"Right." Jayne got in the pedicab. Ocean said she wouldn't
need to tell the driver where she was going.

Charleston had been the northernmost Caribbean port
that lucked into staying attached to a major industrial power
despite itself. The years between the American Revolution
and Second World War had been spent in posturing against
Yankee guns. For a few decades, the place looked as though
it would become civilized if only in the style of military oc-
cupations. But no, the Polaris subs slid away forever like
whales intelligent enough to know a Norwegian whaler from
Green tourists.

Old Charleston didn't mind. Once the generation who'd
made serious Federal money died off, servants would be
cheap again, and they could all return to their subtropical
dreams.

"Wages are now the same as in Mexico. So the women
you'll be teaching piece it out how they can," the pedicab
driver said.

Jayne was a bit shocked that he spoke so openly. Back in
the Midwest, none of the future illegal teachers said in so
many words what they were training for. Judas Girls and various programmatic bugging systems made all the talk go
slant. Jayne knew spreadsheets, basic office programs, a bit of
secured financial transfer systems. She'd come to Charleston
to teach direct body whores and virtual girls accounting and
secure financial transfers, at least as secure as could be had

without strong encryption, which was now illegal if on an un-licensed hard drive. Jayne didn't plan to download her strong encryption program anywhere yet.

"Who are the whores' clients?" she asked.

"Tourists and merchant marines, students at the Medical College. There's a war on with the Citadel."

"War?"

The driver pedaled Jayne across the Cooper River Bridge to a beach community of white peeling wood houses up on stilts, even the ones inland. Palmettos grew like yard weeds— plantains on steroids. A bus pulled past the pedicab and stopped to let off three women, two in their fifties, one in her late twenties.

"They're virtual girls," the driver said. "The manager thought she'd have a couple trained in the bookkeeping pro-grams first. They're just basically numerate, but they know their way around graphic user interfaces."

Jayne didn't think they looked like whores. They looked like clerical people, a bit puffy, in blouses and jeans and sen-sible shoes. "Do they get into body suits?"

"The clients do. Virtual girls run the suit from peripherals and pen-pads." The driver pulled up to the house and locked the pedicab to a giant bolt set in concrete. "I installed the software for them. It's pretty much basic sex industry."

"Why do they have to have women manipulating the suit at all?"

"Guys who didn't want variety wouldn't be going to whores," driver said. "They want a real person to be involved in their pleasure, to care that they get off, to witness it. The older ones get a voice job so they still sound young." He showed Jayne to the back entrance like friends of the family or help. The door opened directly into a kitchen where the three women who'd arrived earlier were making coffee and checking orders. Another woman, dressed in a suit, came down some stairs leading up to a space above the kitchen. She was in her early forties. This woman had an out-front sexuality that reminded Jayne of stray dogs who hung around school and put the mooch on any kid. The driver nodded at her and scrounged around in the cupboard for a cup. "I'm Brandy, the madam," the woman said. "You'll have the room above the kitchen for the summer. I was just checking it."

"My parents might come for a visit. I can't tell them not to." Jayne wished she'd broken completely with her parents, but Ocean said they'd come in handy sometime.

One of the fiftysomething virtual girls said with a real girl's voice, "Bunch of women sharing a beach house, going out with guys. It's all virtual or out-take. You think we want the Citadel guys knowing where to come looking for us?"

The truly young girl said, "We have to move all the time."

Brandy said, "We all have families who don't need to know anything. Ocean tells me you seem to have been celibate for the last three years. You don't have a problem with us, do you?"

Jayne had seen movies about girls who tried prostitution and died, but she had entertained the fantasy. "My mother told me that the woman who taught her what her period was went on to be a madam in Louisville, Kentucky."

"Perhaps my mother knew her. We used to go up for the Derby," Brandy said.

Classes couldn't begin until noon since most of the women worked through until 4 A.M. Jayne hadn't taught a class of real people before, just tutored students. She wondered if they'd know how inexperienced she was. Holding on to her media remote for dear life, Jayne looked at her first class.

She had four students who wanted to learn spreadsheets. All of them were older than Jayne. One was at least her mother's age.

"What do you know about computers?" Jayne asked, sure the question sounded stupid as soon as she spoke it.

Within the week, Jane insisted that she run the virtual machine at least once. "We have a virgin," Brandy told the man who was rigged up at the other end of the modem. The computer showed a naked body on one half of the screen. The other window showed readouts for penile engorgement, alcohol blood level, and a thumbnail picture of the woman he thought he was with. Brandy keyed in a picture of a naked girl who looked apprehensive. The girl in the thumbnail actually moved, shifted. The readout bar said that the machine had her synchronized roughly with the man's suit. He touched her with his hand.

Running a virtual girl required good hand-eye coordination. Brandy said, "You're going to have to talk to him because he's too sober for the machine voices."

The screen was a touch screen. If Jayne rubbed the man's image from throat to knees and clicked the right mouse button, the man had the illusion of full body contact. Clicking the left mouse button brought up the rhythm options: Match His, Random Off by 5 cm, Random Off by 10 cm, Sudden Spine Arching Random. "It's good to vary it. Makes it more real," Brandy said.

Jayne nodded. She opted for matching the client's moves. When she'd asked why the virtual girls didn't wear full body suits themselves, they'd all said that this made them feel more in control. Sitting up, legs together, intensely watching a male having the illusion of sex—a virtual girl ruled.

"Move your hands to my butt," the man said. Default position was around his back. Two dabs of the data pen put hands on his butt. Jayne tightened the arms and switched the rhythm to Sudden Spine Arching.

"You bitch, I slipped out." The man slapped the girl. Jayne worked with both the front and back image to get the man's sensations lined up properly again. She shifted to slightly erratic motions. One button toggled a flexing tube that could only be for clenching the vagina muscles. Jayne hit that. Turgidity was maximal. Jane leaned over the mike and began breathing heavily into it. Click, click on the vagina-squeeze button. A whole new set of animated GUIs dropped down, little graphically moving diagrams of vaginas either quivering, spasming, stripping condoms off cocks, or clamping down in fewer but bigger movements. Jayne started the quivering, then waited until the very moment of the man's orgasm to hit spasm.

The guy went limp, then said, "A virgin, you say?"

Jayne wasn't sure whether she should explain that she was really a first-time virtual girl or what. "You helped me so much," she said. Brandy smiled.

After the man went off-line, the regular girl took over the next client, and Jayne went to the back of the room so she could look over their heads at the screens. From the back of the room, the virtual girls looked like middle-aged computer-graphics designers, fingers and pens and mice flying. Jayne realized they preferred seeing each other to being locked in a virtual suit with a man's fantasy. The screen guy was a tiny thing to manipulate with fingertips and data sticks. Like phone sex, the women mugged for each other between the heavy breathing. The older women seemed to get the most amusement out of what they were doing.

Brandy said, "We have to be careful about carpal tunnel syndrome."

The body whores, all younger women, who lived in the house woke up between noon and 2 P.M., then planned the night's rides out to their clients. Two women, who called each other "roadies," generally shared one car and driver.

In an outlaw twist on Judas Girls, the whores could send out distress signals by switching on a transmitter planted in their jawbones and keyed with their teeth. Teeth clicks to "dun, de, dun, dun" meant the woman was in trouble. The driver was armed and a private security company was on call.

Some of the drivers wore business suits. One dressed like a garage mechanic who could have been driving women home after their car broke down.

The whores never asked Jayne to turn tricks. Unlike the

virtual girls, they didn't like to share opportunities. Virtual girls could work until gnarled fingers couldn't hit the right GUIs, but whores had twenty to twenty-five years if they didn't use drugs, drink too much, or run into Citadel cadets on pussy-stalking missions.

Suzanne was one of the oldest whores, about thirty-eight. When she turned twenty-seven and saw the first signs of age, she'd spent five weeks with her lesbian lover stalking cadets. "At first, we thought, 'shit, they're trained to kill. We're dead meat. They practice on us, stalking armed civilians. That's what they do as soldiers—go to some damned foreign country and stalk armed civilians, get rid of the infrastructure, they say. Whores are good training targets. Those guys hate women. Citadel went private to kick pussy out. We kill them; they kill us. Arrogant little pricks won't pay for it. In the beginning, they just raped us, but we shot one of them, and that was it. The Whore Citadel War."

Oh, it's dangerous being here, dangerous being us. Do you like to get caught? Ocean's voice from memory asked Jayne.

Suzanne continued, "So, I thought I'd be old soon. I might as well die as to spread my legs again. I'd lost all my savings buying into a collections bag, you know, getting rights to collect debts from one of those ads on late-night TV, but all the deadbeats were just flat out uncollectable. Shit, I thought if I could talk guys out of money for sex, I should be able to talk people into paying debts. Wrong. So there I was, venture-capital plans busted, getting old, facing ugliness. So, why not die shooting. It was a bad winter day, the bitch I was with had a heavy double mother thing on the side that I wasn't supposed to know about. Only that had played out, so she was stuck back with me and I was stuck with a cheating whore for bed fodder. So, what do we do? We get the house guns and the nightglasses. We figure, let's go for the really nasty ones. We'd find them in bars bragging how they broke a woman's heart. My girlfriend, she seduced them. I came in and ran them out. We followed the first guy back to the

Citadel. He has a roommate just as nasty, killed a girl in public down at the Market. Cops didn't even bust him 'cause she died with a gun in her purse. Okay, so they're in their dorm room and we're on the roof with the nightscope, thinking we won't make it off the Citadel roof if we shoot. Then again, you can't just shoot them in cold blood, so we called them out."

Brandy, who appeared to have heard this story too many times, came by, and said, "Lucky the whole Citadel didn't go to the meet." She kept on moving out of the room, then came back with a bottle of Lowland single-malt Scotch and three glasses almost like lab measures, but crystal.

Suzanne said, "It was out at one of the parks around one of those gunky old mansions with trees dripping moss. The ground was frost-crunchy. We had a cab. They had a cab. We wore leather and lace. The Citadel guys wore their uniforms. As soon as the taxis went out of sight, we all dived for cover and started firing. I thought I was suicidal until the guns got for real. Then, ladyman, I had a high white moment, all the guys who'd ever hurt me, who'd raped me, who'd refused to pay, out there in the person of one nasty Citadel cadet who was personally trying to kill me. You know." Suzanne almost touched Jayne, but pulled back. "A bullet cracks near your head into the tree behind you. You stare back at a guy who has a gun pointed at you. Suicide's all over."

Jayne asked, "Did he let you live?"

Suzanne said, "I killed him, ladyman. I bared a tit with my left hand and raised my own gun with my right."

Brandy said, "If I'd heard this when Suzanne first wanted to work for me, I wouldn't have hired her." She poured a shot for Jayne, then for herself.

"But, madam lady, the boys never tell anyone when they get called out by whores. They're ashamed if they can't kill us without help."

"You think," Brandy said.

"I'm not wanted, and it's been over ten years."

Without Suzanne saying more, Jayne suddenly realized that Suzanne's faithless lover had died. Suzanne said, "I walked down to a country store to call the cab and decided on the ride back that I needed to be in a house."

Jayne said, "You still go out? Ever with Citadel graduates?"

"Girl-man, it's always with someone like a Citadel graduate. Only I specialize in making sure they're not going to get me. And if I ever feel like dying for real, I'll walk onto the Citadel campus with a gun."

Brandy said, "Suzanne, you've got five dates tonight. Is your bag stocked?"

"Yeah, lady madam. My bag has all its strong girl toys in it." She turned to Jayne, and said, "One of my clients tonight likes to be led around by his dick. You get one of those Chinese handcuffs on a dick, you got the man."

Suzanne's roadie came down then with her own kit bag. She was a small girl who'd just turned legal after being a teenage illegal whore for two years. She still looked like a scared virgin, eyes huge, lipstick slightly smeared.

Brandy said, "Ladies, please take off all your makeup when you come in. I bought the house a couple of jars of eye-make remover that's good to use when you're weary and the room's spinning slightly."

"Or your pupils are spiraling in the dark," the young whore said. "Come on, Suzanne, let's go."

Suzanne picked up her bag of handcuffs, whips, and cock-locks, and sighed. The two women left for the night. After all the body whores left, the house settled into the click of mice and the panting into microphones of the virtual girls. Jayne took each one aside for lessons on keeping the house books in coded spreadsheet.

Every decade or so since 2005, the IRS had offered a tax amnesty program to all illegal businesses that enroll in a coded electronic filing program. The only trick was mastering the program.

*   *   *

Suzanne had been asking her to go to Myrtle Beach on one
of their free days, but Jayne felt slightly uneasy around her.
Suzanne said she'd killed people. On a free day, Jayne went
to the morgue files of the *Charleston News & Courier*, looked
ten years back, and found:

MURDER-SUICIDE OF CITADEL CADETS AND WOMAN

Two Citadel cadets and an unidentified woman died
in a tragic murder-suicide at Orton Plantation early
Sunday morning. Taxi drivers remember bringing the
cadets and the woman to the plantation. Friends of
the cadets remember vaguely that the woman had
been in the dorms. The cadets' names are not being
released pending notification of next of kin.

"Murder-suicides are rare at the Citadel," the
public information officer told the press. "We have
a couple each year. Often suicidal women shoot
themselves near campus, sometimes killing a cadet
in the process, but the death of two cadets is
rare."

Jayne wondered if any tracking programs noticed that
she'd accessed the files. Or if everyone knew already what the
deal had really been.

Jayne walked through the historic district as though she
was an ordinary tourists. The harbor hopped with slant light
on waves. In the distance, Fort Sumter was covered with
scaffolding, transforming itself from a Civil War museum
into something less offensive to the African freighters coming from Ghana and Senegal.

Jayne thought, *History's meaning never stays static.* Then,
*Two cadets and a dead woman. There's always more to what hap-
pens than what you have time to know.*

That night she asked Brandy, "Should I go to Myrtle
Beach with her?"

"Gay women generally don't make aggressive passes. Just be careful."

"Myrtle Beach, not the Citadel," Jayne said.

Suzanne had a car, so they drove to the Pavillion on the Strand. The parking garage took the car by its bumper hooks and took it away into storage. Suzanne said, "Do you know average cars used to have a curb weight of more than twelve-hundred pounds?"

"No." It was one of those factoids that was so meaningless it was probably true.

"Parking. They had to make them lighter to park them without going to heavy machinery."

"Pedicabs are even lighter."

"Yeah, but about thirty miles is max for a pedicab."

Myrtle Beach on a summer night was a sweaty jostle of people who'd be horrified if they knew who they were shoving past. Jayne and Suzanne pushed through the crowd of people in virtual goggles and suits or walking around near naked and drunk, drugged nipples dangling under faces bent by micrograms. Kids lined up for computer games or rides with controls. As they passed two almost life-size fighters, Suzanne said, "Genuine fighter controls."

"Do you want to?" Jayne asked.

"I want to take you into the fun house," Suzanne said. She bought tickets at a booth, swore to them both being adult, and helped Jayne strap on a wrist monitor. The calliope faded as they pushed through the heavy rubber door into the fun house.

The mirrors weren't silvered glass. They weren't mirrors at all but interactive computer screens. What attracted attention distorted itself further into mutations of the body while the reproduced face stayed the same. Jayne appeared in several screens. Her body swelled. The system sensed her interest, Suzanne's interest, and began to lower her clothes.

Naked, pregnant. Suzanne's digital clothes also disap-

peared. Everyone in the fun house became naked and pregnant, then Jayne's belly split open like a seedpod, dripping
babies with guns.

In her memory, she was screaming, lying on a table, her
legs forced into stirrups, the mask feeding her illusions suddenly black.

"Don't feed it. Look away," a man told Jayne, but she was
fixated on the babies with guns. The babies began to go on
patrol, flat images crawling across the floor which Jayne
hadn't noticed before was another giant screen. They
writhed at her feet.

Suzanne said, "If the babies really bother you, close your
eyes and say, "Reset." Her own images turned back into her
clothed self and began to shift toward the masculine.

Jayne closed her eyes, and said, "Reset." The videos displayed her as she was. The image began to swell around the
belly.

"Is that all you can think about?" Suzanne said. Her images
looked like young men now. Her hand materialized a cigar.

"Reset," Jayne said. "I've got to get out of here." Her
image dropped an eyeball. In its place was a miniature camera, naked lens, and metal body, not concealed in a realistic
prothesis like a Judas Girl's. A screen played bodies in coitus.

In memory, a baby cried. *A boy*, Ocean had told her. *You
have to sign the papers.*

There was no getting around hurting someone.

A man looked at Jayne as though speculating on the state
of her eyes. She felt as threatened by her Judas Girl image as
she'd been by the warrior babies.

"Reset," Jayne said again, stumbling for the heavy rubber
door. Her image mutated again. Suzanne grabbed her hand.
The system stripped them both naked. Long tongues thrust
out of their mouths and vaginas, lapping each other, into
each other—vaginas, rectums, nostrils, ears, mouths.

Suzanne said, "That will play for a while," as she pushed
Jayne out of the fun house. As Jayne stood gasping in the hot

night, Suzanne said, "Still obsessed by that baby? Well, you didn't have a horde of them."

"The machine. The image generator."

"It gets a rise out of someone, it goes. Sorry. I thought I'd dominate it."

"You did at the end," Jayne said, remembering the labor through all the virtual delusions, now, finally, her body screaming, the baby's body coming out of hers, screaming.

Suzanne said, "Better that than babies with guns."

"God, why didn't I at least look at him and say good-bye?"

"Ah, I've had abortions. That was before I learned to stick to what I could stand about men."

Jayne didn't know what she wanted. Suzanne said, "Come, let's do something physical. No tricks, just bodies thrashed by machines in space."

They walked down a few blocks and rode the Wild Mouse, a one-car roller coaster that spun on a track as high as a four-story building. Beyond them, the ocean was bouncing moonlight. Jayne looked down at it as the car climbed to the top of its frame, then screamed as the car dropped into its gyrations. Suzanne held her hands over her head through the whole thing.

"Do you want more?" Suzanne asked. "Or are you wiped?"

Jayne realized she needed those adreneline moments. She felt purged, but not quite purged enough. A baby with a gun waited in the back of her mind, angry for being rejected. "Again," she said. Again also postponed the moment where she had to deal with Suzanne's sexuality. Jayne didn't want to insult it, but it made her nervous. She thought of the sexuality as something apart from Suzanne.

Suzanne led her down through the Pavillion as the lights spun and machine grease faded into squealing metal sounds. They reached the Ferris wheel. "It's not intense, but I like it," Suzanne said. "Don't be so nervous. Gay women don't make unwanted passes like guys do."

Jayne remembered that she'd been the aggressor in the sex that impregnated her. "I'm not sure what I want."

"I like having some friends I don't sleep with," Suzanne said. They rode out of the noise below into the silence at the Ferris wheel's peak. It stopped, leaving them swinging gently while other people got on. The beach was a line between the empty ocean and the bodies and lights below them.

"Do you come here often?" Jayne asked. The question sounded weird, a bar pickup line on the top of a Ferris wheel, made to a woman who made her living off of metaphorical desires. Somewhere out behind the electric commotion below them, Jayne's baby was walking, talking, maybe beginning to ask questions.

"Yes," Suzanne said after a pause filled with Jayne's thoughts about the weirdness of her life. "I need a place where I can just be a body in a crowd of people who don't know me."

That's what Myrtle Beach is about, Jayne thought.

They got the car from the lift racks, then drove back through the dark to the house. The beach traffic thinned as they got farther down, then picked up again for the Charleston area beaches. "Many drunks out tonight, even for a weekday," Suzanne said. The moon still rode above them. "You're so tense. You expect I'm going to make a pass at you or that baby stuff freak you out?"

Jayne said, "Both."

Suzanne said, "I made a pass. You didn't notice."

"The whole thing was a pass, I thought," Jayne said. "I'd like to be interested, I think."

"Totally a turnoff. I've been through them bi-curious girls."

Jayne felt strange sitting beside Suzanne, who drove the little car as fast as it would go. She wanted to ask how it felt to kill a man, two men, perhaps her faithless lover, too. What had it been like to survive? What she asked was, "Have you ever been back to the Citadel?"

"Never have felt suicidal enough again. If I really wanted to do it, this time, I'd shoot myself. Or go down in poison. You ever hear of women offing themselves in public? Happens. People pay to see it. I've been studying on the history of what I do. Japanese women, Indian women, everybody's had whores. Seems like dying for exhibition would be less lonely."

Jayne said, "You could ask for euthanasia."

"You're surrounded by people who see you as pitiful and too chicken-shit to take your own poison. With the other, you make arrangements for someone to inherit your cut of the snuff take. Well, that's more the way I'd want to do it. If I ever got that depressed, I'd go in public, leave some money to someone I half-assed cared about."

"There's a lot of esoteric weirdness about your business," Jayne said, wondering if Suzanne knew the word *esoteric*.

"Hey, you want to kill a Citadel boy, I can find you someone to go with, though. You could kill someone sworn to a Judas Girl. Me, I want to quit the business, really. But what would I do that paid so well?"

"You could be a madam like Brandy." Jayne wondered if she was going to try to be too helpful and end up condescending to this woman.

"Shit, I've saved enough money for the license and all, but I don't know if I'm ready to be boss mamma to a bunch of whores like me."

"We should have ridden the Round-up," Jayne said, ducking what looked like the beginning of a depressing conversation. Ocean had told her, You're there to teach what they want, not to reform them. Our clients can't always be people we approve of.

"Next time, girlfriend," Suzanne said. She stopped talking and turned on a radio station to slow songs about cheating men and early mornings filled with rain and cigarettes.

"You bought more of what?" Brandy said to Suzanne.

"More default credit accounts, yes. I got it for three cents on the dollar. I'm a dominatrix. I should be able to collect, and the company gave me software on state and federal collection laws." Suzanne wore red-leather pants, high-heeled boots, and a sleeveless silk top as though she were going out to work her slaves. On her left bicep, she'd tied a tight-braided black-leather cord.

Jayne thought but didn't say, *Your clients volunteer to be bullied. These people aren't interested.*

Brandy said, "You lost money last time."

"I've been a doma for three years now. And I've got this software that dials for me."

Brandy said, "Jayne, could you help her with the computer?"

They went upstairs into the room where the virtual girls fingered their machines and mice. Suzanne stopped at the door, and asked, "Must I run my collection service from here?"

Brandy said, "It's the only place we've got phone lines and computers." She pulled a minitower computer out of a closet, and said, "It's old, but it does have voice mail and an autodialer. See if it will run your program."

The virtual girls all looked up from their own work to see precisely what Suzanne was doing. She shifted uneasily on her booted heels and shoved her thumbs into her pants waistband, then turned to Jayne. "Is it okay?"

"Yes, the database is hybrid disk. You'll be okay." *At least technologically,* Jayne added to herself. She installed the program on the hard drive and looked at the menu when it came up. "We can sort by last payment or by state or by amount outstanding."

"Amount outstanding," Suzanne said. She didn't sit down at the computer, but stared out the window.

"I'll show you," Jayne said.

"Can't you run the machine for me?"

Brandy said, "No, we're paying Jayne to teach us about

computers, not to operate them. And, besides, this is your deal. I'm letting you use my lines for free, you know."

Suzanne said, "I'll give you a cut, Brandy."

"When you earn back what you put in, then we can talk about a cut," Brandy said. She walked away from them to check on how the virtual girls were doing.

Suzanne pulled up a chair and sat down by Jayne, and said, "So teach me."

"How do you want this sorted?"

"By last payment," Suzanne said.

Suzanne had bought $4 million of medium-bad credit. Even at three cents on the dollar, she'd paid $120,000 for it. Jayne sighed as the machine sorted the clients by last payment made.

None of them had paid on their debts in over eight months. Half of them didn't show payment for over two years. Some of them had outstanding judgments. Jayne asked, "How valid are the addresses and connection numbers?"

Suzanne said, "They can't legally sell ones where they know the address isn't valid."

Jayne said, "How can you prove they knew what the fuck the address was?" She saw that the menus were fairly straightforward. A hot link led to information about judgments and defaults and how court-collection procedures worked. Suzanne, if she were willing to pay the filing fees, could take these people to court to attach salaries. Jayne suspected that in many cases, these debtors were working for their keep, getting paid in room and board. Nothing to collect there.

Brandy walked back up to them as they worked over the computer. She said, "Whoring is infinitely more moral than selling bad credit to desperate people."

Suzanne said, "I'm not desperate. I just want to be able to make even more money."

"You could have brought property," Brandy said. "Rental beach property."

"Not much for $150,000," Suzanne said. "I don't want to just be okay. I want to have nice things. I want to be able to treat my women nice."

Jayne knew that Suzanne made a couple thousand a week. She hoped that Suzanne hadn't spent all her savings on this.

Brandy said, "Do you know how the machine works enough now that Jayne can leave you to this?"

"Oh, sure, sure. I'll figure it out. I always figure things out," Suzanne said. The virtual girls had stopped staring, but they each looked back at her from time to time.

Brandy said, "Jayne," meaning come with me.

They walked down the stairs. Brandy said, "I can't believe she did that again. Last time, she only lost $10,000, got some of the people to pay a little bit. But three cents on the dollar."

"Why do people buy the accounts?" Jayne said.

"If you get three people in one hundred to pay their debts and clear their credit records, you break even. So, if you're middle-class or earnest techie, you think, surely three of these people out of one hundred really want to clear their credit. Perhaps they want to buy a car or a house. But Suzanne should know better. Maybe she wants to pretend she's really as aggressive and domineering as her clients want her to be."

"She told me about public suicides for money."

"She can be the most morbid cunt," Brandy said.

"Does that really happen?"

"Yeah," Brandy said. "Suzanne said it was going on even in the nineteenth century in New York City, but now it's an old whore's special. Not all old whores."

"But Suzanne's not old," Jayne said. "And she was just talking about it."

"Maybe she wants pain," Brandy said. "Maybe I should find her a top for a date. Give her a break, let her be submissive. She's just paid $125,000 to get lied to and cried to by people who know she'd be thrilled to collect three and a half cents on the dollar. She's better off doing what she's good at and looking for a better class of lover."

Suddenly, Jayne felt total moral and intellectual vertigo. She didn't know anything about this whoring business, about these people. She was just there to teach them some skills to make their lives go more smoothly. Just because she'd had a baby out of wedlock didn't mean she understood these women at all. "I feel out of my depth suddenly. You're really a madam. Suzanne beats men for a living."

"Puts leashes on their dicks," Brandy said. "You're not a virgin, either. Are you attracted to Suzanne?" Brandy asked. She sat upright in her chair, her eyes on Jayne.

"I'm afraid of that," Jayne said. "I haven't even masturbated since I came here."

"I'd advise a less complicated first girl."

"I'm going to leave at the end of the summer, and you'll still be here. This is just an adventure for me. It's your whole life. And it's just like everyone else's, and it's not."

"I certainly plan on being in business for a long time. We drain off male excesses that might otherwise hurt little secondary virgins. You can be a cock-tease because your man can come to us."

"I didn't mean that to be critical." The isolation intensified even when Jayne said that. Or because of it.

"No. Perhaps you're a cunt-tease, not a cock-tease."

"I don't know what you mean."

"But then you are leaving at the end of the summer."

"I'm an unlicensed teacher."

"People see you as working around a state scam. I'm a licensed bordello operator and people see me as half whore and half glamour queen. My father was a drunk who died when I was a kid. My mother ran a boardinghouse and worked in a mill to keep us looking decent and eating regular. Surviving whoredom and becoming a madam is what brainy girls without help do. When I had my own child out of wedlock, I didn't have an HMO, a nice place to stay. I had to start working. And I raised my child myself."

Jayne almost asked, *Where is the child now?* But she didn't. She'd ask Suzanne later. Brandy turned on the television and called up an old French movie. Jayne decided to watch it, too. It started with a dead girl in a ditch.

"Suzanne likes this a lot," Brandy said. "I'm sorry I accused you of being a cunt-tease."

"I wouldn't know if I were one," Jayne said.

"Oh, being dumb works fine for some people," Brandy said. "Maybe I've been too knowing for too long, though."

The collection program sent Suzanne out of the computer at twelve midnight, nine o'clock Pacific Coast Time. She threw herself in an armchair, and said, "People are cunts."

"When is that news?" Brandy said.

"One woman promised to send money tomorrow, but she was going to make the check out to the real creditor unless I send her an authorization to collect. The program told me how. Shit, I have to send it by registered mail."

"Need a driver for your early-morning clients?" Brandy said. "We're down a driver. Maybe Jayne could drive." Jayne heard the challenge in her words. She wondered if Brandy's apology had been an act or if it just aggravated her that Jayne hadn't even masturbated since she'd been with them.

Suzanne zipped up her debtor's file case. "God, I'm going to be mean. Jayne, you wanna?"

"Ah."

"These guys are all in pretty good neighborhoods. I don't think you'll need a gun, but make sure you take a cell phone," Brandy said. "We've got a quick response contract with Armstead Security."

Jayne said, "Who's going out with you?"

"I won't need a roadie. You'll be just outside. And I know these clients to a man," Suzanne said. She started down the stairs to the supply closet and took out her leather bag of pain and humiliation toys. "Shit, Jayne, you should come watch."

Brandy said, "Suzanne, don't do any permanent damage." She went to her desk and pulled out car keys. Flipping them across to Jayne, she said, "It's the blue Xhoshiba in the garage." She pulled a cell phone out and came around the desk to put that in Jayne's hand. "Armstead is the second speed-dial button. I'm the first."

Suzanne said, "I'm not that upset."

Brandy said, "These are men you're dealing with."

"They're my slaves."

"You don't own them. They pay. It's their choice."

"I can be really dangerous," Suzanne said. "And they'll be tied up."

Jayne said, "If you really think it would be a good idea, I can go in with her."

"Shit, Brandy, they're my livelihood, even more than ever. I won't do any serious damage," Suzanne said.

The night heat pulled sweat out the instant they went outdoors. Jayne asked, "Is the Xhoshiba air-conditioned?"

"I look studly in sweat," Suzanne said. Both her pants and her top were wrinkled where she'd been twisting in her chair in front of the computer. She threw her bag into the back of the Xhoshiba, slid in beside it, and said, "Drive."

Jayne got in front and backed out of the garage, then said, "Where to?"

"Charleston. Just go all the way down to Broad. I'll tell you where to go from there. Don't park in front of the house. After you drop me off, drive down to the Battery and wait for me."

Jayne dropped Suzanne and her bag at the side of an old Charleston house with its front to its own garden. She parked at the Battery, locked the Xhoshiba, and rolled the windows up, sweating in the heat but afraid to lower the windows to whoever was walking at these hours. *What if Citadel cadets on a whore hunt think I'm one? What if they know this is a whorehouse car?*

Two police walking patrol, a white man and a black woman, stopped by her car, checking the license. Jayne wondered if they knew she was a whore's driver. They seemed satisfied with what their link told them, and walked on.

After a while, the nervous waiting made Jayne sleepy, a mammalian urge to sleep concealed through the predators' night. The cops swung by again, arguing about presidential candidates. The male cop swore two of them were real this time.

Jayne wondered if they themselves were real. Perhaps someday, robots or clones would do their patrols, but she suspected that cops, like whores, were cheaper to produce in flesh. Who'd want to risk a ten-million-dollar robot to the street's whims?

Finally, Suzanne came out. Jayne unlocked the doors for her. "Prick," Suzanne said as she threw her black bag into the car.

What did you expect? Jayne thought. "Bad."

"I asked his advice on collections. He laughed. He's probably still laughing. I don't know why I did that."

Jayne's visual cortex played the movie—losing money on the collection scheme, going down to the Citadel looking for cadets but too old for them to pick her out as an obvious whore, falling for a drunk closeted dyke who was looking for someone to help her into the euthanasia clinic. *Or is this me I'm projecting in my mind's eye.* "Where next?"

"I'm going to cancel that date. I didn't spend all I'd saved on the bad-debts collection program. I'm not that big a fool."

Jayne was afraid to ask what Suzanne had left. "So, you want to go back to the house?"

"Let's go out to Orton Plantation."

"At night?" *Where you killed at least two people.*

"It's one giant lovers' lane all summer long. People sneak in. Began to be popular after the killings. People get hot thinking about double sex suicides."

"I'm not driving you there." *Where is the cell phone?* Jayne reached around on the seat trying to find it.

"It's a solved case." Suzanne's smile flashed in the rearview mirror. Jayne remembered Alice's persuasions and mania. But three days from now was August, and summer would be over before Suzanne played out her credit game.

What happens next? Jayne wondered if this curiosity had any subconcious links to wanting to get caught at something. The virtual girls knew their accounting programs; the whores who wanted to speak properly used more middle-class lingo than they had before. Whoring was a job, Jayne thought, not as satisfying as teaching. She could understand Suzanne's wanting to take the rest of the night off, but to the men who'd booked her, that would be as though their secretaries called to tell them they weren't coming in.

"I'm shit at collections," Suzanne said.

"You just started. Maybe you'll get your money back."

Suzanne didn't answer. She reached under the seat and pulled out the cell phone Jayne hadn't been able to find earlier and called her next date. He wanted a referral to another mistress.

"No, slave, I'll come or not as I please."

Didn't seem to work, but from what Jayne heard of Suzanne's side of the conversation, they both playacted a segue that allowed Suzanne to make the gig a bit late and keep her pretense of control.

When the Xhoshiba stopped at the house, Suzanne went into her black bag and pressed a revolver into Jayne's upper arm, barrel pointing toward the left-front windshield. Jayne turned, saw what it was, but didn't take it in her hand. "Is it real? Is it licensed?"

Suzanne said, "Yes. Enough. You looked awful nervous waiting at the Battery, right." She bent over the seat until she could get the gun in Jayne's hand. Jayne's index finger went into the trigger guard.

"Not safe. Don't put your finger into the trigger guard unless you're ready to shoot someone."

"I don't know a damn thing about these."

"Well, I'll take it back then. I thought it would make you feel safer."

For a moment, Jayne wanted the gun, then she opened her hand and let it fall on the front seat. Suzanne said, "Put it in the glove compartment. I can't take a gun in anyway. This guy has a servant search me at the door."

Suzanne came out two hours later with blood under her nails, without her bag. "I hurt my hands," she said. "Can you go back for the bag?"

Jayne went back to the servant entrance and knocked. A man in a black suit opened the door and handed her Suzanne's bag. "We'll appreciate it if Brandy sends another dominatrix next week." Jayne knew she was talking to the servant. When she got back to the car, she turned on the dome light and looked at Suzanne's hands.

"What? Did he complain I didn't hurt him?"

"You pulled your own nails out."

"I ordered him to make me feel better. He's a doctor. He has drugs."

Jayne wanted to get Suzanne out of the car before she called Brandy. "You know, it might be a good idea if you cancelled your other dates."

"No, no. Show must go on. Give me the gun back."

Jayne shook her head. She wondered if Suzanne would come over the seat back and grapple for it, but Suzanne leaned back and asked for the phone. Jayne handed it to her. Suzanne canceled her other dates in a neutral voice and leaned back on the seat. "Bad for my image to come in bleeding."

"You want out of the game that badly?"

"Your basic dominatrix, she can work a few years longer than a regular whore, but I'm getting too old. Happens. I'll end up getting vocal-cord work done so I can sound young and turn into a virtual girl. Stroke out over the machine and end up drooling in some street corner as a moral object lesson. I ordered the damned man to make me feel better."

Jayne took the phone out of Suzanne's hands, wiped the blood away, and called Brandy. "We're coming in. Suzanne's canceled her last three dates."

"Problems?"

"Yes. But she didn't hurt anyone except herself."

"Badly?"

Suddenly, Jayne was angry with Suzanne's hysteria. "Nothing broken except fingernails."

"Oh." Brandy sounded as though she knew precisely how deeply broken those nails were. Suzanne looked at Jayne in the rearview mirror, one quick stab, *tattler,* then leaned back and looked to the left at nothing but the inside of her own brain.

They got back to the beach house; the plastic surgeon was waiting with her nail-bed kit. She worked on Suzanne's exposed nail beds, then laid in natural-colored temporary nails. "If you do anything to these," the doctor said, "you might not grow your own nails back straight."

Suzanne, drugged, laughed.

Jayne expected to be chastized by Brandy for not doing enough, but Brandy seemed too exhausted to care. When the doctor left, Jayne saw that the sun had risen quite a way out of the ocean.

Up all night.

7
Culture Clang

Ocean came down the first week of August to see how Jayne was doing and to take Jayne out to a restaurant that required dressing well. Jayne borrowed a proper cocktail dress from Brandy, who was her size.

When Jayne got in the car, Ocean handed her fake credit and ID cards, and said, "We'll talk after dinner, not at dinner. At dinner, we'll try to sound posh." They drove down to the old part of Charleston and parked in a high-rise garage that collected tourists' cars.

Ocean looked happy, not drunk. She ordered for Jayne and herself: French food with wine for Jayne, tea for her.

The waiter suggested a fake wine, but Ocean said, "Tea works well enough with veal, thank you."

Jayne wondered why she was being tested in upper-middle-class skills. Maybe someday she'd have to hide out among the upper classes.

Ocean said, "What do you think about the presidential candidates?"

Jayne said, "I heard that two of them might be live humans."

"Machines can be difficult sometimes," Ocean said. The waiter brought in the she-crab soup at that point, and they began eating it. Jayne watched Ocean sip it from the side of the big spoon and imitated her. Ocean paused to say, "Jayne, I have some records you might like to listen to."

Jayne wondered if she'd get real music or if she'd get secrets. "I've always found your taste interesting," she said. The soup had sherry in it. Would this little bit drive Ocean into another drunk?

"We've gotten more sponsors for our program," Ocean said, breaking the agreement not to talk until after dinner, but then this could mean anything unless the listeners knew precisely which program Ocean was involved in.

Jayne said, "I'm glad." She wondered if when Brandy's clients met the whores, they first sent their wives eating at such places. The waiters kept coming, whisking away soup the nanosecond it was finished. The second course —fish— followed, just a little decorative piece of fish on the tiniest of green beans, grown that way, not cut out of larger pods. The wine waiter poured Jayne's white wine and brought Ocean her tea with nearly as much ceremony.

"We want more of this," Ocean said, gesturing at the room. "Everyone should have the opportunity to be entertained by their food."

Fish gone, the waiter brought in the veal medallions with a tender red wine. Jayne felt drunk and dislocated from her past and present. In a few hours, she would go back to sleep at a whorehouse. And Suzanne was a credit-collecting whore. Reality wasn't just one thing.

Who were the sponsors? Jayne didn't think she should ask. Ocean dabbled at her food, rearranging it on her plate, while she ate. The waiters darted in at appropriate moments to refill wineglass and teacup and whisk away Ocean's plate after the food circled it twice.

Dessert Ocean ate with passion, a dark chocolate thing that smelt of brandy. Jayne still felt disoriented. She wondered if the people who did her favors, even the huge favor of getting her into a better college than she'd hoped, were quite normal. Or had Suzanne's self-mutilation a few nights back left an emotional cast to even benign events?

Whatever, I'm not in a position to turn down Ocean's favor. So Jayne ate her own dessert and wondered what advice Ocean would give them when they were in a more private place. Ocean paid the bill with her credit ID. After they were back in her car, she said, "You should eat there more often, get used to it. Some of our patrons are very wealthy, but they aren't interested in demeaning themselves. But on the other hand, Jayne, I think you should continue to drive Suzanne. You need to learn how to handle people like her."

"I couldn't stop her. I don't trust her not to get me into some terrible trouble. We'll end up on the Citadel campus with drawn guns or something."

Ocean said, "You have to control situations more, Jayne."

"I should have called Brandy after the first date."

"Suzanne needs to decide whether she's in the business or out. If she stays, better you see the struggle than her roadie and regular driver."

"She wants out," Jayne said. Pretty horrid to risk it all on bad-risk debtors, though.

Ocean said, "We don't judge the uses of our education. We just educate those the state and corporations abandon. Summer is almost over."

Jayne realized she'd gotten an order, not heard a suggestion. "I'll see if I can help her collect on some of the debts, too."

Ocean said, "Sounds sensible."

So Jayne helped Suzanne with her collections and drove her to her clients. "I'm leaving August 29," she told Suzanne, who took this as a challenge.

The clients seemed to respond more to Jayne's assumption that they either wanted to pay their debts or they didn't. If they seemed relieved finally to be in touch with a collector, she didn't ride them for anything other than payments that would equal half payment and half interest. She learned that the collections program gave bad advice about postdated checks and wasn't always current on state collection laws. Since buying bad credit had become a popular home business, Jayne found support groups' mailing lists.

Suzanne watched while Jayne exchanged information and downloaded files from state agencies. She seemed almost awed by Jayne's ability at collecting. Jayne doubted a dominatrix should be so impressed.

"I'm not going to buy any more credit," Suzanne said, "if a mouse like you can outdo me at collections."

"You have to think of it as helping them be good," Jayne said.

"I had an offer to settle for 50 percent of the balance," Suzanne said. "The machine said that would be acceptable."

"The guys selling you this credit want to see you collect enough to get you to buy more. If you could collect 50 percent of the balance from everyone, you'd do great. But if only one in twenty pays you 50 percent back, you're not in great shape unless they're the ones who have bigger than average balances." Much to Jayne's shock, the average balance was around $5,000, too small to justify court costs unless collection was then a certainty. Half the people she'd talked to lived off-grid now as servants or just liars. "It's a mug's game."

Suzanne said, "I want to take you shooting."

"Not at the Citadel."

"No, at a commercial practice range. We can shoot digital boys. Or pop-up targets filled with medical gelatin, find out what stretch cavities your loads give. Pretty neat. I've done it before."

Jayne said, "You've shot real people before, too."

"Double suicide murder," Suzanne said. "I'm meeting my client at the shooting gallery, so you might as well give it a try."

Jayne said, "Can I shoot paper targets instead?"

"You'll seem strange," Suzanne said. "Nobody shoots paper targets anymore. You could play paintball. That's what we're going to do. We're renting a private arena."

"You're going to playact shooting a guy."

"Naked."

"And you're sure the shooting gallery isn't doing a digital of you in action?"

"My client is the owner," Suzanne said.

"I'll stay in the car," Jayne said.

"Not a good idea. The place is crawling with Citadel people, and if any of them check the Xhoshiba's registration, they'll find out where you're coming from and assume what you do."

Jayne wondered if Suzanne was lying. "Nude paintball?"

"He'll be wearing a dick guard and eye protection. I'll be wearing full body armor. Can't afford to show other clients bruises."

The message seemed to be *If you're not going to whore with me, at least you'll shoot.* Jayne hated guns, the whole guy phallic symbol, killer lead sperm, and cold metal business of them. But she was, after all, leaving in two weeks.

Her "Okay" pleased Suzanne. "You'll have to rent something there. They don't let you bring in your own gun unless it's cased, and we don't have a case for the car gun."

When they reached the shooting range, Jayne used the fake credit ID Ocean had given her week before last.

A guy in a suit patted both of them down just inside the door. Suzanne said, "They've got some really valuable weapons here." On her fake card, Jayne rented a revolver for Suzanne like the car gun and signed the alias on a pressure pad. In one corner, a guy was complaining about how difficult it was to qualify for the South Carolina private investigator's license. Suzanne's date came out from a back room, heard who Jayne was, and nodded to her once before disappearing with Suzanne and the gun.

"Would you like a lesson?" a woman who'd been behind the counter asked.

"Can I add it on my card?" Jayne said.

"Sure. It's a certified NRA lesson. If you sign up for ten of them, you'll have passed the training requirements for a concealed carry permit."

"I just want one," Jayne said, giving the woman her card to swipe through the reader again and wondering how many felonies she'd just committed in using it twice in a gun-rental establishment. Could it be illegal to take an NRA handgun lesson under a fake name? Again, Jayne put the fake name on the pressure pad.

Suzanne and her date were at the opposite end of the shooting range from Jayne and her NRA instructor. "You'll pull back until the hammer is cocked, then you squeeze just a bit more, squeeze, don't jerk." The NRA instructor arranged Jayne's wrists so that while both hands held the gun, the wrists weren't lined up side by side, but were slightly offset. "Keep one hand ahead of the other. It stabilizes your gun better. If you have both wrists together"—the instructor moved Jayne's hands to match the description—"you wobble." Yes, the gun was steadier when the wrists were offset from each other.

Suzanne and her date seemed to be loading cartridges into cylinders with their lips. Jayne turned back to her own target and squeezed off a shot that seemed to have hit the target paper, only not in the outlined figure. She listened to the woman and steadied the gun, squeezed when the sights were lined up with the center of the figure. The gun banged and rose up in Jayne's hand again. The instructor said, "Pull back, aim, then fire. You'll hold the gun steadier that way."

Finally, a shot in the figure. Jayne finished off the cylinder, swung it open as she'd seen other people do, pushed the rod, and caught the brasses.

"Don't catch your brasses. People have died catching their brasses."

"Oh."

"What you do in practice is what you'd do under stress. Let those brasses fall."

Another gunful. Jayne's hand began getting tired. "Stop for a moment, and I'll explain temporary and permanent stretch cavities and what sort of load you'll need."

"I don't own a gun," Jayne said.

"You need one," the instructor said. Jayne wondered if the woman thought she was a whore like Suzanne. "All women need them." The instructor began drawing on a pad. One set of wavy lines going from point of entry was the temporary stretch cavity—the flesh shock wave traveling out from the bullet's path. The second smaller set of lines represented the tissues permanently damaged by the bullet's energy—permanent stretch cavity. Jayne thought of stretch marks, while the woman said, "You need ammunition that can punch through a leather jacket and heavy muscles, really do damage. Revolver like this, you need plus Ps."

Suzanne and her date walked out behind Jayne. Suzanne said, "We'll be in the car for a while. Have fun with your gun."

The instructor ignored the interruption, drawing another model of a body with two different stretch patterns. "Safety slugs—problem is that if you're going against someone with lots of muscles, they'll just chop up flesh without doing serious internal damage. He could still kill you."

"Um, do you think I could practice a bit more," Jayne said. She wondered if she could touch a gun again after the stretch-cavity diagrams. Also, she needed to keep an eye out on Suzanne.

Two more gunfuls later, Suzanne came back in, and said, "Come on, you've got to drive us."

Jayne left the shooting range and got back in the car. The man in the backseat smiled at her, which made Jayne very nervous. Suzanne said, "Okay, I'm going to show you both where I won my duel."

Jayne said, "Let me call Brandy."

The man said, "I'm paying to see where Suzie killed her men." He was breathing heavily. "We can play paintball there."

Jayne called Brandy and said, "Suzanne's date wants to see the plantation." Best not to say too much on a car phone. She wondered if the statute of limitations ran out on crimes solved by lies.

"The plantation in the news clipping?"

"Yeah."

"Does the guy really want to?"

"Yeah."

"Tell him it will be $200 extra. And walk with them."

"Brandy says this will be $200 extra."

The man handed over $200 in gold coin without hesitating. Suzanne handed the money to Jayne.

The Spanish moss looked like black ghosts gibbeted in the trees. Suzanne walked ahead of her client. As illegal as carrying a concealed handgun without a license might be, Jayne stuck the car gun in her waistband.

The man said, "Someday, when I'm ready to die, you'll kill me, won't you, you bitch." He pulled a bucket of paintballs out of the trunk.

Suzanne said, "Maybe. If I don't kill myself first and leave you alive."

"I wouldn't like that." The man made a wet sound with his mouth. Jayne thought he'd licked his lips. "How did you do it? Get two cadets and the other whore?"

"Easily. I didn't give a damn, so I wasn't trembling so much I missed when I shot. Jayne, that's the secret of being a good shooter. Don't give a damn whether you kill or not."

"Don't bring me into this," Jayne said.

"Oh, I thought you were part of the deal," the man said.

"I'm just the driver," Jayne said.

"What if I tried to strangle Suzie?" the man said. He smiled. "You'd shoot me then, wouldn't you?"

Jayne said, "I'm going back to the car."

"You'll feel guilty if I killed her before killing myself," the man said.

"And you wouldn't really like it if I killed him," Suzanne said.

Jayne walked back to the car and called Brandy. "I'm half-tempted to leave them here," she said after she explained the situation.

"If you're being dragged into shit you can't deal with, just give her the phone," Brandy said. "They'll need a cab or driver soon enough."

Jayne tried to figure whether she'd feel guilty if either of them died that night. She felt more annoyed at their melodrama. If they wanted to fucking die, they shouldn't be dragging her into it. She walked back with the phone and saw the man putting a gun with a fat barrel to Suzanne's lips. *Whew, just paintball.* "Here's the phone. Brandy said to call when you're finished, but I'm not going to wait for you. Brandy said I didn't have to wait for you."

Suzanne didn't take the gun barrel straight into her mouth, one sign of sense, but took it between her teeth like a horse bit and sucked on it. The man said, "Run away then, little driver. We may not need a ride home."

Suzanne, still licking the painball-gun barrel, rolled her eyes at Jayne and smiled. Jayne turned and walked back to the car. She sat shaking for a few moments, pulled the gun out of her waistband, and unloaded it by picking the bullets out with her fingernails. Then she drove back across the dark night to the beach house.

Suzanne came in, slimed with green, blue, and yellow, just as Brandy was organizing the drivers to go searching. She said to Brandy, of Jayne, "The bitch punked out on me. But it made my slave feel like he was really getting the real goods. Another hundred bucks for leaving him way alone with a killer bitch."

Jayne said, "Don't fuck with my head."

"Honey, I dominate."

Brandy said, "Don't get that mess on my furniture. Jayne won't be driving you after last night."

"Juicy scary brain candy, little unwed mom. Ocean wants her to drive me."

Brandy said, "Ocean will change her mind."

These people are different from anyone else I've known or imagined before. "But let me go back to helping her with the credit collection."

Suzanne said, "You think your politics makes you a wonderful person, don't you?"

"I don't have any politics. I just want to help people," Jayne said.

"What a fucking arrogant-ass thing to say," Suzanne said. "Why do you think someone like you can help people who had a thousand times more life than you?"

"I try to teach people skills they can't get through the standard education system. Brandy asked for people this summer, didn't you?"

"We just wanted people to teach computer skills and better English. That's all," Brandy said. "We didn't ask you to help us more than that."

Suzanne smiled, almost touched the banister to the stairs with her paint-smeared hand, saw Brandy's face, then went off to the kitchen without touching anything.

Jayne remembered the people trying to help her in school, how she felt they more wanted her to be unhappy in their way than hers. "Sorry, but I want to know as much as doesn't swamp me. I need to know as much as possible."

Brandy said, "But I haven't seen you volunteer to be a body whore."

Jayne went to bed during daylight to nightmares of guns and vulvas and Judas Girls and lonely eyeballs freezing outside their sockets.

After that, Jayne was surprised to find Suzanne defending her when she got in an argument over astrology and luck with one of the virtual girls after class.

"Why should you know better than registered teachers

about this? I know you know computer systems better, but they're real teachers in the schools. So when they told us that we shouldn't discount belief in astrology and luck, well, why do you think you know better? And why do you want to knock luck?"

Jayne said, "They want you to believe in astrology and luck so you'll waste your time waiting for the planets and the stars to rescue you."

"My teachers respected us, so I don't think they'd be deliberately misleading me," the woman said. "Told me about how people like us was always happy with our lives compared to them. And my daddy always said you had to have the luck behind you. He won the lottery once for seven hundred dollars."

Jayne wondered how much the daddy had spent on tickets before and after that win. But if the woman believed Jayne, the woman had to face precisely how deep her personal hole was, how difficult to get out. Jayne decided to nod and drop the argument.

But Suzanne had no delicacy. "It's like this, Lucy," she told the virtual girl of forty-nine. "They tell you shit to keep you from crawling your own way out of the hole."

"They said we had easier lives."

"Virtual whoring is about the easiest way going. How close you come to being a servant?"

"My sister's a servant. It's not a nasty life even if she can't save enough to come visit."

"Look, luck's got nothing to do with it, really."

"My daddy . . ."

". . . sucked man balls all his life and thought he doing right well for a guy like him."

"Luck is the only thing that will change us," Lucy said. "I really get comfort from my call-in astrologer."

"Who's about as honest as you are with the guys who call up here."

"What do you want to tell me this for, Suzanne? You're sure dumb about what you can do on your own stick."

Jayne realized that Lucy was too old to benefit greatly from a life-strategy change. Maybe her astrologer, hired out of the limitless pool of actors without licensing or performance contracts, helped her feel better about her circumstances without making her feel bitter or too stupid to test out of her assigned class. Jayne said, "I don't know everything."

"If you knew everything, you'd have tested into a real teaching program," Lucy said, her faith in luck restored.

Suzanne said, "Come out and walk on the beach with me. It's almost nine in California already."

They walked on a boardwalk over sea oats and ghost crabs scuttling over the dunes. Suzanne said, "I've wanted to crack her little belief system, too. But then she's almost fifty. What else would there be for her?"

"She can be a virtual girl until her eighties. The old women seem most amused by it. What about you? What would you do if you could make a lot of money from credit collection?"

"Buy apartment buildings, I suppose. I've paid taxes faithfully so I could qualify for mortgages and all that stuff," Suzanne said. "I don't want to stay in the game as a madam."

"Why did you try the credit game again?"

"I . . . I wanted to prove that I really was a top, in the real world, not just when someone hired me to be the dom. Well, I'm just a fucking whore. You're collecting more of this goddamn money than I am. They'll all quit paying again as soon as you leave."

"You and that guy at the plantation . . ."

"Shit, I'm sorry." Suzanne stared at the moon. "But you don't understand my game."

Jayne felt as though one of her eyes and the brain hemisphere behind it had gone to the Judas Girls and she'd just found out. "You wanted to make him feel you were dangerous enough to kill him."

"Do you doubt I could kill?"

"I don't know if you could now."

"Let's go into Charleston tonight, get drunk together, roam the streets howling at convention, restrictions, regulations."

Jayne hesitated. "Would anyone think we're whores?"

"No, they'll think we're dykes. Bet that's just a bit too scary for you, being mistook for something that can commit suicide by request."

Jayne said, "Depending on the state, I can get it for being an abandoning mother or for having been on school drugs."

"Ah, so you were on school drugs," Suzanne said as she tucked her arm into Jayne's. "I always suspected."

Jayne didn't know what Suzanne meant by that, but she felt further argument would both make her seem like a bigot and would egg Suzanne into attacking her fears that perhaps the people who put her on school drugs were right and that all that she'd done ever after was simply a way of being crazy.

If crazy, then why not howl in the street with this other madwoman? Suzanne led her to the garage, and said, "I'll drive this time."

Jayne remembered that she'd had a good time at Myrtle Beach until they went into the fun house of interactive screens. If she hadn't been so lonely as the only nonwhore in the group, she wouldn't have gone anywhere alone with Suzanne. But because Suzanne was the only person who'd been fairly friendly, Jayne was going through the night toward Charleston.

"We'll have fun," Suzanne said, her elbow out the window. The night smelled like three hundred years of human waste gently degrading back into Spanish moss and sea funk. They went over the high arch of the Cooper River Bridge and dropped down into Charleston. Jayne wondered where the Citadel was from there and suspected that that was precisely where they were going.

Summer would be over soon, and she could get back to finishing her training. Or find another line of work than unlicensed teaching. Not whoring, though. Her sister the Judas Girl had gotten that much into her. Tonight Jayne's options seemed like surrendering to the Judicious Girls or going to Charleston for whatever trouble Suzanne would find.

I was thinking like this when I got pregnant. Almost like nothing really mattered.

Suzanne found a back street and parked. Jayne didn't recognize where they were, only knew that it was not in the best of tourist areas. They went up to a bar guarded by two fat guys wearing business suits with fat ties. Suzanne motioned for Jayne to stay back while she had a whispered discussion with them and handed over a credit ID. The fatter of the two guys swiped the card through his processor and shoved the keyboard at Suzanne for her PIN.

Then it was okay to go in. The guys opened the doors to a long hallway. The floor was clear with lights under it. The hallway was lit with squirming red-neon tubes. "Like walking in through your lover's cunt," Suzanne said.

Jayne wondered if she was going to be seduced tonight. Did the early sex games with her friend mean that maybe this was the way she was? The tunnel opened out into a well-lit bar.

Some of the people were well dressed, wearing what she recognized to be clothes worn by patients who came down for breakfast wearing multicarat diamond and ruby rings. Others wore clothes that had been fashionable ten years earlier. Not much of that era's clothes had held up well. Or perhaps not many people like the styles of their childhood.

The third variety of people in the bar seemed to be wearing clothes they weren't familiar with. Fingers touched the fabric as though surprised, then adjusted either collars or ties. A few of the men didn't know that to keep a tie clean, it went over the shoulder. The women who wore ties knew this trick.

"It's so well lit," Jayne said.

"Charleston's not so big. Everyone has the bad news already."

"Bad news?"

"About looks."

Then the music began. The whole floor was a giant

woofer, bass vibrating through Jayne's bones. A woman began dancing alone in the center of a spotlight. Was this a strip place, Jayne wondered. Then other singles and couples went out on the floor, all sexes in all combinations. Suzanne's eyelids relaxed. She looked like a giant cat giving an approving half blink, eyeball cat kisses. Jayne looked to where Suzanne was looking, thinking that perhaps someone Suzanne loved had walked in, but no, Suzanne wasn't focused on anyone. She looked quickly over at Jayne and smiled.

Maybe this wasn't about anything except having a night out. The floor rumbled. The back wall began playing giant men walking over a landscape from deep inside a brain. Jayne didn't like loud music and crowds. In case of problems or severe boredom, she'd brought taxi money, but the situation didn't seem that extreme.

Two small, thin people came up, a man and a woman. The man had a thin face and the fine lines that came from reconstructive surgery. When he was older, wrinkles would obscure the lines, but now they looked like raised white tracks around his eyes and down around his mouth. If the woman had scars, they were better hidden. The man asked, "You here together?"

"We're here together, but we're not together, if you understand what I'm saying," Suzanne said. The man turned his eyes to the woman, and they shrugged. They stood beside Suzanne at the bar for a while, then the woman took Jayne's chin between her thumb and index finger. She raised Jayne's face, and asked, "Have I seen you around?"

"No."

"You look out of place here, darling."

"I am," Jayne said.

The two smiled at Suzanne and went sliding between other bodies to another woman standing at the bar.

"Well, Jayne," Suzanne said. The music went to a higher pitch, louder but with fewer reverberations from the floor.

Jayne asked, "What kind of bar is this anyway?"

"It's a whore's bar," Suzanne said.

Jayne had visions of Citadel cadets storming the place. "Is everyone here except me a whore?"

"Some are friends. No clients, but some clients know about this place. I've had a few ask if they could come with me. As friends."

"What do you tell them?"

"I tell them whores don't have friends," Suzanne said. "They like that."

Jayne looked around the room again and realized nobody looked older than forty. "Madams and pimps don't come here either, do they?"

"No," Suzanne said.

"And some of the people are from the public brothels," Jayne said. "They don't usually wear clothes like what they have on."

"No, darling, some of them are from prison. They get a night off, work-release, they come here."

"But prostitution isn't illegal."

"Who said all whores were nice?" Suzanne said.

The bartender worked his way over to them, and said to Suzanne, "I thought you said she wasn't a tourist."

"Not a tourist, just naïve," Suzanne said.

"Take her out, she makes people nervous," the bartender said. "If we have a license check, the cops will assume she's not paying the tax."

Jayne said to Suzanne, "What did I do wrong?"

"Asked too many questions. Answered the wrong ones," Suzanne said. Her face had gone hard again, all dominatrix as she found her car keys and paid the bartender for the drinks they'd had.

After they left the club, Jayne said, "So I've ruined your evening."

"Evening's not over yet, and there are other bars," Suzanne said. They crossed a dark cobblestone street. Jayne thought she saw the high-rise garage where they'd left the car, but then noticed another garage just like it to the left.

"Do you know where the car is?"

"Yeah, I know where the car is," Suzanne said. "We're not going to the car yet."

And she can click her jaws and have help arrive instantly. Or maybe not. Jayne followed Suzanne through the streets, wondering if Suzanne was walking somewhere or just pacing in linear fashion. Suzanne said, "They're looking for you because of the hack you did on the newsfeeds."

Jayne didn't understand what Suzanne was talking about, then she realized the only hacked links she'd ever worked with were in the house she shared during her community college years. "What hacks?" Perhaps Suzanne was going crazy or teasing.

"You didn't ask who's they?"

" 'They' are always the law in our world," Jayne said.

"I thought you were the type to hack newsfeeds," Suzanne said.

"Are they really looking for me? I didn't hack the feeds. I don't know programming languages that well," Jayne said.

"Why do you want us to know we're being lied to?" Suzanne asked. "I lived perfectly well when I didn't question what was happening to me. If I lost my money, it was because I was too dumb to know better. And the government protected me from knowing better since I was dumb, and made sure that I'd have something to do by making what I did legal. And you and your kind just make me feel stupid."

"So you took me to a bar where I'd be the dumb one."

"Yeah."

"And you're teasing about the news agents looking for me," Jayne said.

"Do you want to go back to your school out in the nice Midwest and find out?"

Jayne began to wonder how Suzanne would know if the

news agents were looking for her at school. "News used to be free, broadcast through radio waves."

"Were they any more honest then?" Suzanne asked.

"They were supported by advertisers," Jayne said.

"You're just going around making people miserable when they thought they were okay before?"

"I was miserable when I was being lied to," Jayne said. "Nothing was being done for my own good." Her sister felt, though, that she'd been trying to save Jayne.

Suzanne said, "The news agents arrest you all sooner or later. Your life's a bust."

"Where are we going?"

Suzanne smiled and kept walking toward another bar. Jayne noticed that all the men going into it were young and rather military-looking. "No, Suzanne."

"I'll save everyone the cost of keeping us going in prison. I'm going to kill or be killed tonight."

Jayne thought about leaving right then, but she couldn't abandon Suzanne. "Suzanne, you don't have to do this."

"I don't want to be anyone's servant. I didn't make my money back on the bad credit."

"You don't know. People might start paying."

"We've collected $16,000. I willed it to you. Why not? My most recent lover left me in April after I didn't help her with her taxes. Can you imagine that?" Suzanne stopped moving forward.

"Well, what was the relationship if she left you for that?"

"Damned if I know. I always end up with bitches who either cheat the IRS or me."

"Why tonight?"

"Because, baby, you're leaving in a week."

Jayne almost said, *But I wasn't your lover,* when she realized that might have been the problem. "What are you going to do, issue a challenge in the bar?"

"Precisely, babe. Or maybe in the street." Suzanne

grabbed a husky youth by the wrist, and said, "In the street. Duel, what about it?"

"No," the kid said.

"What about watching me take poison and die?"

"She a whore, too? I might sleep with her for free," the kid said. He twisted his hand then and broke Suzanne's grip quite easily.

Jayne found she was embarrassed that the kid wouldn't take Suzanne up on the duel. The rejection had the flavor of sexual rejection.

The kid went on into the bar. Suzanne stood outside. Jayne hoped the moment's challenge and despair would pass, but three guys came out of the bar about two minutes later, just long enough for the story to have spread inside.

"Who wants to get fucked and who wants to die?" the largest of the trio said. He wore Bermuda shorts and a Citadel T-shirt. He jammed his hands into his pockets and smiled.

Jayne said, "She's just kidding."

Suzanne said, "Nobody gets fucked. I duel with one of you, not all. Don't you Citadel cadets have honor?"

"You're whores."

Jayne almost said *I'm not,* but decided denial wasn't going to matter right then. She felt numb in her body, almost as though she watched from above her left shoulder. Suzanne must have the car gun. "No, she's just suicidal. I suggested a parlor, but . . ."

"She's a licensed whore. I know all the Charleston whores by memory. Maybe you're unlicensed, afraid Daddy will find out?"

And this bar always had someone like him in it any open moment, not quite up to going down to the whore bar and issuing challenges but ready to come out for a challenge from a suicidal whore. *You can burn for money. You can burn for love.* The lyrics for "Suicide in Flames" popped into Jayne's mind.

Two of the guys went back inside. The original guy who'd

spoken stood in front of them, smiling an *I can take any two women* smile.

Jayne's stomach twisted. Her body seemed to pull blood back from her arms and legs. *You could bleed tonight,* her hindbrain told her, *so I'll try to keep it to a minimum.* She looked over at Suzanne. Suzanne twisted her eyes toward Jayne and smiled slightly.

"Is this how it's done?" Jayne asked. The challenge and acceptance had a ritualistic feel, but she wanted to be sure.

"Yes," the man said. "You can go now if you're not part of it."

Jayne had no idea of how to find the car. She didn't have the keys, the parking stub. "Suzanne?"

Suzanne threw the keys and the parking stub at Jayne. "Go then, back to the Midwest. She's training to teach," she said to the man.

Do I leave or stay? Suddenly, Jayne didn't want to leave Suzanne, as bad as the situation had gotten, and go out into an unfamiliar night. She looked at the parking stub and hoped she could find the high-rise parking garage that held the car. *How will the news describe this tomorrow?* And the other men had seen her. They were this man's friends. If Suzanne died, they wouldn't come looking for her, but if the man died, then what?

Suzanne was suicidal. The man wouldn't die. Jayne asked, "So where do you go from here?"

"To the Battery," the man said. "I'll take her with a knife."

Jayne wanted to ask them to walk her to the car. She stumbled on the sidewalk as she began walking away, then began running. Maybe Suzanne had left the gun in the car. You can't save everyone, she tried to tell herself. She imagined for a second that they were chasing her down these ragged sidewalks, then slowed down. From where she stood, she saw three high-rise parking garages. None of them looked familiar.

A Charleston police officer stopped his car beside her.

"What's the problem?" He was black, which meant he'd served in the military for the license to live where he wanted.

"I can't figure out which garage I left my car in," Jayne said, amazed that she sounded so normal. A cop had noticed her, not a good thing.

"Let me see your stub," the cop said, his tone adding dumb tourist. Jayne handed him the stub. He shined a flashlight on it, then on her, and said, "It's the seven-story one." He pointed to the left. "Not the five-story one, not the four-story one down on Broad."

"Thanks."

"Not a good idea to be alone at night, ma'am."

Jayne wanted to tell him she hadn't started the night alone, but she just nodded and began walking. About three blocks farther, the same cop car passed her again. Jayne wondered if he'd keep circling her until she reached the garage.

How were Suzanne and the cadet who wanted to kill her getting to the Battery? If they were walking, Jayne could beat them there. She found the garage and gave the attendant the check. He started the hoist and the Xhoshiba came around swaying. Such a light car. Jayne wondered if she could hit the cadet with it and then drive it away. And what gun might still be in the glove compartment?

The cop circled by as she got into the Xhoshiba. If he checked the registration, he'd know a whorehouse owned it. Jayne waved at him as though she was just another lost tourist saved by a cop. She got in the car and drove toward the Battery, wondering all the time if she shouldn't just let Suzanne die as she pleased. After all, people owned their bodies and had the right to dispose of them as they saw fit. She wondered if she'd been taught this in the same civics class that told her that terminal news was less socially damaging than broadcast news.

The news is terminal was a popular tag art scrawl.

Jayne kept going. She checked the glove compartment, but

Suzanne had taken the car gun, or had left it back across the Cooper River if she were determined not to save herself.

Click your teeth and get help. Unfortunately, Jayne didn't have the hardware. She came around toward the Battery and saw Suzanne crouched behind a historical stone. The guy, holding his gun in his hand, was walking toward her.

I can't do anything. Jayne didn't want to witness this help-lessly. She drove the Xhoshiba at the guy. He jumped to the side, but fired at Jayne. She ducked as the front window crumpled, the glass attached in little balls to its safety plastic.

The car is fucked. I might as well go for it. She threw the car in reverse. Things in the underchassis ripped as she backed up to Suzanne.

Suzanne's face was half covered in blood. Her eyes seemed covered with scum. For a second, Jayne was afraid Suzanne was already dead, but she blinked and looked over at Jayne. Her hands gripped the stone and she began to tremble.

The guy fired again. Jayne opened the door, hauled Suzanne in, and then slammed into forward.

When the car hit the guy, he sprawled forward onto the glass beaded plastic sheet that had been the windshield. He'd lost his gun, but he scrabbled toward Jayne.

Suzanne said, "The car's reinforced in front. Hit him again."

Jayne tried to back away from the guy, but he clung to the car. Suzanne crawled forward and twisted his fingers off the dashboard. They both panted. Jayne realized the guy was se-riously damaged.

He fell away from the car. Jayne backed up, ready to try to get away, but Suzanne said, "You've got to finish it."

"We can't drive anywhere if we hit him again."

"The car's reinforced. Go for it."

"You're alive. We can get away."

"Not if he's alive."

"I can't," Jayne said. She backed the car away from the

guy, then saw his gun lying out beyond him. Suzanne saw it, too, and swung out of the car to get it.

As Jayne turned around, Suzanne shot the guy.

"They can't live down getting popped by a whore," Suzanne said.

"But I thought you wanted to die?"

"Getting shot at makes life real interesting again," Suzanne said.

Jayne thought she saw the same cop who'd given her directions, but despite all the damage and blood, he didn't stop her. Maybe the cops weren't interested in whore versus cadet duels. *Just another quaint Charleston custom.* The car got them back across the Cooper River Bridge with the wind smelling of 300 years of human shit ripping them in the face.

"Suzanne, people are going to kill you now," Jayne said. Too many people had seen her at the bar.

"It's between us and the cadets."

"You can't go on like this."

"Fucked up my face, didn't he?" Suzanne dabbed her fingers at her cheek and eyebrow. "The whole thing is fucked."

"What does it matter? You're a dominatrix."

"I shit myself. I thought. I thought." Suzanne's eyes rolled back in her head, and she slid down in her seat. Jayne wondered if she'd helped kill a boy for nothing, decided she'd check Suzanne's condition when the car was safely hidden.

The car died just on the property. Jayne left Suzanne in the car and ran into the house. "Suzanne's been in a duel. I don't know." The whole thing was absurd.

"You can't stay here," Brandy said. "People have been around here looking for you."

Suzanne hadn't been lying. "She's hurt."

"We'll take care of her and the car. You've got to leave now. Ocean will take you away tonight. We've already packed your things."

That sounded like a good idea to Jayne.

Suzanne, held up by two of the virtual girls, was walking

in as Jayne was leaving. "Well, you did the stand-up thing in the end, but too late for my face." She sounded drunk. Drunk probably explained a lot, Jayne realized. She wondered if the world was a better place for having a live whore and a dead cadet in it.

Ocean said, "We just want to get you back to college before you talk to the news agents. If they talked to you here, they'd figure things out. You were just here for a couple weeks, then traveling in virtual. We took care of that. I've got a VRML file of the highlights."

"A cop saw me tonight in Charleston."

"Did you show him ID?"

"No."

"It's a chance we have to take."

"I couldn't just let Suzanne die."

"No, you couldn't. And remember, if she'd really wanted to be dead, she'd be dead."

"What she was hiding behind looked like a tombstone," Jayne said. Despite the heat, she was shivering. "I didn't hack the system in the house I shared." But she'd done work on it.

"Of course, you can't program. You're a mere end user," Ocean said. "Come on. You're going to have to spend a few days in virtual to make this trip seem real. Seeing the VRML on a screen won't be enough."

8
Sewing One's Head Back On

Being in VR was like riding a tricycle through the Sierras. The visuals were deep-colored, finely bitmapped, but the vehicle for crossing the visuals crawled all the slower for the spectacular informational density. When she detached, she felt as though she'd pushed through digital gelatin. Gun jelly, shot by people testing bullet temporary and permanent shock cavities, probably had the same resistance. The suit itself felt viscous as it pulled away from her skin. Ocean, sitting in a chair by the lockers, waited for Jayne's eyes to focus on the real world.

Jayne still saw the real world at 126 dots per inch, but the color was paler than virtual. The 3-D effect wasn't as pronounced, but her hand didn't stick and skid when she pushed back her hair.

Ocean said, "You'll go home to visit your parents for the weekend before going home. The news agents will talk to you there. We want people around who can confirm you've never been a computer whiz. The news agents are as insidious as Judas Girls," Ocean told Jayne. "They'll make you wonder if you're on the right side. Remember, they would have had you limited to life as a clerk, at best."

Jayne asked, "But do they know I'm a former unwed mother?" Everything seemed unreal. The eyeball effect of retina painting lingered for hours, but her memories replaced another person's VRML program in her visual cortex.

Her various pasts wrapped like nested cylinders around the killing. The child cuffed to the tree screamed for help from the teenager who decided to get pregnant who became the cruel mother leaving a child behind in the mountains. Across the state a community college coed surfed through all the news uncertain what was real and what wasn't. Both in the interactive fun house and in a cartoon, she gave birth screaming. Approaching the present, the shell around now's central moment, Jayne saw the dying cadet looking at her. She wondered if he thought she was Suzanne's lover.

At her parents' front door in reality's own polygons, Jayne knew she was forever beyond their idea of her. But, when her mother opened the door and smiled at her as though she'd been foolish but they still loved her, she almost felt herself shrink down to become their own crazy Jayne again, with two eyes and a used womb.

"Sidna was asking about you," her sister said.

Jayne wondered what was so wrong with Sidna's life that she would ask about a nonvirgin who got away with both eyes.

"We told the news agents that you were too dyslexic to do anything with computer code or rewiring," Carolyn said.

"True," Jayne said. "What did Sidna want to know about me?"

"She couldn't believe you were in college after all you'd done," Carolyn said.

"She was happy for you," her mother said. "You could still be friends."

"Is she living in Philadelphia now?" Jayne asked.

"Her husband's working his way up from Coshohocken," Carolyn said. "They're here for a few days."

Hunted by Judas Girls way beyond high school. Jayne suspected she exaggerated, but she didn't really want to see Sidna again.

"A woman needs women friends," her mother said.

"If they're honest women," her sister said.

Living with whores had changed Jayne. After a teenage decade of caring even though she rebelled, Jayne didn't mind what they might be thinking. Being a virtual sex worker seemed more appealing than being a suburban housewife married to someone who'd only proposed after he spied through her false eyeball to see how other people viewed her.

Jayne said, "When will I talk to the news agents?"

"You call them," her mother said. "They've already talked to us."

"What's the number?" she asked.

"You just got home," her mother said.

"I want to get this over with," Jayne said.

Carolyn said, "They're intimidating, and they're right."

"What's worth paying attention to is what makes your life happier," Jane's mother said. "No one needs to be informed beyond that. I stuck their card behind the phone."

Jayne found the card and swiped it through the reader. A man's voice answered, "News Agency."

She didn't need to tell them her last name. The phone would give them that. "I'm Jayne. I understand you want to talk to me about the computers in the apartment I shared at Sandhills a couple of years ago."

The man rattled off her address, where she was going to college now, where she'd been this summer, really, and then said, "We'll send a car."

Ocean said to be as honest with them as possible. *Their rules carve out our econiche.* Jayne imagined the news agents as her dancing partners. They provided the resistance the outlaw schoolteacher pulled against, letting her lean far backward as they swung her around.

Her mother wanted to serve the driver and the chaperone tea or coffee, but they were in a hurry. Trying to posture co-operation with every muscle, Jayne walked out between them. *Ocean said if I hide now, they'll always be watching me. So here I am, poor girl dupe.* The dead cadet grinned at her. She'd fooled him, too. Virtually innocent. Not into getting caught.

The chaperone put on ancient rock about wishing to have been born a thousand years earlier, and they drove Jayne down to the news station. *I am a duped girl, not a man.*

Jayne didn't know if she felt arrested or not. The driver and chaperone escorted her into a room with a big table in the center. The door closed behind her. She guessed they had video on her. That meant she should act natural, but Jayne wasn't quite sure what natural was in this context. She took her teeth to a snag of skin around her thumb. About the time her cuticle bled, a man and woman pushed in a rolling file cabinet. Jayne wondered if they were her interrogators, but they just pushed the file cabinet in and closed the door.

Am I supposed to look in the file cabinet or not? Jayne decided that she ought to leave the file cabinet alone. Was it on her? On the school she was attending? On all the people she'd met.

I should have asked if I could look at it. A woman opened the door. She was older than the others Jayne had seen and dressed in a blue suit. A man, also in a blue suit, came in a little after the woman. While the woman looked in the file cabinet, the man leaned against the wall. He said, "Want a cigarette or water?"

Jayne realized she was thirsty. "Water."

He nodded, and someone else brought the water in. The woman said, "What do you know about computers?"

"I'm not a techie. The apartment we were in, the computer was already there."

"And you didn't report it?" the woman said.

"No."

The man asked, "Do you blame society for the mess you got yourself into?"

"No."

"How did a girl with a school record like yours get into a four-year college?"

"It's a private college, and my community-college grades were good. A woman I met when I was pregnant thought I could benefit from a better degree."

"Ocean Tatum," the woman said.

"You know anything about her?" Jayne, feeling bold, asked.

"She's a drunk," the man said. "Has money, likes to rescue social cripples like yourself."

Jayne flinched, then relaxed. If they were sure Ocean liked to rescue social cripples, perhaps they'd stop at Jayne as the rescued cripple. "I am doing better than expected," Jayne said.

"But you're not a technical girl, are you?"

"Not technical enough to get unrestricted news on my system," Jayne said. "I tried to learn 'Hello, World,' but I got messed up with the punctuation."

The man went to the file box and pulled out a paper file. He opened it on the table and showed Jayne the transcript of a male roommate blaming her for the rigged computer. Jayne realized that while it seemed like his words, she had no proof he'd blamed her. She also realized these people could give her a convincing digital 3-D fraud. His accusation hurt her feelings truly enough. She hadn't realized the guys in the apartment thought of her as a pet they had to keep out of trouble. "I bet he knows who really did it."

"That's our guess, too. You're free to go."

Jayne kept herself from seeming surprised. "Thank you."

"Hacking a news feed isn't worth it. Real news doesn't travel on-line," the woman said. "It isn't disseminated beyond its appropriate auditors at all."

"None of it seems like anything other than entertainment," Jayne said. When she left, they'd make a note in their files about how dumb she was, how cooperative. That wasn't a bad thing to have in the News Agency files.

"How was your summer otherwise?" the man asked as Jayne began to stand. She thought about sitting back down, but realized that would imply she felt they should prolong the interrogation. All she needed to do was give a rhetorical answer.

"It was a bit boring. The details in VR were great, though."

"If we need to talk to you further, we'll look you up at college," the woman said. "The driver and escort will give you a ride home." The driver and escort came to the door, and the man nodded at them.

I'm not into getting caught, Jayne reminded herself. She looked down at the file box as she walked out but it was only identified by an alphanumeric code: AHE-1237. The man smiled at her. She thought about saying just curious, but that didn't have quite the right tone, so she just nodded back at him as though they should expect, after all, some natural curiosity.

"So you cleared things up," the escort said.

"I don't know enough about a computer's guts to do what the guy claimed I did."

"People hack machines all the time," the escort said. "It's pretty petty theft."

"Information is property," the driver said.

"I guess I should have reported it, but I thought they were my friends."

"Thieves don't befriend people who buy hot property," the escort said.

"I know that now," Jayne said. "My parents didn't like those guys anyway."

"You've been quite an embarrassment to them, haven't you?" the escort asked.

Jayne realized this was still the interrogation. "Yes, I guess I have."

"They didn't come to visit you at the beach, did they? You were staying at a whorehouse. If you weren't working, why were you there?"

"Research for a possible school project," Jayne said. Since this wasn't an official interrogation, she didn't have to answer these questions, but not answering would be more awkward.

"Good profession for a woman like you," the escort said.

"Virtual girls have the best of it," Jayne said.

They didn't say more and took Jayne to her front door. Her mother said, "Sidna's here. She's with Carolyn in the kitchen."

Jayne watched the escort and driver turn back. She wondered if Sidna was a continuation of the interrogation. "I'll pass for now. I'm rather tired."

"She just wants to be friends," Jayne's mother said.

Sidna came to the foyer, and said, "I was so very judgmental as a girl."

Following Sidna was Carolyn. "Come on, Jayne, we've all been through different times now. Life isn't so harsh as it was when we were in high school." Her sister was now a Carolina freshman, engaged to a man who preferred a more educated woman.

Jayne thought that Sidna's marriage must be terrible. "You never did finish college, did you, Sidna?"

Sidna didn't answer. Carolyn steered them all to the kitchen. She found a box of cookies and set water on for tea. "Well, here we are again."

Sidna said, "You like your college?"

"I liked community college better."

"Your housemates tried to get you in trouble for the information theft."

"Once style and image and character were copy protected. Now it's information. Used not to be that way. You could have all the information your head could carry."

"Most people's can't carry much," Sidna said. Carolyn made tea in a teapot covered with a knitted cozy. Jayne wondered where on earth Carolyn found such a thing. Her sister put three porcelain cups and saucers on the table, then stared at the teapot as though it would signal her when the tea was properly steeped. Perhaps it would.

"Why did you tease us about joining the Judicious Girls?" Sidna said.

"I was tempted," Jayne said, "but I wasn't a virgin anymore, and I didn't want to sacrifice an eye. And how often are the eyes used to watch?"

"We have graphics-recognition programs now, not physical watchers," Sidna said.

"Who owns that information?" Jayne asked.

Sidna stared at her, then said, "It's the property of our organization."

Jayne said, "I don't know. We have Judas Girls; we have legal prostitution and suicide if you wrecked your life enough or if you didn't get the right DNA to start with."

Carolyn said, "Legalized prostitution often goes with a more rigid morality for the rest of us."

"They take the burden off the rest of us," Sidna said.

"So, yeah, a woman like me might as well be a virtual girl or even a flesh whore. Better than to have ideas."

"Is that why you went down to Charleston?" Sidna asked. She stiffened over her teacup.

Jayne felt insulted by the whole cliché of it: unwed mother turned whore. "I went down to Charleston to help people." No, shouldn't have said that. But it was said, hanging in air vibrated by Jayne's vocal cords.

After the air stopped moving, Sidna said, "I thought I was offering you help in high school."

"I don't like being an object of pity," Jayne said. "That was the most embarrassing thing about being pregnant out of wedlock."

"So you don't like being a pity object," Sidna said. "But you want to help other people. Are you getting a license to be therapeutic in some way?"

"I'm still a student," Jayne said. Sidna, the bored house-wife, could be more dangerous than the teenager with a self-righteous girl gang behind her. "I haven't gotten into a certification program yet."

Sidna said. "You should know what you're going to do next."

Jayne said, "It depends on my sponsor."

Carolyn said, "She's an old drunk Jayne met, but she's rich."

Sidna said, "Nothing worse than the renegade rich. With-out them, the poor would accept their lots or try to test out middle-class. Too much money to be downwardly mobile in an appropriate way, but not competitive with the truly ac-complished rich."

Jayne said, "Without her, I'd be downwardly mobile."

"You had others reaching out to you. You could have turned to us," Sidna said. Carolyn nodded.

"Too late now," Jayne said.

"Wrong. You could go in for a full psychological work-up: IQ tests, mental-health tests. It's entirely possible you could be reclassified. Your college grades would be factored in. It's a Quaker school, isn't it?"

Although Jayne hadn't paid that much attention to religion on campus, she realized it was Quaker and nodded. She'd never been curious about religions.

"My husband can tell me a lot about Quakers," Sidna said. "Petition to be reclassified, why don't you?"

Carolyn said, "The world's a more forgiving place since high school."

The summer collapsed a memory hole that spat out old mo-ments at inopportune times. While as a freshman, Jayne wor-ried about attending classes enough to dream about missing whole semesters of them, Jayne now came back to college a week late. When she worried about catching up, memories of the dead boy crawled across the work she was doing. When her fellow students worried about their debts, Jayne's inner ear heard a woman explain she couldn't pay off debts because she'd scheduled herself for euthanasia next Monday.

In her senior year, Jayne had dinner with two gay guys, one, Mark, who'd been planning to be an unlicensed teacher, and his lover, who wanted him to go to graduate school.

As they sat down together at a table in a restaurant modeled on English Soho pubs, Jayne said, "It's almost unreal. We'll be finished at the end of this year."

"I'm going to continue for a while longer," Mark said. "Aren't you thinking about graduate school, too? There's the possibility of being tested and reclassified."

"I've heard about that," Jayne said. "A woman who used to be a Judas Girl told me about it."

"No one is ever a former Judas Girl," Mark's lover said. "I retested in order to get legal teaching certification."

"But then you have to teach only what's scheduled to be taught," Jayne said. She wasn't sure she'd be a teacher at all if it wasn't a rebellion.

"Doesn't mean you have to obey the law constantly," Mark said.

"I'm tempted by conformity," Jayne said.

"I don't want to do anything yet, so graduate school looks like an option."

"Hiding out in academia," Mark's lover said. "I'm totally aware of why I'm here."

Jayne wondered which one of them would get the Ph.D. first. "I want to get to work. We're looking at last century's systems for working with people who learn differently than average."

"Why not just call them stupid?" Mark's lover asked.

"Because they can learn if you try different approaches," Jayne said.

Mark didn't say anything. Jayne realized he, too, thought about testing out, of slipping sideways back into licensed society again. Within five weeks, a general's daughter, a senator's son, the sister of a media CEO, and the current president's nephew (possibly a real person) had opted for euthanasia. The public began to get nervous about killing off brainy people who possibly could help their families. Sociobiology downloads, streaming movies of the families in their virtual grief, helped sway public opinion on this. The campus opened a gay-and-lesbian chat-line for the first time in thirty years.

The lover said, "But, people, we can't become ordinary citizens. We're too aware."

"I think a lot of ordinary citizens are very aware," Jayne said. Her illegal teaching depended on some subordinary being more aware than usually expected. Ordinary people, a lot of them, Jayne hoped, knew the system lied to them, but accepted the lies as part of getting along. Consumer goods and entertaining theories about the universe made people happy enough. Beyond entertainment, the facts simply made people unhappy.

Mark's lover said, "After we're done here, let's go see a movie. To change public opinion of us, our owners put out a progay costume drama from early-twentieth-century Edwardian times. Based, they say, on real people."

The hero, surrounded by police, reined in his rearing horse, shouting, "I want to surrender." He had not, he reminded them as they pushed him to the ground, fired his pistol. Without letting him change his dirty coat, they took him in to the Secret Service agent who would become his and his lover's mentor.

"Did you know Alexis isn't a woman," the agent said.

"Of course, do you take me for a fool?"

Wrong answer. "Take him away until he's stubbly and lousy," the agent tells the guard. The audience senses that the agent, too, is gay. Why then, in Edwardian England, is he a prominent legal figure? Why is he arresting our hero and his friend?

Our hero lies down on the prison cot. He asks another

prisoner, "So, tell me. Are there lice in here? I know how to get stubbly, but if they don't provide lice, I'm damned if I know how I'll get lousy."

He reaches for his hair and discovers he's been crawled on. Several people in the audience squeal, but he simply puts the louse back in his hair.

Mark said, "They don't want him if he's too fastidious. We're tough, really."

His lover said, "I had to fight my way onto many a high-school bus."

Jayne realized these movie gay heroes were rich top university students. She felt like an invader among the moviegoers, a person whose own heroic story about being caught in the pregnancy wars wasn't ever going to be a movie.

The hero, suitably lousy and stubble-chinned, came back into his interrogator's office. He looked at the older man, and said, "So."

"Don't you think you owe your family discretion?"

"Discretion, yes. A life without pleasure, no."

"Even if that pleasure is illegal?"

"You pick and choose whom to prosecute. Wilde, but not his lover."

"Can you prove to your king that you're loyal despite this inconvenient law?"

At this point, guards bring in the other lover with long yellow hair and stubble. "Why are we here? Are we going to be charged?"

"We want to train you."

For work in His Majesty's Foreign Service. They're deloused and go to all the right parties, meet Harold Nicolson and his wife Vita Sackville-West and their lovers. The lover, who dresses like a woman, learns to be even better at playing his role as seducer. Soon it is the 1930s in Germany and they are both in danger.

By the 1970s they are old men and highly respected. Times change again.

Jayne thought, but didn't say, Where is my movie?

Her son, age four, could start asking questions. That night she dreamed he found her when he was about eleven and said, "Mother, we could have had such fun on welfare together." *So, it goes on from here,* Jayne realized, *with this sticky past attached to my future.* When she signed the baby away, the social workers assured her that the bad old days of adult children inserting themselves in their birth parents' lives weren't going to return.

An organization named Bastard Nation went on the Undernet, converting old files to find its group history about the 1980s and 1990s when the first Bastard Nation began crusading for adoptees' rights. Members of the adoption triad could again start searches for birth mothers and optional fathers.

9
"Mathematically Impossible Objects Made of Glass"

After a year in Houston working with dockside people and three years working with a commune in Chicago's Open Zone, Jayne wondered if her life would forever be moving from one place to another, never attached to anything or anyone.

Ocean sent Jayne to Brooklyn for her next duty assignment with a couple named Renee and Harry.

The plane came in directly over Manhattan, which seemed like a dream: chrome, granite, glass, slidewalks, helicopters, and winking lights. Over the Bronx, the plane leaned over and turned to land.

Then Jayne took a tube and a cab to Brooklyn, which could have been anywhere else. The cab let her out in front of a small row of houses with a hulking big high-rise, studded with antennas and receiving dishes, behind them.

Second from the end of the block was the house where Jayne would live, an Italianate brownstone with wrought-iron railings and a two-story bay. The small house looked intimidated by the huge building behind it. She'd been told that squatters ran a building behind where she'd be staying, but hadn't expected something so huge and weirdly spiked with antennas. It looked like a technical facility that housed decoders.

Jayne rang the doorbell. Ocean told her that she'd be sharing with the couple and a starving artist person who'd been asked to leave the squat because he couldn't contribute to the material fund. Ocean said the couple claimed this person was capable of doing some work for them and wouldn't betray them.

A skinny woman in her forties with dyed black hair opened the door. For a second, Jayne wondered if she was Alice's older sister, with two eyes with heavy eyelids instead of the one and a patch. She seemed to be a bit upset with something about Jayne—youth and inexperience, Jayne suspected. The woman said, "I'm Renee. You must be Jayne. Come in and we'll talk. Harry's out. But then Harry's often out." The quip meant something to Renee, but Jayne decided not to ask what.

Jayne wondered how much space she'd get when she saw the living room piled with books and computer parts. A blond guy in gray leggings or long underwear and a stud-fastened dinner shirt from a thrift store was staring at a computer screen. The tower box was running bare without a case. Renee said, "Heightfield, Jayne, Jayne, Heightfield, also called Height, but never High."

Height looked up from a screen of a half-rendered melted-glass thing filled with boards that turned into swirls inside the glass. He took a long look at Jayne as though she was an object to be memorized, then turned his attention back to his computer.

Renee said, "I'll show you to your room."

Well, better than a bed and trunk in Charlotte. The room was on the top floor, about eight-by-twelve, next to a bathroom that wasn't much smaller. The view was the giant apartment building behind the house.

Renee said, "Crouch and you can see the antennas."

Crouched, Jayne could even see sky. Well, she hadn't come to New York to see tree lines and harbors.

Renee said, "Tomorrow, we'll start your basic English class. Tomorrow night is Harry's salon."

"Do you have a system I can use?"

"Height was supposed to set it up," Renee said. "He can probably manage that now. He's just watching a rendering. I can get him to do it if I say you're interested in rendering, too."

"I'm capable of setting up my own computer, thanks. I just need the box." The only program Janyne brought with her was the illegal cryptography program, but she didn't yet know how to set it up.

"I'll ask him to bring your system," Renee said.

In a few minutes, Heightfield pushed a cart with computer parts into Jayne's room. Her computer would be cased, but Jayne didn't see a monitor. Without saying anything, Heightfield jacked the line in, sat down at the keyboard for a few minutes before noticing that he didn't have a monitor, went back downstairs for a monitor that looked larger than he should have been able to carry, and, before Jayne could stop him and do it herself, set Jayne up on basic services. "You have an ID?" he asked. Jayne, realizing he wasn't going to stop until she was on-line, handed over the real ID she was still using, not the fake ID she had for emergencies.

"I'm going to give you one of my files," he said. "Lathed glass with bottled heightfields, that's my signature."

He pulled a disk from his waistband, stuck it in Jayne's drive before she could answer. Her computer began calculating all the possibilities of light in, on, and through glass objects and solids that expanded in bottle necks and mirrors inside cored blocks of multicolored diamonds, at sixteen frames a second. Jayne wondered how long her computer would be tied up.

"Diamonds are a special texture of mine," Heightfield

said, "but after a while, what I do is make mathematically impossible objects. I want to find a way to make the renderer
work anyway." He pushed a button on the computer and the
image screen folded itself up into an active icon about an
inch and a half square, scan lines slowly coming down, in the
screen corner. "You can go on-line now, but you won't have
full use of memory until the render is complete."

Jayne knew she could abort the render, but that seemed
rude. Height didn't get up and go away as she'd expected. He
sat cross-legged on the floor. His upper body swayed slightly
as though his pulse was rocking him.

The rendering program beeped, displayed its image, and
folded itself back inside the hard drive.

Heightfield said, "Your people gave you a really fast machine."

"I was afraid the render would tie things up for hours,"
Jayne said.

"But things could be faster. We could be seeing direct
retina maps now if the investors hadn't interfered with cre-
ativity," Height said. "Perfect VR."

"Perhaps we just hit a natural plateau," Jayne said. "Technology couldn't expand exponentially, really. Eventually,
we'd use technology to control technology's further growth."

"That's what school tells you. My family also told me that
I shouldn't learn anything that would make me uncomfortable. But shocks and dislocations and cognitive dissonance
make a person creative."

Jayne wasn't quite sure whether he knew what he was saying
or had memorized other people's phrases because they sounded
so good. Jayne said. "Drugs and lies pacify the lower classes."

"Suicide pacifies the crazy classes," Heightfield said. He
unfolded himself, stood up, and left her alone.

The first class met in the basement of the squatters' apartment at 5:30 A.M., before work for the people taking the
class. Jayne felt half-asleep and illegal, the combination that
made her wonder if anyone in the class would prove to be a

great organizer, another underground teacher, or an informer in the making. She was teaching Standard English, again. Given the stigmatization of the other dialects, Standard English by then should have been the primary dialect of all English speakers, but it wasn't.

Street, on the other hand, seemed to have spread everywhere: African grammar on a mostly English base with Spanish in the punch lines.

Her students couldn't test out without a mastery of Standard. Jayne knew some of them would resent the hell out of giving up durational "to be"—that distinction between "he be working when the man come" and "he working when the man be coming." And the smartest of them knew their languages had rules as rigid in their own ways as any in Standard. The street called Standard English "proper."

"You here to learn Proper?" Jayne asked the class.

They all shrugged. No getting away from it.

"I don't call it Proper," Jayne said. "It's just another way of speaking, no more or less. Just that people with some power speak it. They made the language proper. Not the other way around. You never want to be using Proper with your people, but if you speak with Proper-speaking people, it's like matching manners to talk their talk at them."

The faces looked, *oh, shit, another social worker who thinks we're just fine as we are but don't know it.* One, then three grins appeared. They'd heard her trying to talk like them.

Jayne said, "What you really want to do is pass, of course."

The class laughed a little, and Jayne started in on possessives, which Standard English had done screwy things to. She felt like her cheerfulness and humor now was a skit she played well at regardless of internal trepidations.

By the time of Harry's salon the next night, Heightfield had cleared the front downstairs rooms of all computer equipment and set up additional tray tables. He swept the place furiously, then mopped the kitchen floor.

While Heightfield was setting up the last tray table, Harry came in and sat down in the room's largest overstuffed chair and began loading a pipe with tobacco. Renee looked in the room once, then disappeared back upstairs. Heightfield didn't speak to anyone, just took things that were in the way down to the basement or back to his room behind the kitchen. Jayne wondered how large Heightfield's room could be.

When the first salon guest rang the bell, Heightfield disappeared, and Renee came downstairs to answer it. "Heightfield doesn't like politicals," Renee said to Jayne as she went to open the door.

Harry looked up from his pipe, and said, "But he's always depended on the kindness of politicals."

A couple came in. They looked as though they expected packs of Judas Girls and news agents to show up at any moment. The man had been surgically transformed to look anonymous. Jayne wondered if the faint crazing of scars would be singular enough to give him away. The woman was short, thin, with black hair and eyes freshly worked on, the eyelids uneasy on the raw keratotomy cuts. "Sylvia has been busted," the woman said. "We're collecting for her vaccinations."

Renee said, "See, little Jayne, Sylvia has just turned forty-nine. Old and harried by the law."

"They've let her out on parole to her parents, but she's sure she'll serve jail time since she's been busted before," the man said. "We've got to find a way to get her the money without it being connected to us."

Jayne said, "Can't she get in touch with American Civil Liberties?"

"They only look for test cases. The Feds promised her a short term if she just pleaded guilty, but they're going to put her in Bedford Hills," the woman said.

"Bad staph there, and TB," Harry said. "Why didn't she get current vaccinations when we had the warez doctor visiting?"

Jayne wondered if her own immunizations were current enough for a bust. Renee said, "Sylvia doesn't trust warez. You can get shit just walking into a news interview."

"I've been interviewed. I thought I got out well," Jayne said.

Harry said, "Renee's paranoid."

Renee said. "But enough. What immunizations does Sylvia need?"

"AIDS, TB, cholera, influenza, staph, typhoid."

"I thought our health costs were covered," Jayne said.

"She was a tagger, not a teacher," the woman said. *Ah, Sylvia threw away her freedom to paint slogans on walls.*

Three squatter gods from the giant building came in, two guys and a woman. They wore stained shorts. The woman, her hair cropped just as close as the men's, wore a T-shirt stained with black oil splotches. They all were over six feet tall and scarred with tool injuries, not cosmetic keloid work. One of the men had been slashed down the belly. The scar disappeared down below his shorts' waistband. Jayne wondered if being big and scarred made squatting easier.

Renee went back to the kitchen for snacks. Jayne wondered if she should help. After a moment of silence in the group, she did.

"Why would someone be a persistent tagger?" Jayne asked Renee in the kitchen.

"She figured that the only people who were listening to the radio broadcasts had already bought the messages. But did you ever get your politics from a wall? So stupid, really, but then aren't we all?"

Jayne shook her head, then remembered the art tag in the elevator back in Charlotte. But then she had already been converted to rebellion. "I guess it depends on how good the work is."

"And tagging. You're gonna be busted if a cop sees people witness a tag and him watching. But living in a squat builds a confrontational mind-set."

"Here, I can carry that," Jayne said about the huge platter of food Renee kept adding sliced peppers and bean-curd chunks to.

"They all just worship squatters and Harry. It's the most unfucking sensible alliance. We're supposed to be quiet, on the side, living a cover job. Harry hasn't held down a cover job in six years. I have priors already, and get called down to the News Agency when they want to rattle me. And you, you're going to grow up to be us. And we're the lucky ones. We've been able to live in one place for more than three years."

"I think things are getting a bit more liberal," Jayne said, taking the tray before Renee caused a vegetable landslide.

"For you, maybe," Renee said. "I have a record. I'm the woman news agents call in to interview when they're bored." Jayne went back out to the front room and set the tray down on a coffee table. More people had joined the group by then: Some looked like former students, others looked like upper-middle-class kids who'd hidden in marginal neighborhoods.

Harry said, "We need to do more outreach to the working-class community. It isn't enough to work with outlaws."

One of the three squatters who'd come in early said, "Outlaws don't buy the system. Worker drones totally buy it. Maybe they aren't that smart?"

"They don't have the options," Jayne said.

The squatter woman said, "They give you up the nanosecond anyone legal wants to know how they got to know something beyond their scope. These people will sell you. They've got no honor."

Jayne remembered Mick.

Harry said, "We're supposed to be outlaw teachers, not teachers of outlaws."

Jayne said, "I thought it was a little of both."

"People need to know how to rebuild information-broadcast systems, how to build a network that is too flexible and multiplex to be controlled," the second squatter said.

"Hack chips, get the information you want, not just the information you need to do your job better."

"Guns and radios," the first squatter guy said. "Now if you could teach workers how to make guns . . ."

Harry said, "We've thought about that. But most of them want help in learning things that would allow them to test out at a higher class level. They want to stay away from big felonies that can get people who do them gunned down."

The woman who'd come in with the news about Sylvia said, "So all we do is make the system more efficient by helping it recruit the bright few among the poor."

Harry said, "If you're one of those bright poor, then what we did matters."

Jayne went back to the kitchen, and asked Renee, "How often are teachers betrayed by their students?"

"The better a teacher you are, the more likely someone will question what gave your students the second chance."

"But don't our students who rise really appreciate us?"

"They want to be exceptional. If everyone could rise, then rising wouldn't get you anywhere."

Jayne thought about the whores in Charleston. They were interested in rising, too, keeping more of their money and not letting accountants know what they were making. "Are you saying what our underclass students want is the life in the suburbs that I fled from?"

"Yep. If we end up jailed, then those suburbs don't ever get too crowded." Renee laughed.

Jayne thought about the classes she'd taught in the squatters' basement rec room earlier that day. All of them wanted to be classified or reclassified, though the squatter children wouldn't say so directly. "I kept wondering how it would have been to be brought up with squatter life as the norm."

"Eventually you get busted for something utterly trivial, and you don't have a registration card, and you find out precisely how different you'd been brought up," Renee said. "They shouldn't have kids."

"How does the law register the squatters' children if they bust them?"

"As Code 8, menial."

Born crazy through no fault of their own. Code 8 waived the antisuicide laws. Jayne was registered Code 8, clerical on her real papers. Her fake ID had her Code 6, technical. Emergency running card.

The room in front got noisier for a while. Harry's voice cut through as he settled or silenced issues. The three squatters' voices disappeared. Doors opened and closed.

Renee said, "I've already been through probation and weekend jail. I'll be a third offender."

Jayne asked, "Did your students . . ."

Renee nodded before the sentence's end. "You need to start looking for a clerical cover job tomorrow. Normally, we'd just arrange a fake job with sympathizers, but I want you to have a real job on your real ID."

Jayne sensed an edge to all this, a challenge and a will to see her stay busy. She almost told Renee, *I won't sleep with Harry,* but that seemed too catty. She said, "I have to teach during the day and on weekends."

"You can do homework. You've got a computer. A great computer. Heightfield is jealous."

When Jayne came back from her evening class the next day, Renee and Harry were screaming at each other over forgetting that Renee didn't like coffee ice cream. Jayne wanted to say, *But it's only ice cream,* but the fight seemed a ritual of misunderstandings, all tiny and destroying.

They paused when Jayne came in, but then continued. She felt they were rude. Her parents never screamed at each other in front of her.

A few days later, Jayne tried to catch up on her homework. She was doing optical-scanning recognition files, adjusting the program for sensitivity to various letters more likely than other combinations to show up in the texts. Abbreviated minutes turned into "rain," abbreviated milligrams showed up as "nag." She wondered why the files had been scanned from print in the first place. *I should take a break.* She looked up and saw Heightfield standing in her door. She got the impression he'd been in her peripheral vision for minutes. "Can I show you tricks on the computer?" he asked.

Somewhat nervously, she nodded.

When Heightfield brushed fingers by her arms and hands on the way to her keyboard, he made her squirm. He put a disk in the machine and showed her a glass rose unfolding into a matrix of tiny movies. Some of the petals were blank.

"I had a great machine once, better than even this one. The program reacts to available memory," he said. "It knows your machine now and will make the movies simpler so you can see them all."

Indeed, the movies squirmed into broader strokes and sprouted new movies on the formerly blank petals. The movies were tiny figures doing sports-hero things—racing bicycles, climbing rose petals that were also rock walls, riding horses and jumping them across petal veins.

"Did you make this?" Jayne asked, as the rose opened flatter and flatter.

"I found the pieces and put it together," Heightfield said. He pulled the disk out of her drive and looked at her. "The rose is mine. Why are you a political?"

"I'm more a teacher than a political."

"Well, why do it for politicals? Couldn't you test out?"

"If we tested out, the law would expect us to get real teaching jobs and teach what's prescribed."

"People don't need politicals to beat the system. I beat the system without any politics at all."

What Harry said about him went through Jayne's mind, *He's always depended on the kindness of politicals.* She said, "I've never belonged when I was a kid, and now I have a

community I can believe in. Sometimes, it's hard, but I have
it. I mostly believe in it."

Heightfield looked down at the disk, and said, "I could
show you more, but I guess you're busy."

"I'd like to see some of what you do," Jayne said. "Maybe
sometime this weekend."

That weekend, while Renee took Sylvia for her inoculations
against the various strains of prison bacteria and viruses, Jayne
took a break with Harry on the back deck. They stepped out
through the second-floor window onto the flat roof over
kitchen extension to the house. On the roof were wrought-iron
chairs and an expanded-metal-mesh-topped table.

"Why isn't there a door to this?"

"No building permit for a door. We took the house over."

"But do you own it now?" Jayne asked. She wondered if
squatters lived everywhere in this neighborhood. The huge
squatter apartment complex blocked out any view beyond
the vegetable garden between them and the building.

"After we cleaned it up, we bought it for back taxes,"
Harry said. "You don't need to take your cover work so seriously. Want a beer?" He slid in through the second-floor window without waiting for her reply and came back with a cold
six-pack. Jayne took a beer from the pack.

"Renee's not just paranoid," Harry said. "She's becoming
careless. I think she'd be relieved if she were arrested."

"Wouldn't they get you, too?"

"She's never betrayed me except in bed." Harry stared
down at his beer. "Enough of that. How do you like Heightfield?"

"Like him?"

"He's attracted to you," Harry said. He swallowed the rest
of his can as though that would keep him from saying more.

Jayne watched his Adam's apple bounce, the vulnerable
sweep of his throat below the beard. She noticed that Harry
had long eyelashes. She said, "I get lonely sometimes, but not

for people like Heightfield. Being around them makes me feel even more alone."

"We have an understanding in our field, the illegal teaching business, that when one partner goes to jail, both partners are free to find sexual partners on the outside or inside. No conjugal visits. The one who didn't get busted acts surprised and hurt, totally naïve. My first wife left me like that."

Jayne noticed he didn't say which of them had been busted. She asked, "Was she like Renee?"

"Renee's very passionate."

"And you love each other." Jayne felt the conversation circling around her lack of virginity and a man.

"It can be tiring to live with a paranoid."

"But she's passionate."

"Yeah. I guess that's what keeps me with her. Do you think Heightfield would be too passionate?"

"I'm not interested in Heightfield."

"If you're not going to sleep with him, let him down easy. He has very pure lusts." Harry handed Jayne another beer. She noticed that he hadn't opened a second one himself, but she seemed to want the second one beyond thirst.

For a few minutes, they watched three people come out of the squatter apartment to work in the vegetable garden. Jayne looked over at Harry. He looked back at her. "I don't suppose you want another beer?"

"I'm fine."

"Renee's not getting you scared, is she?"

"But how is it that we're not all arrested? This can't be much of a secret."

"Illegal teaching's like drugs. Having a shot at reclassification takes the edge off for the guys in power. We're not as subversive as we think. The squatters, now, maybe that's subversive. But eventually, even they want to regularize their relationship with their property."

Jayne said, "They've just found another way to become homeowners."

"Renee has been difficult this last year. I tried to get her to see one of our therapists, but she doesn't think she's unrealistic."

"Maybe she isn't. That's what's scary?"

"By the time you're Renee's age, it will all be different. The future won't be like this. Political conditions are unstable right now."

"Tolerated, but still illegal if the news agents want to bust you? How is that unstable?"

"Let's go inside. You've got another class to teach."

Harry helped her in through the second-floor window. Jayne felt his hand grip on her shoulder just before he walked away, a squeeze. Brace up. Maybe more. Renee wasn't too different, Jayne guessed, from Suzanne, another passionate crazy. Harry seemed sane. He smiled at her and took the beer out of her hand. For an instant, she was afraid he'd kiss her, then she wondered if she wanted him to kiss her. Heightfield was too weird, Harry too married. "Maybe I ought to be nicer to Heightfield," she said. He finished her beer as though savoring the taste of her saliva mixed in the warm brew.

"Crazies are difficult lovers," Harry said. "Don't make a stupid decision to avoid being alone."

Jayne walked to the squatters' building where she thought about Harry all through the class, making in-class assignments that left her sitting at the desk with an image of Harry's throat playing in her mind.

I haven't had a lover in so long. She wondered if Harry and Renee had an understanding about secondary relationships. As an experiment, she tried to fantasize about Heightfield, not impossible, either, but he reminded her of Mick. She looked at her students, heads bent over the screens of out-of-date laptops found abandoned on the streets and refurbished by people like Heightfield, technological idiot savants.

Jayne's students claimed they never broke news code, perhaps as a form of sympathetic magic: *If I don't read news not intended for me, perhaps the world will ignore how I stole knowledge in illegal classes.* Maybe they didn't trust any news they couldn't confirm with their own eyes and ears.

Harry's throat, naked under the beard. Sex kicked the higher brain functions out of the way and played its nerve music on Jayne's pulse.

Renee still wasn't home when Jayne got back. Heightfield and Harry sat around the table looking at a computer screen. Something bubbled in a soup pot. Automatically, Jayne checked the heat to see if the pot might be about to boil over.

"I hate it when she's late," Harry said. "I worry when she starts talking about her students betraying her."

"But students are the reason you people get busted," Heightfield said.

In orientation, Jayne heard that many of the student informers were really undercover cops, but many wasn't most. Maybe this was a way for the student to join the police or the news agents, study enough to try for recertification and trade the teacher for the job.

"Could she be gone, then?" Jayne asked.

Harry sighed. Bored with political hysterics perhaps, Heightfield went back into his room. Jayne stayed up with Harry, drinking coffee and eating soup.

Renee called at midnight to say she was with Sylvia at a boy house. Harry said, "Renee said Sylvia wanted to get cock before she went to prison. Sort of a last-chance thing."

"Wouldn't any of her friends sleep with her?" Jayne asked.

"Buying it makes you boss. You have to ask to get it from your friends," Harry said.

"Well, Renee's okay then."

"She ordered me not to worry for the rest of the night," Harry said. He put his hand on Jayne's over the kitchen table. The soup bowls waited in the sink. "I brought you here into the middle of an emotional mess. I'm sorry."

The blood heaviness in Jayne's crotch distracted her. Her lips seemed swollen. Harry let go of her hand and ran a fingernail across her lower lip. *He sees it's swollen, too.* Jayne asked, "Are you sure she didn't hire a guy herself?"

"Jayne, do you want the address?"

"No, I don't think so." Jayne's voice was softer than she'd meant.

"Renee won't be back until tomorrow," Harry said.

Jayne felt impossibly bold. "Heightfield will know."

"Yeah, that's what I was hinting at. You're not so nice a girl that you're offended, are you?"

The blood reversed itself. After the body reacted, Jayne realized she did feel insulted. "You said she was crazy. You said she was going to get herself busted."

"I've never been alone," Harry said. "Not for long. I hate it. I can't sleep without a woman's legs twining together with mine."

"I've never slept in a bed with someone."

"I know your history."

"I didn't stay in bed with him after I got myself pregnant."

"She wants to get busted so it's over with. She doesn't have the nerve to leave me on her own."

Jayne almost said, *I'd like to hear that from her,* but that sounded too much like a challenge. His neck under the beard was very pale. If he'd been Heightfield, the veins would have stood out on his temples, but he was fleshier, not fat, though. Where was Heightfield? Jayne wished he'd come in to break the tension building between them.

"Will you stay with me when she's busted? Even the strictest marriages tend to get suspended then."

"You won't have conjugal visits?"

"Too dangerous."

Was Harry going to turn Renee in himself? No, Jayne couldn't operate that way. Too paranoid. She had to trust the community that took her in after she blasted her reputation. "I don't want to hurt Renee."

"What she doesn't know won't hurt her," Harry said.

"You said Heightfield . . ."

"We can go somewhere else. I've got friends with a spare room."

Now? Jayne felt more nervous than a virgin. Anxiety made sense—sex equaled babies. "I'm not on the pill or anything." If Heightfield were trying to listen, he could hear everything they'd been saying.

It was one o'clock in the morning. Jayne thought surely they were both too tired to follow up on this instantly, but Harry reached for her hand, and said, "I'll take care of you."

He was old. He remembered the last blast of techno-optimism before the Mars expedition stretched into a lesson about too-long supply lines.

The buses in Brooklyn ran all night. He took her to a loft near the Williamsburg Bridge where two women opened the door to an ongoing party, assignations for all genders welcomed. If Harry had to pay them, Jayne didn't know. They danced together, slow dances body to body. About eight other couples were also there, some dancing, some sitting in corners talking and kissing. *Renee's driving him away with all her paranoia and her spite.*

Harry pulled her into a small room equipped with mattress and a hookah. "Have you ever smoked pot before?" he asked.

Jayne didn't think this could possibly be good for her lungs, the smoke harsher than tobacco smoke. She wondered what Harry thought he'd get out of this.

They stared at each other for a few moments. Jayne felt lost in her body, her swollen tongue stumbling in her mouth, her brain disappearing into the drug smoke.

If he's doing this to seduce me, I'm scared.

Slow liquefaction. Slow rot.

"The drug is not working the way you think," Jayne managed to say.

" 'Tis okay. We don't have to commit adultery right away." Harry said. He giggled. *Like a pothead,* Jayne thought.

Jayne felt confused. She wasn't sure she wanted to have

him commit adultery at all, but Renee was impossible. And the drug scared her. The world around her seemed like a dream, slow time, and she wondered if she'd remember anything.

"I might have done better without the drug," Jayne said.

After a moment, Harry said, "I'll put you in a cab. You need to get back before Renee comes home."

Jayne blinked. What was this to him? She wanted him to reassure her that it had been okay not to sleep with him. He seemed hostile, body turned away from her.

"Okay, okay," Harry said. Was he hostile, or was Jayne herself angry at him for wanting to betray his wife? Odd. Jayne didn't know what she felt. Her body wanted him anyway, a nasty habit in a female body, she felt.

Harry made two phone calls. One was for the cab; the other was to yet another woman. *He can't stand being alone at night.*

Jayne got back to the house before Renee, but Harry didn't. "Where's Harry?" Renee asked.

"I don't know," Jayne said. She wanted to tell Renee that she didn't have sex with him, but to say that seemed ridiculous. Renee seemed to smell the marijuana smoke on her, but Jayne couldn't tell if Harry used marijuana regularly to seduce women or if Renee had particular memories of that.

Harry came back at noon, looking fed and rested. Renee started when he came in, then curled up in a chair and didn't speak to him. She stayed in the chair for three hours, staring at the stairs leading to the upper floors.

Saying *I didn't sleep with him* wouldn't solve anything. He had certainly found someone else.

The next days revolved around not talking about what hadn't happened. Heightfield stopped bringing disks to her room, so Jayne felt sure he thought she'd slept with Harry.

Then Heightfield came to her room without any disk to share. "Can I come in?" When Jayne nodded, he came in and sat down on her bed. "Is my life really crazy?" he asked.

"Why do you ask me?"

He stared at her and hummed in his nose. The hum wavered, then he said, "You're more my age than either of them."

When she didn't answer, Heightfield said, "Oh, I guess you don't really know much about me."

"You want me to give you my honest opinion on whether you're crazy or not, even though you don't guess I know much about you. What the fuck?"

"You haven't heard the whole story," Heightfield said. Was he offering autobiography as pity object, as seduction? Jayne was beginning to realize he wasn't referring to her unacted-on lust for Harry, not directly or even at a slant, but the pheromones in the air might have made him vulnerable to his own desires and self-doubts.

"Do you want to tell me the full story?"

"I used to watch banks of videos that were the artificial eyeballs of Judas Girls." When Jayne nodded, Heightfield continued, "I figured out how to use the dual processors to render. Some frames were supposed to be watching with the girls, but I'd have bezier patch roses with screws pulled to points as the stems. You know screw forms?"

Jayne felt a double entendre hiss by her ears. She shook her head.

"You have a plug-in that makes threaded screws, then you go to point edit . . . I'm boring you. That's why I wanted to ask if you thought I was crazy."

Jayne felt tender toward him, though she knew she wouldn't if Harry hadn't roused her body. "I don't think you're really crazy, Heightfield." Her tone was way too tender, and she recoiled back from her own words the instant she said them.

"I don't know what you mean by that."

"I don't avoid people. . . ." Not good to say, *just if I think they're crazy.* "I wasn't avoiding you. I was just spending more time with Harry."

"People keep telling me I should do something professional with cee gee or commit suicide for being crazy," Heightfield said. "If this was earlier, I'd be a code drifter. I would have had a community. You know, you're right. You're ahead of me. You have a community."

Jayne boggled, then realized cee gee meant computer graphics. "How are you getting by, though," Jayne said.

"I'm working for Harry now," Heightfield said. "You see me."

But you're just a servant. No, not good to say that. "Why did they ask you to leave the squat?"

"They stole from me," Heightfield said. "They sold my computers. I couldn't get any work done."

Jayne couldn't imagine Heightfield wanting his computers to be public property. But now he was beginning to whine. He was a guy, and guys couldn't get pregnant. She was sorry she encouraged him to talk, but she was lonely.

So she asked, "Were you ever on school drugs?"

Heightfield got up from where he'd been sidling closer and closer to her on her bed and walked to the door. Then he turned around, and said, "Yes, were you?"

Jayne felt that her honesty would lead somewhere she'd regret, but she owed him this. "Yes."

He said, "To me, your life looks really crazy. You're running around the world trying to save it from itself. But then maybe everyone's life is obvious from the outside. Maybe I should do something reasonable with my life before it's too late."

It was too late when he was born, Jayne thought, but she asked, "You said I had a community at least. So why does my life seem crazy?"

"You're sacrificing yourself to people who don't really care the way you do. You want them to fight the structure, to understand and learn how to be more than what the system offers. All your students want is to get a better place in the structure. And Harry is a skirt fucker. He wants someone to be around when Renee gets busted."

When Renee gets busted. "Harry says she's going to be so paranoid she annoys someone into turning her in just to get back at her. And I really didn't sleep with Harry." Jayne felt that even though she hadn't slept with Harry, she'd broken faith with Renee. But maybe from the outside, betrayal on one thing implied betrayal on another.

"I want to feel like I can really talk to you."

"You can do that."

"Not if you're sleeping with Harry."

"I said I'm not sleeping with Harry. He gave me marijuana, and I got confused and scared."

He looked at her and turned his head to the left as though his thoughts unbalanced his brain. "Harry said not to say anything or do anything that would upset Renee."

"You don't believe me? I'm telling you the truth."

"I've never slept with you and I'm not Renee so what business is it of mine?" He left her room then.

We're all nuts here.

A squatter with connections warned Renee, Harry, and Jayne to skip classes. Renee went off to witness that Sylvia surrendered in good health and to bring Sylvia's personal possessions back to the squat.

When the squad cars pulled up, Harry and Jayne went out on the deck to watch while Heightfield pulled all illegal programs off the hard drives and took the disks down to hiding in the basement. Jayne hid her encryption program on a minidisk that fit in a fake quarter.

"Could they listen to us here?"

"I suspect they wanted us to know about the raid. It's not a teaching raid, but it's intended to be . . . educational."

Cops surrounded the apartment building. Three men in gray overcoats got out of a gray car that arrived late and walked into the building as if nobody would ever dream of hurting them. They wore hats—an archaic touch. And overcoats, despite the weather.

"Fedoras," Harry said. "The more the news agents try to pretend they're slacking, the more they dress like twentieth century Nazis. Imitation Gestapo, but they're trained to be more polite these days. But they're not happy to have to be polite."

Jayne felt like she should be hiding, but when she started to go back in, Harry wrapped his fingers around her wrist. "Anyone can be curious. They expect everyone to watch."

And the neighborhood seemed to turn out to watch, circled around the building behind the police lines. A small boy tried to duck through, but a uniformed cop picked him up and held him for a few minutes.

"So we can't continue," Jayne said.

"We don't know what they really wanted. The building is a squat after all."

"Those guys just walked in as though nobody would dream of hurting them. What if the squatters fought back?"

"They're armored under the coats," Harry said. "And if you do hurt them, the police will call in helicopters."

"Meaning they'd bomb a residential neighborhood?"

"They could take out one building detached like that one very neatly. Smart bombs. I've seen it done."

The cops relaxed. Everyone inside was cooperating, letting the news agents scan media, check code locks, set up surveillance devices.

"Don't they have to have probable cause to go in like that?"

"You can raid a squat anytime you want, install any surveillance gear you want. The squatters will have to leave the gear in place. Taking it out after it's been legally installed brings in another team."

"Haven't they been broadcasting?"

The crowd stood around for hours. Finally, after the pretzel and hot dog carts showed up, the three men in long coats came back out with the tall squatter woman that Jayne had seen at Harry's open house.

"Just her?"

"She's been tired for months, and they know it. Jayne, we'll see this here soon. What will you say?"

"I met you at a conference and you offered me a place to stay in Brooklyn while I found work."

"Go back and do that work. Lots of it. Heightfield's cleared the school things off every drive. All he needs to do to get any of us is leave a hard drive readable."

All he needs to do to get any of us is leave a hard drive readable. Jayne knew she could wipe hard drives so that no utility could recover the data.

As the car drove away with the squatter woman, Renee came through the police lines with Sylvia's clothes. She had her head up, her hands holding a bag at her waist, walking through the police as though they were an ordinary crowd. A uniformed cop stopped her. Jayne could see them talking, then he let her go through.

"Oh, Christ," Harry said. "A fucking grandstand thing like that." They both went into the house then, not waiting to see Renee come back out. Harry went to his liquor supply and poured a glass of whiskey, tossed it back, and poured one for Jayne, who shook her head.

Renee came in the door. Her eyes were bloodshot and fixed on something in the distance, pouched skin under them.

Harry handed her the neat whiskey, and said, "Did you see who was in the agency car?"

"Agents and a tired woman. Sylvia considering opting out," Renee said. She tossed the drink back. "I've thought about it, too."

"You don't have grounds," Jayne said. "You're not really crazy."

Renee laughed, the wrinkles suddenly more intense. She looked at Harry, then at Jayne. "You'd like me to be out of here, wouldn't you?"

"No." Jayne didn't want to be the occasion for adultery, not with this tension in the house.

"I . . . can't . . . go on . . . teaching," Renee said, space between most of the words as though she spoke to foreigners. "What can I do with my life?"

"You know I'll support you," Harry said.

"And fuck behind my back."

Jayne said, "Harry said I ought to put in lots of legit work now. Heightfield's cleared our machines."

"Fuck you," Renee said. "Fuck you your youth, your naïveté, your idiot enthusiasm, and all your misplaced pity."

Jayne's head bounced back. Pity, that undercutting thing Jayne herself hated to receive. "I'm going upstairs. If you want me to leave, tell me tomorrow."

Renee smiled again, one mouth corner only. "Oh, shit, stay. He's going to need company after I'm busted."

"I didn't sleep with him."

"Don't you think people see people here, leaving the house together. I have friends who didn't want me to be hurt by someone else, so they told me."

Harry said, "All you know is we left the house together. She came back without me."

Suddenly, Jayne was annoyed with Renee for making such a big fuss. "He scared me with the marijuana. I think I would have slept with him otherwise, though. Satisfied?"

Renee said, "You skittish little bitch."

"Jayne, let me talk to her. Leave us alone, please."

Renee said, "Until I'm gone." She poured herself another drink. "How do I get out of this trap? Oh, shit." She turned to Jayne, and said, "Go upstairs, bitch." Then she sat down on a couch, pulled her legs up under her, and wrapped her hands around her head. She rocked back and forth, muttering, "Oh, shit. Oh, shit."

Jayne wondered if Renee had gone crazy, but she felt colder than she ought to have felt. As she went upstairs, she turned to see Harry embracing Renee, rocking with her. They both cried.

Harry loved Renee, would love her even when he slept

with other women, could betray Renee and love her at the same time. Perhaps because he was caught in her intensity, he needed less complex women. Jayne didn't like to think of herself as a simple woman. But compared to Renee, she was. She wanted to be as complex as Renee, but without the hysteria. But Harry loved Renee. He loved her beyond adultery, betrayal, and hysterics.

It will be so relaxing for her to be captured. She can ask for euthanasia anytime without getting arguments from Harry.

Jayne feared that she'd be the one who walked Renee through the presurrender rituals: lawyers, doctors, injections.

Walking through the police lines to the squat was a sign.

Heightfield, though he'd seemed to have sworn off Jayne earlier, knocked on her door.

"Everyone wanted to protect Renee," Heightfield said. "Only Renee doesn't want to be protected."

"So how do we keep from being busted with her?"

Heightfield said, "I'm not political."

"Oh, Heightfield, you are more than you think."

"I'd die if I went to jail."

"Aiding and abetting," Jayne said, feeling cruel for wanting to scare him.

"Don't. Please let me sit down beside you."

Jayne moved off the bed and pulled out the file of the rose with movies that Heightfield had given her when she first came to Brooklyn. She put it into the computer and sighed.

"Why are you so hard?"

"Why am I here?" Jayne thought about calling Ocean to ask for a transfer, but if the whole house was being watched, a call would link these teachers with Ocean. She closed the rose and opened homework. "Heightfield, I'm not hard, not really."

"I just want to code what I want to code," Heightfield said. "The last century, the last quarter, had a place for people like me."

" 'Open Source lives,' " Jayne said, fixing ram/rain problems. "We're all just waiting now, aren't we?"

"I hate waiting. How do you know about Open Source?"

"I saw it in code comments. What do you want from me?" She knew the instant she spoke. He looked hungry, as though he wanted to crawl back up her body and hold on, screw his dick into her, wrap his arms and legs around her, and let her absorb him. "So, was Open Source something that the news agents thought got out of control?"

It would relieve a lot of tension. If Heightfield didn't seem too weird, an affair with him would make more sense than sleeping with Harry. She wondered if an egg was luring sperm to it, then knew the organization would make sure this time she didn't deliver.

"Open Source was the work of code warriors," Heightfield said. "In the end, they buried their programs in other code."

"I know," Jayne said.

Downstairs, the front door opened and kept Jayne from dealing with Heightfield that night. She heard Renee screaming and strange men's voices. "Do you have tranquilizers? The night's going to be worse."

Heightfield scurried away. Jayne sat doing homework, not sure in this case whether she should be curious or not. She was afraid to face whoever had broken in the door.

Harry came up, and said, "Jayne, come downstairs. Renee did something stupid."

He didn't touch her as they walked down the stairs. Jayne recognized the three men from the afternoon raid. Four other men held Renee, who finally said, "Please, no. I'm sorry. I don't do anything bad." But she didn't stop struggling with them.

The men pushed Renee down slowly. One went outside and came back with a canvas thing with buckles Jayne recognized as a restraint posie, a kind of straitjacket. The three men in overcoats simply watched. When Renee was finally in restraints, one of them said, "ID, please. On everyone in the house."

Jayne said, "Mine's upstairs." One of the overcoats followed her upstairs, then took her elbow and led her back downstairs with her ID between his thumb and index finger. Still holding on to her, he ran it through a scanner and movies and text flashed across the screen. Jayne saw her mother smiling and crying, a VRML of herself whirl across the screen with full biometrics down to blood type and DNA scans. Out-of-wedlock pregnancy, school drugs—she could read the report on his face as much as on the screen. Ocean told Jayne early that the big details couldn't be edited away. The news agent handed her the card back and squeezed her elbow before shoving her away from him and letting her go.

Harry handed his ID over. The man's face turned to Jayne again, smirking. Then he paused for a while, looking at Harry's scrolling life.

"A most lucky man," the man who'd read the ID said. Harry reached out for his ID. The man keyed something on his computer, swiped it through again, and handed it to Harry.

Where's Heightfield? Jayne was almost afraid to think about him. She looked at Harry, who wasn't looking at anything. Renee lay on the floor by a couch, tied in the restraint garment, muttering, her eyes bloodshot. *She looks crazy enough.*

Heightfield came up then. He had cut his beard down to stubble and had shaved his head, but he had his ID with him ready to show the people who'd raided the house.

"I'm their servant. I work for keep," Heightfield said. He looked as mad as Renee.

The three overcoats looked at each other. The man checking IDs scanned Heightfield's and looked at him with pity. "Your family has permanent asylum papers waiting for you if you want to sign in. We can't commit you unless you threaten to kill someone. But you're not that type, are you?"

"No," Heightfield said. "I'm an artist."

He is an artist.

"Mrs. Blaine, we just wanted to ask you a few questions," one of the other overcoats said. He was the oldest of them, a bit heavier than the others. "Why the hysteria?"

"She's been in prison before," the man who'd scanned the IDs said. "Maybe she thought we knew more than we do now."

"We could talk to her friend, Sylvia," the oldest man said. "Sylvia's not too happy to be going to Bedford Hills. Maybe she could explain why the hysteria."

"We just wanted to talk to you," the third man, who'd been quiet, said.

"Don't lie to her," Heightfield said. "Her sense of reality is shaky enough."

"Honest, boy, we just wanted to talk to her," the older man said. "But now we want to know why the hysteria."

"We can interrogate ex-felons chemically," the third man said. The four uniformed policemen looked sick.

Harry said, "Renee, do you have a lawyer you want me to call?"

"Fuck, yes," Renee said. She closed her eyes and curled up tighter, defeated by her husband, her paranoia, her suspicions of what chemical interrogation would do.

Jayne felt her bladder beginning to twist. "I have to use the toilet," she said.

"Sure." The man who'd gone upstairs with her nodded to the police. One of them walked her to the toilet and watched. The news agents had been more courteous. Jayne felt they'd bust her, too, before the night ended.

When she finished, she went back, and told the overcoats, "I have to log in more hours." Work, some desperate routine, seemed like a haven now. She would have to wait to see what happened to Renee under interrogation, whether Sylvia would betray all of them.

Sylvia couldn't betray her, Jayne realized. Sylvia had been busted before Jayne came to Brooklyn.

For a moment, Jayne wondered if the overcoats were right, that she was some foul promiscuous crazy bitch kicking against a reasonable society. Then she went upstairs and faced the awful work she had to do as a licensed home worker and realized she had only one life, one sex, and while society had given her life, it hadn't given her a particularly good reason to keep it and would willingly kill her if she only agreed.

Fiercely, she refused to accept society's verdict, but the temptation to surrender to their opinions and lie down and die was there.

After the police took Renee away, Harry came upstairs. He said, "I'm sorry."

"What happens next?"

"They book her, sentence her if she pleads guilty immediately, remand her for trial with an ankle strap if she doesn't plead. Then, one day, they'll call her back to trial."

"Sounds like Kafka."

"That's why a lot of people plead guilty to avoid the waiting."

"You love Renee."

"Yes, but I can care for you. I can make you ready for someone who'll really love you."

Jayne shook her head slightly. Harry smiled, a flinch grin. She said, "Will she be sentenced as soon as she pleads?"

"They still strap on the ankle monitor, but they give her time to arrange her life, get the inoculations. Jail's not intended to be lethal to everyone."

"What if she opts out?"

"She won't do that," Harry said. Jayne sensed the weakness, his need for Renee and his resistance to his need, and beyond that, the arrogance that made him the center of his own known universe. "She manipulates me with that, but she won't do it."

That night around two o'clock, Jayne woke up and couldn't sleep. She went on-line to the innocuous programs available to one of her class, willing to be distracted. At 3:38, she fell asleep holding the computer keyboard between her hands. When she rolled in her sleep, it turned itself back on and woke her. She went off-line, shut the machine down. Five A.M.

At eight, the three men in the overcoats came to bring Harry Renee's clothes. He stood holding them as Jayne came down. She knew immediately that Renee had died that night. Had been killed.

"You didn't ask me," Harry said. "You didn't let me try to talk her out of it. I could have talked her out of it."

"She had the right as an ex-felon facing further charges to request euthanasia, and our psychiatrist thought she seemed psychotic enough."

How odd. They make Harry seem pitiful and unreasonable. Jayne wondered if perhaps they were lying, if they'd just killed Renee without her consent.

But probably not. The men looked from Harry to her as if soliciting her to volunteer for her own death. For a second, she felt that deadly charm, then fought it, and realized she would never stop fighting it.

10
Reality Analogs

Jayne walked down to the Williamsburg Bridge that afternoon. Now she felt trapped forever in another woman's hysteria. Renee's suicide said, *I don't trust anyone and I hate you all, so I'm going away to never ever talk to anyone ever again ever.*

The bridge strings sang. She took the walkway, a raw steel thing welded in place against the older girders, expanded metal showing the cars below. A twentieth-century song popped into her head, "It's so easy, so . . ." and the rest faded.

The world whispered, *Die, you don't fit in, die,* and some people obeyed. Jayne wondered if Renee could have lived through prison again, if she even would have been busted had she not sought it. However madly, Renee had controlled that situation; she'd made them bust her and kill her. Maybe that was better than going from place to place knowing that the news agents built a bigger and bigger file, toying with her and waiting until she could bring them the maximum possible betrayals.

A man walked up to Jayne on the bridge. She recognized him as one of the trench coats, the man who'd run her ID through the scan. "I was following you," he said.

"I'm glad you didn't lie. Are you going to throw me off the bridge?"

His head jerked back, his chin tucked down and his lower lip drooped slightly. "We don't do that. I want to talk to you."

"Can I say no?"

"Yes, you could say no, but I think you need to listen." The wind lifted his hat slightly, and he took it off and put it in the crook of his left arm. His blond hair lifted slightly in the wind. His polished shoes, his gloves and hat, and the black overcoat made Jayne felt shabby. He used a voice tone she used on students when they weren't paying attention.

She knew he was recording her.

"Okay, who are you that I should listen to you?"

"Agent Patrick Drury," he said. "You know I'm an information-control officer. I've been studying your case. We suspect you're involved with illegal teaching. You're not technical enough to be a code sifter, are you?"

"I do optical character recognition work at home," she said.

"Very industriously, too." He smiled. "We've sent it to you to see what your teaching schedule was. Most illegal teachers download the work after they teach."

If she could get through this interview, Jayne needed to get that information back to Ocean. "I'm not teaching."

"Yes, legally, we'd have to prove that, wouldn't we? Are you so sure we can't?"

Jayne almost said, *So, arrest me,* but that sounded too much like Renee. "You haven't arrested me."

"I'm going to proposition you. Not sexually." He smiled sexually, though, or perhaps it was his excitement at her fear. She stood, cold, rooted, listening to him while the steel underfoot dragged away her body heat. Jayne knew what the proposition was. He wanted her to inform. She flushed, not quite sure why she was embarrassed.

"You've had rough breaks. You shouldn't have been put on school drugs." The guy was cute. He sounded sympathetic, and Jayne almost wanted to go anywhere other than back to Harry's house.

Suzanne's voice seemed to speak to Jayne, *Oh, he's good.* She was glad she'd known Suzanne. Drury's approach had the flavor of pity compounded by ritual humiliation tainted by sexual excitement. "I can't talk to you." She sounded weaker than she wanted to sound. "You people killed Renee."

"Renee was tired of living. Do you want to be that way at forty-seven, husband bringing his mistresses home to live with you, no way to get out of the life, busted and a repeat offender? Jail time certain. There you have it. Your forties. Do you want it? You've never had a stable relationship in your life, moving from place to place."

"I haven't done anything, I just live there." They all thought she'd slept with Harry. Weird, she felt that she might have except for his strange and desperate moves, the drug. But she hadn't, and that gave her an odd sense of pride. He'd had other lovers. Why did Ocean send her there?

Backing away seemed necessary and foolish. She took a few steps backwards, then ran off the bridge, knowing he could follow, knowing she looked absolutely guilty.

He didn't need to follow her. He could track her by satellite and Judas Girl eyes.

And, for an instant, the bridge had been too tempting, too. Why throw herself off to a painful splat when suicide could be had at any health center?

Instead of calling Ocean directly, she thought she could route the call through the Charleston whorehouse, call Suzanne, whose voice in her head had stopped her from falling for the guy. Drury would know where she was.

She fumbled with her secondary phone card, the fake untraceable one, not sure she should use it or not.

Get one of the virtual girl numbers, don't go straight to Brandy or Suzanne. The woman on-line remembered Jayne and managed to get the call transferred to a secure line.

Brandy said, "This better not fuck us up."

"Get in touch with Ocean. Tell her or somebody to call back here." Jayne read the number, tracing the digits with her index finger to keep them orderly. The old disorder popped up under stress.

"Don't explain," Brandy said.

Jayne hung up. The world had her trapped in this phone booth. Until the phone rang, she had no reason to leave it. She slumped against the side wall, looking out to see if anyone was watching her. The street seemed neutral.

The phone rang. Ocean asked, "This line is secure on my end. What is it, Jayne?"

"I ran. A guy, a news agent named Patrick Drury."

"Well, you ran. What did he say to you?"

"He said they knew I was an outlaw teacher from the pattern of my homework posts."

"Not necessarily lying, but I suspect Renee's hysterical terminus made them suspect everyone in the house. Harry's who they're really after."

"What do I do?"

"Go back to the house. You have students who need you. We'll have you posting all through tutoring sessions. Just do one on one for a while. I'll send in a seducer for Drury. I've heard about him before. We have some very good people for this, medically enhanced. Very good. You'll be amused."

"Just go back to . . ."

"Yes. If we transfer you now, you'll look guilty. We want you to have as much of a normal life as possible."

"I didn't fuck Harry."

"I was hoping you might fall in love with Heightfield."

Jayne felt insulted. "Heightfield?"

"Go back, dear. It will be okay. You'll look like you were scared straight."

"I have a record with the news agents now," Jayne said.

"They have as much on over fifteen million people. If you get really tainted, we'll put you in a place where we pay them off, but as of now, you're more valuable to us where they simply ignore all but the most flagrant actions."

"Then I'm too tainted for places where news agents actively hunt down illegal teachers?"

"We didn't want to give you something that difficult. Harry didn't tell me how poorly Renee was doing."

"So, you want me to continue as though nothing had happened."

"Yes. You'll surprise yourself."

The phone booth opened. Jayne walked to a subway and took a train back to her compromised house. She was a temporary creature dissolving in the universe. The complexity of living organisms and their institutions broke individual lives down and made them vanish. But Jayne's life wasn't over yet. She comforted herself with the thought that in ten thousand years, not only she, but this society would be gone.

She decided she didn't need to say anything to Harry about the news agent or her phone call to Ocean. And she would go to Heightfield. She needed someone, but not Harry.

As Jayne walked from the subway stop to the house, she began to hate Harry, and wondered how she could control this hate. As she saw the house, she wondered how she could live though the whole mess.

But these people are my side. I won't inform on them. That thought did not make her feel good enough. She took out her door key and opened the door. Harry sat in the darkened living room, crying still, his hands moving over one of Renee's dresses. Jayne nodded at him, went upstairs to her little room.

She heard footsteps on the stairs and couldn't tell if they were Harry's or Heightfield's. Which one? She turned slightly where she'd thrown herself on the bed.

"Jayne?" It was Heightfield.

"Oh come in." She wondered if they'd end up screwing each other out of pity. Heightfield came in and sat down on the floor with his back to the wall, knees up. Jayne made a move to turn on a light, then saw that he'd been crying, too.

Her idea of a pity fuck seemed trivial and tasteless. Going through with it would have really made her feel like trash. "Heightfield, are you okay?"

"My name's really James. I don't want to go on being Heightfield. I want to change my life before I can't."

Renee's suicide reflected differently in his life than in Jayne's or Harry's. "So, what could James do that Heightfield couldn't?"

"I could go home for rehabilitation."

"I don't know what's right for you."

"Unusual in a political," he said.

"Harry said you've always depended on the kindness of politicals."

He didn't answer. His hands, dangling out over his knees, twitched.

"Couldn't you be both James and Heightfield?"

"I've been asked to inform."

Jayne almost said, *So have I,* but somehow couldn't quite as that would sound like mockery. "Would you inform on me?"

"They'd just ask you to testify in exchange for dropped charges. They're really after Harry. Election year or something. The guy who talked to me said they'd like to show that surrendering would be safe for illegal teachers. They won't even put him in jail."

"Nobody's ever informed on him."

"He picks his students really well. Never just takes people like Renee did."

"Took you in, though."

"Renee did that," Heightfield said. "I really should just go home. Get rehabbed."

Jayne realized Heightfield's parents were rich, upper-class. Rehabilitation for Heightfield wasn't what it would be for her. "You'll hate yourself if you inform, no matter what they do to Harry or me."

Heightfield said, "I think I'll stay Heightfield for just a while longer. I want to see what happens."

Jayne said, "And if this place is bugged, don't they have all the evidence they need?"

"I make sure no place I live in is bugged. My parents might be looking for me," Heightfield said. "Sometimes, I wish they really were."

In the morning, after breakfast, Jayne went back up to her room to work on her home assignments, the endless rounds of formatting tables, checking scanned text, running legal searches in the areas where she had a license. About noon, Harry brought a woman upstairs, and said, "Here's Naomi."

The woman was extremely attractive, full eyelids and lips, with high cheekbones. She looked like she'd just gotten out of bed. Jayne looked back at Harry.

"It's not what you think," Harry said.

"Harry, go on downstairs. I'll introduce myself," Naomi said. She looked slightly dark, and her voice was soft. Jayne recognized the flavor of whore about her. Naomi nodded at Harry who left. Naomi said, "I knew Renee, but not well enough to know it would come to this."

She can seduce anything, Jayne thought. Suzanne hadn't gotten Jayne to bed, but Naomi could. "And Harry?"

"I'm not here for Harry," Naomi said. She sat down in Jayne's only chair in a flurry of legs. "I'm here because of you."

Jayne hoped Heightfield was right and the house wasn't bugged. Naomi smiled as Jayne flinched back against the wall behind the bed. Jayne said, "I don't think anyone needs to chaperone me."

Naomi said, "Well, it would look bad, wouldn't it, a woman in a house with two men, third man maybe calling on you?"

"Can we talk like this?"

"How do you feel?"

"Guilty. Even though I didn't sleep with Harry while Renee was out with a woman friend who was going to prison. I know what it looked like. And she was so bitter. What do you do when people are old and bitter?"

"Let history take you away from the present."

"I feel like history ate me alive. And nobody and nothing noticed."

"I'm here. We need to take a walk tomorrow."

"I knew whores once. Were you ever . . . I'm not trying to be insulting, but . . . it's like even I could sleep with you. Everyone could sleep with you." Jayne wanted to insult Naomi just enough to push her away.

"I'm perfectly adaptable," Naomi said. Jayne wondered then if Naomi started life as a man, but those operations were illegal now.

But then, so was unlicensed teaching for money.

Naomi rose from the chair and nodded at Jayne, then left her. Jayne realized she hadn't told Naomi that Patrick Drury, the news agent, also approached Heightfield.

Jayne went to emergency tutoring. She picked four of her best students: a young mechanic named Phillipe, who knew enough about computers to run her home work routines but not enough English to run them without correction; Roxanne, a fourteen-year-old Appalachian girl who was a maid in a Prospect Park house; Popcorn, a probably quadroon guy who seemed to deal in car parts; and an old woman, well into the years where suicide was permitted for mere obsolescence, who called herself Nana. Nana just wanted to learn Spanish for fun.

Nana was afraid of turning on computers, but once the machine and program was set up, she and Phillipe could work as a team on Jayne's home work while Jayne tutored Roxanne in standard dialect English.

"Ah cain't speak like this at home," Roxanne said.

"They'da make fun a'me." The past tense was a bare-breathed thing between the *they* and *make*. Jayne knew all dialects with adequate lexicons were equal, but this girl couldn't get a good service job without more prestigious English.

Roxanne bent over the tape recorder, speaking the diphthong drills, not the broad vowels, "I," not "Ah." She played them back.

Nana looked up from the computer, and said, "Much better, dear."

Roxanne said, *"Tu madre,"* Spanish picked up on the street or back in some Southern mill town where the West Virginians leaving the played-out mines met the Mexicans leaving played-out fields.

Popcorn said, "Yeah, talking the Man's English."

Jayne said, "I'm not forcing you. You're paying to be here."

"Could go to a skill doctor and get motor-trained on something legal, but no, I gotta pick up proper English so as to deal with the ecological chop shops down Philly."

Nana, not missing a keystroke, said, "We don't want to hear about that, Popcorn."

"Well, I never been saying it, then."

Jayne wondered, not for the first time, if Nana was a senior teacher assigned to observe her during this job.

Meanwhile, Naomi and Patrick Drury came in and out of the house, Naomi seducing Patrick away from Jayne's room, taking him out for serious talks when Jayne had her students visit the house, letting him pry through Jayne's things when Jayne was gone. The house smelled faintly of Clorox and musk.

A thoroughly professional seductress, Naomi left Jayne feeling sexually stunned, then anxious. While the brain didn't recognize a rival, the body did.

Patrick Drury thought he'd found the perfect informant in Naomi. He sat in on one of Harry's at-home days, a day where nothing illegal got spoken though hints of the illegal drifted slantwise through the conversations.

Jayne and Heightfield found themselves tangled in bed as though the chlorine and musk rotted their brains like erotic gas. *Precisely,* Jayne thought as her body went irrational on her. Then she lay sweating by Heightfield, who seemed to have taken her passion as life rendering his code. *Another woman was getting it, and I had to compete with her.*

If Naomi started as a woman. Naomi so seduced her news agent that Jayne again wondered if she'd been born male to play with guy fantasies so well.

Heightfield carefully removed the condom from his cock, then held it pinched shut as he took it to the toilet. "I saw them floating out at sea when I was a boy," he said. "Like miniature angels waving in the water. I wonder where they go now."

"They burn them," Jayne said. She hadn't really wanted an affair with Heightfield, especially not after he'd told her the news agent approached him, too, but the come and musk odors spoke straight to her body. Competition, and so she competed, but the mind outfoxed the ovaries this time.

Renee dead, Harry seemed shattered, watching Naomi with the news agent, Jayne with Heightfield. He brought over the squatter woman one night and they squabbled all through breakfast. Then he wasn't there nights.

While Naomi wove her seductions, Ocean sent word that Jayne should slip out of the house, not telling anyone, especially not Heightfield.

But Ocean wanted me to love him.

A baby, a lover, Jayne abandoned them both. She took Heightfield's disks with her. *Forever on a glass rose's petals.*

Her Appalachian student, Roxanne, likened memories that circled forever in one's mind to a banjo playing in the back of the brain, hard over soft, steel over cat skin.

And in memory for comfort and for lust, Heightfield. And

Jayne couldn't find out whether he felt bitter or if being abandoned was the usual course of things for him.

"He went back home," Ocean said when she brought Jayne to her own home. Jayne stalked around angry until she finally cried.

11
"Her Life and Times as a Mainstream Honky"

Then in the next decade, people began to hack media, rearranging the plots. Occasionally, a diamond landscape appeared in the background, or a cliff poured itself into a glass bowl while the heroine did the unexpected. Jayne wondered if Heightfield himself was responsible or if he'd influenced others.

Then that stopped—those responsible busted or converted. Jayne wished she knew for sure.

Fifteen years after her stay in Brooklyn, thirteen years of living in Philadelphia, Jayne took off from her students and her cover job to spend two days walking. She saw a white rose translucent in front of the rising sun, and wondered if she still had Heightfield's movie-filled rose. She began reconstructing her time in Brooklyn. Remembering took the raw events and sorted them to an order she could live with. Finally, this time, forever, perhaps, until the next thing that evoked memory from a different angle.

On the second day, between West Philadelphia and Third and Delancey, memories and present sights played back and forth in Jayne's head. She couldn't erase the past even by living beyond it. If she walked away now, however she'd remembered the past, the news agents would have their own version of her past and could always hold her legally accountable for it. But the present opened onto dogwood, small-flowered magnolias, and Belgian block pavers in colonial streets. She'd always found older American cities the most comfortable. Places where people had lived under regimes before democracy and automobiles reminded Jayne that people would live on through whatever the future brought.

As she walked back from Center City, one of her last year's students, a city dancer who took classes to be able to check his accountant's work, saw her on the street. "Whatcha been doing?"

"Thinking about when I lived in New York," she said, wondering if he was doing better because of her classes but unsure about asking.

"New York. Why'd you leave?

Jayne said, "Philadelphia's like lunch."

Her former student boggled for a moment, then said, "Yeah, and New York is a party. All the important things happen there first."

But I'd rather skip parties and have lunch than skip lunch and have parties. Jayne didn't tell her former student this, just smiled, and said, "I didn't live in New York. I lived in Brooklyn."

She lived four blocks away from the warehouses on Lancaster where the ecological chop shop and Data Reverse Engineers did business disguised as illegal dance halls. Jayne taught the chop guys who weren't crackers basic literacy, as tedious as anarchist rhetoric could get, and some computer skills that the crackers found too basic to mention. The collaboration between the chop-shop street crews and the crackers seemed odd, but one of the guys who did disassembly on data and car parts said cracking didn't pay all the bills.

And so home to the third-floor walk-up with a tiny balcony overlooking two-hundred-year-old houses. Four blocks north, Mantua was now urban mall, mixed-use apartments, stores, and trolleys. A short block of nineteenth-century two-story slum houses survived inside the large building as history and playground for children whose parents worked and lived in the mall. The mall complex was almost fifty years old and had begun to resemble the old Mantua, with dead whores in the service passageways.

But Jayne's neighborhood hadn't changed visibly since the rehabilitations of the 1980s, only more cable under the street, more central air in the apartments, more photoelectric cells on the roofs.

All that memory exhausted her. Jayne locked her apartment door and braced it against anyone who might kick in a door during the night.

But the central air wasn't on yet, so Jayne opened her windows. Through the night, she heard the chipping noise the repointing robots made as they climbed her building brick by brick, nicking away corroded mortar and smoothing in new plastic stuff that was supposed to last thirty years and be utterly watertight. And as far as she knew, they could be laying communications bugs and wires. Jayne never discussed anything illegal at home.

All stations could be temporary. Home was as long as it lasted. *I should get sleep; I have too much to do.* Jayne listened to the chipping robots for hours before she could get to sleep.

Her sister Carolyn e-mailed Jayne Sidna's phone number. Carolyn, still in North Carolina, had married a man who'd forgiven her Jayne's out-of-wedlock pregnancy. Jayne never understood why this made Carolyn so grateful. Carolyn, who seemed afraid to visit earlier, decided now was right for a trip to Philadelphia. And they could both see Sidna.

Jayne, who'd visited home on a regular basis as ordered by

her superiors in illegal education, agreed, but put Carolyn off. She was working putting together visuals for a graphics-news company, but she had her weekends and evenings free. It would make more sense to have Carolyn visit when she wasn't teaching, but Jayne felt that while her sister's visit would be a minor stress during school time, it would ruin her holiday.

After two weeks, the usual subliminal terror of being busted faded, leaving the older terrors Jayne thought she'd forgotten: the fear of being the scapegoat, the certainty that the reasonable adults around her would suddenly start chanting again, against her. Being illegal balanced her with a real fear, a real resistance. Being just another citizen threw Jayne off-balance.

The fear returned with the classes. She walked into the back courtyard of the ecological chop shop under the canopy of old bedsheets and painters' cloths and looked at the strangers in the group, then at the students she'd worked with before. Spies possible among the first; ingrates among the repeats.

Holding the laser pointer and mouse, she opened with a variant of the Big Speech since some of the students had heard the Big Speech before.

"I hope you can all get out of this what you want. From those of you who've had classes here before, you know I want you to test up and do better economically. If what you got was more money, then I hope you learn to get even more money after this class.

"But that isn't all there is. I want to bring you certain freedoms, too."

Jayne looked at them more closely. One of the guys who'd just learned to read last year was paring his nails with the knife on his tool set. She decided that was enough of the Big Speech.

And so, into the material. *Rhetoric and its discontents*, thought Jayne.

*   *   *

After her classes started up again at the ecological chop shop and the paranoia settled back to its usual dim whine, Jayne e-mailed Carolyn back with a full plan for the visit and went out and bought an air mattress, one of the big thick ones, for Carolyn to sleep on. Then she purged her computer of all news-code hacks and kept looking out for people who'd bust her anyway.

Five nights that summer, Jayne dreamed about the son that she'd never seen. And Carolyn wasn't ready to visit quite yet. Family matters.

At night, Jayne watched bats ambush bugs drawn to the streetlights, the bats flying through the lit spaces with their backs to the electric glare. Red-tailed hawks screamed around the sky over the Art Museum. Philadelphia seemed to be retreating from the prong Nature sent through Fairmont Park. Bats, opossums, deer, foxes, raccoons with opposable thumbs—all lived in Philadelphia now.

Jayne amused herself thinking that raccoons would evolve against human selective pressure. Those clever hands that sprung traps could do even more. She sometimes wished she'd been born far in the future as a superintelligent raccoon. Or perhaps she could have been born just far enough in the future where things were different than the present with its restrictions, its petty meanness. Jayne's ideal, though, would be to live in a loop that went from 1963 to 1972 over and over, without leaving.

In September, Carolyn e-mailed to say she could finally get away. Would arriving day after tomorrow be a problem?

Jayne e-mailed back: *No, I've had the mattress since spring. Is my nephew coming?* Carolyn said she never traveled without her son. Jayne sent the instructions she kept for visitors who'd be arriving either by train or airplane. Either way, they ended up at Thirtieth Street Station and transferred to either a jitney or a pedicab from there. Or walked, but Jayne didn't imagine Carolyn would walk.

Outlaw with family and obligations. Jayne's life varied dramatically from a media outlaw's, but most real outlaws she'd known spent time buying toys for their families.

But in the end, her nephew didn't come. Carolyn made vague excuses from Thirtieth Street, but Jayne suspected that the family feared she'd make too big an impression on the boy. Carolyn took a cab. When the buzzer sounded, Jayne went downstairs to let Carolyn in. Her sister looked nervous on the ground, but as they walked up the stairs to Jayne's apartment, Carolyn looked even more uncomfortable.

When Carolyn saw Jayne's apartment, she burst into tears. Jayne didn't want to understand, but Carolyn said, "It's so little."

"But I have a balcony," Jayne said. She wondered what Carolyn would have thought if she'd seen the loft buildings on Lancaster.

"And you don't have any protection service."

"I buy students' cards from time to time," Jayne said. "You have to have one to activate a university police box." She only did that when she was out late.

"Can I use your system?" Carolyn asked.

Jayne had removed all the secondary data disks that she used for teaching. Carolyn shouldn't notice anything about Jayne's subscriptions either. She set Carolyn up in e-mail and watched her sister type the numbers for a suburban address.

Sidna. Jayne felt like her sister was using her to see Sidna and wondered why Carolyn hadn't gone straight to a place where she'd feel more comfortable.

"Could you have stayed with Sidna?"

Carolyn looked around the apartment and fixed her eyes on Jayne's secondhand futon chair. "If I stay here, I'll be sleeping on that?"

Sidna wasn't in. Jayne said, "You can sleep on that or the air bed. Let me show you the balcony." The space seemed suddenly way too small. As they stepped out on the balcony,

Carolyn said, "The houses are too close together. Do you have rats?"

"Not here." Jayne did see rats in the other streets near the warehouses. She opened the balcony door. She wanted to change the subject as suddenly as possible. "How's the family?"

"You'd worry them a lot less if you didn't live here," Carolyn said. "Dad's been retired."

"Oh."

"Yeah, they retired him early. He's trying to get permission to start his own business."

Jayne realized her dad was in his sixties, but couldn't remember exactly when he was born. "I hope they let him."

"Why don't you go back to live with them? It would be cheaper for all of us."

"Why?"

"Because then you could be there to take care of them if anything happened." Carolyn looked at the balcony door turn-bolt as if trying to weld it shut, then went to the terminal to see if Sidna's machine had replied to her. It had sent a time when she'd be running a voice program. Jayne said, "If I can find my microphone."

"Don't you use voice?"

"Not particularly," Jayne said. Her sister had some serious reasons to want to see her old one-eyed Judas girl leader. Carolyn had a problem and was turning to Sidna for help. Jayne realized she'd forgotten that people like her sister had problems they took as seriously as the outlaws took the threat of jail. They weren't used to life-threatening problems, so they made the most of the ones they had.

Sidna lived in Chestnut Hill. Jayne had never been to Chestnut Hill the whole time she'd lived in Philadelphia, but Carolyn was paying her way by taxi and suburban train.

What they passed was ordinary Philadelphia—half bombed-out, half an amusement city for people who couldn't afford New York. But seeing it through Carolyn's eyes, it looked monstrous, broken-out windows and buildings coated in ads, then streets full of people who kept to themselves in tiny enclaves they'd carved out of abandoned buildings. Finally, the train went through sections of row houses where the rich were block-busting in reverse, buying up small houses and tearing the houses down for bigger new houses and streets. Jayne suspected that Carolyn approved, but she didn't want to ask.

When they got beyond the edge of gentrification, Carolyn said, "This looks better." The houses looked like they'd been well taken care of since the Civil War. "Sidna said it wasn't like Philadelphia, at all, really."

"But it's really part of the city," Jayne said. "If the slums had expanded, they'd be up to here by now."

The slums had stopped expanding when people who would have moved to Philadelphia couldn't do things like that anymore. Not that people didn't sneak in. Jayne suspected her own permissions to live in Philadelphia were dubious, but she was qualified as a computer-tech home worker, was white, had been born into middle management.

"Here," Jayne said. Carolyn got up before the train stopped, just as though she'd been conditioned to stand when someone said, 'here.' The station was in a shopping district filled with people who looked like they didn't belong to Jayne's Philadelphia. Center City was over somewhere, and West Philadelphia wasn't something they thought about. The shops around the train station looked prosperous, as though nothing had changed since the twentieth-century, revisionist chrome and plate glass. No rock-throwers out here. From the middle of the twenty-first on through the turn of the century had been their kind of time.

Carolyn said, "Now this is where you should be living."

"I'd have to have a car. I can walk to all my clients," Jayne said. "I don't need a car."

"But if you had a car, you could live out here." Jayne had

to admit it was pretty, but she'd never owned a car in her life and suspected she'd be a terrible driver now.

Sidna picked them up in a car that looked like something out of the 1950s: big, winged, boxy, dual-fueled, and poky. She got out of the car without taking off her dark glasses and stood with her arms wrapped around herself waiting for them to come across the parking lot to her car. Jayne thought that to Sidna, turning forty was a curse. The world had shifted around her.

So this is what an aged Judas Girl looks like. You've lost an eye, and it isn't fashionable anymore. The younger girls have security chips that don't require mutilation.

As soon as Carolyn opened the car door, both she and Sidna seemed to relax. Jayne felt disguised as a usual person, an outlaw in a dress at church, sweating at the preacher.

"I've had the work done at Sheie," Sidna said. Jayne knew immediately that the work was something cyberbionic that fed visual data into the optic nerve and that Sidna's operation wasn't quite successful.

Carolyn looked at her sister and shrugged the slightest of shrugs. *I came to Philadelphia for my own binocular vision.* "Fish and salamanders can regenerate their optic nerves," Sidna said, a comment that would have sounded insane if Jayne hadn't already guessed the context. The natural world with its oozy regrowing mocked Sidna. Jayne wondered if Sidna had her blind technical eye replaced after the surgeons failed to restore vision to her left eye. She also wondered about all the various people who'd watched through it, whether they'd been bored most of the time, what kind of person saw that younger version of herself shrink away from Sidna at the party.

Carolyn asked, "Can they try again?"

If not, a rude question. Jayne was still tempted to ask if they'd put the artificial eye back in.

"I'm taking steroids through my eye. I think I know how a man feels," Sidna said as she gave the car's ignition her fin-

gerprints. Before they pulled completely into traffic, she said
to Jayne, "I know where your son is."

Jayne felt her whole body turn robotic. "For how long?"

"Since Carolyn told me we should look each other up,"
Sidna said. She'd used her contacts to get something on
Jayne in case she ever did have to deal with her. "We could
get you together," Sidna said. "He lives in New York City."

Jayne wanted to ask if Sidna had ever looked him up, or
sent a Judas Girl to broadcast the face. "Have you talked to
him, yourself?"

"No. Why would I? You're his mother. You should talk to
him. He's as unrealistic as you are."

Jayne found herself hoping her son had not gone into illegal teaching, and that wish, rising suddenly, frightened her.
"How so unrealistic?"

"He thinks he can run for office."

"That works for local political offices," Jayne said.

"He's meat," Sidna said. "A program is as predictable as
its committee. Committees are more predictable than single
individuals. Committees can watch each other."

Carolyn got in the front with Sidna; Jayne got in back.
Sidna backed and wheeled round, pointing her good eye just
over Jayne's head, then swiveling around to use the rearview
mirror. The car moved through the commercial district and
then into the neighborhoods. Sidna's house was a two-story
brick set closer to the street than Jayne expected. The garage
was camouflaged to look like more rooms, with tables and
lamps showing in the street-side windows. They drove
around back and into it.

First a mudroom, with bootjacks and a potting bench, then
the kitchen. Jayne thought it was a predictable layout and noticed that the dirt on the potting bench looked dusty. They
went on into the kitchen and began milling around looking at
each other, Carolyn and Sidna talking about other Judas Girls
they knew and what had happened to them. Jayne realized she
hadn't heard about Sidna's children. No children then.

Sidna's husband, Jack, stuck his head in the door about then. The husband looked at the women as though suspecting them of gossiping about him, and backed away. He looked like a freeze-dried version of the kid he'd been at the wedding. Only now he had a one-eyed barren wife.

"Carolyn, you'll stay for supper, of course," Sidna said, as though Jayne would equally of course find her own way back to Powelton Village.

Though neither Carolyn nor Sidna had mentioned it, Jayne realized that Carolyn would be having her own eye worked on at Sheie and trusted that Jayne, the poor sister, would nurse her afterward.

The old Judas Girls wanted their eyes and the strict lifestyles back both at the same time. Eye surgery and reaction. But if the old regime hadn't been so restrictive of technology, perhaps this operation could have been perfected sooner.

Perhaps in most people's lives, the restrictions were still as bad as they'd ever been, only Jayne had escaped them by living in a subculture where prison's only threat was dying of a disease, never the stigma of having been jailed. A person who'd survived prison in some circles was more desirable than someone who had never been tested that way: superior stock, strong disease resistance, and tough enough to win whatever fights came down.

The light slanted into the approaching evening and made everything look dramatic. Carolyn said, "Sure we'll stay for dinner."

"Unless Jayne has other plans. What, no classes tonight?"

"I don't teach." Jayne felt fortunate that Sidna hadn't noticed her before now.

"Oh." The tone was, *I don't believe you; I don't not believe you. Perhaps you washed out as an outlaw teacher.*

When the women began to make dinner, the husband sat down on a stool by the porch door to watch them. Sidna had the whole array of cooking toys: pesto mortar, Mouli food mill, bread machines and kneading troughs, marble slabs and candy-pulling hooks. "Jayne, could you get the broth out of the freezer and thaw it after I finish with the fish heads?"

Japanese suribachi, the proper knives and scissors for anything from chicken to sashimi to boning lamb legs. Jayne couldn't imagine that Sidna tediously used all these hand tools, but Sidna pulled down the food mill and put some fish heads in the microwave. So this was the suburban thing—microwave and hand preparation.

The conversation stopped as if everyone was listening to the fish brains cooking out the horrors of being caught. The husband stared at Jayne's belly as though he'd heard about her out-of-wedlock child. The microwave binged. Jayne thought about pretending not to know how to use a microwave anymore, but went ahead and thawed the soup. She noticed that Carolyn wasn't the person asked to help.

Without being asked, though, Carolyn did set the table while Sidna whisked ground fish heads and various spices and fluids into the broth. The husband moved over to the dining-room table as Carolyn called for Jayne to help her by bringing in the soup plates. Jayne had expected them to be warmed before using at the table, but Sidna didn't seem that particular. Sidna carried the tureen in by herself. Jayne wondered if she was supposed to do heavy lifting so soon after surgery. Carolyn moved to help her with it.

Jack didn't offer to help at all. He still had a barren one-eyed wife. The place reeked of no children. Jayne wondered if they were child-free by choice, but it didn't feel like that. Jack said, "I'll serve." He kept looking at Jayne, who found her arms had folded themselves reflexively over her breasts. *Cover us from him.* Carolyn sat down, but Jayne found herself locked in Jack's gaze. She felt that he saw her as a way to humiliate his wife. And she suspected he thought she'd cooperate. No, he knew she'd cooperate. *Arrogant bastard.*

Sidna said, "Well, sit down, Jayne." Jayne sat down near Sidna, which seemed to surprise both husband and wife. *No matter what I think of her, I won't be used as an accessory to his nastiness.* She felt more sexually skittish than she'd actually been last time she'd been a virgin.

Carolyn said, "Jayne, I'd like to ask you if I could have you help me through the operation."

Why not ask these people to help? Isn't she one of your Judas sisters? I don't have the time; I don't want these people in my life, Jayne wanted to say, but she couldn't be that cruel. "Why didn't you ask me at home?" Carolyn didn't reply. Sidna and Jack looked at the food, each other, the soup tureen. Because Carolyn wanted witnesses if Jayne did say no. *I'm either going to be decent about it, or a bitch.* "My apartment's such a small place."

"It's near Sheie," Sidna said. "We'll help you."

"Oh?"

"I know you think I made your teen years difficult," Sidna said. "But I thought I was doing the right thing. And we tried to bring you into the group." Carolyn nodded.

Maybe childhood is over and I've been carrying a grudge too long? "Okay, but when?"

"I've got an appointment to be examined Monday," Carolyn said. "I arranged that when I was in North Carolina after I got the group newsletter."

A newsletter full of the doings of old Judas girls with their search for renewed vision and morality, Jayne thought. "Okay." Her parents would approve. So would Ocean. "But has anyone gotten back full vision?"

"In Japan," Jack said. "Did Sidna tell you she'd located your son?"

"In New York," Jayne said.

"It must have been brutal to have given away a child," Jack said.

"Not really," Jayne said. "I was relieved, actually." She wasn't sure she spoke accurately, really.

Sidna said, "I hope he never hears that."

Jack said, "The eye operation requires a lot of licensed biotech. But the Judicious Girls are paying for it."

"I can't believe people's parents let girls have an eye removed in the first place," Jayne said, fairly reckless now. Why did conservatives draw out her most radical side?

"It was for our protection," Sidna said.

Jack said, "Chinese people bound their daughters' feet to make them more attractive."

*To make girls feel vain about being seen through. To make girls feel important, that their safety and virginity matter more than full eyesigh*t. Jayne thought about the watchers, bored, possibly contemptuous, watching the monitors full of girls' glances. She said, "Binding girls' eyes." What a horror to have been the most important Judas Girl in high school, then to grow up.

"I wanted to try it," Sidna said, her voice very tired. Jayne wondered how she patched her life together these days, cooking, doing whatever. Sewing would be difficult with only one eye, but perhaps one could adapt.

"I learned a lot about my wife before I married her," Jack said.

Jayne said, "If you knew how to evaluate what you saw."

"Are you really that cold about your son?" Carolyn said. "Mother talks about him, wonders how he is."

Jayne wouldn't confess her ambiguity. "I'm really that cold."

Sidna said, "Don't worry about the dishes. I'll call service for that."

The people who did service for Sidna's neighborhood must have been on her street when they got the call. Or prepared for the call and waiting. The dinner party sat around talking about more Judas Girls while Jayne leaned back in her chair and wondered if they'd be leaving before service arrived. But the doorbell rang promptly, and a man and two women in black uniforms came in. They moved like the puppeteers in Japanese puppetry—visible but not calling attention to themselves. Jayne recognized one of them as the woman took her plates away. Jayne had taught her and doubted the woman could test out. Obviously, the woman hadn't. So, this was the work the woman was fitted to. Just before the woman reached the kitchen door, she stuck her fingers into the leftovers on Jayne's plate and scooped some of them to her mouth.

The two others scurried around the kitchen, quickly cleaning, washing dishes, going through the refrigerator and taking out all the items past pull-date. As the woman Jayne taught ate Jayne's scraps, she looked over her shoulder and saw Jayne was staring at her. She stared back at Jayne. Jayne felt embarrassed for noticing anything.

One of them, really, the woman's eyes implied. Jayne wanted to deny it, but what had the teaching been for the woman? Just another humiliation, this time one the woman had to pay for. Jayne looked over and saw Sidna smiling slightly. She looked from Jayne to the woman, who vanished into the kitchen with more plates.

Sidna said, "She seemed to know you."

"I know lots of people in West Philly," Jayne said.

"Like the people at Thirty-ninth and Lancaster," Sidna said like a woman who'd lost a car and knew where it went but couldn't prove it.

"They run a dance hall. I suppose it's unlicensed."

Sidna leaned her head back and flared her nostrils. "So. You'll take care of your sister."

"I'll take care of my sister while she's recovering from surgery."

"Jayne's apartment is almost nice," Carolyn said, "but it's so tiny." Jayne wondered if Carolyn would want her to rent something bigger during this eye surgery.

"Carolyn can't afford to pay for attendants afterward," Sidna said, "so you won't need a larger place. And it's close to the hospital."

"HMOs don't cover that. It's experimental," Jack said, meaning, *I paid for it, and she's still half-blind and sterile.*

"The Judicious Girls can't get the best surgeons and have

anything left over for aftercare. Our resources are limited," Carolyn said.

"So I'll be the unpaid attendant," Jayne said. She wondered if the crew in the kitchen could overhear them. She imagined their thoughts, *Not really a worker, just another middle-manager bitch who screws up but who still gets to avoid service detail.*

Sidna said, "But she's your sister." A middle-manager-class girl who fucked down. Jayne wondered where Mick was now and what he had thought of her when she used him to get pregnant. "I've already bought an air bed. I guess I can let Carolyn have the bed."

"We could buy a real bed," Carolyn said. "You've just got a futon thing."

"So when were you thinking of having this surgery done?" Jayne asked.

"The doctor said he could do it next week," Carolyn said. "Otherwise, I'd have to come back in November."

Jayne leaned back and closed her eyes. She had her cover job and classes to teach. Maybe the weather would heat up again and Carolyn would buy her an air conditioner. Maybe Carolyn would feel differently about life when she could see in three dimensions.

"Great. Okay, okay." Sidna said, "We'll be over to help." Jayne opened her eyes to see Jack wink at her. He reminded her of the cadet she'd helped kill in Charleston.

During the next couple of days, Sidna began behaving civilly to Jayne, asking her over with Carolyn. Jayne tried to dodge the engagements. She had her work, her students, and didn't want to spend time with her childhood bully.

But Sidna and Jack finally met her for lunch the day before Carolyn's surgery while Carolyn was in for preop testing. And Jayne began to wonder if her memories of childhood were as real as she'd thought.

"So it comes to wondering who was the villain of the

piece," Jayne said, crumbling bread into the juice left on her plate. She was across the table from her old bully and a guy who reminded her of a cadet dying on the windshield of the car she'd been driving.

How had that really happened? Jayne was sure the cadet had died looking at her—only that she had the vivid memory in her head next to an image of Suzanne walking in a long coat under Spanish moss with a gun in her pocket, something Jayne had never seen, she didn't think, but the false-memory image was as vivid as what she remembered of the real death.

"What are you thinking about, Jayne?" Jack asked.

"Nothing much," Jayne said, aware that she was lying and feeling slightly guilty about her suspicions of them. But then, she knew she was tired, sneaking around to rearrange student schedules while Carolyn and these people poked into her life.

False memories. Perhaps all four of them twisted high-school memories, breeding monsters out of images others might correct as total fabrications.

Here, then in the past, Sidna's eyes moving over the party, Sidna blending with Suzanne, dominatrixes both, in their own ways. Powerful among women, what an odd fate the Judas Girls had, but only powerful among middle-class and upper-middle-class girls, watched by half-insane guys working their way through college.

How much attention did anyone really pay to those monitors? Jayne suspected the whole thing deteriorated into a fraud only a few years after it was started. As a mutilating initiation ritual, taking girls' left eyes out to install monitoring devices hadn't lasted as long as binding girls' feet or female circumcision. Now the monitoring devices read off the optic nerves, maybe didn't exist at all. Perhaps the whole thing had simply been to trick women into being mean to each other and making fools of themselves.

"I was afraid you would refuse to take care of Carolyn," Sidna said.

"She's my sister," Jayne said. Her people wanted her to have strong family ties.

When Carolyn went in for surgery, Sidna drove them both to the in-patient procedure unit and put her car in the free garage for the duration.

"Let's walk back to your apartment and wait until they call us," Sidna said. "We have plenty of time before they bring Carolyn up from recovery. And then she'll be there for two days."

Jayne really didn't want to spend time with Sidna. She had other things to do. "My apartment is awfully small."

"So I've heard," Sidna said. She made a move to take Jayne's arm in hers but didn't force it when Jayne stepped back. When they reached Lancaster, Sidna looked up the street at the warehouses, then at Jayne.

Jayne said, "They have dances there, from time to time."

Sidna said, "I wondered where those were in relation to where you live."

"Not far," Jayne said, turning onto Baring. Neither spoke again until they'd walked to Jayne's apartment.

Sidna went straight for the terrace and opened the door. "It is beautiful here, really," she said. "Your neighbors seem to care."

"I've always thought so."

"Houses are still cheap here. Have you thought about buying one?"

"No."

Sidna sat looking west from the doorway and didn't say more, just sat, gradually making the silence uncomfortable. Jayne wondered where the surgeons were in Carolyn's eye socket.

"Could you bear a child for us?" Sidna asked. "You could buy a house with what we could pay you."

Jayne wondered for an instant if Sidna thought she'd sleep with Jack, then laughed.

"No. Seriously. Look at your life. You're working yourself to exhaustion just to live here. We could offer you a chance to own property. You could get a protection license and rent rooms to students."

"Why would you ask me? We didn't like each other."

"I'm trying to help your sister. It's an opportunity for you."

"No."

Sidna slumped over and picked at her shoes, then looked back at Jayne, who was standing in the kitchen. "I can't imagine that you took us all that seriously."

"I was scared of you. As a child."

"Well, thank you for that," Sidna said. She turned her attention back to her shoes, took them off, and began picking at her toenails. Her feet looked as though they'd been half-bound, deformed little toenails twisted up. "I'm supposed to be a mother."

Jayne, feeling reckless, said, "I'm not supposed to be one."

"Little drug sluts can breed, and I can't."

"So why do you want me to bear your child?"

"You'd just provide the womb."

"Fuck off."

"I can do you more damage than you know. And I can shield you."

"You want me to carry your child to term for that attitude?" Jayne felt her body stiffen, all the little minor pains fade as adrenaline whipped through her. "And you ask me this while I'm taking care of my sister, who wouldn't have had this stupid problem if she hadn't admired you so much."

Sidna put her shoes back on, and said, "Guess it wasn't such a good idea after all." She pushed by Jayne and went into the living room and pulled out a virtual rig, goggles and gloves. She sat down in Jayne's best chair and pulled them on. Like a mime, she gestured through the air, blind in both eyes, for the moment.

Jayne wondered why Sidna didn't just get a one-eyed goggle.

*   *   *

The new artificial eye in Carolyn's head looked like a real Judas Girl eye, the iris realistic, the white a bit too clear, no blood vessels to match the bruised eyelids.

Carolyn saw light as soon as the doctor removed her bandage.

"Your mind will have to learn how to use it," the nurse said. "Seeing light is a good sign."

Sidna said, "I know after this morning that you've been gloating at us, half-blind . . ."

Jayne sighed and look away. She doubted this was other than another experiment, at her sister's expense, and dreaded the emotional letdown Carolyn would be facing.

"No, Sidna, I never gloated. Do you miss your eye now, or the power?"

Carolyn said, "Please don't fight. I want to recover in peace."

Jayne thought Carolyn could have done a better job of that if she hadn't brought Sidna into the deal, but then Carolyn undoubtedly trusted Sidna better than she trusted her own sister, who'd been so embarrassing when they were all younger.

"Sidna asked me to bear her a baby," Jayne said. "I guess that's why Jack was leering at me."

Sidna said, "In vitro. We were offering you a chance to get the down payment on a house. This isn't a surprise to Carolyn."

Suddenly, that was tempting, but Jayne knew she could be moved or have to leave Philly at any moment. Perhaps she should be leaving now. She had the strange urge to flee, leave for a contact point and never call home again, but felt it was just from the stress of overworking.

Carolyn said, "Jayne, was that so terrible a thing to ask? You didn't think about any of us when you got pregnant the first time."

"Maybe you should stay with Sidna while you're recovering."

Sidna said, "You'd be welcome, Carolyn," as though Jayne was being impossible.

"I'm going to see again, I'm sure. I want you to be happy for me, Jayne. You're my sister."

Jayne felt bullied, yet guilty. Her pregnancy back in the past had embarrassed her sister and made Carolyn also a target for teasing and gropes, but Jayne's stomach turned with the idea of Sidna's genes in her uterus, or of her ova taking in Jack's sperm. Did Sidna even have ova for an implant? Crippled eye, crippled ovaries—probably that was it, or she wouldn't have cared that Jayne's child turned out well. "It was a mistake then. I can't see any reason to repeat it."

Sidna said, "And you were cold to give your child away without regrets."

"No, I didn't regret it. People then had me convinced I couldn't do anything with my life alone, much less with a child. Even if I'd moved to a haven."

Sidna said, "You can't say that you *have* done anything with your life." She smiled, *gotcha*. Jayne couldn't defend herself without admitting to breaking numbers of restrictive code-and-licensing laws. And even if Sidna knew what a good teacher Jayne could be, that only proved Jayne was dangerous. What was being an unlicensed teacher?

Carolyn said, "If we'd known you'd have turned such a prude in your middle age, I wouldn't have told Sidna it would be okay to ask."

"It wasn't okay to ask," Jayne said, feeling stubborn but shaky. Money to do something else with. She almost asked how much. Then she remembered how nasty Sidna had been to her as a girl and the temptation abruptly died. Carolyn began heaving. Jayne grabbed a curved pan and put it under her sister's chin, catching vomit from heaves that seemed almost like sobs. Sidna watched. Sidna didn't catch vomit.

"When I was pregnant, I threw up like this all the time," Jayne said. A nurse brought the proper medication to stop Carolyn's heaves. She said to Jayne, "I'll bring some ice."

Carolyn asked Sidna, "How much vision did you have at first?"

"None," Sidna said. Jayne realized Sidna talked Carolyn into the operation without having had any vision through her own new eye at all.

Carolyn cupped a hand over her good eye. "I can see light and shadows even now."

Practicing neural reconstruction, practicing medicine. Jayne wondered if the operation would be perfected only in time for these women to see their grandchildren as they died. Each time, a better connection. Finally, someday, the machine-woman interface would work. Then perhaps the fashion would be for extra eyes, one in the belly, one in the back of the head.

The doctors came in and admired their handiwork. They waved fingers, flashlights, and white coats, then went out chattering to each other.

Sidna said, "Do you need company?"

"I'm going to call home, tonight," Carolyn said.

"I'll drive Jayne home, then I'll come back."

Jayne decided she was tired of them, and it was time to see the old gang at the ecological chop shop again, wash the middle-class hypocrisy out of her brain. She looked again at her sister's new eye. Shouldn't they be regrowing eyes from undifferentiated cells these days?

The children who could be the makers of such eyes were growing up. If they didn't get all the stimulation and information they needed by age twelve, they'd be so tangled in catch-up that they'd never have the knowledge base for that jump into invention.

All her students ever did was try to catch up to the middle-class around them. A good goal, but not enough. For high-wire acts of the mind, people needed to start young on the lower ropes and needed, even more, to believe that the high wire was possible. Rules chilled invention, making the ideas move slowly between the minds that needed them.

"She needs to rest. We older women don't recover from these things like young girls," Sidna said. "Let's go."

When Sidna dropped Jayne off at her apartment, she realized she could just walk back to Sheie and Carolyn, but the car created a weird dislocation between her sister and where she was now. Sidna drove off. Although Jayne knew her sister had more reason to feel isolated and alone, wounded in a strange city, Jayne felt suddenly lonely, almost sorry that Sidna had driven off. She called to see if her students wanted to go back to meeting at the ecological chop shop.

The first person she called told her the guys there had been busted and chipped.

"Not a good idea to go see them," the man said. "They might think it was you who did them."

Jayne felt nervous about assembling her students anywhere, and called off her classes.

After checking her e-mail—nothing—she walked down to Lancaster and the ecological chop shop, feeling defiant about needing contact with her side, feeling like she just didn't care. Raymond, the skinny tall guy with graying hair and oil-stained fingers, answered her code knock.

"Thought you were avoiding us since the bust," he said.

"I just heard a half hour ago. When did this happen?"

"Well, last night over a car. They had us so cold we couldn't do nothing but say we were guilty. We pleaded; they chipped us and turned us loose. You moving your students out and all made me wonder if you saw it coming."

"I didn't. Man, that was quick. They chip everyone that fast?"

"Saves housing," Raymond said. "We got guys coming who can operate under oil so the chips don't register that they're out of you." Raymond pulled up his shirt to show a bruised hole and raw tattoo on his belly. "They stick it under your skin in the fat."

The warehouse behind him, usually full of disassembled cars and computers lit by banks of hanging fluorescent lights, was empty of everything except a soundstage. Otherwise, it was stripped and dark. "Busted then," Jayne said. "What are you doing?"

"Getting rehabbed for houseboys, I guess. Or something like. You never got got?"

"I've always had the feeling they know but just haven't had time to bust me yet," Jayne said. *They do know, don't they?* The news agent in Brooklyn knew.

"Don't hardly keep you in custody at all. They'll just chip you and cut you loose. The judge said chipping was more humane, that sending guys to prison was like cruel and unusual, but I think they chip you so you'll lead them to your friends."

Jayne wondered if stopping by had been a mistake. Another of the former car thieves climbed up on the stage and began playing slow riffs on a clarinet.

Raymond said, "I don't think they can hear through the fat. It's just a location device. They say they keep us tapped by satellite."

Jayne wondered if removing the chips under oil would do any good. The police still had computerized fingerprints, retina scans. If the chip didn't move, they'd find it, know who it came out of. The next time the person got busted, he'd get hit with an additional felony charge for interfering with supervision.

But then, if a person was tired of waiting for that second bust . . .

Jayne said, "My sister just had a mechanical eye put in that's supposed to feed to her visual cortex."

"One sister a Judas Girl. The other an illegal teacher. Both boss girls, really."

Jayne said, "I thought I was one of you guys."

"I didn't give you up, you know. You owe me," Raymond said. He pulled up his shirt and tapped the tattoo over his chip, then pulled his shirt back down. "We wonder if it monitors drugs. Jaycee's been trying to see."

"Taking cars off the street, you were helping the city."

Raymond looked at Jayne as though she'd just gone stupid. "All in all, your particular fuss is just something between managers. We pay you guys for the classes, but then something always happens so as it doesn't matter. News agents always want to know how we got the info we weren't supposed to have, so we have to go around and about to get retested, wait for an amnesty, see if we'll make quota. Say I apply for the retest during amnesty time, then I got news agents wondering why I thought I could pass whether I test up or fail. You still get paid, right?"

"Not that much," Jayne said.

"Somebody's getting money. Ain't you, ask questions. Me, I gotta go clean a house." He began looking for his keys and train pass on a table covered with dusty wrenches and screwdrivers and spark gap gauges. Jayne remembered when the tools were clean or oil-stained from recent work, when the whole place rang with tools on metal and loud music.

Jayne asked, "Was learning to read again totally worthless?"

"No, babe, or I would have let them have you," Raymond said. "Reading, it's okay." They walked out together, and Jayne walked back to Thirty-eighth Street and turned south toward the Sheie Eye Institute. *Neither God nor Devil* popped into her mind. She noticed she was being followed by men who dressed in black with black sneakers and data glasses, this season's fashion in news agents.

I'm about to be busted. She didn't know why, because she'd visited Raymond, because the woman she'd taught hadn't been able to escape servitude. Renee's words popped into her head, *It's always your students.* She thought about going back to her apartment, to take the bust there, not in front of her sister.

Jayne felt like she was watching herself from a distance, a tiny figure walking by the old sculptures of doctors in metal coats. She stopped for a second by the sculpture in the center of the garden, spray of parts coming together in a butterfly. The men paused, waiting. They grinned. They'd bust her anyway. She was their bad guy.

Forever in a garden . . . a green thought in a green shade . . . But Jayne couldn't turn into a plant. And so out, not looking at them again, to see her sister as though nothing was going to happen until it did.

Jayne wondered why family felt like any kind of refuge, but any other kind of running would only get more people put under suspicion. She was their bad guy, and they were very pleased with themselves following her up to her sister's room. Jayne wondered if they thought her family had failed to socialize her properly and so didn't care that this might upset her sister. Maybe her sister wouldn't be upset to see Jayne busted.

Afraid that Sidna would be there to witness, afraid that her sister would approve of the bust, Jayne turned the doorknob to her sister's room. A woman who was dressed in street clothes, not a nurse, was with her sister. Sidna was not there. Jayne felt stunned by how grateful that made her feel. The news agents came in the room. Jayne noticed how much taller they were than she.

Carolyn, perhaps taunting, perhaps not knowing what was going to happen next, said, "Jayne, I can really see."

"I'm happy for you." Everyone was the center of her own universe.

Jayne waited. They were not so cruel as to read her prisoner's rights in front of her sister. In their eyes, they were the good guys.

Again, Jayne felt like she was watching this happen from above, a small woman taken into custody for teaching people skills they had no use for. Taken into custody for trying to free people from trapped lives. Taken into custody for reasons and guilts that spiraled around her. Renee's voice said almost audibly, *you get tired of waiting, of waiting to be busted again.* One of the news agents put his hand on her arm, and she nearly collapsed. "We'll let you know where we're taking your sister," they told Carolyn. "Perhaps you can get other family members to come up and help."

Just outside Carolyn's room, the world started swirling. The news agents jerked her up as she started to slump and slammed her against the wall. The people passing looked but went on.

Before finishing the beating, the agents pulled her arms behind her back and cuffed her. Hospital people—orderlies, nurses, doctors—and visitors walked by. The horror of the beating was that they didn't really lose control and beat the shit out of her. They were roughing her up; they were in control.

Three more bounces, and they were done. She walked out between them feeling as though she would vomit at any moment.

"You'll get off with probation this time, you know, because we can't prove enough."

Jayne realized that was why they beat her. They knew more than they could prove in court, and they had to punish her more than simply implanting her and turning her loose.

"My sister," she said.

"She has friends who'll take better care of her than you would," one of the news agents said. Now that the deal was done, he seemed bored. Perhaps he wanted more melodrama out of the bust, hysterical running through the streets.

Jayne kept thinking about the people passing her beating, seeing it, passing right by it.

When they arrived at the agency, one of the agents ducked her head down as Jayne got out of the car, and said, "Data entry, sigh." Now she was something to process and processing an arrest was a bore.

After a matron did a quick scan of her body and patted her down, the two agents who arrested her put her in a holding cell with a couple of unlicensed junkies and a woman who'd killed a man. The unlicensed junkies were teasing the woman who'd killed her lover. She didn't know now if she'd done the right thing, which the two skinny junkies thought was hilarious.

Jayne said nothing, wrapped her arms around herself, and sat down on a bunk, hoping the bunk didn't belong to anyone. The toilet, a steel thing like a giant cooking pot, was in the open. She needed to use it, saw that there wasn't much toilet paper left. And so had wet fingers when the matron came to take her up for retinas and fingerprints.

This time they took away her clothes and gave her a gray uniform with shoes that didn't quite fit. Another matron issued her a blanket and pillow.

"Could we have more toilet paper?" Jayne asked.

The woman said, "The junkies plugged everything up with it. We had a flood. After we get them out or you out to a private cell, we'll give you toilet paper. You're in one of those teaching frauds, aren't you? You have a lawyer."

The first question was hardly a question. The second, Jayne wasn't sure the woman was telling her she had a lawyer or asking if she had a lawyer. "I don't know."

"One's here for you, if you want."

"Yes, I suppose."

"We'll arrange it," the matron said.

About midnight, a physician's assistant came by to give Jayne a series of inoculations and prophylactic gamma globulin.

One of the junkies who'd appeared to be sleeping opened her eyes and watched the needle going in.

Before the night court arraignment and sentencing, her father came to visit her. *They brought him up here so he could be with me just after I was busted.* So the family agreed on putting her away.

But Jayne's anger dropped away. Her dad looked old and confused, and she remembered that the company he'd worked for had retired him. They sat together in a room with metal chairs and a metal table screwed into the cement floor. He'd brought a violin case. For a second, Jayne thought he'd brought it for her, then he said, "I've finally taken up the fiddle. Your mother keeps wanting to call it a violin, but . . ."

He pulled the violin out of the case, and with trembling hands, put on a brace that allowed him to hold the violin directly under his chin. "I wanted you to hear me," he said, as if this might be the last time.

Jayne nodded. He looked so old. "I'll stay for the trial," he said.

"I'm just going to plead if they'll leave me alone," Jayne said. "They'll tag me, put me on probation. I've never been busted before."

"Do what you have to," her father said. He looked fierce for a second, then held the violin in its brace against his chest and played fiddle music against the jail, against time, an awkward man playing "Farmer in the Dell," with a bow that trembled.

Jayne said, "Thank you for coming, Dad."

He looked at her across the fiddle and almost cried, then with ceremony, unscrewed the brace from the fiddle body, put it in the case, then put up the fiddle and bow. "You're my daughter. I had to."

Jayne thought, *I have a son I've never done this for.*

12
"In the Office of the Virtually Real"

By midnight, Jayne was in front of the judge. "The first sentencing is swift and lenient," the judge told Jayne. "You have good family connections, you show remorse, and have some skills. We've sold your contract for suspension to Entities, Inc."

From the small country of prison, Jayne pleaded across the borders to the other world in the rest of the courtroom. A strange young man watched her. She knew almost before he came up that he was her given-away son. The judge allowed a family visit. The young man kept coming with her father and sister.

Sidna told him. Jayne knew that, too. Family connections, the son had done well despite having a bad mother and a dumb father. She wondered if she'd like him, felt hostile that he would show up at such a time, felt guilty that she hadn't tried to raise him herself, as a whore, as an outlaw teacher. He was thin, with eyebrows that reminded Jayne of Mick's scars and a long nose, his father's poor white Anglo-Saxon face. But he wore a suit and a large thin watch on his wrist.

"I'm your son. My name's Roger. Mother, we could have had such fun on welfare together," the young man said, a fast hard quip to Jayne's stomach. "You could ruin my career."

"No, it was really better the way it was, for you," Jayne said. Her father put his arm around her waist and pulled her away from the young man.

The guards watched them all with lazy eyes, knowing Jayne was in too much shock to try anything and surrounded by good citizens, her family. If anyone tried to physically assault her, she thought the guard might do something, maybe stop it, but if these people struck her verbally, so what. The guards lived in a physical world. Jayne's stomach squirmed against the coming implantation. She wondered what diseases she'd picked up before the inoculation took effect.

Her father said, then, "He's done so well, your son. You should be proud of him."

Jayne said, "All I did was bear him and give him away." Her lips felt thick. *My family is putting me away.*

Her son said, "Entities, Inc., is a very interesting place. They do politicians."

An insane assignment for a political, Jayne thought, but then everything about her life seemed loony to her now. Entrapment? "Did you, did you help get this for me?" Her son had amazing confidence for a bastard. *They want me implanted for my own good.*

"You are my mother. I can't believe you're entirely stupid."

"I must be an embarrassment to you," Jayne said, not entirely caring, not entirely not caring. They talked at her, the words buzzing, stripped of meaning.

When the matron came to lead her away for the implanting, Jayne found herself relieved. The prisoner mode fit better than mother, daughter—embarrassment (again) to the family, even more of it than before the arrest. Being Prisoner JA45897 in the matron's hands was better.

"You'll be out in no time," the matron said, making that almost a threat, as she turned Jayne around a corner with a slight twist to Jayne's upper arm. "Your family can take you home in about three hours. You can go to work on Monday."

Jayne wondered then why the family visit before the implanting, then decided the family visit was a psychological trick, but wasn't quite sure if the trick was on her or her family.

Not quite one of those marked people yet, but now the matron took her into an anteroom with showers. "You'll shower and put on the first gown so we can get to your belly, then put the other gown over that. Pass me the clothes."

But they're my clothes, Jayne almost said. Another couple of women came in and waited for Jayne to strip and shower. "Use the purple soap just above your belly button," the matron said.

Navel, Jayne wanted to correct her, but didn't. The shower didn't have a towel, but rather a hot air blaster that Jayne played over her body before putting on the first gown, then the second. The matron handed her paper slippers, then took her by the arm and led her behind the anteroom to where three medical technicians waited with the scalpel that would open her up to the tube that would implant the homing device. Jayne noticed that the two other women guards were behind her, and a fourth woman appeared. For an instant, she wondered if fighting would make it hurt less, then she lowered her head and let the technician take away the gown that closed in back. Outnumbered, she climbed on the table and closed her eyes as one of the technicians stuck her right hand with an IV needle. Another technician, a woman, put sheets over her breasts and hips, exposing her belly. A cold tickle, then the punch of a needle. Jayne felt her belly around the navel go numb, then a tugging as they opened an entrance for the laparoscope. Something cold moved inside her and then warmed to body temperature. Jayne swore she'd be able to feel the lump forever.

They used glue to stick her together again, then moved her to a gurney. Jayne opened her eyes as a jail orderly moved her to the recovery room. She looked back to see another woman prisoner climb onto the table.

Her father came to see her in recovery. He seemed genuinely sorry that all this had to happen to her when her sister was recovering her full eyesight so well.

Jayne couldn't tell if she was remorseful or not. She was still in shock, and sleep seemed the best escape. Perhaps they arranged night court for a reason. The prisoner escaped into sleep and woke up a different category of being.

Jayne didn't know whether she wanted to tell her father she forgave him for not warning her to run or whether she wanted him to forgive her for all the family embarrassments. She fell asleep against the decision.

In her dreams, Jayne was a resident of a small country in high mountains that had a peculiar death penalty. Any residents of the country who tried to leave would be killed, but unless they did try to leave, the occupiers treated them civilly and said the occupation was for their own good.

On Monday, Jayne's probation officer, a young guy about twenty-three, came by to take her to her job. He said, "You doing okay?" as though she was just another human being recovering from minor surgery.

"They took my computer," Jayne said. "And I'm still sore."

"Don't worry, the thing's only about the size of a walnut. Think maybe they're hazelnut-sized these days. And they put them far enough in so you don't twiddle them."

"Twiddle them."

"Yeah, like find it under the skin and start twisting. Don't, but then it's probably down far enough. If you'd been a guy, they'd have implanted you below the navel, but in case you have kids, they don't want to have to operate again."

"So it's in forever," Jayne said.

"Look, you'll be monitored at random intervals, just to make sure we know where you are. We don't listen in. Can't. Sound doesn't transmit through fat all that well."

"Oh."

"And we'll shock you if you don't stay either at work, shopping in your neighborhood, or at home for the first six months. We'll discuss easing travel restrictions then."

Jayne knew every illegal act in her neighborhood. "They know at the office? Where you're taking me?"

"They'll know. You aren't the only one. The company likes to get bright people cheap."

Jayne tried to remember the times in high school where anyone ever called her bright. "I still feel numb."

"Protective trick the mind has. When you're ready to feel more, you will. Put some time between the bust and your future. You'll eventually forget you've got the monitor in your belly."

Isn't that what they want?

The building had been a high school in the twentieth century. The population it had served shrank after the Removals. and the school system sold the building. The present owners had gutted the giant shell and rebuilt around an interior courtyard filled with plants that throve in low light. Jayne could walk to work.

The building had almost no exterior windows and felt like a jail. Jayne realized she'd always known it was there but hadn't let it register on her consciousness because its semiotic messages were "big," "control," and "outside excluded." Her mind bounced off it earlier even though it had always been in her neighborhood.

Her probation offficer took her elbow to steer her through the ground-floor maze to an elevator at the core of the building. The elevator was a clear-plastic-walled pod that clung to the courtyard wall. At the fourth floor, they had a choice of doors. One opened out onto the fourth-floor Entities lobby;

the other onto the skywalk around the interior courtyard. The railing around the skywalk was not quite chest high.

Jayne wanted to ask, *Do people jump,* but resisted the temptation and followed this guy who had charge of her life into the Entities office.

The first week, Jayne did optical character recognition processing. The company was putting together the position spec for a new candidate and had scanned in quotations from Madison and Jefferson to insert into their candidate's speeches. Her other job was proofing the 3-D rendering of the candidate, making sure that the shadows fell properly in the blended shots.

The guy who was working on the congressional database said, "When you have a meat candidate, you can't really set policy properly. With an entity candidate, you get consistent policy."

The woman who was the only programmer who joined the juniors at lunch said, "We're trying to come up with a more progressive social policy."

Jayne said, "But meat candidates run for local office."

"Yeah, because they have to go to events in air," the congressional-data guy said. "Our guy is running for national office."

"We're getting some interesting sponsors," the woman programmer said. "But most of the time, it's just programming. I guess for you, it isn't even programming."

The equipment was beyond what Jayne had worked on before. She wondered if it was state-of-the-art or if she had all along been teaching her students obsolete techniques. The virtual rigs that promised to turn anyone into a data manipulator hadn't been invented. Instead, each subsystem seemed to have its own programming language and an interface to the next programming language, all of these broken into modules so that only the computer could put it all together.

Researchers found that without a minute touch of pulse

visible from time to time in the neck, a candidate was not credible. The better the illusion of meat, the better the candidate did, even if the entire voting population knew they decided between data puppets. A viable candidate breathed irregularly, sweated in outdoor rallies. Eyes had to show saccades.

Jayne found herself forgetting what she was doing in the technical challenge of optimizing the variables in the candidate's eye movements. She caught herself forgetting why she was at Entities, Inc., and thought, *They busted me to the bone.*

After a week, she joined the people who ate lunch in the commons room. The programmers and systems administrators ate in the greenhouse in two different shifts, and the five top bosses either ate in their offices or vanished into lunch meetings in restaurants miles away.

The people she worked with used odd names, perhaps even their legal names. They were bright and verbally aggressive. Frank's Eddy was the guy who ran the analysis of the *Congressional Record.* By the third week, Frank's Eddy asked at lunch, "Why did you do what you did?"

The collective question was backed by a full collection of stares. All talk stopped. Jayne wanted to model these stares, with their undercurrents of meat randomness, into the candidate and his audience when he asked a question that might trap his opponent. "Because I felt like people were being cheated out of what they were capable of learning."

Frank's Eddy asked, "Were you so educated that you could tell?"

"I was more educated than I was supposed to be."

Another tech asked, "Did it make you happier?"

Jayne wondered if she'd have been happier without what she'd learned, but she couldn't imagine lacking curiosity. "I'd have preferred it if my student hadn't turned me in."

"As long as it worked for you, then," Frank's Eddy said.

Jayne said, "Does learning always have to be practical?" She remember Heightfield's video roses.

"Why make the servants unhappy with their lot in life?" a woman dressed in long clothes said.

Jayne remembered a book she'd read, by a twentieth century writer about a pavement artist who knew the stars. "I love knowing things myself. Why would knowing something more make them unhappy?"

"A student of yours turned you in, you said," the woman in long clothes said. "Maybe he wasn't looking for pure intellectual pleasure."

"She," Jayne said. "It was a woman. She saw me at a friend of my sister's. In Chestnut Hill."

"A pickup crew, that's all your education did for her, put her on a pickup crew?" Frank's Eddy said.

Jayne remembered the long-skirted woman's name now, Andromeda, Meda. Meda said, "You're middle-class, Jayne. You wanted to confuse having a romantic outlaw life that paid halfway well with doing good."

"I did it to do good," Jayne said. She didn't want to expose her school-drug past to this woman.

The others at the table left her statement about wanting to do good hanging in the air. Jayne felt that she was dangling from it, and strangling.

The others began talking about other things, teasing Frank's Eddy about his latest girlfriend. Jayne, listening, realized things had changed if an office staffer could have a live-in girlfriend. *But weren't we the ones who changed the morals?*

"Now here you are, homing beacon and shockers in your belly forever," Meda said as they used the women's toilets. "Would you want to be hacked?"

"Why do you ask? You think I was making a living off of being an outlaw?"

"It's an interesting technical problem," Meda said, washing her hands and peeling soap out from under her nails.

Roger began visiting Jayne about twice a month. She doubted he did it to make her feel guilty for abandoning him.

What she was involved with, at Entities, intrigued him. Being meat limited a politician to offices where air appearances and small-scale deals still meant something.

Still, he seemed frustrated with his unrepentant mother. Jayne doubted it was sentiment, but rather that he had no leverage over her, no way to force her with guilt and sentiment to tell him everything about his superiors, the programmed entities.

He's my son, all right. While he intrigued her, she refused to get gooey. His side had put the spike in her belly.

After the fifth Sunday of lunches, she asked, "I'm not going to go gooey on you. Giving you up was the best thing I ever did for any human. So why do you keep coming back to Philly to take me out to dinner?"

He said, "Why do you keep coming?"

Because she was lonely without her outlaw connections? Because she was curious about what she'd spawned all those many years ago? Because she was too broke to turn down free restaurant meals?

And because Meda stalked her head offering to hack the spike. Her son was her major reason not to hack the spike, which implied sentiment. Jayne refused to be gooey about a baby who'd grown up into a stranger who took her out to lunch on Sundays. Jayne said, "I'm curious about you. This doesn't imply a maternal relationship the way you might like."

"Fair enough," Roger said. He poured her a glass of red wine and watched the waiter set up the entree. They were on Sansom Street on a block filled with restaurants and desk-ornament shops. "I couldn't imagine that you'd want to help me, could I?"

"Are you watching me just to keep me from embarrassing you?" Jayne felt cynical and hurt at the same time.

"If all I cared about was not getting embarrassed, I'd simply have you watched, Mother. Why are you being so difficult?"

"Difficult about what?"

"I'm for the community above family," her son said.

"And so am I," Jayne said. She stuck the wineglass against her teeth to avoid saying more. Why had this lunch gone here? She wished they could coax the sound waves back into their mouths. Slowly, she realized he wanted her to sabotage her work at Entities. *How terribly female to do it for my cub. Shit.*

"The spike doesn't have to be forever," he said.

She drank. He ate. Then she cut her meat while he poured wine and drank it. "Ah, man, my son," she said.

Wineglass at his mouth, he looked at her above the wine pouring into his throat. Young, aggressive, willing to fight programs with meat, what a son she'd had. She saw how others must see her, utopian dreamer with attitude.

Outside, he slipped a piece of paper in her pocket and said, "You need to meet other people."

The address her son gave her was on Lancaster Avenue, up from the former site of the ecological chop shop, a storefront filled with broken clocks, ancient computers from the last century with corroded hard drives filled with operating systems now illegal to use, and lamps without shades that took bulbs that hadn't been made in the past fifteen years or more. *In the neighborhood, so okay by the spike,* Jayne thought. Jayne rang the bell and wondered if her location was illegal even though it was within her allowed shopping perimeters.

A small man in a three-piece suit, somewhat stout, opened the door and looked at her without speakiong.

"I was given this address by a meat politician in New York," Jayne said.

"Ah, do you say so? You're spiked. I can't hack them, you know. I can only diagnose them. Come in." He left her to look over the lamps and antiques, then came back and said, "I'm ready."

Jayne lay down on an antique medical-examination table

covered with fresh paper. She thought, *a parody of the implantation,* and wondered if the various electrodes he fastened on her belly would inform on her. He looked at her, then brought an ultrasound probe against her belly, looking at the screen, not her. The spike, in her subcutaneous fat, appeared in various echo distortions.

"It doesn't broadcast continuously," the man said after turning sharply to see another display.

"I've never tried to see if it would shock me if I went out of bounds."

He manipulated a keyboard behind Jayne's head, the click of the thing echoing some signal that went out to the geosynchronous police satellite overhead. She felt a slight shock.

"What did you do? The devices that shock cost more."

"I taught illegally." *I helped kill a man; I may have helped drive a woman to suicide.* "I'm now indentured to Entities, Inc. My son wants me to help him."

"A meat bit player in today's arena. Elected officials were always puppets distracting you from what was really going on." Then he stopped talking and continued to read the data flowing through her skin, then told her she could pull down her shirt and go.

Technical people would play with the data. Jayne realized she'd met another underground. Maybe she should pretend this visit never happened. Life was going along smoothly enough. *I am not just going to be a puppet in their game.*

She and all the other spiked people on Lancaster Avenue walked under the police satellites to where they were supposed to be walking.

The following Sunday, her son took her walking. On Mantua Bridge, he said, "Forget I'm your son, if you have to. I want your help."

"Can I think about it?"

"Hell, Mother, you can even say no."

They walked through the Art Museum. Jayne realized she

hadn't been there since she'd been spiked. Her son led her to the armor displays.

She could imagine him in armor and smiled. Strange challenges young men wanted to take on—meat against the system. But then, she'd taken on the system herself in having him in the first place.

Back on Mantua Bridge, she said, "Yes."

13
Subverting the Frame

After making up her mind to help her son, Jayne did nothing further for six months. Even so, Roger began to spend more time with her. Jayne thought he must understand that with a spike in her belly, she couldn't do everything soon. He began arranging with her probation offficer to take her around the city and even up the Delaware Valley to New Hope on the archaic train. She went to the back of the train and watched the city disappear. He came and stood with her and didn't say much until they were walking from New Hope to Lambertville, eating ice cream on the bridge.

"So," Jayne said.

Her son said, "Mother, sometimes you seem almost reckless. I'm not running for anything right now."

On the way back, his cell phone rang, a woman. He turned away from his mother to answer it. But Jayne could tell by his voice that her son was sleeping with the woman and that he wanted Jayne to know. It annoyed her a bit, then she thought, *Good for him.*

The trips had a flavor of reward and of some attempt to figure her out, to get her to like him better. But then he, too, was placing his career at risk. Jayne figured that if she'd been younger and not his mother, he would have seduced her.

Jayne began to be proud of him and charmed by his combination of boldness and anxieties. He was definitely doing more than the public-relations minimum of helping his disgraceful mother. Given his curiosity about other things, Jayne read his lack of probing into illegal teaching as tact. Or self-protection. Either was good.

He said nothing more about his request, even on Mantua Bridge. She didn't either, but one spring day at work, Jayne began walking around the building at random, to see where the spike stopped her. The walking fed her restlessness. For the first time, she hated the spike.

And when she felt no twinges even at the edge of the parking lot, she felt annoyed with herself for taking it so seriously. She suspected the granularity of focus was much less specific than she'd been told. Or the intervals between watching much larger. What was the spiked population of the United States these days? People were spiked for offenses ranging from multiple trespass to marginally justifiable homicide.

Over the next couple of days, Jayne explored as much of the building as possible. In the basement, she found three locked rooms, one with the flat plate and red sensor of an old smart-card system, and a storage area filled with old desks and computer components. She rummaged through the desks and found a flat keycard, black on one side, gray letters on a white field on the other, the initials of a company long since out of business.

If it's a smart card, the battery is probably dead, she thought, but then she rubbed the dirt off it a bit more and saw two tiny dull gray patches, each the size of a pinhead, on the top-left-hand corner. She wondered if the man in the peculiar shop might know what to do with it.

To see what might happen, she laid it against the red sensor on the lock plate. Nothing happened. No alarms. She looked at the door hinges and figured the door should swing out. A gentle pull got no response. Still no alarm.

Probably nothing worth getting at.

* * *

"I can't give you much for it," the man in the electronics shop said, turning the card over in his hands.

"Has the battery run down?"

"Oh, quite."

"Could you recharge it?"

"If I can find the specs for it. You might be surprised at the cost for such information."

"What about if you recharge it using the most likely voltage for such a thing?"

"Bring me something I might like from the room it might open," the man said. He went into the back of the shop for a moment, then came back and tossed the key to Jayne in a high, wobbling flutter.

Her hand snapped it from the air—*so, it's a game with him.*

He said, "Remember, if you're going exploring in old spaces, the past can invade the future. Not that the past isn't always invading the present."

"Which past?" Jayne said.

"Whichever past you make it," the man said. "Some things disappeared in 1993; others hid later behind slash star."

"The commented out sign for C code," Jayne said.

He looked at her as if a bit surprised or very surprised and hiding it well. "Can you hack C?"

"I kinda know what a program looks like and how to compile it."

"Pity you wasted your time teaching losers. You could have been a lot more dangerous data mining."

"I wanted to help others."

"No, you wanted to see the others you were helping and see yourself helping them." He sounded like he was angry with her. "And perhaps you wanted to be busted? Some people actually like the humiliation they'd otherwise have to pay good money for. Code doesn't betray people; people betray people."

"All people?"

He sat down at his counter, looked at the things in the display case, and didn't speak for a moment. His hands dangled in front of him. Jayne noticed a tiny round scar on the back of each of them, carpal tunnel syndrome surgery, she suspected. He saw she was looking at his hands and raised them, turned them palm-side out to show long scars, down, not across, his wrists. "Friends stopped me. Exploration of the possibilities, but I didn't want to just make a dumb gesture. I wonder if my carpal tunnel surgery failed on purpose." He lowered his hands and said, "Go, be dangerous with your data dumpster diving, if that's what's behind your locked door. Don't get caught, and bring me the prime parts."

Jayne wished the people on her side weren't so often weird.

The keycard worked on the door, which opened with rusty screeches and signs of termite damage. Jayne suspected she could have cut through the door instead, but didn't know what maintenance the room's machines got.

No human being seemed to have been in the room in at least a year, perhaps longer. Air conditioners ran; various light arrays on the backs of computers and switches moved. Jayne noticed that the electric cords had been modified so that they were screwed into UPS sockets, which in turn were fastened by screws to the wall sockets.

A cleaner about the size of a duffel bag came out and began snuffling dirt. Jayne watched it coming closer to her, then swerve around, still sucking dirt with a funnel-shaped snout flattened at the end to fit into crevices.

One wall was a bank of monitors, twenty of them, most looking at interiors of houses or golf courses, moving as though in a walking human body. *Judas monitors,* Jayne realized. She wondered if she could have watched through Sidna's eye from there, but it was now missing. One of the monitors played white noise. Two were black. Another eyeball approached Sheie Eye Institute.

Jayne wondered if the rest of the machines were as obsolete as the monitoring screens still running even though no humans cared to watch anymore. She went farther into the room and saw other monitors that appeared to be sleeping, yellow indicator lights still showing through the dust. She looked back at the monitors in the wall rack. The two black ones showed no signs of even being sleeping. Did the monitors simply fail, or did the monitor get turned off remotely when it no longer had live feed from the artificial eyes?

The other monitors shifted perspectives, different eyes, different women. Jayne wondered when she'd see the eye scheduled for removal again. She went up to one and brushed one of the lower screens free of dust and saw the woman's ID number change as the screen shifted to yet another Judas Girl, a hand shaking a girl child who was obviously screaming.

Jayne knew she could do nothing to help that child, so she turned her attention to the machines in the other racks. Seven were set up with mice and live monitors. She jiggled a mouse and saw a prompt waiting for a password. Another mouse and she saw a machine endlessly rebooting itself. *How do I get in?*

Whoever had used the fifth machine had been careless. And it was set up for the sort of user who might forget passwords: automatic telnet links to other machines; ssh, without needing a password for authentication to what looked like a monitoring system. But the user name wasn't familiar, though that proved little. Many people used other names for log-on. The operator had trusted that no one bad could get to the keyboard.

Jayne began exploring the limits of the user who'd left himself logged on. She changed his password and left everything still logged on. If the account was still used, the guy would know if he logged off and tried to log back on. Something would happen. Security would check this room; the account password would be changed again.

Crackword. This was an old UNIX system despite all the add-ons to keep the users away from the guts of the machine. Jayne could run Crackword on the system and see if whoever set root had been careless.

She also could run top if she could get a basic systems terminal shell. She could; she did; the system behind the account she had open was enormous. She saw the processes she'd left running, user names she recognized, user names she wasn't supposed to know. Someone had to be monitoring this. She saw the top process that she was running. *If someone is monitoring this, I'm busted.*

If I'm not busted, I'll run Crackword on it.

She closed top and explored the guy's home directory further, his private programs, then looked at his projects. *I could just copy a project and telnet to this machine, work on it from my desk when people weren't looking.*

How can I disable top? Eventually, alarms would go off. If a human wasn't monitoring the system, surely a machine was.

Jayne looked over her shoulder at the views from the various fake eyes. Nobody was monitoring that. She went back upstairs to see if she'd be busted, then worked the rest of the day on Entity's presidential candidate without trying to telnet to the basement machine.

Under the interface is a twentieth-century system—and I'm not busted yet. Five o'clock, the spike would let her go home.

The next day, she found a candidate who was running against a meat candidate in a state too far away to affect her son's campaigns. She copied the files onto the machine and account in the basement and began to destroy the subtle eye saccades that made a virtual candidate seem credible.

The next day, she trapped an interactive session from someone who had another account that worked on the California candidate and found that the password seemed to have been sent in clear, uncoded, no secret.

For five days, she simply rebuilt the other candidate.

Someone else was improving his chances against the meat candidate; she was writing a shadow program that would make him untrusted. Only if she dared try the password could she switch the work she'd been doing to the worker assigned to help him win.

Jayne's fingers cramped the first time she tried to type in her coworker's password. Her body didn't believe this was safe.

Listen to the body.

She went back into the basement room and saw no signs that the dust on the machines was any different. Another Judicious Girl monitoring screen had gone black, the eye removed from its victim.

They can't just be ignoring my intrusion.

She walked over to the machine where she'd changed the password and logged on in the second user's name, then copied her shadow files over the work the other graphics modeler had done. *Boom. Maybe it's safer not to involve my machine in any way.*

In November, the Entities, Inc., president won the election; the minor candidate in California lost. The managers opened the greenhouse for a party and called in two caterers with Ethiopian and Californian food and wine. Through the swirl of people laughing, Jayne noticed two men and a woman in the corner of the greenhouse against the building wall, one man standing with his back to the crowd, the other two sitting. The woman saw Jayne looking their way and flashed a short smile at her, then looked back at the man standing in front of her.

They lost in California yesterday. Jayne decided to see if her suspicions were right. She went to them and stood for a while listening to see if she could pick up the conversation. The group went quiet, then the man standing said to Jayne, "You've heard that meat candidates won a lot locally, didn't you?"

"Don't they generally win locally?" Jayne said.

"They won elections they shouldn't have won," the man said.

Jayne, feeling very rash, said, "You don't think anyone tampered with the vote, do you?"

The woman sighed. The group went quiet again. "Nobody tampered with the vote," the other man, the one sitting, said. "It's just . . ."

"We really don't want to talk about it," the woman said.

"By the way," Jayne asked, "who won clerk of court in Manhattan?"

"A dumb meat kid," the man standing said, "but he wasn't running against anyone we've got a contract for."

"Maybe it's the Zeitgeist," the woman said. "Or people are beginning to want to see their candidates in the flesh?"

Jayne wondered if she'd affected anything at all. Whatever, she had to feel like she was doing something.

On Mantua Bridge, she congratulated her son for winning, and said that she'd helped a meat candidate in California win, though she still wasn't entirely sure she'd done anything.

"When one's subverted, people begin looking more closely at all the candidates."

Jayne hadn't considered that. It made her feel better. They walked to the Art Museum again, not speaking further of what Jayne was doing until they were back on Mantua Bridge.

"I thought Entities, Inc., was running the candidate against me," her son said.

"Maybe it's something in the Zeitgeist," Jayne said. "A butterfly in Texas flaps its wing to build a hurricane in Florida."

"Subvert one candidate in California and another candidate loses in New York. "

"The human won in California, too," Jayne said.

"When you taught, did you think you were making significant changes in the way the world worked?"

"I mostly hoped I was making a significant change for some of my students. When I was younger, I wanted to change the world."

"I'd love to do it all by myself," her son said, "but I don't think changing the world's in the clerk of court of Manhattan's job description." He smiled slightly.

"How do we find out who is running the candidates?" Jayne asked. "All I know are the Entities candidates, and only the ones I can access on the computer I found in the basement."

"Or the ones you are assigned to work on."

"I don't want to risk that."

"You could have subverted the president."

"So? Another program would have won."

"Satisfying ambitions by committee is very difficult," her son said. They left Mantua Bridge and began talking about the Chinese furniture's clean lines. He slipped something into her pocket, a data coin drive of a root-hack-and-mask program. To possess that was more illegal than anything Jayne had ever done.

The drive slipped into a carrier that itself cost Jayne all the memory chips she could steal from three idle machines in the basement. The fence took the coin drive to the back with him and told her what it was when he came out. Jayne suspected that he'd made a copy of it, but there was no way she could tell. She came back from the shop on Lancaster Avenue and slipped the coin drive into the carrier, popped the release with a crochet hook, looked at the thing, and wondered why she was doing this for her son. For anyone.

Teaching had been dangerous, but it felt honorable, an end run around the system that, without Ocean's help, would have left her as deprived as her students. But this? Human politicians led to the system that replaced them. How could other politicians lead to something better?

Whatever. Jayne couldn't imagine machine entities leading to a better system, either. Imagination leveled by committee, all was maintenance.

She even wondered if hacking root would be more dangerous than what she'd done in the past. Her two collaborators, son and fence, had more to lose than she did, really.

Down in the basement, the woman who beat her daughter when Jayne first saw the old monitoring screens was looking at her daughter sleeping. A hand brushed up against the eye, crying. Jayne wondered what had happened since she'd last looked at the screens.

Enough of that. Jayne pulled on thin latex gloves, illegal in themselves without a prescription, and pushed the coin-drive carrier into a port in the back of the computer and selected the drive. She watched as the program loaded itself, running flickering over the machine too fast for her to read anything, almost too fast to grasp that numbers and letters were flying down the screen.

Then the machine stopped, displayed characters: ex%itII91&#Q9. Root's password. Jayne copied it down, found the mask program, and installed that, exited the program, exited the user, and started back again.

Root. Password: ex%itII91&#Q9. The machine opened to her, every directory hers to cruise.

She opened a program that monitored users and processes. She was invisible, disguised as processes on three other machines that had root, vague shadows split into too many parts to pull together.

Jayne trembled. She began reading the client files. *Remember everything.* Notes were much too dangerous to take.

That evening, she took the carrier back to the shop on Lancaster and left the coin drive in it. If her son's fence didn't make a copy the first time, he could now. The thing was much too dangerous for her to keep.

"I used gloves," she told the man.

"Gloves keep things so tidy. No fingertip sweat, no skin

shedding DNA into the spaces between keys." He popped the coin drive out of the carrier and put it in a basket sitting by the swipe card reader. He put the carrier back in a drawer. Jayne doubted either would stay where they'd been put once she left the shop. "Wipe with alcohol if you didn't use gloves before."

Jayne remembered isopropyl bursting the paramecium cells decades earlier when she was a girl.

In the middle of this, Ocean died in South Dakota in the middle of nowhere and was cremated. An ex-student who'd gone on to test out from class of origin came to tell Jayne in person. Jayne felt the death as almost an intrusion.

"She wanted you to have some of her ashes," the woman said, handing Jayne a small sealed ceramic jar the size of a thimble.

My sister sees binocular again; my mentor's dead.

"We want to keep in touch with you," her ex-student said, now obviously in the unlicensed teaching hierarchy herself.

"When can I get the spike out?"

"We'll make your life safe even with it. You can work in administration," the woman said. "Students are the ones who betray you."

"Some of them," Jayne said, smiling slightly.

"Successful ex-students rarely betray their teachers."

"Rarely." Jayne wondered if Ocean had really died. After the woman left, she tried her alternative channels and found that the woman hadn't lied.

I don't know whether to grieve for the woman or for having drifted away from her over the years. Ocean had rescued her; condemned her; and died so that all the things Jayne wanted to ask were impossible questions now.

Her life before Ocean had been terrible. She was now in a life after Ocean. Jayne wondered if she should drift out of her connections with the unlicensed teaching world. She'd been busted; she was doing other things.

Everyone could find her through the spike.

She found herself missing Ocean now that she couldn't contact her again. The loss built from day to day rather than diminished. She woke up from a dream where she talked to Ocean again to find herself crying.

And so to work, where she couldn't talk about the loss at all, even how she shouldn't be feeling so much of a loss since she'd drifted away from Ocean over time.

But on Mantua Bridge, she could talk to her son about the old woman who'd rescued her from her threatened future, a rescue that left her in a legal twilight forever.

Her son said, "I guess I'm not helping matters, either, but you were already outside the law when I found you."

"I miss her. I miss that I'll never be able to talk to her again, even though I'd hardly been talking to her in the last couple of years."

"If I dropped out of your life, would you miss me?" her son asked.

"You'll probably have to. I'm dangerous to know, right. I have root now. Got any meat friends running for office where we've got the candidate going against them?"

He didn't say anything. Jayne wondered if there was another conspirators' circle she shouldn't know anything about. Then he said, "What if I found out more about the people you were working for as an illegal teacher?"

"Do you think that would hurt me? Or help me?"

"I don't know anything about them really, other than they don't like the way the country works and aren't willing to change it by lawful means."

Subverting a program to win an election is lawful means? Jayne thought, but she didn't say anything. They were off the bridge. She wondered if it was really true that the spike wasn't reading all the things she'd said to her son.

Meat candidates began winning the fringes of the political universe like mice inhabiting computer printers and shorting out the motherboards by shitting on them.

* * *

In the basement, the girl in Screen Number 8 was crying. Jayne looked more closely and noticed a number that looked like a net number. She wondered if it was still current.

A hand reached out below the fake eye and slapped the girl. Jayne froze for a second, remembering her mother beating her, and went on the computer. She looked back over her shoulder, got up, and jotted down the contact number. But how would she explain what she'd done? How did she see what was happening to the girl?

The screen cycled on to the next artificial eye, and the contact number changed.

Jayne turned back to working on sabotaging yet another program candidate. She wondered if doing this was more important than saving a single child from what must already be a bad childhood. How better could she make it if she intervened? Would anyone listen to her if she did report child abuse?

Meanwhile, Carolyn could see again. Her parents sent Jayne a thank-you card on the anniversary of the surgery.

Sometime later, her father came up to see her. Jayne wondered if this was the anniversary of her arrest, but made no attempt to check. Her father slept on the air bed and watched sports shows all day while Jayne was at work. She thought about getting a virtual sports rig for him, but that seemed almost obscene, her old father trying to be a sports program.

Her son came up to visit then, and they all took a pedicab to the restaurant on Sansom.

"You're doing well at the job, I hear," her father said. Jayne forgot about her probation officer most of the time—he never made home visits and only came to the office once a month. The news agents trusted that their spike would keep Jayne from running off. Jayne found her hiding place, lower than where she was supposed to be, not horizontally farther away. The spike seemed insensitive to depth. Perhaps there was enough noise in the system that going down to the basement wasn't noticed.

And Jayne had considered also that perhaps they knew precisely what she was doing, but she would go ahead and do it anyway.

Her son said, in her thinking silence, "Mom's really okay, you know. Why didn't you protect her better when she was a child?"

Jayne looked at her father. Would it have even been possible?

"I worked," her father said. "I didn't know I'd have to raise the children, too. I thought Jayne's mother was taking care of that."

Jayne said, "I didn't know how to be discreet." *And I still don't. I want to help the child I see getting beaten.* She said, "Times were different then. Women raised the children. People wanted stability again after all the turn-of-the-century madness."

Her son said, "It's not an either/or proposition. Human beings are not binary machines."

Her father said, "If I could do it over again, I would have told Jayne how pretty she was. Give her more self-confidence. I wasn't good at building self-confidence in her. I didn't know."

Jayne loved her dad, was exasperated by him, and knew it was entirely likely that she'd hurt him again, without quite meaning to. Being told she was pretty wouldn't have been enough.

The otherness of other people. She wondered then about who she might be in her son's mind.

So then, what was going on in the child's life on the screen that nobody cared to monitor? How many years had old Judas Girl eyes sent their signals to complete indifference until Jayne found the basement room with the bank of monitors still scanning? The woman perhaps forgot that she transmitted the child's screaming to anyone—decades after the monitoring equipment was installed and years after losing an eye to stay safe was considered a good trade.

Jayne watched the monitors and realized all these artificial eyes and their women lived close. She saw university buildings and construction on Market.

The crying child was in the neighborhood. The woman left her house to climb into a car one day while Jayne watched— Hamilton Street, near Thirty-second, above the Gardens, where trains used to come and go. A man smiled from the driver's wheel and touched the woman's cheek. She leaned into the hand, huge against the cheek below the Judas eye.

Adultery, perhaps. So the woman completely ignores her monitor.

So, the next weekend, Jayne went walking until she found the house where the little abused girl lived. Her spike read all this as in her neighborhood, exercise, okay, not an attempt to escape. Was the spike as ignored as the woman's artificial eyeball that monitored her at random intervals?

She saw the little girl playing with other children and watched for a while to see if the girl was being treated unfairly. They all went to the common gardens that had been in use for over a century and began playing hide-and-seek. The garden was dotted with small buildings used for storage and heaps of cornstalks and beanpoles.

Whatever else was happening to the girl, the other children appeared to be treating her fairly. In fact, she seemed to be maybe a bit bossy.

Jayne watched them until one of the parents came looking for them and scattered them all for lunch at their various houses.

Maybe it's nothing more than a couple of angry days that happened to coincide with the monitor being on.

The man who'd come to the garden looked at her as though wondering about her motives.

Jayne smiled at him and went on back to her apartment.

The ecological chop shop and Data Reverse Engineers was completely gone, the building sealed with police tape and locks, the next time Jayne looked. She didn't continue up to the junk shop where the man with the electronics connections did business.

A week later, she heard from the street that the guy, who'd been spiked, tried to take it out and died screaming. Jayne doubted that anyone really knew what happened. She realized the spikes were that worst of all reinforcements, the intermittent one. *One week, you could go anywhere, leave the country, travel to Asia. The next week, you'd crumple to the ground if you walked to Center City.*

She wondered how well they read through walls or floors, and how well they read in the subbasement where the woman who lived at the end of Hamilton Street was arguing with her daughter and pacing the floor. Jayne didn't see any blows this time.

Maybe the beatings were rare events but clustered, so Jayne had seen the cluster, but not the general trend of the mother-daughter relationship. *And maybe I'm afraid to say anything because someone would wonder why I was down here and discover the program for scattering root's top overview of who was using the system.*

Jayne discovered that some computer systems in distant places still used ssh. In some variations, it required a password for entry. She began to be sorry that she'd given up Crackword, but wrote a dictionary-testing program to see if that and a couple of numbers insertions would give up any new machines. Soon she was on a machine in San Diego and one called Engine3 in Indonesia, and moved some of her programs to the remote machines, not sure whether that made her easier to trace or more difficult. The she remembered her encoding program and installed it on Engine3.

Somewhere along the way, she picked up a trick to log in

to her ghost programs from her own machine, download her stolen files, and exit, leaving a pattern maker to undo the randomizations other programmers gave their entities. She sensed almost subliminally that the basement was dangerous.

As their clients' programs began losing elections, Entities began cutting back on staff. Jayne heard from her probation officer that her contract had been sent to an auction house. "You may have to leave Philadelphia," he said, "but we'll help with a new apartment."

Jayne wondered if she was being watched. She went back to the basement and saw the woman at the end of Hamilton beat her daughter again. The daughter seemed incapable of fighting back even though Jayne had seen her being bold enough with the other children in the public gardens.

And once I leave here, I can't help her anymore. Then Jayne realized she hadn't helped the girl at all. She'd just vicariously sympathized.

When she went to her remote machines, she found that clumsier crackers had also found Engine3. Other programs were running on it, and one of them was using her encryption program or another like it. The other cracker programs weren't protected by the program that masked the running processes.

Jayne began to feel doomed, but she didn't think she'd committed any capital crimes. Arrest's seductions played on her—that sense of knowing finally, even though the answer wasn't the best, the sense of being stopped in this crazy over-working. It would be over, and the questions of doing good and doing enough good would stop. The authorities would make her stop. She couldn't possibly work this hard in prison.

She shut her computer programs on Engine3 off and removed the mask program before someone not as responsible as she was discovered it. When she looked back the monitoring screens from the Judas Girl eyes were going off one by one. *Fluke? Or am I being watched? Have I always been watched?*

If the electricity is going off, I'd better get out before the door freezes. Jayne left everything still up and went to the door. As she got through it, the lights behind her began to shut off. She could salvage down there if she brought a flashlight. Nobody would notice now if the computers went missing.

The next day, the smart card didn't work. Jayne wasn't quite ready to break through the termite-riddled door. Jayne listened for news in the office about anything that would clue her in to what was going on. Her programs on remote would still be working even though she'd disconnected from the machines. She suspected that Entities, to save money, cut power to areas of the building that were supposed to be abandoned.

If management knew she'd been the one playing on those machines, they didn't seem to care, but then they were selling her off.

"It's not really slavery," her probation officer told her. "It's like a work contract. The people who own it can't do anything untoward to you, and the government still pays you what you've been getting all along and arranges to help with your rent if necessary."

"Can your office buy my contract?" Jayne asked her son at their next lunch, not waiting for the moments on the bridge.

He said, "I'll try to help, but we can't buy our relatives."

"I'm not your mother of record," Jayne said.

"With Sidna knowing?"

Jayne realized, yes, it wasn't safe for him to arrange for her to be bought. She began hoping that the underground teaching establishment would buy her. She could work in administration. Her ex-student who'd come to tell her of Ocean's death had said something about that. But maybe that was on top of the support job. The teaching had always been on top of the support jobs.

*   *   *

Soon, I could be gone from Philadelphia. Jayne went to see if the girl at the end of Hamilton Street looked okay. She waited around the time that schoolchildren came home, then noticed a person watching her. It occurred to her that there was an easier way to find out what the woman was like, whether child-beating was an anomaly or a habit. She e-mailed her sister to ask Sidna about the woman, said that she'd noticed the eye without saying how.

Sidna e-mailed back, not her sister, asking her why she wanted to know anything about a Judas Girl.

Jayne found a quiet battery-operated saw and cut her way into the old basement computer room. She worked in the dust and brittle plastic to pull machines into pieces she could smuggle out. If Sidna was suspicious of her, being more cautious and losing the salvage of the basement machines to someone else was pointless.

The fence was nervous when she came in with so much stuff. He went back into the shop and stayed back out of sight for fifteen minutes, then came back with the word, "Barter only."

Jayne didn't know what to want out of the clutter in the cabinets. She said, "Do you have a way to read a Judas eye?"

"There are some things one doesn't want to take," the man said.

Jayne knew that the equipment she needed was still in the basement machine room. The program didn't have to run on precisely that hardware; it just had to read those signals.

Sidna showed up to take Jayne to lunch; Jayne didn't feel like she could make proper excuses fast enough. She had a brief fantasy of running for it, but then Sidna was walking into her workspace.

"You know, there was a monitoring station for Judas Girls here once," Sidna said.

Jayne wished she had run for it. "Someone told me they saw old monitors in the basement once."

Sidna said, "Vision is fading in my fellow eye. This happens sometimes after an injury to one eye. The other eye goes, too."

Maybe her own miseries will stop her from making trouble for me, Jayne hoped. "Can't they reverse it?"

"They're not sure of the mechanism," Sidna said. "Your sister asked me to take you to lunch. I've made reservations at the closest best place."

Whatever had happened to Sidna, she had money to use against Jayne. Jayne nodded and followed Sidna out, feeling as though she should have made excuses, feeling strange for not having simply sent the woman away.

But I don't know what she can do. Or what sorts of monitors were in that basement room. Maybe the news agents know everything? She remembered the day she fooled the news agents only to come home and have Sidna pick her story to pieces.

Sidna had her car parked in the employee parking lot. She opened the passenger-side door for Jayne, then got in the driver's side, but didn't turn on the motor. She said, "Your son turned out remarkably well for someone sired by a school-drug person on a school-drug person. The drugs Mick got were supposed to damage his chromosomes so that he couldn't breed."

"He didn't take them," Jayne said, figuring that after all these years, that couldn't hurt him.

"Surprise, surprise. How many people were escaping us?"

Jayne didn't know. She hadn't been a trusted member of that community. "Lots, I suspect."

"Nobody trusts you, do they?"

Neither of them spoke. Sidna still didn't start the car. She said, "I'm going blind, I tell you. Blind. And you think it's funny."

"I don't."

"You lie. I did this." Sidna stabbed her right index finger at her dead eye. "I had this done to make myself safe from the Micks of the world." She punched at the eye again, coming closer to the artificial surface. "Because I wanted to be a good girl. I was fighting evil."

Jayne was glad she'd never feared herself so much that she'd put out an eye to keep her impulses monitored. She wondered if Sidna understood the implications of what she was saying.

"And now I'm going blind. It isn't fair."

Jayne said, "Where are we going to have lunch?" She suddenly worried that Sidna would drive her beyond what the spike permitted and that this day the satellites would be looking for her.

"You asked Carolyn about a friend of mine, Evelyn Nesbit. I thought it would be fun to find out why, so we're having lunch with her."

Jayne thought, *She would be a friend of yours.*

Sidna pulled on a headset with a camera that aided the view from her right eye. Jayne knew she should feel pity, but instead the woman looked monstrous, with a glassy-tipped snout over her face. Sidna turned to look at Jayne, and said, "Not very pretty, is it?" and turned on the car.

They parked in front of the Hamilton Street house. Sydna took off her headgear and began to get out of the car. Jayne thought again about running. How hard could it be to run from a woman more than half-blind? But then the young girl came to the door. Her face was bruised. Jayne got out of the car, realizing that she had to do something, there, then. The computers in the basement were gone. Her program that turned entities back into obvious machine dreams lived on several other computer systems. All she could do was either try to save herself or this young girl.

The girl said, "I fell, and I'm staying out of school today."

Jayne said, "Your mother hit you. Isn't she usually more careful about leaving visible bruises?" Jayne was shocked at how matter-of-fact she sounded.

"That's slander," the woman said. Jayne had never seen her before, just had looked through her fake eye.

"Jayne knows," Sidna said.

"The child is impossible," the woman said. "She has hysterics."

Jayne looked at the girl, and said, "I saw you being beaten through the camera in your mother's eye."

The girl looked at her as if wanting to ask why Jayne hadn't done anything. Jayne added, "I'm sorry."

"How did you find out?"

"Bank of receivers in the basement of where Jayne worked. I'd forgotten about them until Carolyn called me saying her sister claimed to have spotted you. Jayne's not normally one to be curious about Judicious Women."

"Nobody has been monitoring you people for years. And nobody cares what you do or what happens to you."

"Or to the child," Evelyn Nesbit said.

"I care about the girl," Jayne said. "Whatever she's like, she doesn't deserve to be hit in the face like that."

"Jayne is a convicted criminal," Sidna told the child.

"My name is Louise," the girl said, hot with dignity.

"You'll grow up to be just like Jayne," Sidna said.

Prison would be better, Jayne decided, than any further dealings with Sidna. "Was my looking illegal?"

"You stole a keycard," Sidna said.

"I found a keycard," Jayne said, hoping that Sidna would be too technologically illiterate to understand how old and drained the card was. Louise moved her lips, then didn't speak. She kept her eyes on Jayne.

Sidna reached across the couch where they were sitting and took Jayne's chin in her fingers, moving them across Jayne's face. "Wasn't your mother right to beat you? You grew up to be such a bad girl. You're glad I'm going blind."

"I wouldn't wish it on anyone." Jayne knew she was lying. *Yes, go blind. You've always depended on the vision of others.* And she felt guilty. She looked at Evelyn and made a sudden guess. "Was your surgery a failure, too?"

Evelyn said, "The orbital bones were too corroded for it to be safe."

"None of the men took the Judas Girl thing as seriously as you did. What dumb thing can you get women to do to their girls next—bind their feet, put out their eyes, train them to corsets, pierce them, brand them?"

"Beat them?" Louise asked in a low voice.

"She's a bossy, aggressive girl. It's not right," Evelyn said.

But she's still my mother and you have to go away, Louise's face seemed to say.

Jayne wondered how far she could walk until the satellites noticed. She said to Louise, "I'm sorry I didn't say anything sooner, but I didn't know how bad it was. Your mother was only monitored intermittently, and I wasn't sure of what I was seeing."

"She beats me at least once a week. Sometimes not this hard."

And, even now, what can I do? Jayne decided to walk out. If they tried to stop her, she'd fight them until they killed her or had her arrested. "I don't think I want to stay for this lunch," Jayne said. She rose.

Louise said, "I want to come with you."

"To prison," Sidna said. "Yes, follow her. You'll end up in a juvenile hall, in a foster home."

Evelyn looked at Sidna, looked away.

"I'm going to prison, but I'll tell them about you first."

"I know where to hide," Louise cried.

"Go then, hide. You'll starve to death. People will get you who'll make your mother look like an angel," Sidna said. She groped for her eyepiece. Jayne wondered how much of the blindness was psychosomatic, how much the magnifier helped at all.

Louise jumped and snatched the magnifier away, stamped it with her small foot. Jayne winced. The child probably did herself more damage than she'd done to the eyepiece.

"Come now," Jayne said. They ran toward Mantua Bridge

with the two women behind them unable to keep up. *No, they know the satellite is paying attention to me today.* Jayne flushed further with anger. Sidna had bet that Jayne would be too afraid of prison, of hurting her son, too subdued by their hate. Or just couldn't imagine that anyone would prefer prison to being subjugated to her will.

If they know what I've done . . . but then Jayne hadn't done anything for her son, directly. *No doubt, just run.*

They got much farther than Jayne thought she'd get, to Boathouse Row. *We have no friends here,* Jayne thought as the pain started. She said to Louise, "We have to go back a bit. I'm starting to be captured."

"So, the old bitch wasn't lying," Louise said. She stared at Jayne, who was bent over, uselessly, as the pain was from nerve induction.

"Yeah, yeah. I've got to step back a bit."

They both heard the sirens wailing as the police came to get Jayne. Louise said, "You do have to leave me."

"You have to tell them what's been happening to you. I suspect they'll try to work it out with your mother." In the end, freedom for the girl had been short and brief. *But what should we have done, sit there with her mother and Sidna, accepting it all forever?* Jayne moved back the way she came, and the pain seemed to ebb slightly but didn't completely go away. She then felt a shift in the current and found that she could barely move. But she could speak. "It won't be all the way as better as you could imagine, but at least someone doesn't think you deserve to be beaten."

"Will you die now?"

Jayne laughed. "No, we don't have to die. We can go on. Time will take them away from us. You'll be able to do without your mother someday."

Louise said, "If she doesn't kill me. She said she'd kill me if I exaggerated about her hitting me."

"You were in most danger when nobody had any idea it was happening." Jayne hoped that was true.

"Mom told me she might send me away and nobody would love me. She does love me. My father doesn't love us anymore."

"One never knows."

The police got out of their squad car and came up to Jayne. One held a scanner with a readout, a blunt clublike thing. He pushed it into Jayne's belly and nodded to the others. "So, you tried to steal the girl."

Jayne said, "Her mother was beating her."

"That's not what her mother said," the cop with the reader replied. Jayne felt the current in her body shift again, no pain, no sluggish muscles. She wondered if they'd beat her in front of the girl. Maybe since they were regular city cops and not news agents, they wouldn't beat her at all.

"My mother beats me every week," Louise said. "She told me she'd kill me if I told anyone."

The cops looked at each other. Jayne said, "Her mother's a Judas Girl. Her eye still works, at least did the last time I watched her beat her daughter or go off with a friend." She didn't want to let the girl know her mother had a lover, but she hoped the cop would understand her intonation.

"You want to go home now?" another cop, a woman, asked the girl. "Or do you want to go to Juvenile Hall until we can get this straightened out?"

"I want to go somewhere safe," Louise said. She said it so plainly and with a nearly tearful dignity. "Please."

The cops looked at each other. "We'll take this one in, and you see about the kid," the cop with the probe said to the woman cop.

Louise began crying hard. Jayne said, "Please believe her," as they cuffed her hands behind her back, an unnecessary ritual now that they had the spike in her belly.

The cop with the probe unlocked the cuffs and put them on in front. "If you were watching this shit, why didn't you call someone earlier?" he asked, but Jayne appreciated the gesture and hoped that all would work out for Louise. *Somehow.*

And somehow, she'd survive prison herself. She suspected eventually, even being in prison would be normal, a place she lived through, in.

She had skills she'd stolen from the world. Even in prison, she'd find a use for them.

14
The End

One morning after prison, Jayne worked with her house-mates pointing the brick on the two-hundred-year-old building on Spring Garden Street. Skin withered to crepe, hair mostly gray, Jayne knew that she looked old beyond what slight remedies like wrinkle creams and exfoliants could manage, but she liked doing physical work with the kids. Suzanne looked even older, and she still went down to Center City every Friday night to Victor/Victoria's.

Jayne had been able to keep her defiance in prison. Now she taught legally, and some of her students were fellow parolees from the secret cell there that her son exposed and pardoned her for starting.

Time to be nice to the old bitches.

As she walked down to the community center, she noticed three young girls, one black, the others the mixed race most of America seemed to be now that the ghetto barriers were down. The news agents portrayed her in media as someone they'd shown mercy to, a pity object. But somehow, Jayne had become more than that, and these weren't the first young women to come to see if she was flesh, not digits.

So now she was a folk hero, and the news agents cut the digits different these days. And people again hacked graphics code and wrote their own stories. She'd come back to a new neighborhood in the same buildings, pardoned from the crueler time and sentence.

Another young girl came up to her just as she was about to enter the community center, and said, "You really are real? Even if it gets bad again, you don't have to give in."

"No, *you* don't have to give in," Jayne said. The young girl smiled at that. Jayne remembered when Louise visited her. Jayne's intervention had meant something, just not everything. Louise said she had to learn how to survive her mother herself, despite all the interventions that followed.

The young girl looked defiant, and then grinned broadly at having gotten attention from her heroine.

So defiance continues. Jayne didn't feel particularly responsible for it today. Some time from now she'd be dead. Whatever, if defiance continued in the right proportions to the force against it, all would be well. Until the human race was gone, someone would defy authority.

"I'm glad they didn't break you and turn you informer," the young girl said. Jayne wondered if the girl knew how much Jayne's media life missed. Engine3 in Indonesia never was part of it. Having a real, breathing president of the United States was part that never made media. Her life filled up beyond what she could recall in a day or two of musing, or even a week of deep introspection. No way to cover it all in a week's miniseries.

Odd, to come to realize that the news agents were not so wrong after all to say that reality is constructed.

But who's to construct it?